THE
WORLD
TURNED
UPSIDE
DOWN

THE WORLD TURNED UPSIDE DOWN

A NOVEL

STEVEN MENDEL

atmosphere press

Dedicated to Margaret, my life muse

CHAPTER 1

Rough hands gripped her arms and dragged Abagail out of bed. She tried to scream. A cloth was shoved into her mouth. The world went dark as a rag covered her eyes. *They are going to kill me*, she thought. Calloused hands held her arms down to her sides and turned her, wrapping her body tightly in a sheet.

Abagail tried to hear the whispers of her kidnappers as they hoisted her on their shoulders. Feeling the fast pace of their movement, she wriggled and pushed against the hands that gripped her, but they held tight. She tried to figure out which part of the palace they were in by the route they were taking, but there were too many turns. The kidnappers stopped and repositioned her. Suddenly her head was pointing down. Her panic spiked, thinking she might fall, but they held her tightly and started walking again.

By their uneven gait, Abagail knew they were going downstairs. Their footsteps echoed on the stone stairs that went down for an eternity. The air was wet from a steady *drip, drip* of water and permeated with the odor of rot.

Then they stopped, lifted her off their shoulders, and lowered her to the ground. Abagail's feet touched a cold, stone floor. The blindfold and gag were removed, and her hands and feet freed. Her eyes unused to the dark, Abagail could barely see her captors as they silently slipped away.

Abagail was alone, standing in the darkest place in the world, certain she was still in the palace but with no idea where. Unwrapped from her covers, she was cold and wrapped her arms around her body to stop the trembling. Suddenly, out of the darkness, a huge figure walked toward her. She wanted to run. Her legs were free but felt as heavy as tree stumps. Her mouth was open, trying to scream, but no sound came. And still, the man approached her.

He grabbed her arm and dragged her down a long corridor. She tried to resist, but the man was too strong. A door creaked open, and he pushed her into a room. The door thudded closed and the lock clicked into place.

"Let me out," Abagail cried, hearing the sound of footsteps fading and then silence. She pushed frantically against the heavy door, but it didn't budge. "Please, let me out. Why are you doing this?" She continued to bang on the door with her fists until her knuckles were bloody and her voice gave out. Exhausted, she slid down to the floor with her back against the door. Abagail couldn't tell how much time had passed, and it was so dark she didn't know if her eyes were open or closed.

Abagail heard a sound. She couldn't tell from where but was sure of it. Someone or something was breathing. It was alive but what was it—an animal...or something else?

Balling her trembling hand into a fist, promising herself no one would ever carry her away again, Abagail focused her eyes across the room and could just make out a tiny figure. "Hello," Abagail whispered. The small shadowy figure didn't move or speak.

"Show yourself," Abagail said with as much courage as she could muster.

A figure shuffled slowly in the darkness. Abagail froze. It was something tiny—child, dwarf, or some unimaginable creature.

Then she saw that it was an old woman with wild, matted hair, clothed in rags that hung from her malnourished, bent-over body. She slowly moved toward Abagail.

Sensing the old woman wasn't a threat, Abagail sat on the wet floor, hugging herself to keep the cold from seeping into her body. "I'm going to get out of here," Abagail said out loud. "As soon as Princess Margot finds out about this terrible mistake, I'm getting out."

"All right, my lady, when the princess comes for you, will you put in a good word for me?" asked the old woman in a halting voice. "While you're waiting to be rescued, would you want the food they left for you or can I eat it?"

Abagail was speechless.

"The food," the old woman said, and pointed to two wooden bowls.

The larger one was filled with a grey-brown mush, the sight of which made Abagail gag. The smaller one was filled with water. She pushed the bowls towards the old woman, who quickly swallowed the food and drank the water in one big gulp.

Abagail curled into a ball and rocked back and forth, telling herself that this nightmare had to end. She pulled her dress up to cover her shoulders and remembered it was the new dress made for the ball. Abagail and Princess Margot had been so excited that they decided to sleep in their new dresses. Abagail drifted off to sleep dreaming of music, food, wine, and laughter.

Where am I? Abagail woke in a confused daze, contemplating the cold stone floors. A faint light from a little window too high to look out of illuminated the room's only furnishing, a beat-up bed with a rough straw mattress. *How long have I been sleeping?* Abagail thought.

"I'd say the good part of a day," the old woman an-swered.

Abagail jumped. She had forgotten about the old woman and wondered if she had spoken aloud. It was just a thought, not meant to be heard by anyone.

"You can tell how much time has passed because they feed us once a day," the old woman explained. "There's only been one meal since they put you here. They should be coming back soon."

Abagail's stomach growled at the mention of food. She remembered the food she gave to the old woman and wished she had it back. Being in such a dark place was like living in her own mind; the outside world didn't exist. The sound of footsteps came toward the door. A key was thrust in the lock, and the door opened.

Abagail was on her feet, ready to hug her princess and leave this cave-like cell and the old woman buried in the earth. Instead, the large, scary man who first pushed her into the cave stood in the doorway, holding two wooden buckets and a ladle.

The old woman rushed past Abagail and held her bowl out. The man filled the old woman's large bowl with the same mush as before and dipped the same ladle in another bucket to fill the smaller bowl with water.

Abagail walked up to the large man and in her calmest voice said, "This is a terrible mistake. I should not be here. Talk to Princess Margot." The guard ignored her and headed for the door. "Please," she pleaded.

Before the guard closed the door, the old woman picked up Abagail's bowls and spoon and thrust them forward. "The poor girl is in shock and doesn't know what she is saying. Give her some food and water. I will make sure she eats it," she said with a toothless grin.

The man shrugged his broad shoulders and filled Abagail's bowls.

CHAPTER 2

Princess Margot stared at Abagail's empty bed, willing it to provide the answer. *Where is Abagail?* The sheets were all tangled up and lying on the floor along with her blanket and pillow. It looked like a wrestling match had taken place. Margot looked in the adjoining room. *Where is she?*

Margot walked quickly out to the corridor, lined by nine bedrooms to the left and seven to the right. Margot walked down one side of the corridor and up the other side, opening all sixteen doors and calling out Abagail's name. A sense of dread began to creep in. By the time she finished checking all the rooms on the floor, she was really worried. "Abagail!" Margot shouted loudly, but there was no response.

Margot ran down the grand staircase that led to the reception hall. "Your Majesty," one of the maids called out with a bow, but Margot didn't stop. At the bottom of the stairs, Margot turned left into the main dining hall. She rushed by three maids setting up for that night's state dinner. The maids scurried out of the way, bowing and saying, "Your Majesty, your Majesty."

"Have you seen Lady Abagail?" The maids shook their heads. Margot ran back up the stairs, unsure where else to look.

For as long as Margot could remember, she and Abagail had spent their days together. Yesterday began with the both of them eating breakfast together, talking the whole time.

"You are the fortunate one," Margot had said.

"Me?" Abagail replied. "You are the princess."

"Yes, but your life is your own, mine is already all laid out for me."

Abagail, knowing what Margot was referring to, ate quietly. Tomorrow was the day Margot was to meet Prince Leo of Spain, who she was to marry. It was an arranged marriage.

Margot was right. She may be the princess and I am just a lady in waiting but at least my life is my own. "The prince might be wonderful."

"I met him once when I was young. They say he is very handsome. I hope so," Margot said and started to laugh.

Abagail began to giggle also, sending the both of them into a fit of uncontrollable laughter.

The day proceeded, but it was unlike any other day. The two of them played a game of cards, talked, and laughed more. But as the hours passed, the excitement was accompa-nied by dread. Their world was going to change. They both decided to wear their new dresses, bought for the ball, to bed. *What happened to Abagail in the hours since then?* Margot wondered.

Margot heard talking in her mother's sitting room. Bursting into the room, she asked, "Mother, have you seen Abagail? I cannot find her anywhere."

The queen faced her mirror while her personal maid arranged her coiffure. She didn't turn around to look at her daughter. "Do not concern yourself about Abagail. Are you ready for tonight?"

"Where did Abagail go? She just disappeared."

"Abagail knows you will soon be a married woman. It is time to leave your childhood behind."

Margot gasped. "But Abagail is my only..."

The queen abruptly pushed her servant's hand away. "Enough!" she shouted. "You are a woman now. It's time to leave girlish things behind."

Margot bolted from her mother's room, ran down the hall to her bedroom, and flopped on her bed, crying. Life without Abagail was unimaginable. She hated her future husband. He was the reason she was being separated from her home and her life-long best friend.

I will find Abagail, she thought. *I will talk to my father, the king.* Margot wiped her eyes, washed her face, and, with her shoulders pulled back, walked quickly through the palace to find her father.

The king's door was closed. A sentry standing outside put his hand up. "I am sorry, my lady, but the king gave strict instructions. He is not to be disturbed under any circumstances."

"I command you to enter his room and let his highness know his daughter must speak with him now. Is that understood?"

"Yes, my lady," the guard replied, but he didn't move.

"Well, what are you waiting for?" Margot said, her voice rising.

"Your Majesty," the guard sputtered, "I have strict orders the king is not to be disturbed."

"Do you know who you are speaking to?" Margot's voice was getting even louder.

The soldier was paralyzed between two contradictory royal orders and couldn't decide which one to obey and which to disobey.

The door swung open. The king's advisor stuck his head out. "What is going on? Oh, your Majesty," he said, then bowed.

"I need to talk to my father now," Margot said loudly.

"Who is that?" the king's voice boomed out.

"Father, I need to speak with you—it is very important," Margot replied.

"Of course, my dear," the king answered. "Come in."

As Margot walked toward the door held open by the king's advisor, she turned her head slightly and over her shoulder said, "The next time show some respect to a member of the royal family."

"Yes, your Majesty," the guard said meekly, bowing deeply.

"What is it, my dear?" the king asked without looking up from the pile of papers in front of him.

"I have something very important to ask you." Margot waited. A few seconds later the king lifted his head and met his daughter's gaze. "Father, it is private."

The king turned to his advisor, who bowed and left the room. The king walked over to his daughter and put his arm around her. "You must be very excited. Tonight is the ball and you will see your future husband."

"No, father, it is not about the ball or my marriage. I cannot find Abagail. She has disappeared and..."

"Ask your mother," the king said abruptly as he removed his arm.

"I already did, and she told me Abagail is gone from court and is not coming back."

"If that is what your mother said, you have your answer." The king waited. "Is that all?"

The king's reply was like a punch to Margot's stomach. Not what he said but the way he said it. Her father always treated his daughter like she was special. He always had time for her and took her concerns seriously. Now her concerns were dismissed as childish. A line had been crossed. Margot was no longer an indulged child.

What did I do to be treated like this? she asked herself.

Margot knew that her father was under tremendous pressure. All the talk in the palace was about the endless war with Spain. What Margot didn't know was that her marriage was an honorable way to end the conflict. King Charles agreed to a payment of 200,000 crowns to the king of Spain as a war reparation disguised as Margot's dowry to end the war. With the people in a rebellious mood, the clergy fighting among themselves, and parliament resisting his attempts to raise more money for the war, the very existence of the monarchy was endangered. The king had no choice but to accept the terms offered by the Spanish king.

Meanwhile, in her dressing room, the queen sighed and, looking at her reflection in the mirror, thought about her daughter's future. She remembered when she left her home to live with her new husband. How frightening it was. It seemed like a lifetime ago. The queen could not show how upset she was to her daughter. It would only make it harder for her to do what she had to do.

I have to be more patient with Margot, the queen told herself. She looked in the mirror and was startled by how old she appeared.

Queen Henrietta wanted to tell her daughter that over time you find a way to accept your fate and, if you are lucky, you may even fall in love with your chosen husband. But she kept her counsel, not wanting to give her daughter false hope.

CHAPTER 3

Abagail slumped in a corner of the cave, as far away from the old woman as possible. She laid on the cold wet floor, crying, and couldn't remember ever feeling so alone. Abagail realized her only clothing was the dress meant for the coming ball. *How stupid of me. This dress is useless.* The hem was filthy. It was already covered in dirt and, in an attempt to look seductive, her shoulders and bosom were exposed. It didn't even keep her warm. Memories of life with Princess Margot floated through Abagail's mind: trying on new clothes, going to balls, eating delicious food whenever she wanted, laughing and talking with the princess about nothing and everything. The dress was a reminder of the life stolen from her.

Time passed. The old woman was right: the only way to measure how long she had been locked up was by the daily meals. Abagail began to look forward to when the guard brought the food and water. She tried every way to get him to talk to her.

"How long will I be here?" she asked, but he didn't reply. He simply doled out the mush in her big bowl and poured water in the smaller one. Then Abagail tried an easier question. "Can you please tell me what day it is?" The guard met the question with stony silence. When the guard brought food and water the following day, Abagail desperately tried to make eye contact. He looked past her as if she didn't exist, and Abagail began to wonder if she did.

Then one day, a young guard brought the food and water. He looked to be about her age and didn't avert his eyes. Abagail seized the opportunity and asked, "Do you know why I am here?"

To her astonishment, he answered, "No, I don't. It is forbidden to speak with prisoners."

To Abagail, this short exchange was miraculous. The

young guard made her feel human. He actually smiled—or Abagail thought he did. She wasn't invisible after all. Abagail, desperate to hold on to something positive, gathered pebbles and placed them in a straight line. Guessing she'd been locked up for a week, she placed seven pebbles in a row. That night, in a dream, Abagail and the young guard ran in a field covered with beautiful yellow flowers.

The next day, Abagail almost cried when it was the large older guard who brought the food. *I can't do this*, she thought. She took the two bowls, hunched up in a corner, and fell asleep. According to the pebbles, it had been nine days since her arrival at the cave and nothing had changed. No word from Margot or anyone else from outside. Her world was this dark, cold cave shared with a silent, crazy old woman. Abagail stood up and stepped on the hem of her dress, nearly falling as she did. *Stupid dress.* It was dirty, wrinkled, and now torn. Was it really only nine days ago that she and Margot had dressed for the party? She had to speak to another person before she forgot how.

"Why are you here?" Abagail asked the old woman, who didn't seem to hear the question or else decided to ignore her. Abagail turned away, feeling defeated. One day melted into another until time itself seemed to disappear. Abagail tried once more to talk with the old woman. "Why are you here?" This time she spoke loudly and stood directly in front of the old woman.

The old woman looked surprised, as if she forgot there was someone else in the cave. "Who are you?" she asked.

"I am Abagail, Princess Margot's lady-in-waiting and her friend." Abagail hesitated. "I thought."

"Ah yes, Princess Margot and Abagail," the old woman repeated. "Abagail, where is she?"

"That's me, I'm here." Abagail sighed. It was no use. She shuddered, realizing she may be locked in here forever with no one to talk to. The old woman was muttering to herself.

Abagail walked closer and heard her muttering, "Abagail, Abagail." *Just repeating the last thing she heard,* Abagail thought.

Abagail walked to her corner and turned her back to the old woman. Suddenly someone was touching her, tapping her softly on the shoulder. When Abagail turned, the old woman's face was so close it almost touched her. Abagail pulled back. The old woman stared at her, saying, "Abagail, Abagail," over and over again.

"That is right, that is my name," Abagail said loudly, losing her patience. Then she saw tears in the eyes of the old woman and felt awful for yelling at her. Abagail took her bony hand and held it. To her amazement, the old woman lifted her hand and gently stroked her face. Abagail tried to pull her hand free, but with surprising strength, the old woman wouldn't let go. Then she opened up Abagail's hand and gently kissed her palm.

"I am so sorry, my dear, so sorry."

"What are you sorry for?" Abagail asked.

The old woman repeated, "I'm sorry, so sorry."

Maybe trying to connect with someone was too much for the old woman? "It is all right," Abagail said.

According to the pebbles, it was her fifteenth day in the cave when the young guard brought the food. Abagail walked right up to him and stood so close, they almost touched.

"What day is it?" Abagail asked in an exasperated tone.

"Tuesday," he replied.

Abagail almost shouted out with joy. Another's voice—a human being responded to her. "What is your name?"

"Frederick," he answered. His face turned red and he quickly walked away.

Abagail had won a great victory. Hearing another voice in response to hers was like looking into a mirror and seeing her reflection.

The young guard stopped, turned, and started to walk

back towards her.

He wants to talk some more, Abagail thought. "Frederick, my name is Abagail. Do you know why I am here?" Her heart leaped for joy—finally a sane person to talk to.

He didn't respond or even look at her. He poured the mush and water in her bowls and without another word walked out.

Abagail's hopes dashed, she took the bowls back to her corner.

The old woman grinned as she ate her food.

Abagail smiled back. It was time to try again. Could she somehow connect with the old woman?

Abagail took her bowls and walked over to sit next to her. "How long have you been locked up here?"

"Since you were two years old," the old woman said.

What was the old woman talking about? *Every time I ask a question all I get is nonsense.*

"It was two weeks after you turned two, August ninth, after your birthday," the old woman said.

"How do you know my birthday?" Abagail asked, feeling a chill go through her body.

The old woman shook her head and mumbled, "I'm sorry, so sorry."

"Sorry for what? What are you sorry for?"

"It's all my fault," the old woman said. "I tried to run away."

"Run away, run away from who?"

The old woman put her bowl down and looked right at Abagail. Tears were running down her cheeks. "I did not want you to be hurt."

"You knew me when I was a baby?"

The old woman started rocking and held her arms out as if cradling an infant. "Shush, little baby girl. Everything is going to be all right. Mommy will take care of you."

Something deep within Abagail moved as a distant memory was shaken loose, but the memory hovered, un-formed, unnamed.

"I'll take care of you. No one will hurt you now," the old woman said.

"Why were you sentenced here? What did you do?" Abagail asked sternly.

"What did I do?" The old woman hesitated. "I disobeyed the queen. I took care of my child like any mother would."

"What child? What are you saying?" Abagail demanded, louder than she meant to.

"I was lucky not to be executed on the spot. It was only because I was so close to her that my life was spared."

"Close to who?" Abagail swallowed.

The old woman opened her eyes wide and looked directly at Abagail. "She wanted to take my child, my little baby, my Abagail."

Abagail gasped and asked, "What do you mean?"

"I am the queen's sister. We were both pregnant," the old woman said.

"Mother?" Abagail asked, the word slipping out. The word hung in the air and at that moment Abagail knew it to be true. This crazy old woman was her mother.

The old woman looked away.

Abagail took a deep breath. "Mother," she said again, almost choking. That word was so full of emotions; a declaration of love, anger, betrayal, and, most of all, confusion. Abagail asked very quietly, "Why were you put here?"

"I never gave up hope. The years passed and I thought about you and prayed every day to see you again before I died. Even in this hell hole God is present and answered my prayers."

Abagail reached over and hugged her mother, feeling her bones beneath the thin, worn dress she wore. Whispering this time, she asked again, "Why were you sentenced to this place?"

CHAPTER 4

The old woman took a step back, breaking her embrace with Abagail. "Let me ask you a question." The old woman didn't say anything for a few seconds. She just stared at Abagail.

"All right," Abagail said, confused by the sudden change in tone. "Ask me what?"

But still her mother stared and didn't speak. "What do you want to ask me?" Abagail said, getting impatient.

"What did the queen say when you asked about your mother?"

"What do you mean?" Abagail could hear her heart pounding.

"How did the queen explain to you what happened to your parents?"

"I never asked," Abagail said, and a sense of shame came over her. "I never asked," she repeated.

"You never asked," the old woman said in a shaky voice. "Where did you think you came from?"

Abagail felt accused of some horrible crime.

"You never asked?" the old woman repeated.

"I don't know. I just accepted I was where I was supposed to be."

"Didn't you ever wonder?"

"Well sometimes, when you say it, it sounds so wrong. I was a young child when all this took place. You said it yourself it was right after my second birthday..."

"Yes, but as you got older and now, you are a young woman, and still you did not ask?"

The old woman was incredulous.

"What did I do that was wrong? What are you saying?" Abagail's voice got louder.

"What I am saying," the old woman spoke very slowly,

emphasizing each word, "is at some point in your life you were old enough to ask and you did not."

"But..."

"You did not want to know. You became part of the campaign to silence me, to wish away my existence." The old woman abruptly stood up and walked to the farthest corner of the cave.

Was Abagail's mother right? Did Abagail take part in a conspiracy of silence? *Why didn't I ask about my parents? I just accepted my life as it was. The imprisonment in this cave must be my punishment. It was all part of the illusion that I controlled my life.*

The old woman and Abagail stayed as far away from each other as possible and did not speak for a whole day, not a word. A thought came to Abagail that wouldn't let go. It insisted on being spoken and wouldn't allow her to wallow in wounded silence. Standing near where her mother was sitting, Abagail waited for her to raise her head, but the old woman sat facing the stone floor. "Mother, I don't even know your name." Abagail bent down and saw tears in her mother's eyes.

"Beatrice," the old woman said in a hoarse whisper. "Beatrice, my name is Beatrice. No one has called me that for years. I am Beatrice and I am your mother. Please forgive me, child."

"Will you forgive me?" Abagail asked.

"There is nothing for me to forgive, being here so long I feel like I've been forgotten."

"I still do not know what we did to be locked up."

"For your part, it was being born. For me, it was my stubbornness that ruined both our lives." Beatrice rubbed her face and Abagail waited. "Queen Henrietta made you a companion for her daughter rather than sending us into exile," she continued.

"Exile?"

"Yes."

"Why?"

"It's a long story and I will tell you everything, but now I need to rest." The old woman closed her eyes and fell asleep.

"Of course." Abagail also needed time to make sense of what she just heard. It was blinding, like going from total darkness into a bright light. Could it be true? Why would the old woman lie? She did know her birthday. Was it really possible that for fifteen years her mother was living so close without a word or any kind of hint from anyone?

Her mother slept for what seemed like days. She was so still. Abagail tiptoed across the cave and bent down to listen for her breath. Her mother can't die, not now. Abagail couldn't imagine feeling more alone after being ripped out of her life and thrown in this dark cave. If her mother left now, how would she survive?

Her mother coughed and jerked her head forward. Abagail yelled, "Help! Help!" but her mother raised her hand.

"It's all right my dear, I am fine. Is there any water?"

Abagail jumped up and ran to her corner, grabbed her bowl, and tipped it so her mother could drink.

"Thank you, my dear," her mother said, wiping her mouth on her sleeve. "I did not mean to frighten you."

"I thought...I thought..." Abagail muttered and began to cry.

"There, there," her mother said, putting her hand on Abagail's shoulder. Abagail bent her neck so that her cheek was lying on top of her mother's hand.

"I thought I lost you...again."

"To see you and talk with you after so many years, it's a miracle. I have dreamed about this day and prayed for it. I have had hundreds of conversations with you in my mind. You have kept me company and kept me alive. I have waited too long for our reunion. No, I am not going anywhere, not any time soon." Beatrice stood up. "We have much to do."

"We do?"

"Now we begin your education." Her mother smiled. "You have lived a full and rich life in the royal court, but it was all based on a lie. You do not know the most basic facts of your life—who your parents were or how you ended up where you did. You lived in a kind of a cave also, cut off from the world and your past. I have lived my life in my head. When it comes to being with other people, I am ignorant. I don't remember how to talk with people, eat with a fork, or how to put on a dress. I would like to help you have an internal life, a life where you know who you are and where you come from."

"I would love that, mother," Abagail said, tasting that word, *mother*.

The old woman suddenly stopped talking and went to her corner. Without saying a word, she pointed at the other corner. Abagail moved there. The footsteps of the large guard bringing food and water stopped at their door.

When he left, Beatrice stepped over to Abagail. "It's best if they think we are not too friendly."

"All right," Abagail said, not sure why, but it sounded right.

Abagail and her mother sat very close to each other. In a hushed voice, her mother told Abagail the history of their family. "You come from a distinguished lineage. My mother, your grandmother, was Mary Queen of Scots, the sovereign of this country before she was executed."

"Executed," Abagail said, "why?"

"Mary and Elizabeth were half-sisters, same father—King Henry VIII—different mothers. Elizabeth was three years older and was the next in line for the crown."

"But to kill your own sister?"

"Yes, it was terrible. They were rivals for the crown."

"There was no other way?" Abagail asked.

"Elizabeth tried. She sent Mary into exile and forbade her from getting involved with politics, but Mary did not obey."

"What does that have to do with why we're locked up?"

"Our lives have been dictated by the past." Beatrice laughed bitterly. "My sister, Henrietta, tried to break the pattern of the past. Instead of sending the both of us into exile, she kept us close, making you a companion for her daughter, Margot, the princess."

"Are you saying I belong here in this hole?"

"I'm not saying that at all. My sister, your aunt is trying to do her best, but only knows what has been done before."

"Wait, I hear someone coming," Abagail said, and they stopped talking. Abagail stepped quickly to the other side of the cave. Her mother, not making eye contact, stared blankly.

"Tell me more," Abagail said when the halls were silent again.

"Henrietta, despite all her efforts not to, is repeating her mother's story. She has all but killed me. Locking me up and erasing me from the world is a kind of murder."

"You speak like there was no choice."

"I have come not to blame my sister. Her behavior was determined by her past as was mine. It is what she knew, what we both knew." The old woman sighed and shook her head.

"And what about us, are we to live the rest of our lives here?" Abagail took her mother's silence as a yes.

"Like my mother, I refused to give in, forcing my sister to silence me and you."

"Are you saying it is your fault?" Abagail asked, feeling more confused than ever.

"No, but I did have a role to play. I kept up the rivalry with my sister, competing for..." Beatrice stopped.

"Competing for what?" Abagail asked.

"I was the same age you are now. What do girls your age dream about?"

Abagail shook her head.

"Love, romance, marriage—those were the things that occupied our every thought. We were both smitten with the same boy. I remember first meeting him at a ball. My sister and I were together. He asked me to dance. We danced the whole night, causing a scandal."

"Why?"

"Because my sister was meant to be his bride, being the oldest. Their marriage was already arranged."

"I don't understand. You mean Queen Henrietta didn't marry the king?"

"Well, he was not the king at that time. He was the prince." Beatrice could tell by the look on her daughter's face that she didn't understand.

"So, what happened?" Abagail asked.

"Prince Charles married the sister he was meant to, and I became the maiden-in-waiting."

"Waiting?"

"Waiting for the prince to become king so he could do as he pleases."

Abagail waited for her mother to explain, still not understanding. Her mother smiled, raising her eyebrows, and nodded ever so slightly. Abagail turned the phrase over in her mind: *the king could do what he please.*

"You and King Charles were..."

"Yes, we were lovers, and I do not regret a minute of it." Beatrice's face took on a defiant look. For the first time, Abagail could imagine her mother as a princess, a proud young woman.

"What did Henrietta do?"

"We all pretended that no one knew."

"So, what happened?"

"You, my dear, you happened."

Chills ran through Abagail's body and she thought, *my life was a mistake, and I am the reason two sisters became enemies.*

"I went to a convent until I gave birth."

"I was born in a convent?" Abagail had the impression of leaving her body and floating, looking down at the both of them. This was someone else's life story, not hers.

"The nuns offered to care for you and raise you. I refused and insisted that I return to the court where I belonged." Beatrice saw the dazed look in her daughter's eyes. "Is this too much? Should I stop?"

"No, no, go on." Abagail insisted.

"I came back to court. I did not know what to expect but I had the youthful belief that everything would work out." Beatrice stopped and took a drink of water. "I was naïve and terribly wrong."

"What happened?" Abagail asked.

"That's when my sister—by that time she was Queen Henrietta—proposed that you would be in her daughter's service as a lady-in-waiting. You would be well taken care of, raised alongside the princess, and I could live at the palace and see you whenever I wanted. But only on the condition that no one could know I was your mother."

Abagail became angrier the more she heard. "And you accepted that, giving up your baby, me?"

"Where could I have gone, live by myself with an infant and no husband? All I knew was life in the court. I was your age with a baby and no family. So, yes I agreed."

Abagail felt cold inside. Her life was something to be haggled over, a thing to be negotiated, and looked at her mother with disgust. At that moment, Abagail hated her, and stood up to move to her corner, refusing to look at her mother.

They didn't speak for the rest of the day.

The next morning Beatrice patted her daughter's back. "I probably told you too much too soon." Abagail stared at a spot over her mother's right shoulder.

"Tell me when you are ready to hear more." Beatrice hobbled back to her side of the cave.

Abagail sat very still, but her mind was working furiously, trying to make sense of her mother's story. Born in a convent to a woman who slept with her sister's husband. Then another thought hit her—she and Margot were half-sisters. Did Margot know? What would Abagail have done in her mother's situation? Seventeen years old with a little baby, no husband, and only knowing an extravagant lifestyle? She had so many questions. But there was something more pressing to discuss with her mother.

CHAPTER 5

Abagail took Beatrice's bony arm and whispered, "Mother." The word moved a feeling of belonging inside her. "Mother, we have to find a way to escape this place."

Abagail expected her mother to respond with disbelief and even scorn, but instead, her mother resolutely said, "I have a plan."

"You do?" Abagail responded excitedly.

Beatrice spoke slowly and deliberately. "The only way out is through the guards. We have to disarm one of them and get his keys when he delivers the food." Her mother leaned back, closed her eyes, and was perfectly still, reminding Abagail of a corpse.

"Mother are you all right?"

Eyes closed, the old woman flexed her hand, demonstrating life.

"How do we do that?" Abagail asked, suddenly flooded with doubt.

The old lady put her hand up and softly whispered, "In a moment."

Abagail looked at her mother slumped against the rocky wall and tried to imagine her when she was young, clean, and beautiful. But she couldn't get past the old, unwashed, frail, woman in front of her, more dead than alive. Then, as if woken from the dead, her mother opened her eyes and sat straight up.

"We have to take our time, but that's the one thing we have plenty of." Her eyes sparkled as she let out a small laugh. "We wait until that young guard brings us food."

"But can we overpower him?"

She held her hand up again. "Give me a moment. It's exhausting to talk after so many years of silence." After a pause, her mother continued. "We can do it if we have knives."

"Knives?" Abagail asked. "Where do we get knives?"

"We make knives from the handles of our spoons."

"How?" Abagail asked in a strained voice, her heart pounding.

Her mother sighed at needing to explain. "We scrape the handles of the spoons against the wall until they are sharp."

"Then we'll tie him up," Abagail said, her face brightening with hope.

"No, that won't work. We have to kill him." Her mother said this without any emotion, her sallow countenance unchanged.

"Kill him?" Abagail was shocked by the matter-of-fact way her mother endorsed taking a life, and saw in her the regal manner of a queen.

"We either kill him, or we spend the rest of our lives buried in this hole."

Abagail paced, thinking it through, but there didn't seem to be another realistic way to escape. "So how do we sharpen our spoons without the guards noticing?" she asked.

"They do not see us—to them we are not a threat. We are just a crazy old woman and a helpless young girl. We have to lure that young one into the cave."

"I know what to do to make him want to come into the cave. A little smile and my hand on his arm then once he is in the cave we can both pounce and bring him down," Abagail said.

"It would be better if he was already on his knees. I will pretend to be deathly sick, unable to stand. You ask for his help when he comes with the food. When he kneels down next to me, you stab him in the back, and I'll stick him from the front."

Abagail could feel the blood drain from her face as she imagined the scene. Without speaking of it again, Abagail sharpened her spoon handle and then her mother's against the jagged wall. Her mother was right, the guard did not notice as she sharpened the spoon handles into knives.

Every day, Abagail prepared to rush up to the young guard and plead with him to help the old woman. The line of pebbles grew longer and still no sign of the young guard.

"Will he ever come?" Abagail asked her mother.

"Patience my dear, patience."

Abagail's eyes teared when her mother advised patience, sounding like a real mother, reassuring and comforting.

Abagail went from feeling like she was drowning in a bottomless swamp of time without a beginning or an end, to counting the minutes to freedom. Abagail tried to keep herself ready by going over the plan again and again. But her resolve weakened every day as the older guard brought their food and water.

Beatrice had the opposite reaction. Making an escape plan gave her hope. The fact that Abagail was back in her life meant that miracles happened. *Maybe I will leave this place alive,* she thought.

CHAPTER 6

One day, the door opened, and the young guard carried the buckets of food and water into the cave. Abagail froze, her mind blank. She heard her mother groan and that snapped her out of the haze. She sprang up to the young guard.

"Help," she said. "Please help us. The old woman is very sick. I do not know what to do."

The young guard stood there, not moving. Abagail touched him gently on the arm and guided him further into the cave.

They stood over her mother, who was groaning loudly. "What do you think?" Abagail asked the guard. "She's been groaning like this since last night. What is it? Do you see anything wrong?"

The guard knelt down and bent over to get a closer look at the old woman. His back was to Abagail. She turned her spoon to the sharpened end, poised to strike, and stared at his back, her hand trembling—she couldn't do it. Suddenly the guard began wrestling with her mother. Abagail couldn't see what was happening. His body covered her mother.

The young guard sat straight up and turned toward Abagail. A whoosh of air left his body. He grabbed his stomach with both hands and blood oozed between his fingers. His mouth moved but no sound came out.

Abagail closed her eyes and with all her might thrust the spoon in him. It made a sickening sound as it sunk into something soft. She pushed the spoon in with all her strength. Opening her eyes, Abagail saw him grabbing his throat, trying to pull the spoon out. Blood spurted out of his neck. He fell forward onto her mother, whose bellow rattled Abagail to her marrow. Abagail rolled the guard to the floor and onto his back. His eyes were wide open, unfocused, and lifeless.

Her mother was covered in blood, but Abigail couldn't tell whose blood it was. She looked closely and saw blood trickling out of her mother's mouth.

Abagail turned away as her stomach rose to her throat. She vomited violently. She wiped the puke from her mouth and waited. Her mother's mouth moved but there was no sound. "Mother, tell me what to do."

With a great effort, her mother managed to raise her head. Abagail put her ear as close to her mother's mouth as possible, straining to hear her. "Go, leave me." Then her mother's head fell back, and her eyes had the same unfocussed look as the young guard. Abagail's face was as close to her mother's mouth as possible. There was no breath. She put her fingers gently on her mother's neck—there was no pulse.

Abagail kneeled with her mother's head in her lap. She sat, frozen, then remembered what her mother told her to do if something happened to her during the escape. Abagail was to escape without her. Her mother had Abagail promise to follow the escape instructions and had committed them to memory.

Abagail looked at her mother one last time to sear her face into her memory. She kissed her on the cheek and pledged that she would live on in her mind and her story would not be forgotten. Abagail got up and took the ring of keys from the young guard's belt. Her eyes trained on the cave wall to avoid looking at his dead, bloody face.

CHAPTER 7

The door to the cave was wide open and Abagail simply walked out into the hallway. She found the staircase where they had carried her down and very quietly walked up. There was not another person in sight. Abagail was outside. It was dark. She inhaled deeply. Breathing outside of the cave was like diving into a clear, cold stream. She closed her eyes then opened them quickly as the image of her mother lying in a pool of blood on that cold, hard floor came back. Leaning over with both hands on her knees, her stomach went into spasms. This time nothing came up. Her stomach was empty.

Her gown was splattered with the blood of her mother and the guard. Dry blood covered her hands and stuck under her fingernails. Evidence of the murderous deed was written on her body and clothes. Realizing the sharpened spoon was still in her hand, she threw it far from her in the tall grass and swallowed the bile that rose in her throat.

Her instinct told her to run as fast and as far as she could, but that would only bring attention to herself. She needed to hide—but where?

Abagail had only lived in two places: the palace with the princess and the cave with her mother. Both places provided her with necessities. Now, at the age of seventeen, she had to find her own way in the world, and above all else, she couldn't be found.

As Abagail thought of her next steps, something her mother said came to mind: "The less you have, the more you have to use what you have wisely." Abagail crossed over to the sharpened spoon and hid it in her dress. Now, how to cover up the blood? There was no access to water to wash herself, and even if there was, she couldn't just take off the stupid blue dress. Scooping up handfuls of dirt and rubbing it on her clothing may have made her look like a dirty mess, but at least the blood was mostly hidden. *Hide, so you can live,* she thought. Live, so you can pay back those who killed your mother and robbed you of your life. Live to avenge.

CHAPTER 8

Abagail stumbled toward town, hugging the buildings and trying to be invisible. In the near-empty streets of the city, people stirred, beginning their day. The sky began to turn from black to blue. The light of the rising sun was her enemy. London was waking up. It was time to get off the street and find a place to hide.

Exhausted, Abagail could barely keep her eyes open. She found an alley, crawled behind a stack of hay, laid down next to it, covered herself with some loose hay, and fell into a deep sleep in which she dreamt of drowning. No matter how fast she swam she couldn't reach the surface. Her life was slipping away as she sank into the cold, dark depths. Abagail was ready to die, almost welcoming it—finally, the rest she so badly yearned for. Just as she was preparing for her death and the end of her suffering, her body began to float, breaking through to the surface. Sweet air filled her lungs and her eyes opened.

Abagail laid in her hay bed for a few moments, but her hunger wouldn't let her rest. She couldn't remember the last time she had eaten. Standing made her dizzy. Almost falling, Abagail stumbled out of the alley into a busy street. People went about their business, walking and talking. Some bumped into her like she was invisible as they hurried on their way and others whispered to each other when they saw her dirty dress and wild hair. She waited for someone to shout, "There she is. Yes, that's the one." Every look in her direction was an accusation. Every conversation between two people was a plan to return her to the cave. But incredibly, nobody accused her of murder, and nobody came to drag her back to jail.

As Abagail walked aimlessly through the city streets, the delicious aroma of baking bread over-powered her. Almost fainting from hunger, Abagail managed to stagger to a bakery doorway and leaned against the door, unable to take another step.

The door seemed to open itself. "Yes, miss. Can I help you?" A heavy-set, middle-aged woman from inside the bakery held the door open for Abagail, who stumbled in. The woman looked at Abagail and shook her head. "You look a mess. What happened to you? No, don't tell me. I do not want to know but you look like you can do with something to eat." The woman took a roll from behind the counter and handed it to Abagail. "It might be a little hot. It just came out of the oven."

Abagail took the roll and devoured it in two bites. It was the best thing she ever ate.

"Well, you sure made quick work of that. When was the last time you ate?" the woman asked, giving Abagail two more warm rolls.

Abagail ate one and held on tightly to the other.

"Don't worry, dear, nobody is going to take it away from you."

Abagail was so grateful she started to cry and tried to thank the woman, but the words stuck in her throat.

"Can you talk?" the woman asked. "I guess not. Well, dear, you can't go walking around half-naked. Come closer, dear, no one's going to hurt you here." The woman ap-proached Abagail and saw that her dress was bloody. Putting her hands to her mouth, she gasped, "Oh my, what happened to you?"

Abagail didn't know how to answer.

"Let me see, you are about the same size as my daughter." The baker took her hand. "Come with me." Abagail followed the baker to a small bedroom behind the bakery. The woman rifled through a trunk and pulled out a dress "Here it is. It is not new, but it is clean. I was thinking about giving it away, so I washed it just yesterday, like I knew someone was coming who would need a dress. My daughter cannot fit into it anymore and you look like you can use it. What is your name, dear?"

Abagail didn't respond. Her voice wouldn't work. All she could think of was the taste of the warm rolls melting in her mouth.

"Oh, right, what am I thinking?" She handed the dress to Abagail. "Speaking of washing, I dare say you could do with some cleaning yourself. Wait here."

In no time the lady returned, carrying a wooden bucket. "Here's some hot water and some soap and a towel. Take that dirty thing off, do not be bashful."

Abagail took the soiled dress off and covered herself with the towel. The woman touched Abagail's gown immediately, feeling the quality of the material. Where did she get a dress like this? But the woman didn't ask. What would be the use? She couldn't give her an answer. "When you're clean and dressed, meet me in the front. I have to get ready to open."

Abagail's skin awakened as the hot water ran down her back. The soap smelled like fresh-cut flowers. She rubbed the soap into a lather and slowly washed, not missing an inch on her body, and washed her hair twice. The scent of the soap lingered. She dried herself and put on the new dress. It was well used, a little too big, and worn in places, but it wasn't covered in mud and blood. Abagail felt like a new person as she walked to the front of the bakery.

"Well, aren't you pretty? I'm sorry I do not have any shoes to give you."

Abagail took the woman's hand, opened it up, and kissed her palm.

The woman became flustered. "You do not have to do that. I am just being a good Christian. I have to open up the bakery soon. You are welcome to stay."

Abagail shook her head and headed for the door, then remembered the spoon. She turned at the door and picked up her old dress.

"You can leave that here, dear. Do not worry about it."

Abagail gave the kind woman a big smile. She held onto

her old dress, felt the spoon in the pocket, and slipped it into the pocket of her new dress.

"Wait one minute," the woman said, and handed Abagail a bag full of warm rolls. "Well, good luck, and may God be kind to you."

Abagail left the bakery, overcome with gratitude. She couldn't remember the last time someone had been so kind to her. The bit of food gave Abagail some energy, and with the energy came hope.

The baker, by her kindness, posed a question for Abagail. Why would someone be kind to someone they never met?

It was time to make a plan. First things first, Abagail needed to find a way to get out of the city, then to support herself.

CHAPTER 9

The queen was enraged, her neck flaming red. "What do you mean they escaped? How is that possible?"

The marshal bowed his head, preparing himself to take the blows of his queen. "It seems," he said quietly, "that they were able to fashion wooden spoons into weapons."

"Wait a minute. Are you saying that this old woman and young girl were able to overpower a guard?"

"Yes, your Majesty," the marshal said, barely loud enough to be heard.

"And who is this incompetent guard? I want to speak with him."

"Well, your Majesty, he was killed."

"Killed, they killed one of my men?" The queen raised her voice even louder.

"Yes. And the old woman was killed as well."

"What did you say?" the queen screamed, spittle flying from her mouth. "That cannot be. No, no that cannot be," she repeated, collapsing in her chair.

The marshal was so stunned by the queen's outburst that he was momentarily speechless. "The old woman attacked the guard along with the young lady. It looks like the old woman was killed fighting the guard."

The queen held tightly onto her chair to prevent herself from falling off.

"Your Majesty, are you ill?" the marshal asked. "Should I call the physician?"

"You are sure my sister is dead?"

"Your sister? I don't understand."

"The old woman, you are sure she has been killed."

"Yes, I am sure."

The queen put her hands over her face.

The marshal was not certain, but he could've sworn the

queen was sobbing. He heard her moan, "What have I done?" a number of times.

The marshal had no idea what to do so he did as he was trained to do, standing at attention and waiting for further orders. He stood until his back hurt and his legs began to wobble.

The queen finally lifted her head and asked, "Where is the young girl, Abagail?"

"Gone."

"Gone," the queen repeated. "How?"

"She took the keys from the guard, opened the doors, and walked out."

The queen took a deep breath and, using the last of her energy, was able to ask, "I assume you have men looking for her?"

"Yes, your Majesty."

"I want her found and found immediately. And I want her brought to me unharmed. I hold you personally responsible to see that she is caught quickly and not hurt. Do you understand, marshal?"

"Yes, your Majesty."

"Who was the guard that was murdered?" the queen asked.

The marshal mumbled, dreading what was sure to come.

"Speak up, man. What is his name?"

"Your Majesty, his name was Frederick Westbrook."

"Frederick Westbrook, I never heard that name before. How long has he worked for the court?"

"Well, your Majesty, he was not officially working."

"What do you mean not officially working?"

"He is the son of Albert Westbrook, the regular guard. He relieves his father from time to time."

The queen's mouth moved but no words came out.

The marshal stood at attention, trying his best not to move. He stood that way for several minutes, which felt like hours to him.

Finally, the queen hissed, "I want Abagail found immediately. And I want to speak to this Albert Westbrook. Is that understood? Do you think you can handle that, marshal of the royal court?"

The marshal felt his blood turn to ice and, using all the restraint he could muster, he walked slowly out of the hall.

The queen fell back into her chair and remembered when this tragedy began many years ago, when she and her sister, Beatrice, were pregnant at the same time.

*

"I have the solution," the queen had said excitedly to Beatrice. "Your baby will be brought up in the palace and become a member of our family. Our two babies can grow up together."

"You want to take my baby away?" Beatrice asked, her voice shaking with fear. "Never, you will not take my child and ruin her life like you did mine."

"What are you talking about—ruin your life? I am trying to save it."

"Save it?" Beatrice grunted.

"Yes, save it. What will you do? How will you support yourself and your child? Who will take you in, a disgraced mother with a bastard child?" The queen breathed deeply.

"Beatrice, just listen for a minute," she tried again. Her younger sister sobbed. She put her arm around her shoulders. "I'm proposing that your child live in the palace, and you would live here as well."

Beatrice raised her head and wiped the tears away. "I can see my child?"

"Of course," the queen continued.

"But would she know I'm her mother?"

"I don't think that is possible." The queen removed her

hand from her sister's shoulder. "It's for the best. Your child will always be cared for and you can see her whenever you want." The queen paused.

Beatrice's silence was taken as acceptance by the queen.

The two baby girls were born a few weeks apart. First Margot the princess, followed by her companion, Abagail. They both entered the world with their very different futures all planned out. They each had a wet nurse and they spent all day lying side by side in their cribs. Everything worked out, at first.

Beatrice would spend hours gazing lovingly at Abagail, mesmerized by her. "Isn't she beautiful, Henrietta?" she would ask her sister, the queen, not believing that she had given birth to such a perfect baby. The most perfect child ever born was hers, but she never felt like the baby fully belonged to her and that began to hurt.

King Charles never acknowledged Beatrice or her baby. He was unfailingly polite and friendly to his sister-in-law, but showered all his attention on Margot. It was as if he forgot or pretended not to know that Abagail was his daughter. Beatrice was relieved. If the royal couple wanted to pretend that what happened never did, it was fine with her. It was an unspoken but hard and fast rule that no one was allowed to break the iron code of silence regarding Abagail's patrimony.

As the girls got older, Beatrice couldn't quiet the questions in her mind. *Why are Margot's needs more important than my daughter's? Why do I always come in second to my sister? And now my daughter is following in my footsteps, acting as a servant to her sister.*

The questions persisted and it was on Abagail's second birthday that Beatrice decided to take her baby and leave the palace. She would just walk out and make a life—a real life—for herself and her baby. She couldn't be part of the charade any longer. What kind of person would her daughter grow up to be if she didn't even know who her mother and father were?

Two weeks after Abagail's birthday, Beatrice woke up early, picked up her baby, and simply walked out of the palace. It was only when the palace was out of sight that she realized she hadn't any money, a destination, nor a plan.

Beatrice just wanted to get far away from the palace and her sister. The only alternative to hiding in town was going into the forest, but she was afraid of the forest and opted for wandering the town streets. While Beatrice tried to hide and come up with a plan, the palace was in an uproar.

The queen's advisor knocked as softly as possible on the queen's bedroom door. In all his years of service to the crown, this was the first time he interrupted the queen before she was out of bed. "I'm so sorry to disturb you at this early hour, your Majesty."

The queen sat up in bed, pulling her robe up to cover her bare skin. "Yes, yes, what is it?"

"Princess Beatrice has left the palace, your Majesty, and no one knows where she is."

"What, how? Check the nursery. Go, quickly now." The queen panicked and, to the horror of the court, ran out of her room and partially down the corridor with her robe flapping open behind her. Then the queen did something even more shocking. She yelled to the advisor, who immediately stopped when he heard his mistress and ran back to her. "Check on Princess Margot, hurry."

The advisor ran fast for someone who hadn't run since he was a young boy. He burst into the nursery. The beds were turned over and the two wet nurses and the nanny were frantically searching for something—or, more likely, someone. The advisor prayed silently. Oh, please don't let it be Princess Margot they're looking for. His prayers were answered.

Out of breath, he ran back and entered the royal chamber with a bow.

"Well, what did you find?"

"Princess Margot is safe and sleeping," the advisor said.

"Thank God for that," the queen responded.

"But..."

"But what, man? Come on, spit it out."

"The baby Abagail is not in her bed."

"Find her now. Fetch the marshal and tell him to use all his men to locate Princess Beatrice and the baby."

Two hours later, Beatrice was found sitting on the ground in an alley near the town square. Her baby was wailing from hunger. Abagail was immediately taken to the wet nurse. Beatrice was brought before the queen.

"Did you really believe you could kidnap the child and escape?" the queen asked.

"If she is my baby, how can I kidnap her?" Beatrice, with her eyes down and shoulders hunched, didn't look at her sister.

"I can't believe we have to talk about this again. I have explained to you many times why it's better for you and Abagail that no one learns the circumstances of her birth."

Beatrice stood very still, then said, "You pretend to care for me and my daughter, but it is really only you and your family you are concerned about."

"How dare you say that. All I am thinking about is your and Abagail's welfare."

"You can tell yourself that if it makes you feel better, but we both know that if the truth comes out about my 'indiscretion,' I would have to leave the court."

"Exactly, that's what I've been saying."

"But it's not me you are worried about, it's yourself."

"What do you mean?" the queen asked.

"Your line of succession is challenged by Abagail."

"Nonsense, that's utter nonsense. Your baby has no father. What right does she have to the throne?"

"You and I both know who her father is." Beatrice felt her courage rise. The resentment of her and her baby's life thought of as an embarrassment to be swept under the rug erupted.

"If you say what I think you will, you will be sealing your fate. So be careful, little sister." The queen held her breath.

Beatrice, for her part, didn't blink and met Henrietta's stare with her own. "I cannot do this anymore, living my life based on a lie," she finally said.

"Think before you speak. Your future is in your hands."

Beatrice was quiet for a moment. "It is killing me. I have to speak."

The queen waited silently, but inside two words kept repeating—*Do not.*

"You and I both know the truth. Now it needs to be said out loud. The father of my baby is the king, Charles, your husband."

"No!" the queen screamed. "That is a treasonous statement and unless you retract it you will pay the price for your treason."

In that moment, Beatrice reclaimed her life. "Abagail's father is the king." She repeated it loudly. It was exhilarating to finally speak the unspeakable. She never felt more powerful.

"Retract this traitorous statement! I beseech you."

Beatrice shook her head.

Queen Henrietta rang a bell and a servant appeared as if by magic. "Fetch the marshal and tell him to come here right away." When the servant left, the two women were alone. "You leave me no choice sister. I beseech you again to reconsider. You still have time before you throw your life away."

Beatrice stood with her arms crossed, not uttering a word.

"Yes, your Majesty?" the marshal asked as he walked into the chamber.

"Escort Princess Beatrice to the cave."

CHAPTER 10

Abagail didn't know it, but she was being closely watched. Spencer Stokes was well known in this part of town. Parents told their children—especially the girls—to keep their distance. They'd say don't talk to him and under no circum-stances ever go with him, no matter what he says or what he promises to give you. Everyone knew Stokes grabbed what he wanted without a thought of the person he may hurt. His prey were the fragile elderly, the innocent young, the unsus-pecting, and the vulnerable. A confused, pretty young girl, aimlessly walking all alone in the street was an offering on a platter.

Spencer couldn't figure out her story. She dressed like a poor person but had the grace that came from money and breeding. He was content to follow her and wait for his opportunity. Abagail walked and walked. He held back, always keeping her in sight and making sure he wasn't spotted. When she walked down a dead-end street, it was time to act. He looked around. The street was deserted. Spencer leaped at his chance.

"Are you lost, miss? Can I help you?" he asked in his most innocent and friendly way.

Abagail jumped. Where did this man come from? Not paying attention to her surroundings and distracted by her mind replaying the terrible scene in the cave, she had no idea someone had gotten so close to her.

"No, I'm fine," she said. The man was scary even though he was smiling. The way he looked at her made her feel naked and exposed.

He took a step closer and Abagail could smell the alcohol on his breath, his sweat, and something rancid. A worn, shapeless jacket hung limply on his thin frame. His eyes were his most notable feature. They burned with a raging fury that Abagail would never forget.

He grabbed her arm, pinching her, still smiling, and said, "Come, let me help. I can get you something to eat and find a nice warm bed for you to sleep in tonight."

Abagail jerked her arm, but his grip tightened. "Please let go. You're hurting me." Her heart raced and she could barely breathe.

"No need to be frightened," he said, smiling still, letting go of her arm. "I'm just trying to help."

Abagail tried to get away from him, but he stayed right behind her, maintaining the same distance between them. She looked to the left and then to the right—there was no way out.

His smile disappeared. He rubbed her face with his un-shaven cheek and kissed her neck.

She felt his scratchy stubble on her cheeks. "No," she said. "No."

He pressed his body against her, pinning her to the wall.

Abagail tried to free her arms but couldn't. Afraid of the authorities finding her, she didn't scream.

With a quick movement, a rope appeared, and he tied her hands behind her back. She wriggled her hands, but the knot just got tighter and hurt her wrists.

"Stop fighting. You're not getting out of it. So, why don't you just play nice. I'll make sure you enjoy this too." He licked his lips and laughed.

Abagail felt his hands rubbing her breasts through her dress. He began unbuttoning her top. His rough hands were all over her body. He grabbed and pinched her breast so hard that she let out a squeal, which seemed to excite him even more. She bit her lip to keep from making any more sounds. He pulled her dress up. Abagail felt a sharp pain between her legs. His face was touching hers. His breathing quickened as he entered her.

Abagail felt herself floating away, imagining she was back in the cave with her mother. Her mother and Princess Margot were talking, having what seemed to be a pleasant conversation. Then the young guard appeared with the spoon sticking out of his neck. He was alive but transparent; she could see right through him. Princess Margot disappeared. Her mother was lying on the floor in a pool of blood. Then Abagail was floating in that pool of blood too. Her eyes snapped open and it took her a moment to figure out where she was and what had happened to her. Then she remem-bered being dragged into a makeshift shelter, more of a pile of garbage than a house.

No longer tied up, Abagail thought she had experienced an awful nightmare. But the bruises on her wrists were real and she felt sticky liquid between her legs. When she pulled her hand away it was red with blood. There was a taste of blood in her mouth, and she remembered biting her lip. She shivered, naked in the cold. Where did that man—that monster—go? Abagail put her hands out in the dark, found her dress, and tried to put it on. Her only thought was to get away before he came back. In the folds of her dress was the spoon. Wrapping her hand around it, she felt some of her strength return. Her hands trembled getting her dress over her head. Then she heard him.

"Where do you think you're going, princess? Are you ready for some more? I am."

When he leaned into her to rub his hands on her body, Abagail didn't hesitate—she clutched the spoon and aimed for his eye. He turned away at the last second and the spoon sliced his cheek. She pushed the blade in as hard as she could and brought it down. He let out a horrible scream as he staggered and grabbed his face. "I'm going to kill you," he bellowed, "I'm going to kill you!"

Abagail gathered up her clothes and ran as fast as she could. She heard him yell after her, "I'm going to find you and kill you."

CHAPTER 11

Abagail ran and ran. When she couldn't run anymore and thought her lungs would burst, she kept running, and when it felt like her legs would fall off, she thought about that man and ran some more. She ran through the streets to the outskirts of the city past the farms and didn't notice the people staring at her. Abagail ran into the forest and kept running until hidden by the trees. Stopping, she leaned over with both hands on her knees, her heart pounding, her breath coming in short bursts. She tried to be quiet, to hear if he was following her. The only sound was the echo of that man's voice in her head, bellowing like a wounded animal: "I'm going to kill you."

Abagail took a deep breath and heard the gurgling of water. Using the sound as a guide, she came to a stream and drank the water, which was cold and sweet. She took off her dress and sat gingerly in the water, trying to cleanse herself from the blood, dirt, and stink of that awful man. The cold made her gasp but after a few minutes she acclimated.

The night sky was covered in stars and the moon was a sliver. Abagail looked around. The world was in total silence and she was alone; alone in these woods, alone in the world. *Get up and keep moving*, she told herself, but her legs were weak. *I have to put as much distance as possible between me and that monster.* She decided to sit for a while and rest before walking again. Startled awake, her panic rose and she realized she must have fallen asleep. The sun was shining down through the trees, and the sound of a wagon disturbed the silence.

Abagail crouched behind a bush and watched the two men on the wagon, one older and the other younger. They talked comfortably, seeming to know each other well. Abagail felt a strong urge to approach them. She never wanted anything so much as a ride in their wagon. To sit and rest while getting away from what happened yesterday seemed like a miracle. Abagail shuddered, reminding herself to trust no one. Crouching lower, she watched the wagon as it moved out of sight.

CHAPTER 12

Spencer rinsed his raw, throbbing wound. He put a dry piece of cloth on it and pressed softly. The bleeding wouldn't stop so he tried pressing harder. It hurt like hell. The cloth turned bright red. He threw it away and put another one on. It took several cloths to stop the flow of blood. He vowed to find and kill her, but not before he made her suffer. He had to wait for the wound to heal before he went out in public— attracting attention to himself was the last thing he wanted.

By daybreak, the wound still throbbed but it had stopped bleeding. He was able to do without the cloth. It was risky to go out in public, but he couldn't sit inside forever and let that bitch get away.

On the street, he found himself in the middle of a protest march. These protests were becoming weekly events. By their banners he could see the marchers were apprentices grouped by their trade; weavers, tinsmiths, carpenters, and silversmiths. They were followed by peasants, unmistakable in their country clothes, and then—he couldn't believe it— clergymen bringing up the rear. What was the world coming to? Their banners held high, with slogans like "People First," "End the War Tax," and "Freedom of Worship." They were all happily marching along, merrily singing like it was a holiday.

Then he saw the king's men. *It's about time they cracked down on these damn troublemakers,* he thought. He moved further into the shadows and waited for the soldiers to start breaking heads. But the soldiers weren't paying any attention to the crowd filling the street. Instead, he watched as they spoke with local residents and shopkeepers, showing them a drawing of a young girl. He walked by some soldiers questioning the owner of a nearby blacksmith shop. He casually walked past the blacksmith, trying to hear what was being said. He couldn't see the drawing but knew it was that bitch who had cut him.

"No, I already told the other ones I did not see a strange girl. I have to get back to work now." The blacksmith walked back to his shop. Spencer waited until the soldiers walked away to question someone else, then went into the smith's shop.

"Why are you not marching with your comrades?" Spencer asked.

"I do not have time for that nonsense. I have a business to run," the blacksmith replied.

"I know what you mean. What were those soldiers asking you about?" Spencer tried to keep his voice casual.

The blacksmith straightened up from shoeing a horse, annoyed. "They are looking for some young girl who escaped jail and killed a guard."

"Killed a guard, you say. Is there a reward?" Spencer asked, licking his lips.

The blacksmith stopped hammering the nail to the horse's hoof to look up at Spencer and noticed the wound. He mumbled, "Yes."

Spencer no longer cared about how he looked or what people might think about him. "How much?" he asked.

"One hundred," the blacksmith said. He wished this man would leave. He made the blacksmith nervous. For some reason, his thoughts went to his wife and young daughter. "I've got to get back to work," he said, and pumped the bellows to stoke the blazing fire. He never turned his back to Spencer and kept his eyes on him until he was out of sight.

CHAPTER 13

Abagail followed the path the two men on the wagon took. The path led away from town and that awful man. It wasn't much of a road. It would disappear at times when the grass grew over it.

As Abagail walked, her thoughts returned to all that had happened since being thrown into the cave. Trying to get the image of her mother dead on the floor out of her mind, Abagail searched to recall a good memory. They had such a short time together. But in that short time, her mother did take care of her. Abagail escaped thanks to her mother. She paid for Abagail's freedom with her life. It was impossible to forget how her mother blamed herself for their imprisonment. Abagail wondered whether her mother no longer wanted to live and felt a heaviness in her chest.

"Beatrice," she said her mother's name out loud. "Beatrice," this time louder. "Queen Beatrice," shouting as loudly as she could. Her mother was not going to be forgotten; her name would not be erased. "Queen Beatrice and Princess Abagail," she said softly, not really believing it. All these years denied her birthright, lied to by the royal family, who had pretended to love her. Tears gathered in her eyes, not tears of sadness but of anger. *Princess Abagail—that is who I am. That is who I've always been.* Exhausted, Abagail laid down and fell asleep.

Abagail slept the whole day. At first, upon opening her eyes, she did not know where she was. It was so dark and quiet it was like being back in the cave with her mother. Abagail panicked, then realized she was in the forest. *Safe for now,* she thought, *but I will not survive if I can't follow these simple rules, walk at night, sleep during the day, and above all else, find food.*

CHAPTER 14

"Frederick is dead." Albert stood in the kitchen, the biggest room of the house, with his head bowed in front of his wife.

Clara screamed at him. "No, no you're wrong, it cannot be. How? Why? Where is he?"

Albert felt his wife's eyes bore through him. "He was taking my place at work." His brain shut down and he couldn't say any more. He stood completely still, one large hand clasping the other as if he was in church, accused by God of his son's murder.

Clara swooned and Albert took her arm to keep her from falling.

She pulled away. "Do not touch me. Never touch me again," she screamed.

Albert's arms fell to his side.

"Why him and not you?" Clara asked in a strangled voice.

They had already lost three of their eight children. Two during childbirth and Sarah just three years old when she was taken away during the great sickness last summer.

Clara desperately searched for a reason why her babies were being taken away. Was it something she or her husband did? The first loss of a baby was horrible. The second in childbirth was even more painful. But when Sarah died at three years old, Clara nearly reached her breaking point.

And now the murder of her oldest, Frederick. The only explanation was that God was punishing her. But what did she do to deserve his wrath? Clara walked out of the house, blind to those around her and deaf to her four living children yelling, "Mother, mother, where are you going? Mother, why are you crying? Do not go. Do not leave us."

Albert bent down to comfort the little ones. "Your mother's not feeling well," he said, trying to sound more in control than he felt.

Clara walked through the city, past the farms until she reached the edge of the forest. It was getting dark out and she didn't remember how she got there. Her mind wouldn't stop asking painful questions. Why was Frederick working for Albert the day he was murdered? Albert wasn't home that day. Clara knew and had always known but pretended not to—he was with one of his whores. God is punishing her for closing her eyes to her husband's sins. She was as much to blame as he was. Throwing herself on the ground, Clara cried, looked up at the stars, and could not stop asking *why*? The stars didn't answer. The animals in the forest were silent. The moon didn't even acknowledge her question.

The next day, Clara went to church and asked the priest, "Why?" She needed to know. *God must have a plan.* To think that the death of her children was random was unbearable. If that was true, what was the point of living?

Albert couldn't bear the pain and the sense of guilt he felt when he was with his wife. When Clara asked him to accompany her to see the priest, he had no choice but to go.

"God wanted it to happen and there was nothing you or anyone else could have done to prevent it," the priest said with great solemnity. The priest droned on. "It is God's will. He works in mysterious ways and we who are merely human could never understand." Clara bowed her head and softly cried. "Your children are in a happier place now under God's protection." Clara let out a sob.

When Albert—following his wife's lead—lowered his head, he did it so he wouldn't have to look into the red eyes of the fat priest with his empty words and phony wisdom. A man who never did a hard day's work in his life, and never had a family or raised a child. Spouting "wisdom" about how his son's death was all part of God's unknowable plan was just another one of the lies the church spewed. Albert knew who killed his son and he would avenge his death.

Albert couldn't bear to stay at home, silently accused by

his grieving wife, and he couldn't return to work. So, he spent his days at a tavern drinking, not coming home until late at night when his wife and children were asleep.

Stumbling in late one night, he saw an envelope with the queen's seal on the kitchen table. The letter summoned Albert to an audience the following day with the queen. "Her Majesty probably wants to offer her condolences," Albert explained to his wife the following morning. In the past, it would have been one of the highlights of her life, her husband having a private audience with the queen. Now Clara was acting as if she hadn't even heard what he said.

Albert knew this audience with her Majesty may be more than an expression of regal sympathy. It could also be about why a sixteen-year-old boy was working as a guard in place of his father. Albert was not afraid. The worst that could happen was him losing his job. He would almost welcome it. His heart had gone out of his work.

CHAPTER 15

Abagail filled up on water, drinking so much her stomach felt like it was going to burst. The occasional woodland animal darted through the bush, but by the time she reached for her spoon, they would be long gone. From the corner of her eyes, she began to see animals as they approached, tiny birds or large insects, but once she turned her head they disappeared. Were they real or was hunger making her see things? The one real thing was the growing ache in her stomach along with constant dizziness.

The day was coming to an end and Abagail should have been walking the road as night set in. But she couldn't even muster the strength to sit up. Closing her eyes, she prepared to say goodbye to the world. Her dreams were not about her mother or the monster who hurt her or Margot. Abagail dreamt of only one thing: food. A whole table full of delicious things to eat. The dream comforted her. This world was just too much for her. Abagail imagined the grass and earth covering her body, keeping her safe and warm. She would sleep forever in the soft folds of the earth. Abagail was ready to find peace, so when hands began shaking her, she resisted opening her eyes. But the shaking didn't stop.

"Miss, miss, are you all right?"

Abagail heard a girl's voice from far away.

"Go get mother and father. Be quick."

Abagail drifted off again.

Then a stronger pair of hands took hold of her arms. "Wake up," a man's voice commanded.

Abagail shot up, her eyes wide open. She moved her hands quickly to find the spoon. *I will die before I let him hurt me again*, she thought.

"Easy, miss. We want to help you," the man said.

Abagail breathed hard and her vision was blurry, but she

was just able to make out four figures—two small ones and two larger ones—standing over her.

"Let me handle this, Frank," a woman said. "Are you hungry, my dear?"

Abagail was frozen with fear.

"Jeffrey, go to the wagon and bring some apples and some cider, bread and cheese," the woman said to a boy.

Abagail ate the food and drank the sweet, cold cider. She ate and drank and then ate and drank some more, feeling full for the first time since this whole nightmare began.

"When was the last time you ate?" the man asked.

"A long time ago," Abagail said in a hoarse whisper.

"Do you have a place to sleep?" the woman asked with a pleasant smile.

Abagail could only shake her head.

"You can stay with us in our wagon," the woman said. "Jeffrey, you've been asking to sleep outside for the whole trip. Well, tonight you're going to get that chance."

"What about me, Mama?" asked the young girl. "I want to sleep outside too."

The mother sighed. "You both will get your wish tonight and sleep outside."

Hearing this simple exchange between a mother and a daughter affected Abagail deeply. Propping herself up, she stumbled as she tried to stand. The man took her arm. She pulled back. He didn't tighten his grip but gently helped her to her feet. Accepting his help, Abagail made it into the wagon.

For the first time in what felt like forever, Abagail had a dreamless, deep sleep. Lying still with her eyes closed, she felt as if she was moving although she was perfectly still. Something carried her along and then she remembered the wagon and the family that fed her. The air in the wagon was suffused with the aroma of fresh flowers. This must be a dream. How can a wagon have a garden? If this was heaven, Abagail embraced her death.

"Miss, miss, wake up."

It was the same child who roused her earlier. Abagail tried to ignore the soft voice, wanting to prolong her sense of well-being.

"Miss, miss."

The peaceful state Abagail was experiencing shattered. Not sure what was waiting for her, she opened her eyes and braced herself. A young girl leaned over her. The girl's red hair framed a face full of freckles. "Mama, mama, the lady is awake," she shouted.

Abagail felt glued to the bed but managed to lift her head just enough to see a woman crawling in her direction. The woman sat by Abagail's side. She had the kindest blue eyes Abagail had ever seen.

"We were worried about you. You've been sleeping for a whole day," the woman said.

"I'm sorry," Abagail said and began to get up, propping herself on her elbows.

"No, I'm not asking you to get up. Lie back down. You must be very hungry. Theresa, get some bread and cheese. You don't have to do anything but rest and eat and get your strength."

Abagail tried not to cry but her eyes filled with tears. "Thank you, thank you," was all she could manage to say. Abagail ate slowly, telling herself to taste the food. It was delicious. The cheese had a soft, creamy texture and a nutty flavor. Her tongue tingled from a surprising kick of pepper. The bread was crusty on the outside and soft on the inside and even the cold water had a unique flavor. Abagail finished eating and tried to keep her eyes open. There were so many questions, but her eyes began to flutter as she eased into a peaceful slumber.

For the next two days, Abagail lived in what she imagined heaven must be like. She felt safe, cared for, protected, and even loved.

The family knew nothing about her. Abagail hadn't told them the story of her life, either the distant past or the more recent, nightmarish last weeks. They didn't need to hear the stories to know bad things had happened to her. The scratches and bruises all over her body told the mother enough.

The strangest thing was that underneath all the signs of her recent battles was the silky texture of Abagail's skin and the softness of her hands. The red splotches Maria knew so well from her own hands, earned by years of hard manual work, were not visible. It was obvious Abagail did not spend her life cooking and cleaning. Hers was a body—even with all the bruises—that could only be someone's who lived a life of luxury.

Jeffrey and his sister Theresa worshiped Abagail completely and without reservation. The sister and brother believed that Abagail was a gift for them dropped from the sky. They spent their time together listening to Abagail's stories about beautiful princesses, brave kings, and evil queens. Her very presence seemed like a fairy tale come to life to the two children. Found in the forest rescued from danger, the maiden, Abagail was a princess. They couldn't wait to curl up sharing their bed in the wagon with their magical friend. And Abagail reveled in this special place, a place of food, laughter, and love.

CHAPTER 16

In all the years Albert worked for the crown, he had never stepped foot in the throne room. The first thing he noted was the room's size. To call it a room was not accurate. It was big enough to host a horse race. Albert had the unique and uncomfortable experience of feeling small. The queen, even sitting on her raised throne, was taller than he was. He had to look up to talk with her. There were people coming and going and speaking in low tones. But the queen was focused on Albert. *Do not be intimidated*, Albert said to himself. *Remember what you are here for.* And with that, he straightened up, threw his shoulders back, and found a stance that was not too uncomfortable.

Queen Henrietta sensed Albert's strength and determination as soon as he walked into the throne room. She decided at that moment the big man would have a role to play in finding her niece, Abagail.

"I am sorry for your loss," the queen said.

"Thank you, your Majesty," he replied.

"It must be a very difficult time for you and your wife."

"Yes, my wife is beside herself," Albert replied.

"But it must be even more upsetting for you, knowing that your son should not have been in the cave in your place."

Albert took a deep breath. So she knew Frederick was not officially a palace guard. He was not going to make excuses or ask for her forgiveness. He kept his eyes down and didn't respond.

The queen remained quiet as well.

Albert finally looked up and met her eyes.

"I have a proposition for you," the queen said. "I want to offer you a chance to catch the killer of your son."

Albert took a step sideways to maintain his balance. The words almost knocked him off his feet. Of all the things he imagined the queen would say, he never imagined this. His greatest wish was granted.

"Well, what do you say?" the queen asked.

"What do you have in mind, your Majesty?" Albert asked.

"I have the marshal already looking for the escapee."

Albert couldn't help himself. He made a face, betraying his doubts about the marshal's effectiveness.

"I can see by your expression that you feel about the marshal the way I do. He is throwing a wide net, maybe too wide to catch a single fish. I want you to be more thoughtful and talk to people one on one and see what you can find out. I will double your pay. What do you think?"

"I would do it for no money, your Majesty."

"I know that," the queen said.

"Thank you," Albert said with great feeling.

"There is one condition." The queen paused and looked at Albert intensely. "You must swear that you will bring Abagail back alive and unhurt." She kept Albert in her gaze. "No harm must come to her. Can you swear to that?"

"Yes," Albert said.

"Let me hear you swear to it."

"I swear I will not hurt the escaped girl, Abagail, and I will bring her back to the court alive."

"Excellent." The queen clapped her hands. "One more thing, your search must be kept a secret. No one can know you are working for me. Not even your wife can know. You are to report to me only."

"Yes, your Majesty."

"I know you are good at keeping secrets from your wife." The queen smiled.

Albert's self-confidence wavered. He heard the unspoken threat. The queen knew his secret. He'd been having an affair with a neighbor whose husband was away fighting in the never-ending war with Spain. With this information, the queen could upend his family at any time, and he didn't doubt for a minute that she would.

"Return tomorrow and we will go over some details," the queen said. An attendant appeared out of nowhere at Albert's side and guided him out of the throne room.

This was his chance at redemption. He was not a believer, but old habits die hard. In his mind, he made a deal with God. *If I catch this killer, I will be the kind of man I know I can be. I will be faithful to my wife, be a good father, and not put myself first.* Maybe there was justice in the world after all.

The next day, Albert returned to the palace. To his amazement, the queen got up from her throne and led him to a far corner of the room, to a bookshelf where she lifted a book from the shelf. The wall opened up and she walked through the opening and out of sight.

Albert didn't move. He didn't know what to do.

"Come in," the queen said from the other side of the wall.

Albert took several tentative steps into a very dark room. He had to squint to see the queen sitting behind a simple wooden desk. He heard the door close behind him with a muted *whoosh*.

Albert looked around. The room was just big enough for the desk and chair and two additional chairs. The room was plainly furnished, no regal trappings, no banners, no paintings on the walls, and no throne. Even the desk and the chairs were simple and practical.

The most surprising thing was what the queen did next, gesturing to a vacant chair for him to sit. Albert hesitated. He couldn't believe it. Was the queen really inviting him to sit down with her? He wasn't sure he heard what she said. "Sit down," the queen said again, and this time there was no mistaking it. Albert was indeed invited to sit in her presence. He sat.

"If you are going to work for me you might come across some very sensitive information. I need to trust you. It is important that you tell me the complete truth. In this room and only in this room we will dispense with court protocol. Do you understand?"

"Yes, your Majesty," Albert said.

The queen smiled. "Well, I guess it will take some time for this to work."

"Yes, your—" He stopped, smiled, and looked at the queen. "Yes," he said.

"Good," the queen said. "Now to the business at hand. First, I am going to give you a copy of my seal. This way everyone will know you represent me. If you are challenged by any official of the court, show them this."

The queen took her ring off and pressed it into a jar of soft wax, making an impression on a piece of paper, which she then handed to Albert. She opened a drawer in the desk and took out a purse, giving it, too, to Albert. It was filled with coins.

"This is not your wages. This is for expenses. And one last thing," the queen said, ringing a bell. The door opened and in walked a woman small in stature, with large brown eyes and very short black hair. "This is Lucia, who will be your partner. Lucia has been involved in many special projects for me."

Lucia smiled and gave a slight bow.

"But your Majesty..." Albert started to say, but he was quickly cut off.

"I know you assumed you were going to work alone but as I thought more about it, I concluded that Lucia will assist you in questioning women. Women feel more comfortable talking to another woman. And Lucia also knows how I work and what I expect. Is there anything else?" the queen asked, meaning the audience was over.

"No, only thank you, your Majesty, thank you very much." Albert bowed and walked out, knowing that Lucia's job was to keep an eye on him and report back to the queen. He was fearful that the fate of his family depended on his catching this Abagail and delivering her unharmed to the queen. Now he had to deal with this Lucia.

"What do you think of him?" the queen asked Lucia after Albert left.

"My first impression matches yours. He is big and strong and I'm certain he is motivated to find his son's murderer. But I do question whether he has the skill and the subtlety to carry out this investigation. Are you unleashing a bull on a very delicate mission? And will he be able to restrain himself when he is face to face with his son's murderer?"

The queen leaned forward and said, "That's exactly what I am doing. I want a bull to stir things up. Who could be more motivated to catch our escapee than the father of the murdered boy? Let him lead you, and then control him."

"I understand," Lucia said. "There is something else that needs your immediate attention."

"What else?" the queen sighed. "What palace plots are being hatched now?"

Lucia took out her notebook. She didn't really need to refer to the book, but it reassured the queen. Lucia knew the prop was necessary to get the queen's attention. Lucia, who was sold to the court as a little girl by her parents, made it her life's work to know the queen. Lucia didn't regret being sold and saved from the grinding poverty of her family. "It is not what is going on in the palace but what is going on with your subjects."

"What do you mean?" the queen asked.

"There is growing discontent among the people about the ongoing war with Spain. And some are blaming you." Lucia hesitated.

"Blaming me, but why?"

"There are those who will take any opportunity to disparage the monarchy. And you are unfortunately vulnerable in this situation. You are suspected as being a Catholic sympathizer."

"After all these years, I do not believe it. I am so careful not to offend the English church. I work doubly hard for this country, especially now that the king is not well."

"That is true, your Majesty, but the people don't see the work you do. And the fact that you are more visible than the king is a source of suspicion among some."

"Suspicion?" the queen asked.

"Yes. The fact that we are at war with Spain, your country of birth and mine, and that you are more visible than his highness strengthens the case that you are the real ruler of this country."

"These people, do they really pose a serious threat to the crown?"

"It is difficult to say. The parliament is more and more resistant to raising taxes and imposing more fees to fund the war. The crucial question is, can all the different opposition factions unite?"

"Thankfully, we will soon announce the end of the war with Spain and hopefully that will silence my critics."

"Really?" Lucia asked. "I am surprised. How did this come about?"

"The king and I have decided to keep it a secret for a while longer. The most serious challenge to the throne right now is Abagail. Her parentage makes her a rival to Margot's claim to the crown. That is why finding her is of the utmost importance. Use this prison guard as you see fit. Lucia, find Abagail."

"He seems very sure of himself and he's not at all happy about having a partner, especially a female partner," Lucia observed.

"I want you two to work together and for you to keep an eye on him. No matter how much he denies it, the temptation to avenge his son's death is strong and I want Abagail alive."

"I understand, your Majesty," Lucia said, bowed, and left.

CHAPTER 17

The next morning Albert set out early, eager to get started. For the first time since that awful day of the escape, he had a purpose in his life, to catch the one who killed his son. He knew his wife would never forgive him, but maybe he would be able to live with himself. His plan was to re-trace Abagail's steps during her escape to understand where she might have gone. He started in the cave and sat for a few minutes, closed his eyes, and tried to picture what happened that day. The image of his son lying dead on the floor with a wooden spoon in his neck crowded out everything else from his mind. He couldn't stay in the cave one more second as his rage built. He was angry at everyone, especially the queen and her agent, Lucia. He was not going to wait for his so-called partner. Let her contact him.

He had to move. Once outside, he was finally able to breathe. Again, he tried to imagine what it was like for Abagail. She probably stood at this very spot. He looked around. There were no landmarks from this vantage point. Where would she go from here? Central London seemed the most likely direction. He was getting ready to walk down the hill toward town when he saw something glitter in the grass. He bent down, brushed the grass away, and found his keys. The keys he gave to Frederick to work for him the day he was killed. Albert held the keys in his hand, closed his eyes, and asked for his son's forgiveness. He wanted to believe finding his keys was a good omen.

With renewed resolve, Albert walked to town. Someone must have seen this young woman, a stranger most likely covered in blood, desperate, scared, and alone. He would interview every person who lived and worked in the area as well as those he met walking through the neighborhood.

Four hours later, exhausted and frustrated, Albert had

nothing to show for his efforts. He found most everyone unwilling to talk and the few who did claimed not to have seen an unfamiliar girl covered in blood walking by herself. The people he spoke to—most of them women—seemed afraid. If they were telling the truth, then Abagail was invisible. He thought of what the queen said about women being more comfortable speaking to another woman. He would try again tomorrow with Lucia, but now it was time to go home.

The queen paced the throne room with impatience when Lucia told her of Albert's decision to work without her. "How dare he go off without you? I told him you would be partners. Don't worry, Lucia, I will straighten this out."

Lucia knew better than to challenge the queen directly, especially when she was upset. In her calmest voice, Lucia said, "I'm not worried. Abagail murdered his son and Albert feels responsible for his death. So of course, it is very personal. He will come to me in a day or two and ask for my help. When he does, then we can truly be partners without resent-ment."

"I will give him two days to arrive at this himself but if he does not then I will order it," Queen Henrietta agreed.

CHAPTER 18

Albert held the envelope with the queen's seal that had been delivered to his house earlier that day. It was a summons to the palace from Lucia.

"Come in, Albert. I am glad you could make it on such short notice," Lucia said, standing at her doorway.

Albert was taken off guard by her opening the door herself. Was Lucia an aristocrat? And if so, what rank and what was the protocol to follow when he addressed her? He bowed slightly just to make sure. Walking in the room added to his confusion. The room was designed in an understated but elegant style distinct from the regal style of the throne room. The room seemed to serve no purpose other than just to sit in. There was no bed that he could see, and the fireplace was too small to be used for cooking. Albert heard of these sitting rooms, called parlors, but this was his first time actually being in one.

"I thought we could meet again under different circumstances and get to know each other better." Lucia smiled, pulled up a chair by a fireplace, and, without any ceremony, sat down. She pointed to an empty chair. "Please sit."

Albert sat. The chair groaned under his weight but held together.

"Would you like a drink?" Lucia asked.

"Yes," Albert said, maybe a little too heartedly, grateful for the offer.

"Would you like red or white?"

Albert didn't know how to respond. Ale was his regular drink. "Whatever you're having is fine," he said.

"We'll start with white," Lucia said. She rang a little bell and a servant entered. "A bottle of white wine and two glasses."

The servant returned, opened the bottle, and was ready to

pour when Lucia said, "We'll take care of it." Lucia took the bottle, poured them each a glass, and said, "Now we won't be disturbed."

As soon as the servant left, Albert blurted out, "I think we should question people together."

Lucia smiled, deciding not to remind him it was the queen's idea, and thought to herself, *men's vanity, tread lightly.* "Good idea."

"Good," he repeated. "We'll start tomorrow morning. What have you found out so far?"

Lucia considered how much to share with Albert given his reluctance about working with her. If it was her, she wouldn't want a "partner" picked by the queen. Lucia would wait and see if they could really work together before telling him anything significant.

"I don't know how much you know about Abagail and the royal family?"

"I know nothing," Albert said.

"Their relationship is complicated and goes back a long way." Lucia paused and noted that Albert was listening intently. "Abagail was a lady in waiting for Princess Margot."

Albert nodded and took a drink. He knew this.

"But Abagail was much more than a princess's attendant. She was very close to the princess, more like a sister. They were born around the same time. Abagail is just two weeks younger than the princess."

Albert was getting restless. This seemed more like palace gossip than anything else. He sighed. "What does this have to do with our bringing her in?"

Lucia was not going to let him decide what was and wasn't important. "Why was Abagail imprisoned in the first place and what was her relationship with the princess, the queen, and finally, the old woman? Do you think those questions are important for us?"

"Yes," he said a little meekly.

"Abagail was treated like a member of the royal family. There's a rumor that she is, in fact, the queen's niece, Princess Margot's cousin."

Albert was taken aback. He brought the cup of wine to his lips but didn't drink. "The queen's niece. I had no idea. Who is her father? Why was she imprisoned and who is her mother?" he asked, hesitating. And then it hit him. "The old woman, of course, that explains a lot of things." He took a long drink of white wine.

"What do you mean, what kinds of things?" Lucia asked.

Albert wiped his mouth. "Well, for example, how were they able to carry out their escape. It takes a lot of planning and trust to attempt such a thing. And..."

"Yes, what else?" Lucia asked.

"I got to know the old woman pretty well. She was already in prison when I started working there. We never talked, but for the twelve years I saw her every day."

"Yes."

"At first the old woman seemed to have gotten worse, more hostile when Abagail first joined her, but then her mood quickly improved. The two of them formed a tight bond and they had an ease together."

"Why is that noteworthy?" Lucia asked. "All they had were each other, sharing that small space."

"Because in all the years I worked there, the old woman never warmed up to anyone else who shared her cell." Albert reached for the bottle, but when he picked it up it was empty.

"Don't worry, we will get another," Lucia said with a laugh and rang the bell. "How about we try a red this time along with some food?"

"A toast to our partnership," Albert said when his goblet was full. Then he blushed, wondering if he went too far.

"To our partnership," Lucia said with a big smile, and was surprised by how much she really meant it. Lucia never had a partner before and thought it must be the wine talking.

They ate in silence. The meat was tender, the potatoes well-seasoned, and the string beans sweet with a nice snap. It was one of the best meals of Albert's life. He put down his knife and fork and pushed his plate away. "I was wondering if they had help?" he asked.

"You mean someone on the inside?" Lucia replied.

"I was thinking more of the outside, but I guess it's possible on the inside too, though I cannot think who it might be."

"What makes you ask that?"

"Well, I was just thinking whether there could be supporters of Abagail who would want her to become queen. Could an old woman and a young girl really plan and carry out that escape on their own?"

"Mm," is all Lucia said, taking the opportunity to get a good look at the big man sitting in front of her. Maybe she underestimated him. Lucia fantasized for a moment about being wrapped in his strong arms and feeling his strength. What it would be like to be with such a big man?

"Why was Abagail locked up in the first place?" Albert asked.

"That is the strangest part. No one I spoke to knows."

Albert tried but couldn't hide a yawn. "It's getting late and we should probably get an early start tomorrow. That was delicious, Lucia. The best meal I've had in a long time, a very long time," he said.

"Yes, I enjoyed it too," Lucia said with a slight smile.

Albert felt the wine as he got up slowly with both hands holding the table edge. He swayed a bit and Lucia stood up and grabbed him around the waist to steady him. She was strong, especially for a woman of her size. They stayed in that position for a few seconds longer than they had to. They let go and both realized that a line, if not quite crossed, was at least acknowledged.

"Good night, Albert."

"Good night, Lucia."

Early the next morning, they met in town at the street crossing closest to the palace. They decided to divide the work. Albert would take one end of the street and re-question people, and Lucia would knock on the doors on the other side of the street.

CHAPTER 19

Abagail looked at the children asleep in the back of the wagon. She thought about whether to continue to travel with this family. Their parents talked softly in the front of the wagon. Would it be possible for her to blend in with this family or would that put them in danger? That was the last thing Abagail wanted to do, but traveling solo was too risky. A young woman traveling alone stands out and is vulnerable. But if she was caught with the family, they could be sentenced to prison, the family broken up, or even worse.

"Beautiful night," Abagail said, climbing over bags to get to the front of the wagon.

"Yes, it is," Maria agreed.

"Are the children finally asleep?" Frank laughed. "They sure give you a workout."

"They're wonderful. I really enjoy being with them."

"It's great, the way you play with them. It makes the trip easier for us. I can tell they're having a good time," Frank said.

"It's the least I can do. You saved my life."

"We just did what anyone would do," Maria replied.

They rode in silence. The three of them listening as the horses' hooves hit the ground as they pulled the wagon.

"What's that wonderful smell in the back of the wagon?" Abagail asked. "It's like living in the middle of a lush garden."

Frank and Maria exchanged looks.

Abagail felt the mood shift from warm and peaceful to tense and guarded and saw Maria give her husband a slight nod. He shrugged his shoulders and whispered to Maria, "Why not?"

Maria straightened and looked directly at Abagail. "You must keep what we tell you to yourself. No one—and I mean no one—can ever know."

Abagail was confused and couldn't imagine what could be

in the wagon that was so dangerous and for a moment wondered whether they were anti-government conspirators. *Are they Papists? Is the wagon full of gunpowder and bombs?*

The couple assumed Abagail's silence meant she was considering whether to agree to the condition insisted on by Maria.

"I don't believe in violence," Abagail offered.

"Violence?" Frank laughed. "We are the victims of violence. We are just trying to make a living, feed our family, and continue working in our trade. A trade that was my father's and his father before him."

"I don't understand," Abagail said.

"It's very simple. What we have in the wagon, what you smell, are the ingredients for making soap," Maria said.

"Soap?" Abagail asked, waiting for the two of them to start laughing. But the looks on their faces told her they were serious.

"Yes," Maria said. "We make soap and the aroma you smell comes from the fragrant ingredients that we use."

"Why is it so dangerous to sell soap?"

"You haven't heard?" Frank said.

"No," Abagail replied.

"The king sold the exclusive right to make and sell soap to a group of large soap makers for a fee of 20,000 pounds a year," Maria said with scorn and disgust in her voice. "And he issued a decree that only the monopoly can make and sell soap."

"The king can do that?" Abagail asked.

"He can and did," Frank grumbled. "And if anyone is caught making or selling soap they can be fined or even put in prison."

"Why did he make this law?" Abagail asked.

"Because he needs money for his fancy balls and hunting trips," Frank answered.

"And don't forget his wars. He needs money to pay for his

glory," Maria added. "If you're even caught with the means to make soap you can go to jail."

Without thinking, Abagail blurted, "No, I cannot believe it. The king would not ruin people's lives just for glory and fancy parties. And he certainly wouldn't throw people in jail for making soap."

Maria and Frank stared at her. "You sound like you know him," Frank laughed. He waited for his wife to laugh but she didn't. Maria looked closely at Abagail, remembering how soft her skin was, like a princess.

Abagail felt Maria's stare and wondered if this was the time to tell them her story, but decided to hold back. The last few weeks changed her view of the world from trusting everyone to trusting no one. The kindness of this family was making her question her new belief. Once her story was said out loud, it could never be taken back. "Will you get caught with a wagon full of soap?"

"What choice do we have?" Frank asked. "We have to eat and we lost our land."

"How did you lose your land?" Abagail asked.

Maria turned around and stared at Abagail. "Where have you been, locked up in a cave?"

"You might say that," Abagail answered.

"Come on, Maria, it is not her fault," Frank said, and then asked Abagail, "Do you really want to know?"

"Yes," Abagail said.

"Well, my family farmed the commons for as long as anyone can remember."

"As did mine," Maria added.

"We all did. Nobody owned the land—we all shared it. We were not wealthy, but we grew enough to feed our families and, if it was a good year, we would take our products to market." Frank paused.

"There were not many good years," Maria said.

"That is true," Frank said. "But we knew how to grow

enough for us to survive."

"What happened?" Abagail asked.

"One day the lords decided the commons were not to be shared. The land was for sale and we were run off the land that we farmed for as long anyone can remember," Maria said with a bitter laugh.

"How horrible. What did people do? How were they able to support themselves?"

"Ah, that is the question," Frank said. "A lot of people moved into town to look for work."

"And a lot could not make the change and never recovered," Maria said. "My father, for one."

"It is true," Frank said. "Luckily my family made and sold soap along with farming. So, when the land was stolen from us, we started selling it full-time."

"And now they took away our right to make and sell our soap, so who knows how long this will last?" Maria sighed.

"We do this trip twice a year and we haven't been caught so far." Frank crossed his fingers.

"How do you hide the soap from the king's men?"

"You've been in the back of the wagon for two straight days. Tell me, where is the soap?" Frank asked proudly.

Abagail was hesitant to answer Frank because it seemed so obvious to her.

"Well, where do you think?" Frank insisted.

Maria tried to signal him to stop talking by touching his arm, but it was too late. She wanted to know who this young woman was before revealing any more family secrets. Frank turned to Maria with a puzzled expression. He thought they agreed to tell Abagail about the soap.

Frank looked back at her and asked once again, "Well?"

"In those two big boxes on either side of the wagon. That's where the wonderful aroma comes from and there is no other possibility."

"See," Frank said loudly. "I told you it would work." He put his arm around Maria and gave her a squeeze.

Maria smiled slightly.

"Why don't you go back there and look and tell me what you find. Don't worry, you will not wake the children."

Abagail was not sure why he wanted her to do this, but she complied and crawled to the back of the wagon, quietly opening the cover of the closest box.

As soon as Abagail was gone, Maria whispered to her husband, "We should be careful how much we tell her."

"Why?" Frank asked. "I thought we decided we can trust her."

"I'm just not sure about her. Did you hear the way she talked about the king? It was like she knew him personally."

"Know the king personally? Come on, you are letting all this sneaking around get to you."

"We do not know anything about her, not really," Maria said. "Do not tell her where the soap is hidden. Not until we know more about her."

Abagail uncovered the large box full of flower petals and was blasted by an overpowering flood of sweetness. She stuck her hand in, thinking her fingers would feel the hard surface of the soap. Her hand went as far down as it could go, but her hand never touched anything hard like soap, just silky-soft flower petals. Being disturbed, the petals' aroma filled the air. It made her gag, it was so sweet. In the second box it was the same, petals of flowers, no soap. Abagail was confused. If it was not in the boxes, where was the soap? Her confusion was about more than the hidden soap. Frank and Maria's talk about the commons and having their land taken from them made her head hurt.

There was so much Abagail took for granted. Of course, she knew that someone grew the food they ate in the palace; that someone cooked, served, and cleaned up afterwards, but the tasks were never connected to real live people. She wondered if Margot ever thought about the real people who made their life of comfort possible. Abagail felt a clutching in her chest and realized that something beside her mother was stolen from her by the royal family—the chance to live a real life.

When Abagail climbed back to the front of the wagon, Maria and Frank did not turn around to greet her. They rode in silence. There was no more talk of soap. The warm camaraderie of a few minutes ago was gone. All of them felt the yawning gap between the couple and the young mysterious woman. Abagail decided to tell them her story. She spoke without interruption for what seemed like two hours. She told them of her upbringing in the palace, her sudden and inexplicable jailing, meeting her mother, her recent escape, and her dangerous journey. Even omitting the rape, which was still too painful to speak of, her story seemed too fantastic to be true even to Abagail.

Maria and Frank did not interrupt once. They were too stunned to ask any questions and if they had, Abagail would not have had the strength to answer them. Arriving at the part where they found her passed out and starving in the forest, she stopped abruptly. Without saying another word, Abagail crawled to the back of the wagon and immediately fell asleep.

CHAPTER 20

Spencer sat alone in the corner of the tavern, sipping his watered-down ale as he thought about what he would do to the tart who sliced his face. The atmosphere in the room suddenly changed with the speed of a quickly moving storm. A big man entered the tavern. Immediately, everyone in the place recognized he was on official business. The big man sat facing the doorway with his back to Spencer. When a tankard of ale was brought to him, he had a long conversation with the waitress, who shook her head several times, seeming eager to get away. The man reached into a pocket and pulled out a piece of paper. Spencer saw the waitress straighten and almost bow. She seemed to become more amiable and they talked some more.

Spencer caught a quick glance at the paper. It was a drawing of *her*, the one that cut him.

A customer called out, "Sadie, can a man get a drink here?" The thirsty man's companion elbowed him and nodded in the direction of the large stranger talking to Sadie. The thirsty man decided to walk to the bar and get his own drink.

The big man slowly turned his head as he surveyed the tavern's patrons. Nobody made eye contact with him. When he looked in Spencer's direction, Spencer ensured his body was at an angle to hide the scar, still red and raw on his face. Spencer felt the eyes of the big man staring at him. He wondered what the waitress had told him. How much did he know? Spencer was not going to wait to find out. As soon as the stranger's gaze moved away, Spencer quickly walked out a side door. It took all his concentration to not look behind him to see if he was being followed. He didn't stop or slow down until making a sharp turn into an alleyway, where he pressed his back against a wall. He waited for two minutes then peeked out onto the main street. He heaved a sigh of relief. There was no evidence of the big man.

Spencer touched his tender scar and winced. He felt a trap closing in around him. He decided it was time to act and find the bitch who did this to him and pay her back. It seemed like half the world was looking for her. The town was crawling with the king's men and now the big guy as well. Spencer had an ingenious idea. Instead of doing all the work himself to track her, he would follow the big guy and let him find her. When an opportunity presented itself, he'd give her what she had coming. Spencer smiled.

CHAPTER 21

Abagail woke up groggy with the remnants of sleep still clinging to her. She felt that something monumental had happened and then remembered last night. Was telling Maria and Frank her story a mistake? She noticed the wagon was not moving and clambered to the front. Maria and Frank were gone. Did they sneak off and inform the authorities? Maybe there was a reward for her. The horses were tied to the side of the wagon, grazing peacefully. It was unusually quiet. The children were nowhere in sight. Abagail looked around, spotting Frank and Maria talking intently as they sat on a blanket. She walked toward them. They were so involved in conversation that they did not notice Abagail until she stood next to them. The two children were playing in the water. The scene was so peaceful and the couple so relaxed, she thought for a moment maybe she hadn't told them her story and let out a deep breath.

Maria shielded her eyes from the sun to look up at Abagail.

"Come, sit, we're having breakfast," Frank said.

Abagail sat.

"You must be hungry," Maria said. "Do you want something to eat?"

"I'm not hungry." Abagail took another deep breath. "To tell you the truth I am unsure what to do next. I cannot go with you to the capitol. Now you know why. I do not know what to do."

"Well." Maria smiled. "Frank and I have an idea."

"Maria's brother lives close by," Frank said. "He lives by himself and we are certain he would be willing to let you stay while we deliver our soap."

"He lives alone?" Abagail asked, her voice quivering, wondering what this man, Maria's brother, would expect of her.

"Yes, there's nothing to worry about," Frank said. "James studied for the priesthood."

"He left the seminary before he was ordained. It almost killed my father," Maria said. "He was the smart one in the family and the one who was supposed to be successful."

"Why did he leave?"

"Maria's brother always lived in his own head," Frank said.

"He has strong beliefs and has the courage to live by them," Maria retorted.

Abagail could see that Maria's brother was a source of tension.

"Anyway," Maria continued. "James is very honorable. You would be absolutely safe with him, right Frank?"

"Yes, absolutely. As safe as living with a priest." Frank laughed.

"Safer," Maria added. "It's a perfect solution. His house is out of the way. You can stay there while we do our business in the capitol and when we're finished, we'll come and get you."

"I do not know. It is very generous of you, but should it not it be James' decision?"

"We should reach his place early tomorrow," Frank said. "You both can make your minds up then."

"Out of the water!" Maria yelled to the two children. "We are leaving."

Jeffrey and Theresa came running, dripping wet, laughing, and spraying the adults as if they were two dogs shaking off water.

"You're getting Abagail all wet," Maria said.

"It's all right," Abagail said. As a matter of fact, it was wonderful to hear the two children laugh. She was right to trust this family. They had only been kind to her.

They all clambered into the wagon. Frank harnessed the horses and off they rode. Abagail chewed on some bread and cheese in the back of the wagon. The two children had their wet heads on her lap. For the first time since being thrown into the cave, Abagail felt hopeful.

CHAPTER 22

Spencer waited for Albert to show up again to lead him to his prey. He spent the night curled up in a fruit seller's stall, covering himself with bags used to transport fruit. Figuring he'd return to where he saw Albert yesterday, Spencer hid in a corner between two buildings that gave him a clear view of the street. Spencer moved back into the shadows when he saw the big man walking in his direction, but he was not alone. A short, dark-haired woman Spencer had never seen before was with him. Who was she, and why was she with the big man? He watched as they spoke and then separated. She crossed over and walked down one side of the street and the big man walked down the other side. Spencer couldn't follow them both, so he decided to follow her.

Lucia felt confident they would be able to find Abagail for her queen. The unmistakable aroma of baking bread interrupted her thoughts. Someone was awake at this time and could be questioned. Lucia walked over to the bakery down the street, its door slightly open. "That's a wonderful aroma," Lucia said, greeting the plump woman inside the shop.

"Yes," the woman said with a smile, "it is our best advertisement. The rolls taste as good as they smell."

"Well in that case I'll take three," Lucia said.

As the woman wrapped the rolls in a piece of paper, Lucia reached into her pocket for coins and said casually, "I heard there was a girl wandering around here four days ago. I'm sure she was hungry, and I imagine the smell of your rolls baking would have brought her in here."

The woman behind the counter stopped suddenly to look at Lucia busily counting out her coins.

"How much do I owe you?" Lucia asked with a big smile.

The woman said with a quaver in her voice, "I'm not saying I saw anyone like that but if there was a young woman alone in these streets this time in the morning, I would say she could be in danger."

"In danger?"

"There's a certain man who..." The woman turned pale and froze mid-sentence as if seeing a ghost.

Lucia turned to see a man walking quickly past the bakery with his collar up, hiding most of his face. Lucia turned back to the woman, but she was gone. Lucia called out, "Miss, miss, where did you go?" There was no answer. Lucia tried again. "Miss, how much do I owe you?"

A voice came from the back of the store. "Leave three coins on the counter and go, please go."

Lucia walked quickly out of the bakery and looked down the street in the direction of the man who just walked by. She was sure he had frightened the woman in the bakery. Lucia went to the end of the street and looked in all directions, but the streets were deserted. No sign of the man.

Was the woman in the bakery trying to tell her something? Lucia half-walked, half-ran to where Albert should have been but didn't see him. They had agreed that if either one of them found something important, they would consult with the other. But the man was getting away and time was running out.

Lucia couldn't wait for Albert any longer. She went back to the bakery. An open sign was posted in the front window, but the door was locked when Lucia turned the knob. She walked around to the back of the bakery and peered through a window, but there was no light and no movement. No more than fifteen minutes ago, Lucia had been speaking with a woman in this very store. Now there was a deathly silence, the woman disappeared, as if sunk beneath the waves of the ocean.

Lucia's skin tingled. She sensed something terrible had taken place. She walked to the back of the bakery and tried the door, but it too was locked. She used her elbow to break the door's glass pane. The shattering glass was loud enough to wake the dead. Lucia carefully reached in to undo the lock on the inside so as not to cut herself on the jagged glass. She opened the door and tip-toed inside. It was too dark to see the interior of the room after coming in from the light. She stood still, waiting for her eyes to adjust. Taking a step, she almost tripped over a large bag of flour and just managed to stop herself from falling. There was a knife on the counter. Lucia picked it up and moved to the front of the bakery, holding it tightly by her side. Then she froze, not believing the scene before her. The baker woman was lying in a river of blood, her head at a strange angle. Lucia bent down and saw that her eyes were wide open, her face frozen in fear. Lucia heard a slight noise coming from right behind her. The last thing Lucia remembered was the taste of bitter bile rising in her throat, then blackness.

Albert was hoping that Lucia had better luck than him. He was thinking about taking a break when he heard someone calling to him. A boy he'd never seen before ran up to him.

"Hey mister, you better come quick. There's trouble, big trouble."

Albert followed the boy as he ran down the street the way Lucia went earlier. The boy stopped at the bakery but didn't go in. Albert was right behind him.

"What is it?" Albert asked as the boy pointed to the bakery then ran away. But Albert already knew. He smelled death. He kicked the front door so hard it almost came off its hinges. He walked inside, and the smell became stronger. The front of the bakery looked fine. He rushed to the back, almost slipping on the blood-covered floor. A woman was lying in a way that no living person could, her head turned at an unnatural angle. Lucia was on the floor next to her, not moving. Albert bent down, picked Lucia up, and carried her outside. He wasn't sure she was still alive. He thought he detected faint breathing. He ran as fast as he could to the palace carrying Lucia in his arms.

His mind was going around and around with one thought. *Please don't die.*

Spencer walked quickly through the city streets, bloody hands stuck in his pockets. It wasn't until he was in the forest that he washed the blood from his hands in a stream. As he scrubbed at the blood, he thought, *why didn't the baker woman tell me from the start what she knew? I wasn't going to kill her, just rough her up a little.* She had started to yell and wouldn't stop. I couldn't let her do that. I covered her face but then she yelled even louder. I thought when I punched her in the face that would be the end of it, but it wasn't. I grabbed a knife and shut her up for good. Then that little dark-haired one ran into the shop like some kind of hero. She didn't see me in there, so I didn't have to kill her. At least I don't think I did. Now, here I am on the run, getting no closer to finding the one who attacked me, and there will be a price on my head too. "Bitch," he said out loud. You started it all and now you will pay for it.

CHAPTER 23

"Uncle James, Uncle James," Theresa and Jeffrey yelled as they jumped off the wagon before it stopped. They ran toward the house from which a tall man with a thin, sad face emerged. The two children ran towards him and his face lit up.

"Whoa, whoa," he said, laughing. "You two are getting so big. I don't know if I can lift you anymore." He picked up one child and then the other and laughed, twirling them around.

"Don't kill your favorite uncle before we say hello to him," Maria said brightly. The man put the two children down so he and Maria could embrace.

Frank stood behind Maria. When she separated from her brother, the two men held out hands for a handshake, but the thin man pulled Frank into a hug, which Frank awkwardly accepted.

"Come in, I was expecting you a few days ago. How long are you staying?" He saw Abagail and abruptly stopped speaking. His expression changed from happy, accepting, and open to suspicion. He stared at Abagail for what seemed to her several minutes.

"This is James," Frank said. James looked her straight in the eye and held out his hand. She'd never met a man who would shake her hand as if they were equals. With the men in court, everyone knew instantly where the other person stood. Either they were a servant or an aristocrat. Depending which they were, you either curtsied or barely acknowledged their presence.

"My name is Abagail."

"We cannot stay long, we got delayed," Maria interjected. "The four of us have to move on today," Maria said.

"Oh mother," Theresa said. "Can we stay until tomorrow?"

"Please, please," Jeffrey chimed in.

"I wish we could," Maria said. "But we have to push on, it's getting late and we have work to do."

"You can at least stay for a meal?" James asked.

"That we can do," Frank said. "But after we eat, we have to go." He turned to the children. "Your mother's right, people are expecting us. Maria, help James prepare the meal and we will load the wagon."

Abagail watched Maria and her brother walk back into the house. James looked nothing like his sister. They were opposites. Maria's round face, even at rest, was always ready to smile. Her laugh came easily. James' long face seemed to always be on the verge of a frown. Maria was plump, while James looked like he was carrying the burdens of the world on his shoulders. Abagail was lost in her thoughts and didn't realize she was standing all alone. Where did Frank and the kids go? She followed the sound of the children's voices to the back of the house, which was dense with many trees, and still didn't see anyone. Where were they? Then, like magic, they appeared as if they popped up from the earth. It was only then she realized the voices came from a hole in the ground, its entrance covered in branches.

Jeffrey emerged. He held the end of a wooden box almost as big as him. Theresa held the other end. Abagail ran over and helped Theresa lift the box onto the grass. Abagail peered down the dark entrance for an instant and immedi-ately felt cold and lightheaded. Sitting down on the grass so as not to faint, she took short breaths, which made her even dizzier.

Frank leaned over her. "You look like you've seen a ghost," he said.

Abagail shuddered, because that was exactly what she saw, a ghost. The ghost of her mother. "The cave," was all she could say.

Frank's eyes lit up. He understood. "Sit until you feel better?"

"Yes, I think I will do that," Abagail replied. She closed her eyes but opened them right away—closing them made her head spin. After a few minutes her breathing slowed, and she was able to stand with just a slight wobble.

"Feeling better?" Frank asked.

"Much," Abagail answered. "What is in those boxes?"

"Ah, the boxes," Frank said, smiling. "What's in the boxes, children?"

"Soap," they both cried out at the same time.

"What? I thought I said they were hidden in the wagon," Abagail said, feeling annoyed at being lied to.

"Now you're really going to learn where we hide the soap," Frank replied.

Theresa and Jeffrey ran to the wagon. By the time Abagail and Frank caught up with the children, they were already loading the soap into the back of the wagon.

"All right, you two finish loading the soap," Frank said, "and then we'll see if Aunt Abagail can find it. See you in a few minutes."

While the soap was put into the wagon, Abagail and Frank walked a little. They sat on a log together.

"Are you sure it's all right with James that I stay in his home?" Abagail asked.

"I'm sure. James is a fine man. Besides, he would do anything that Maria asks him to."

"They seem very close."

"My Maria is more like a mother to him than a sister."

"What do you mean?"

"Their mother died giving birth to James. Maria, being the oldest girl, took on the job of caring for James and their two sisters."

"What a responsibility," Abagail said.

"Yes, their father was not ready to care for four children on his own. He was a bitter, angry man who took to the drink after his wife died. It got pretty ugly at times."

"Father, we are ready," Theresa shouted.

"All right, we are on our way," Frank shouted back. Then he turned to Abagail and said, "Enough of this sad story. Let us have some fun."

"All right, Aunt Abagail, find the soap," Theresa said excitedly.

"You have five minutes. Let us see if you can find it." Jeffrey smiled.

Abagail looked at Frank, who just smiled and shrugged his shoulders.

The boxes they carried, now empty of soap, were lying beside the wagon. Abagail climbed into the back of the wagon and went right over to one of the large boxes filled with flower petals. She opened it, looked inside, stuck her hand as far down as it could go, and once again felt nothing. It was the same with the second box, no soap. Looking carefully around the back of the wagon, she thought there was no place to hide anything. There were no shelves, no hidden corners, just a small pile of clothes. *You can't hide two hundred bars of soap in a pile of clothes,* she thought, but she went through them because that was the only other possibi-lity.

She climbed out of the wagon and said, "I give up. It must be magic. How do you make hundreds of bars of soap disap-pear?"

"Can we show her now, Poppa?" Theresa asked.

"Yes, go in the wagon and show her our secret," Frank said, still smiling.

Abagail followed the children as they crawled in the back of the wagon and watched as they each pulled out a loose board from the wagon's walls. The loosening of the board caused a few bars of soap to fall out. There were really two walls—the outside wall was for show, and the space between the two walls was large enough to store the soap.

"I never would have guessed," Abagail said.

The two children laughed and jumped up and down. "We showed her where we hide the soap," Theresa said to her father as the three of them clambered out of the wagon.

"Yes," Jeffrey chimed in. "We showed her."

Between the rows of hidden soap, Abagail spotted stacks of pamphlets also hidden in the false wall. She glanced quickly at them and saw by the title and the illustration on the front cover they were religious, most likely puritan. If Frank and Maria got caught selling soap without the king's permission, they would be fined and maybe imprisoned. But to be caught with illegal religious material, critical of the state church, execution could follow. Abagail pretended not to see the pamphlets and did not ask about them.

"How did you ever come up with this clever idea?" Abagail asked.

"I wish I could claim it as my idea, but it was handed down from my father's father to him, then to me," Frank said. "In this world, you better have a plan."

"Come on in," Maria shouted then. "It's time to eat."

Abagail was starving as she realized she hadn't eaten since last night. The children were excited to be with their favorite uncle and their brand-new favorite aunt. They talked non-stop throughout dinner.

Then in no time, the family was off. Abagail waved to the children as the wagon got smaller. Here she was, alone with a man she has just met, alone in his house. *What have I done?*

CHAPTER 24

"I will clean up the kitchen now that they have gone," James said.

"I can help," Abagail said, greatly relieved. It was the ordinariness of what he said that let her relax just a little. Instead of going into the kitchen, James walked out the door. Abagail didn't have a clue where he was going, so she took the opportunity to walk through the house that would be her temporary home. The walkthrough didn't take long; three rooms—two small bedrooms and a fairly large kitchen with a table that could fit six. Two beds and a small bookstand completed the furnishing. She couldn't help but compare the house to the palace and the cave. *This is the way most people live,* she told herself. Could she be happy living a simple life in a house like this?

Abagail went outside, looking for James. *Is he hiding?* Then a disturbing thought—he could be waiting in the bushes beyond the next bend, hiding, ready to jump on her and have his way. Taking a deep breath and tightening her grip on the wooden spoon still in her pocket, she continued looking for him. Abagail saw him walk into a clearing and disappear. If he was going to attack her, this was the time. Feeling like a deer flushed from hiding and exposed in a clearing, Abagail looked around, trying to spot him, then realized where she was. This is the cave, where Frank and the children fetched the soap.

James stood at the entrance of the cave and didn't seem to notice her. She watched him as he concentrated on what he was doing. He hummed a tune while he stacked boxes. He turned and saw Abagail.

"Oh, I was not sure you were coming so I just started." His voice trailed off and Abagail could see he was self-conscious.

"How can I help?" Abagail asked.

"Well," he said, looking around. "If you could drag those

three boxes down here, that would be a big help."

Abagail walked up to the stack of boxes. She tried to move them, but they wouldn't budge. It was like they were nailed to the ground. Feeling his presence before she saw him, her hand went back to her pocket and grasped the spoon. Her heart pounded and her bodice was soaked with sweat.

"No, I didn't mean all three at the same time. That's much too heavy. Only one at a time." He smiled.

"Here," he said, putting his hands on the top of a box. "You grab a box by the top." He moved the box with a rocking motion. Abagail gave it a try, feeling clumsy at first, but soon figured it out. They worked together. She moved the boxes down to the entrance of the cave and he stacked them. They got into a rhythm and Abagail began to worry less about his intentions.

"Well," he said. "That is all for now. Thank you very much for your help."

As they walked back to the house, Abagail became nervous. The big unspoken question was, where would she sleep tonight?

James sat down on a log. "I'm not ready to go in yet. It's a beautiful night. How about I get a fire started?"

Abagail sat on a log across from James, relieved that the sleeping situation was delayed. He coaxed the fire tenderly and the lines in his face changed in the orange glow of the blaze. Abagail saw that this very serious man had the features of a young boy. Could this man be trusted? He was Maria's brother and Frank spoke of him with real respect. But he was a stranger, and not only was she alone with him, but they were going to sleep in the same house.

James, looking across the fire at Abagail, had his own questions. *Who was this woman really? The story his sister told him was fantastic, a kind of fairy tale. A poor damsel passed out in the forest found by two children and brought back to life. Was she really a lady-in-waiting to the princess and with no reason thrown into a dungeon and then escaped? And now this mysterious, beautiful woman is sitting across a fire from me behind my house.* In the dark, he allowed himself to look at her directly. What he saw was a tall, slender woman with dark brown hair tied up in a loose bun. He loved the way the loose strands of her hair moved across her forehead.

They sat quietly. James for his part was used to being alone and Abagail allowed herself to experience the evening air. It was comfortably cool. The night sky was filled with brilliant stars that seemed so close you could almost touch them. Abagail started to relax and leaned back. "I hope it is all right with you, my staying here?"

"It is fine, I'm glad for the company," he replied.

The both of them stared up at the sky, working hard not to look at each other.

The silence went from being comfortable to awkward.

"Your sister says you were a priest," Abagail finally said.

James didn't respond.

"You do not have to talk about it. I just thought..."

"No, it is all right. Officially I am not a priest. I left the order just before I was to take the vows." James paused. "It was not for me."

"Why not?" Abagail asked.

"I guess you can say that all those years of training to be a priest resulted in my being a non-believer." When Abagail didn't say anything, James asked, "Are you shocked?"

Abagail was a little shocked but was also very interested in this strange man. Instead of answering his question, she asked, "Why?"

"Where do I start? I understand from my sister that you served in the royal court, true?"

"Yes," Abagail answered.

"Do you believe in the divine right of the king?"

"I guess so, yes. I do not know, I never really thought about it."

"Well, you have the advantage over me. You know the king and queen personally, yes?"

"Yes."

"In your opinion, do they seem like they are chosen by God, and are different than you or me?"

Abagail thought about it and was certain of her answer, yet found herself unexpectedly reluctant to say it aloud. She recalled how the queen's mood would change, her casual cruelty and callous use of other people. She also remembered the king's cowardice in the face of the queen's accusations that he spoiled Margot. And most of all there was her imprisonment and her mother's life spent in a cave on the queen's whim.

"No, they seem like regular humans." Abagail took a deep breath. "They are just born into special circumstances." Hearing her possibly treasonous thoughts spoken out loud, Abagail shuddered.

"Exactly," James said enthusiastically. "And I want to tell you that priests are no different."

Abagail was speechless. The idea that the queen and king were just like everyone else shook something deep within her. And to hear priests were no different from anyone else was like being told fish talk or people were made of straw.

James interpreted her silence as an invitation to continue. "If what we are saying is true, and if the whole world is based on these false beliefs—what is true?" He didn't wait for an answer. "What I believe to be true is that we are all the same. The king, queen, and priests are no different than you or me. Except for an accident of birth, as you said. You or even I could be a king or a queen and, if that is true, the very foundation of our society based on the divine right of kings is undermined."

James challenged her idea of the world in one powerful statement. It was, in one word, heresy.

"If I believe these things," he went on, "which I do with all my heart and mind, then I could not join in the spreading of lies."

Abagail felt herself floating. It was like the ground she walked on evaporated before her eyes and still she could not trust herself to say anything.

James was not finished. "Our leaders, the ones who make the rules the rest of us have to live by, are people just like you and me, fallible, who often make decisions based on their own self-interest. What right do they have to tax us and ask us to die for them? They have created a system based on lies as we struggle to make a living and feed our families, while they live their lives supported by us, without a thought about where the money comes from."

Abagail couldn't take her eyes from James. His face was red partly from the reflection of the flames and partly from the ideas burning inside him. While he talked, he wasn't looking at her but at someplace in the mid-distance, a place that only he could see. His passion was contagious. Abagail was drawn to his ideas as a moth to a flame.

"And," James went on, "the church is a big part of this deception. People are going hungry and still, churches get built. To what purpose?"

"But there are good priests," Abagail spoke up, "kind and caring."

"I'm not saying all priests are dishonest. There are good priests. I have met them but that's not the point. The whole system is corrupt and set up to keep people down. The church is in many ways worse than the kings and queens. They profess to be above the everyday concerns of this world. Their only concern is to serve God. If the king is the ruler in this world and God is the king of the other world, we just go from serving one ruler in this life to serving the other for eternity."

The profound truth in what James said sounded right, but with all her heart Abagail didn't want it to be true. Not only was her life a sham, now it seemed the sham of her individual life was part of larger sham. It was like the very ground beneath her opened up.

"I am sorry if I upset you," James said, taking a deep breath. "You have to understand that I spend a lot of time alone. So, when I have someone to talk to, I get carried away."

"It is all right," Abagail managed to say.

"Anyway, it is time to go to bed," James said casually. He put out the fire and started to walk toward the house. Abagail followed. The things James said were careening in her brain. Her world had been turned upside down and inside out. All the pieces that had their place were shaken out and rattling loose in her brain. What is there to believe in? It was not until they were in the cabin that Abagail remembered to be afraid and put her hand in her pocket to touch the spoon.

James pointed to a bedroom and said, "That is your room." He pointed to another room and said, "I will sleep there."

Abagail let out a breath and the tension left her body. But she still propped a chair against the door.

CHAPTER 25

Albert picked up Lucia's cold, limp hand, covering it with his. Leaving her bedside was very hard for Albert but the doctor came in and said she needed privacy. Albert didn't like the doctor. He had a skinny body, a neck like a chicken, and a face stamped with a permanent scowl. Albert left reluctantly but not before he swore a silent oath to Lucia that he would not abandon her and would avenge the man who did this.

Albert left the palace more determined to find Abagail and whoever attacked Lucia. If those he interviewed before were intimidated by him, this time around, they crumbled in the face of his intensity. He did not accept one-word responses but still was unable to find a witness to the attack in the bakery or anyone who had seen a young lady in a dirty dress wandering the streets. He pushed and pushed and there was one name mentioned by several people Albert spoke to—Spencer Sykes, a man with a large, fresh wound on the right side of his face. There was a general belief that if something untoward happened, he was likely involved. But nobody Albert questioned had any reliable evidence that he was involved in either Lucia's attack or Abagail's escape. At last, Albert obtained a name and a description of the man who might know something. He had to find this Spencer Sykes.

The blacksmith, like everyone else, was initially reluctant to talk to Albert, but Albert was relentless and eventually the blacksmith opened up.

"After I was questioned by the marshal's men a man came by my shop."

"What did this man look like and what did he say?"

"He looked, I don't know how else to say it, he looked evil." The blacksmith shuddered.

"Evil," Albert repeated and thought, *That is our man.*

"This might sound crazy, but he had the look of a wild,

hungry animal."

"Did he have a gash on the right side of his face?" Albert asked.

The blacksmith hesitated.

"Oh, you would remember," Albert interjected. "It's a large wound that goes from his ear to his jaw. You can't miss it."

"I remember now. The right side of his face was partially covered. His face was almost all covered the whole time we talked. I never did get to see the right side of his face. It was like he was hiding something."

"Did you get the impression he knew where this escaped girl was?"

"I'm not sure about that but he seemed to take a great interest in her. I remember, he asked how much the reward was for her capture."

"Had you ever seen him before?"

"I do not think so."

"Did you get his name?"

"No," the blacksmith said.

"Well, thank you. You have been very helpful," Albert said.

Albert's mind was full of questions. *Spencer Sykes, who are you and why are you so interested in Abagail?* Then it hit Albert like a bolt—the man in the tavern. If he closed his eyes, he could see him sitting in the corner with the right side of his face against a wall and out of sight. The man in the tavern who disappeared was Spencer Sykes. He was sure of it. They were in the same room and Albert let him slip right through his fingers.

CHAPTER 26

James was too excited to sleep. He hadn't spoken with another person about his ideas in such a long time; he had forgotten how much they meant to him. He wondered if he talked too freely. Abagail seemed interested, but you never know these days, what with Catholics in hiding and Protestant sects fighting each other, everybody was looking for someone to torture and behead. Just an innocent word on her part could bring the authorities to his door. Then there was the soap he was hiding for his sister. If the authorities found out what he was hiding in that cave with the soap, they would have to hang him three times; once for blasphemy, again for treason, and a final time for illegally trading soap. James smiled. The arrival of Abagail brought something into his life he didn't even know he was missing.

Abagail laid in her bed next door, also wide awake. She never heard someone talk the way James did. Her brain was overloaded, drunk with his words and passion. She would never see the world in quite the same way again. Abagail had played by the rules her whole life without being aware there could be different ways to live, and look where it got her. It was by breaking the rules and escaping from the cave that her life really began. The things James said made so much sense, they seemed so logical, but led to a completely differ-ent way of thinking about the world. *I wonder what tomorrow will bring,* she wondered as she floated off to sleep. Abagail was surprised how excited she felt about the prospect of spending time tomorrow alone with James.

The next morning, they felt awkward around each other, no longer having the cover of darkness. In the harsh glare of the sun, James felt exposed. Abagail took his renewed silence to mean he regretted being so open with her.

They went about getting ready for the day. Abagail went

outside to wash her face and James stoked the fire in the stove. He put two pieces of bread on the grill and cracked two eggs into a pan. After letting loose a torrent of words last night, he didn't know how to start the simplest conversation at breakfast.

They ate in silence. When they finished, Abagail took the dishes. "You cooked, I'll wash the plates."

The spell was broken, and James was able to find his voice. "Look, about last night, I hope I did not upset you. I really do not know you and…"

"No, no," Abagail said as she gathered the dishes. "It was…" She hesitated because there were no words to de-scribe what it was like. "It was like nothing I've ever heard."

"Oh," James said, sounding disappointed.

"It was very—" she tried to find the words, "very eye-opening."

"Eye-opening," James repeated. He wasn't sure what to make of that. "I'm going to feed the animals," he said, and left.

Abagail stood over the washtub, trying to figure out what had just happened between them. What she wanted to say was that his ideas were thrilling, and wanted nothing more than to continue talking. Abagail was on her way out to empty the dirty water and tell him exactly that when James burst in and ran right into her. Some water slopped over the side.

"Oh, I am sorry, so sorry," James said.

"Is there something wrong?"

"Yes, there is. I do not want you to think that I am sorry for what I said last night. I believe every word and I am glad it was you I said it to."

"I feel honored that you trust me enough to speak the way you did."

"I do trust you. I think you and I have lot in common," he said excitedly.

"We do?" Abagail couldn't think of one thing that they could have in common.

"For one thing, neither one of us really knew our mother."

"You're right," Abagail said, feeling her shoulders slump.

"And" James continued, "we both reject the path that was laid out for us, and we're on a journey to find our own way."

"I can think of another thing we have in common," Abagail said.

"Oh, what's that?"

"We each have a secret that, if it would be known, could get us beheaded."

"You are right. At least I think I know what your secret is. Would they execute you for escaping from prison?" James could see that Abagail was upset. "Oh, my sister told me. Do not worry, your secret is safe with me. And what about my secret? Is it safe with you?"

"Of course, but your sister does not know the whole story."

"No?" James was surprised.

"Do you want to hear it?"

"If you are up to telling it, yes." James settled into a chair.

Abagail wanted to open up to James as much as he opened up to her. His ideas about the world were the most personal things he could share. The only thing Abagail had to share was her life story. She related her life story, beginning with being thrown into the cave up to the killing of her mother and the young guard, but once again left out the rape. It felt impossible to talk about it to a man she just met and the whole incident made her feel ashamed.

James seemed lost in thought. "So, how did you survive? All those days since your escape."

"I almost did not, but thanks to your sister's family and a few other kind strangers I managed."

James shook his head. "Unbelievable."

Abagail switched the conversation to him. "What about your offense?"

James laughed ruefully. "You heard it last night. I am all talk, but the wrong kind of talk will get you in trouble. To speak against the king and the church, people have been jailed, tortured, and executed for less."

"Then there is the soap," Abagail laughed.

"Right, the soap. The whole kingdom is threatened by my family's soap trade." James joined in the laughter.

The awkwardness of the morning was forgotten.

"Do you hear that?" James stood absolutely still.

"I do not hear anything."

"Horses, I hear horses and it sounds like they are coming this way."

Abagail heard them now and started to panic. "What are we going to do?"

"You have to hide. Come with me." James took her hand as they ran to the back of the house.

Abagail saw where they were headed. "No, I cannot."

"You have to. The cave is the only safe place." They arrived the entrance of the cave and Abagail froze. James turned and took a few steps back to the house.

"You are not coming with me?"

"No, I cannot. Someone has to stay and deal with these horsemen."

"But I cannot go in there."

"Do not worry. I will come and get you as soon as they leave. Now hurry, the horses are getting closer." He guided her into the cave. "Do not come out. Wait for me. We do not know who they are or what they want. Now go quickly."

And Abagail was all alone in the dark once again. Her body dropped to the cold floor and she wrapped herself into a ball, trying to protect herself. But with the damp cold of the packed earth and the odor of rotting vegetation seeping into her body, her life force was once again draining.

CHAPTER 27

The water pressed down on her. Lucia tried swimming to the surface, but her arms were not strong enough. The current was taking her. Her life was under the water's control. A kind of peace came over her, her body relaxing, like melting into the water. And then without trying she started to rise to the surface. It was as if the water that held her down was now pushing her up.

"Lucia, Lucia," someone called her name. Blurry, human-like figures hung over her, which made sense since she was looking at them from underwater. Someone touched her arm, but it was not part of her dream. She opened her eyes to an explosion of pain.

The first thing Lucia saw clearly were Albert's broad shoulders. His hand rested lightly on her arm.

"You are back," Albert said, starting to get up. Lucia grabbed his hand and tried to talk but all she could do was make a croaking sound. Albert bent down so his ear was next to her mouth. "Say it again. I did not hear you."

Lucia took a deep breath and with all her energy whispered, "Water."

Albert picked up a pitcher from an end table by Lucia's bed and poured water into a goblet.

Lucia's head exploded as she tried to sit up a little. It was impossible. She didn't realize she was crying until tears ran down her face. Her throat was so dry, she felt desperate and at that moment death was desirable. Then Albert did something that seemed like a miracle to Lucia. He held the cup in one hand and with his other slowly lifted Lucia's head.

Lucia never tasted water so cold and delicious. With great effort, she was able to say, "More," and the second cup tasted even better. Lucia let out a big sigh and Albert carefully laid her head back on the pillow.

"Do you want me to get a doctor?" Albert asked.

Lucia shook her head, which ignited explosions in her skull.

Albert took her hand. He wasn't sure what else to do. Shouldn't a doctor see her? They should know she is conscious. He slowly and carefully tried to retrieve his hand from hers, but as soon as he moved his fingers Lucia opened her eyes.

"Stay," Lucia whispered hoarsely.

Albert stayed at Lucia's bedside, holding her hand. He listened to her breathing and closed his eyes. He saw the baker lying dead on the floor with all that blood and the horror of seeing Lucia not moving, not knowing if she was alive or dead. His eyes flew open. It took a few seconds to remember where he was. Lucia was sleeping, her eyes moving quickly under her lids. She moaned and the sound pierced Albert's heart. He started to unlace his fingers from hers, but Lucia held on tight. Albert did not want to wake her.

"Hello," someone said in a voice that sounded miles away.

Albert jumped. Was he dreaming? He looked down at Lucia, who said, "Hello," once again, a little stronger this time. Here eyes were open and she was trying to sit up.

"Wait, do not do it on your own. I will help." Albert carefully put his hand under her head and lifted her. "Do you want some water?" he asked.

"Please."

"How do you feel?"

"Better, my head is pounding but I do feel better. What happened?"

"You were attacked and struck on the head," Albert replied. "Do you remember anything, anything at all about your attacker?"

Lucia closed her eyes. "No, it's all a blank."

"You were in a bakery," Albert said, trying to prompt her.

"A bakery, yes, I remember. The baker was lying in a pool

of blood." Lucia shivered. "How awful. Is she dead?"

"Yes," Albert said, gently resting his hand on her arm.

Lucia cried softly.

"Can you remember what you and the baker were talking about?"

Lucia wiped her eyes. "The baker became very upset describing a man who could do unspeakable things to a girl on her own. A man walked by her shop window at that moment and the baker stopped talking, clearly frightened." Lucia closed her eyes.

"Take your time," Albert said, "try to recall as much as you can."

"I owe my life to you," Lucia said. "If you had not found me and brought me to the palace, I would have ended up like that baker."

Albert stroked Lucia's hand, searching for the words to say what he was feeling. He looked away and spoke haltingly. "No, I owe my life to you. I have not always been a good man and the people I should have protected...I failed." A sob came from someplace deep inside him. "I have made promises I did not keep and acted in a cowardly way." Albert let go of Lucia's hand, his head down, his arms hanging at his side. "I might have saved your life, but I feel it is me who has been saved."

"What do you mean?" Lucia asked.

"You gave me the chance to do good, to do right, and for that I owe you everything," Albert said softly.

Lucia's eyes fluttered. "I have to sleep."

Albert wasn't sure how long he sat holding Lucia's hand, but was how the queen's attendant found him.

"The queen will see you now," the court attendant said.

Albert walked into the royal chamber. On his way in, the marshal walked out. He looked upset and gave Albert a long, disdainful look. Today, Queen Henrietta was in her full regalia, dressed in an elaborate outfit. In a green dress with billowing sleeves, a fashionable high collar set off by a striking gold necklace, her crown, sepulcher, and seal of office, she looked in every way like a queen. Albert bowed, and the queen asked, "Do you have any news? Tell me you've made some progress, please."

"I have, your Majesty," Albert said.

"Yes, yes, tell me. I have a meeting to attend."

Albert told her about the man with the wound and how he may lead them to Abagail.

"That's all fine and good but how do you plan on catching him?"

"Well," and here Albert told himself to tread lightly, "we can split up the search. The marshal's men can search for the man who attacked Lucia while I continue to pursue Abagail." Albert could see the queen was considering his idea. "We have a good description of the man and we know his name and where he was last seen. The marshal has the manpower to flood the town with leaflets and go from door to door."

"You think that will work?" the queen asked.

"It should, your Majesty." Albert bowed.

"I will instruct the marshal to cease looking for Abagail and direct him to find the man you speak of—what's his name?"

"Spencer Sykes, your Majesty."

"Are you any closer to finding where Abagail is?"

"No, your Majesty, but I think..."

"I do not care what you think. I want results."

"Yes, your Majesty."

"Is that all?" the queen asked, but before Albert could answer she waved her hand in dismissal, turned around, and began speaking with her advisor.

It wasn't until Albert was already out of the palace and walking toward town that he realized the queen hadn't asked about Lucia. It was like Lucia didn't matter because she was indisposed. He told himself to never forget that the queen only valued those who were of use to her. He could feel his usefulness coming to an end if he couldn't report any progress soon.

CHAPTER 28

James got back to the house just a minute before the horsemen arrived. He looked around the house and noticed that there were table settings for two. He quickly put one dish and a cup away just before his front door was flung open. Four men in soldiers' uniforms crowded into his small kitchen, their hands resting on their swords.

"We are here on the king's business," the tallest soldier said in a voice loud enough to address a large crowd. "I am Captain Nugent, and you are ordered by royal decree to answer all questions fully and truthfully. Do you understand?" the captain bellowed.

"Yes sir," James said in his most respectful voice.

The other soldiers wandered through the house. James could hear them opening drawers in the bedroom and dumping the contents on the floor. It took all of James' self-control to keep his eyes on the captain.

"Who lives here with you?" the captain asked.

"No one, I live alone."

"Live alone, mm, isn't that strange? What is your name?" he asked. Then one of the other soldiers went over to the captain and whispered in his ear. "If you live alone why do you have two beds that look like they were slept in?"

"My sister and her family visited me, and I have not had the time to clean the bedroom they used." James could feel sweat dripping down his back.

"Mm," the captain said again. "Are there any other buildings on your land? And who owns this land?"

"It was my father's land and when he died it came to me," James said.

"And your name," the captain said in an imperious way.

"James Collier, sir."

"And my good man, how do you make a living, being that

you live alone?"

James realized that the captain had to regain the upper hand, so he played the humble serf. "You asked before about other buildings on the property. I do have a small barn where I keep my animals and I have a garden. Do you want to see it?"

"No, that's all right." The captain turned to the two other men. "Did you find anything?"

"There are a lot of books."

"Books? Show me these books." They all squeezed into James' bedroom. He had a small bookcase by his bed with three shelves filled with books.

The captain picked up two books. "What are these books for?"

"I do not know what you mean," James said.

The captain's face turned red and he stroked his moustache. "Do not get mouthy with me," he said, tipping the bookcase over so all the books fell to the floor. "Show me your bible," he demanded.

James went through the books quickly, hoping none of the soldiers knew what the titles referred to. They were the kinds of books that could get a man beheaded. He found the bible and gave it to the captain.

"Well," he said, "I see it's the King James version, that's good." The captain's demeanor changed suddenly. "James; the name of our dearly departed king, the same as yours. You were named after him, that is good."

James could not take his eyes off the books strewn on the floor. A pamphlet written by John Lilburne, a prominent Leveler, was in plain sight.

The captain was looking right at the pamphlet in the middle of the floor but he didn't seem to recognize the name of the author. "Don't worry about your books. We just have to check them. You have to be careful these days with all the papists around." He smiled and turned to the three other men. "Instead of just standing there, help this man. Pick up the damn books." The captain took a long, lingering look at James and the books and said, "All right, men, we are finished here."

The captain and the other soldiers joined their comrades, who were waiting outside. The captain mounted his horse. He sat erect, like he was posing for a painting. He cleared his throat and spoke with the same official tone he had upon their arrival. "The king is looking for two people who are enemies of the royal court. One is a young girl named Abagail and the other is a man, Spencer Sykes, with a large wound on the right side of his face. They are both wanted for murder and under no circumstances are you to help them. It is your duty to tell the authorities if you see either one. The penalty for violating this order is death. Do you understand?"

"Yes sir," James said as sincerely as he could. The captain stroked his moustache and looked at James again for a few seconds, turned his horse around abruptly, and galloped off.

As soon as the horsemen were out of sight, James ran as fast as he could to the cave. "Abagail, Abagail," he called out. But there was no response.

Abagail had been transported back to the cave with the old woman, her mother. To Abagail it didn't feel like she was imagining it—she was there. The time that passed since her escape was a dream. This dark place was her reality and there were only two people in her world, her and her mother.

Abagail was cold and hungry and, more than anything, terrified. She couldn't actually see her mother but felt her presence all around her and inside her. It was like her mother was everywhere, everything and nothing at the same time.

She saw herself holding the spoon over the young guard, the spoon entering the soft flesh of his neck, and how his body contorted when she thrust the spoon in with all her strength. Blood streamed from the young guard's neck. The cave began to fill up with his blood. Out of the blood her mother slowly emerged. Her mouth moved but Abagail couldn't hear her. Abagail watched her mother sink into the blood. Abagail let out a scream and fainted.

James never heard a sound so awful. He ran as fast as he could. "Abagail, Abagail," he shouted as he entered the cave. He saw her lying on the ground, unmoving. She couldn't be dead, he told himself.

CHAPTER 29

Albert spent the good part of a day questioning anyone who might have seen Abagail. He came up with nothing. He had no idea how to proceed and had nothing to present to the queen. He was stuck and there was only one person who could help him—Lucia.

He could not face the queen with no progress to report. He passed a tavern and told himself he was going in to question the patrons. When he walked in, he ordered a drink—*just one*, he told himself, but he knew it was a lie. Sitting heavily at a table, he downed one jug after the other, trying to drown out the condemning voice in his head. Finally, he reached the numb state he was trying for. He leaned back and fell off his chair. His head made a thudding sound as it hit the floor, but even that didn't arouse him from his drunken stupor.

Sean started working in the tavern two years ago when he was eleven, wiping off the tables and mopping the floors. He learned there were drunks and there were drunks. Most drunks spent whatever money they had but those who somehow kept a few coins were fair game for every hustler that came along. It could be a pickpocket, a prostitute, or just someone acting friendly helping the drunken man up while relieving his pockets of any extra coins. A roaring drunk was going to part with his money sooner rather than later. That's why he was so surprised that no one approached this big man lying right on the floor with his mouth wide open. He looked at Mr. Miles, the owner, expecting him to call his mates to drag the drunk outside, but he didn't. Everyone in the bar walked around the man, leaving him alone, and Sean knew for a fact that there were enough thieves and pickpock-ets in the bar at that moment to fleece any number of drunks.

Sean went up to Rosie, who worked behind the bar sometimes serving drinks and occasionally providing other services in the room upstairs. She was always sweet to Sean after she found out he was an orphan. "Who is that big man?" Sean asked.

Rosie leaned in close and Sean could smell her sweet perfume. In her lowest voice, she whispered, "He works for the queen. He's looking for that girl who escaped from the jail and killed a guard. They say the guard was his son."

Sean went back to wiping tables and walked around and over the big guy on the floor. Two hours later, the big drunk tried to get up. He couldn't do it on his own, so he leaned on a chair for support, but the chair slipped out and he landed back on the floor. He started to get up again and began to wobble, almost falling.

"Sean, don't just stand there, help the man up," Mr. Miles said, as if it was Sean's fault the man was on the floor.

Sean ran over to help him up. Albert leaned on Sean's shoulder. He was so heavy Sean stumbled and they almost fell together, but Sean was just able to angle him over to a table where he half-fell, half-sat into a chair.

Albert put his head in his hands and rubbed his face. He turned his head, looking at all the other customers. Everyone who was staring at him quickly averted their eyes. Then out of the corner of his eye, he saw him. The man with the wound opened the door to the tavern and looked in. Albert closed his eyes to clear his vision and when he opened them again, he was gone.

Albert called the boy over and told him to take a very important message to the palace. "Can you read?" he asked the boy.

"No sir, but I have a good memory," Sean said.

"I'm going to give you a message to take to the castle and give it to a lady called Lucia. Do you think you can do that?"

"Yes sir."

"What's her name?" Albert asked.

"Lucia," Sean said proudly.

"Very good. Now listen closely because I'm going to ask you to repeat it. When you find Lucia, tell her that Albert is following the man with the wound on his face. You got that?"

"Yes, sir."

"Repeat it."

Sean did.

Albert gave Sean a crown coin and said, "This is for you to keep now. When you deliver the message to Lucia and only to Lucia, I'm going to give you another just like this one." He took out another crown and showed it to Sean. "Now go, boy, run as fast as you can."

Sean took off but after a few steps he heard the man calling, "Boy, come back."

Sean almost kept running. Two crowns was the most money he ever had at one time and he didn't want to have to hand it back. But he turned and walked over to the table. The big man was standing, still a little wobbly. He leaned over to Sean and gave him the queen's seal. "If anybody stops you just show them this and they will let you pass."

Albert watched the boy run out of the tavern. Then, stumbling, he wobbled out of the tavern, staggered down one street and up the next. He turned a corner and there was the man. "You there," Albert bellowed, "stop in the name of the queen." Everyone in the street turned around except for the man from the tavern. He buried his head deep in his coat lapels and kept on walking. Albert ran to catch up with him, grabbed the man's shoulder, and spun him around. "Where do you think you're going?" He stopped when he saw the man's face. He didn't have a spot of hair on his face and no scar. He looked nothing like the man Albert thought he saw in the tavern. Albert rubbed his face and mumbled, "Sorry, thought you were somebody else."

CHAPTER 30

Margot just began to eat her soup when the letter arrived. She opened it and her face lost all its color.

"What is it, my dear?" Prince Leon asked.

"My father is very ill. The queen says it is crucial for me to return home as soon as possible." Margot tried to read the look on her husband's face but, as usual, his expression didn't change. She had been married for a little more than three months and her husband was still a stranger. Waiting for him to say something, she finally asked, "What do you think?"

"Of course, you have to go. I'm sure your father and mother need you, and I imagine there are a lot of things to take care of." The prince picked up his spoon and without saying another word continued eating his soup.

Margot had to use all her willpower not to scream. His tone was so even and unfeeling it drove her mad. It wasn't until dinner was finished and the dishes cleared that Margot brought up having to return home again. "I have to leave as soon as I can."

"Certainly, tomorrow I will have my personal secretary make the necessary arrangements." Prince Leon smiled. He wiped his mouth, making sure he patted his wispy moustache with the napkin. Duty done, he got up from the table, went around to where Margot sat, and kissed her on the head.

Margot knew where he was going. He was going to drink a brandy and smoke a cigar with his personal advisor. He might spend the night with his current mistress if he had two drinks or share her bed. If he drank too much, he would spend the night alone in his own bed. Although the news was not good, the thought of returning home filled Margot with joy. For the first time since arriving at the Spanish court, there was something to look forward to.

It wasn't until preparing for bed that she realized they

never discussed whether her husband would accompany her home. This foreign country and her husband would never be home to her. There was a soft knock on her door. She knew by the knock that it was her husband and why he came to her bed chamber this time of night. Taking a deep breath and opening the door, she found him leaning against the wall for support. His eyes were glassy, which meant he had two brandies rather than his customary one. He stumbled into her room and without saying a word took off his clothes.

CHAPTER 31

Abagail's eyes were still closed but her mind began to stir. The desire to keep her eyes closed to avoid her worst nightmare of finding herself back in the cave was strong. *What did happen these past months? Was it all a dream?* She thought she felt the sensation of her hand moving. No, it wasn't her hand—the hand belonged to someone else. Questions streamed through her mind. *Where am I? Who is this person holding my hand?* Abagail's eyes opened of their own free will and the first thing she saw was the friendly face of a familiar man.

"How are you feeling?" the man asked.

"I don't know," Abagail said.

"You have been unconscious for some time. Do you remember what happened?"

"No."

James told her about the men on the horses, and that she had to hide in the cave. She must have passed out because this cave reminded her of being locked up in the cave with her mother. In her fog, Abagail couldn't believe James was talking about her. This was not her life. Then as if a light shone on Abagail's dark corners, she came to see it was an accurate depiction. At that moment there was nothing more important to her than making a different life, a normal life. Looking at James' kind face and warm eyes, she said, "I would like to stay here with you."

James was confused. "Of course," he said uncertainly. "You are. You are staying with me until Maria and Frank come back and then..."

"No, that is not what I meant," Abagail said, interrupting him. "I mean forever. I'd like to live here forever."

"Oh," was all James could say.

They never spoke again about what Abagail said the day

she fainted. As the days passed, though, James did not forget it for one second.

CHAPTER 32

The next morning, Margot rode in a carriage on the first leg of her trip to London. This part of the journey was to the northern Spanish port at Santander and would take three full days of hard riding, followed by a two-day boat ride to Portsmouth England and, lastly, a day's carriage ride to her destination, the palace.

"Mother," Margot whispered upon seeing the queen. Margot wanted nothing more than to be enwrapped in her mother's arms but that wasn't what a princess did, not even in the privacy of the queen's bed chamber. They walked to each other and it was the queen who held out her arms. Henrietta was ecstatic to embrace her daughter. Margot didn't have to tell her mother what married life was like each disappointment, each compromise, each instance of swallowing rage was written on her face for her mother to see. They hugged for a long time.

Margot broke the silence. "How is Father?"

"Not well, my dear. Not well at all."

Margot took a deep breath. "What do the doctors say?"

Queen Henrietta laughed bitterly. "What don't they say? You ask four doctors for an opinion and you get six diagnoses. The only thing they agree on is that the king is very, very sick. Each one is more certain than the next that he knows the best treatment."

Margot felt lightheaded. "I have to sit," she said, and collapsed into the chair in front of her mother's powder table. Her reflection in the mirror was shocking. It looked like she had forgotten how to smile. She picked up a bottle of her mother's perfume and brought it to her nose. The sweet aroma reminded her of being a little girl. She and Abagail would sneak into this room, sit on this very chair, and giggle quietly as they tried all of her mother's lotions, perfumes, and powders. Margot looked up at her mother, "Can I see him?"

"Yes, but not now. There are too many people around. Later tonight will be a better time."

"Why all the secrecy? I had to use the side entrance to enter the palace. There was no escort to meet my ship when it docked. Why?"

Henrietta lowered her voice without being aware she was doing it. "It is always a sensitive time when there is a possibility of one ruler giving away to another."

"Why should it be sensitive?" Margot was confused. This was not like her mother, whispering, sneaking around the castle, and so afraid.

"The war with Spain is over but the country is in debt. There is still unrest, and when there is unrest there are rumors."

"Rumors?" Margot asked.

"Questions of succession to the crown."

"Do I have rivals?" Margot, caught unaware, always understood she was unquestionably next in line for the throne.

"My sister, your aunt Beatrice, had a child out of wedlock, a girl." The queen watched her daughter closely. *Would it be better to get it all out now or to deliver the news piecemeal?*

"Oh my God!" Margot said, suddenly alert. "All this time and I had no idea. All I remember about Aunt Beatrice is that she died when I was a baby. If I ever did see her, I was too young to remember. Is her daughter making a claim for the throne?"

"Wait, there is more." The queen hesitated.

"Tell me please so I know what I am up against."

"It is not simple, not simple at all." The queen held her hand up and said, "I will tell you all of it, but you must promise not to interrupt me or walk out before I finish. Do you agree?"

"Of course, why would I walk out?"

"We will see, but promise me no matter what you hear you will stay until the story is finished."

The more her mother talked the more nervous Margot felt. "Yes, I promise I will not interrupt or walk out."

"As I said, your aunt, my sister, had a baby out of wedlock and this baby, who is now your age, has a claim to the throne."

"How could she? My father is the king." Margot waited for an answer. Her head was spinning and although she was already sitting down it felt like she was falling.

"You said you would let me finish," the queen said.

"All right, Mother, I understand." Margot could feel her face getting hot.

"Remember you promised not to interrupt." The queen looked at her daughter and waited for confirmation.

Margot took a deep breath. "I promise, I will just listen."

"As I was saying, this other girl, roughly the same age as you, could have a claim to the throne."

"How? Unless we had the same..." Margot could not finish her thought.

"I can see by the look on your face that you have figured it out," the queen said.

"How could he? I mean to you, to me?" Margot asked in a choked voice.

"Margot, my daughter, you have to ask that question? I have heard about your husband's activities. You do not think something like that can be kept secret."

Margot's face got hot and her eyes began to fill with tears. She could not look at her mother. "But how could you know?"

The queen let out a small, bitter laugh. "It is my business to know what happens in all the important courts."

"You mean you have spies in the Spanish court?"

"Yes, and they have their spies here. I prefer the term 'agent.' I employ agents at this court also."

"Why in your own court do you need agents?" Margot asked.

"You need eyes and ears in your own court most of all. Otherwise, how do you know who is plotting against you?"

"Lucia is one of your agents," Margot stated rather than asked.

Henrietta laughed. "What makes you say that?"

"The way the two of you meet alone so often and she is obviously more than a lady-in-waiting."

"Good for you. You are very observant. And when you become the queen Lucia can be retained as your eyes and ears."

Margot didn't reply but felt revulsion about the whole business.

"So, to return to our topic I need you to just listen. This is hard for me to talk about. So, please, no interruptions." Henrietta looked at her daughter, who nodded.

"I promise."

"When I learned that Beatrice and I were due to give birth at the same time, I made a decision that I have come to regret. Her baby was to be raised right alongside you. The child must never know who her mother and father were. I hoped it would work out for everyone. But it did not turn out that way."

Margot held her breath, and when she finally exhaled, one word came out: "Abagail."

"Yes, Abagail."

"Oh Mother, how could you? We grew up together never knowing we were sisters."

"Half-sisters," Henrietta corrected.

"And her mother? I don't remember anyone that could have been Abagail's mother."

Henrietta took a deep breath. "This is the most difficult part. Abagail's mother, your Aunt Beatrice, has been in prison for years."

"What, in prison?" Margot repeated in disbelief.

"Let me explain," Henrietta said. "I gave her the choice—either leave the court and live on her own with her baby or live at court under the condition she wouldn't tell Abagail she was her mother. Beatrice agreed to live at court but insisted on telling Abagail. Beatrice wouldn't promise to cease, so I threatened her with prison. I never thought my sister would be so stubborn, a few days at most, maybe a week in the cave and I was sure she would understand the logic of my proposal. But after two weeks of being imprisoned I made her the same offer, but Beatrice refused it. It was as if my sister wanted to return to her cave."

"That is so cruel. How could you?"

"I did it for you, so there would be no question about who your father's successor would be."

Margot jumped up. "Oh no, you are not using me as the reason. I never asked you to do it. You disgust me." Margot bolted from her mother's bed chamber as the queen predicted, slamming the door behind her, and went to her bedroom. She lay in bed, wondering how she could be so ignorant of even the most basic facts of her own life. Her father, a philanderer. That explained his cold attitude towards her. Her mother, incredibly cruel, her aunt imprisoned, her best friend her half-sister. Her entire life was based on an elaborate web of lies and unbelievable acts of cruelty.

CHAPTER 33

Spencer the hunter became the hunted. The king's men were everywhere, handing out pictures of him. They had his name and his description including the gash on the right side of his face. It was just a matter of time before he was caught. He had to leave the city now. As soon as it turned dark, he headed for the forest.

The forest reminded Spencer of his childhood. It was not a happy memory. His father died when he was seven. No one ever explained how, but as an adult Spencer came to understand that it was suicide by drink. Staggering home drunk one night, he had fallen and hit his head, leaving four young children and their mother alone.

Spencer knew, even at his young age, the best way he could help his family would be to set off on his own, one less mouth to feed. So one night, he walked away from his family and never returned. He went to the city where there was opportunity, but nobody was interested in taking on a skinny nine-year-old, so he did what he had to, to survive.

Spencer grew up an outsider and learned to use this to his advantage. He would evaluate every situation with one question—how could he use it for his gain? By blending into the background, observing the people around him, picking out the most vulnerable, he was always ready to take advantage. He started out shoplifting, mostly food. He got caught a few times, and was punished with a smack, a kick, and a warning. As he got older, he moved onto to breaking into homes and taking the little that people had. The only plan he ever had was pounce. Grab what you can and get away.

Spencer vowed to never return to the miserable little house of his childhood, but now it was the only place he could think of. He had no other place to go. He walked all day. By the smell in the air, he knew he was close. It was just over the next rise. His old home came into view. It looked even more shabby than he remembered. Time was not kind to it. His pace quickened. Who was that in the front of the house? A woman he didn't recognize. Could it be his mother or one of his sisters? No, it couldn't be. As he got closer, the woman spotted him and called into the house, from which a man emerged.

"Sorry to bother you," Spencer said as he approached, "but I wonder if you know the people who used to live here?"

The man grunted. "No."

"Are you sure? Because I used to live here, and I have not been back for quite a while." Spencer tried to smile and lightly touched his scar.

The woman replied, "Yes, there was a mother and her three children."

"That must be them. Do you know where they are?" Spencer asked.

The woman hesitated and glanced at her husband, who said, "They were thrown out because of failure to pay rent."

Spencer didn't ask if they knew where they went. He turned around and walked away. He didn't want to hear anymore. He knew it would only be bad news. He had a strong urge to hurt someone.

"Wait, wait."

Spencer stopped, turned, and saw the woman waving towards him.

"Come back," she shouted.

Spencer walked back down the hill toward the house.

"I'm sorry we were so rude," the woman said. "You know the way things are these days, it is hard to trust people. We are eating soon, and we wonder if you would like to join us, nothing fancy, just some soup and bread."

"I would like that very much," Spencer said. He hadn't eaten all day.

"Good, very good. You can wash up out here." The woman pointed to a pump.

The couple bent their heads and prayed before they ate. When they were done eating, the woman poured the remaining soup into Spencer's bowl along with the last piece of bread.

Spencer ate it all. "That was delicious," he said. He started to get up to leave when the man put his hand up.

"Why not sit for a while, unless you have somewhere to be," the man said.

Spencer sat back down.

The man cleared his throat. "We were thinking that if it was agreeable to you, uh..."

His wife cut in. "We would like to offer you a job. It is harvesting time and we can use the extra help. You can work for your room and board. Three meals a day and a bed. What do you say?"

Spencer was taken back by the offer. It was a perfect way to blend into the countryside and shake off the big guy who was looking for him.

The couple took his silence as a sign that he was considering the offer. The man finally said, "If the harvest is a good one you could have a share of the profits. What do you say?" He stuck out his hand.

Spencer shook it. "You got yourself a deal," he said.

The farmer almost smiled. "My name is Ezra Morton, and this is my wife Ruth."

"My name is Samuel, Samuel Moore," Spencer said. "You can call me Sam."

"Well, Sam, we start tomorrow at sunrise."

CHAPTER 34

Sean had never seen anything like it. The ceilings were as tall as the tops of buildings. The walls were covered with paintings like in church, but this was like no church he'd ever seen. He was looking at a picture of two laughing, naked ladies sitting on a blanket, eating grapes like it was the most natural thing in the world to have a laughing, naked picnic.

A man roughly grabbed his shoulder. "What are you doing here boy?" He slapped Sean on the side of the head. "Be gone with you now, leave."

Sean thought of running off when he remembered why he came in the first place. "I have a message for a lady."

"A lady, what is this lady's name?" the man asked.

Sean had to think, and then it came to him. "Lucia, her name is Lucia."

"Are you sure about this? If I find out you're lying, you'll be in big trouble."

Sean puffed himself up a little and said, "Yes, I'm sure. It is a very important message."

The man said, "All right, give it to me, and I will make sure she gets it."

"Oh no, I was told to only give it to her, and anyway it is not written down—I had to remember it," Sean said proudly.

"You cannot just walk in the castle and expect to see an aide to the queen. Come on." He grabbed Sean by the elbow and began dragging him out. Sean tried to plant his feet to stop him, but he wasn't strong enough. Then he remembered. "Wait, wait," he said, "I have something," and he freed his hand and pulled the queen's seal from his pocket.

The man stopped dragging him. "Where did you get that from? If you stole it, boy—"

"I did not steal it. It was given to me by the man who paid me to give the message."

"Lucia, do you know this boy?" the man asked a woman quickly walking by.

The lady turned and looked at Sean for a second, then shrugged her shoulders. "Never saw him before," she said and walked away.

"That was Lucia, boy, and she has no idea who you are." The man hit Sean's head so hard he saw lights flashing like a hundred candles being blown by the wind.

"Wait, miss, wait!" Sean yelled after her. "You know Albert. Albert sent me."

Lucia turned quickly and walked back to Sean. "Let this boy go," she said to the man, and took Sean by the hand. "Where is the message?"

"It is not written down. I am supposed to tell you."

"All right, come with me," Lucia said. She took Sean by the hand, led him down the hall, and opened a large wooden door with animals carved on it. "What is the message?" Lucia asked.

Sean couldn't hear her. His heart was beating so loud he was surprised the whole world didn't hear it.

"What is your name, dear?" Lucia asked in a calm voice.

Sean couldn't speak. He was in the throne room. The actual room where the king and queen ruled the world.

"Well, Sean, what was the message that Albert wanted you to give me?"

Sean shook his head to loosen his tongue. "He said—" Sean swallowed. "He said that he saw the man with the wound." Sean smiled, proud that he remembered the message.

The lady turned red and grabbed Sean's arm. "Was that all, the whole message?"

"Yes, ma'am," Sean said.

"Wait here, I'll be right back."

Sean was all alone in the throne room. He took a step toward the throne and waited for someone to yell, "Hey, you, what are you doing here?" but nobody did. He walked until he was standing close to the throne. He stretched his arm, his finger lightly touching the throne before he pulled his hand back quickly. He would remember this day for the rest of his life. The day he touched the throne.

Lucia ran down the hallway, made a turn, and was out of sight. She came back after a minute and Sean was sure he saw the blade of a long knife sticking out of her coat. "Let us go, show me where Albert gave you the message."

CHAPTER 35

Sean saw him first. "There he is." He pointed to Albert, who was sitting on the ground with his head in his hands.

"Thank you, Sean," Lucia said. Her head pounded, she felt dizzy, and she was out of breath. Lying in bed the last few days had left her weak. There was no rush. Albert didn't look like he was going anywhere. Lucia took a moment to recover from the brisk walk when she noticed Sean hadn't left her side. "You can go now," she said.

"Well, Miss, I was promised, you know, if I delivered the message."

"Oh, I understand. How much were you promised?"

"I was promised ten crowns."

Lucia reached into her pocket and took out a ten-crown piece. "Here, for a job well done."

"Thank you, Miss," Sean said, smiling.

Lucia sat down on the ground next to Albert and asked, "Did you lose him?"

Albert lifted his head and, squinting in the sun, muttered, "I don't know," in a low voice. "I don't know."

"What do you mean?"

Albert looked into Lucia's eyes. "I don't know if I really saw him or if it was my imagination."

"Imagination brought on by drink," Lucia said with disgust in her voice, turning to walk away before she remem-bered he saved her life. "I have a job for you."

"What do you mean?" Albert muttered.

"Do you promise to do exactly what I tell you?"

"Yes, I promise." The big man answered Lucia as if she was his mother, eagerly exchanging his freedom for someone to give him some direction.

Lucia helped him stand up. "You cannot live your life full of regret and blame. I will help you get your life back if you are ready to really change." Lucia looked up at Albert's blotchy red face and asked, "Are you ready to change?"

Albert kept his head bowed, feeling as if he couldn't speak.

"I need an answer from you, Albert. Do you want to change your life?"

It took all of Albert's strength to say, "Yes."

"Good, we must go to the palace. I have an audience with the queen. You will come with me. While I am with the queen you will clean yourself and someone will bring you new clothes. When you finish, wait for me outside of the queen's stateroom."

"Go to my rooms and an attendant will bring you clothes," Lucia said when they got to the palace. "The queen is waiting."

"Your Majesty," Lucia said, bowing. "I am sorry to disturb you at this time but there are very urgent matters to attend to."

"What is it?" the queen asked in a low voice.

"The unrest throughout the kingdom is growing. The Levelers are growing and getting more organized. The absence of his royal highness, the king, at public events is commented on."

"What kind of comments?" the queen asked.

Lucia swallowed and stopped talking. Just uttering these words sounded treasonous to her ears. "There is talk of overthrowing the king."

The queen sighed. "Surely our enemies are not powerful enough to pose a serious threat to the monarchy."

"Not by themselves. There are reports the Puritans and the Catholics are forming a coalition with members of the parliament and the Levelers to oppose his highness."

The queen came to life. Lucia had her mistress' full attention. Her body rigid and her eyes wide open, the queen spoke in short, direct sentences. "We must have supporters. The noblemen, the army, and the merchants are still loyal."

"Yes, of course, most of the nobility and the larger

merchants support the throne but the military is split."

"What do you mean split?" the queen asked.

"I would say the majority of soldiers would swear their allegiance to the crown, however."

"Yes, go on," the queen insisted.

"Some regiments have mutinied and gone to the rebel side. Fighting between loyal soldiers and the traitors has erupted. The apprentices and poorer peasants are the most fervent supporters of the Levelers and are reportedly arming themselves."

Queen Henrietta sat quietly. "The longer my husband hangs on to life, the more vulnerable the crown. Margot has to ascend to the throne, then this rebellion will end. I know the king would agree. The future of the monarchy is more important than any single life—even the life of a king."

CHAPTER 36

Dinner was over. James and Abagail sat outside in front of the house. A good fire was burning. Now was time for James to ask the question that has been on his mind all day.

"Do you remember what you said when you woke up in the cave?" James asked.

"I was just coming to and was all upset..." Abagail's voice trailed off.

"Oh," James replied. "So, you did not mean it, when you said..." James hesitated. "When you said you wanted to live with me."

"I did mean it, but I do not know if it's possible."

"What do you want, Abagail?" James asked.

"What do I want?" Abagail repeated, then slowly said, "So many things and yet I have a hard time naming them." She looked at James, who returned her gaze with warm eyes, inviting her to speak. "I want answers so I can know my story and make sense of my life."

"Answers to what?"

"Like what really happened between my mother and the queen? Did Margot know about my mother being locked up? Did she know where I was? Is the king really my father? What changes if Margot and I are truly half-sisters? And so many more questions." Abagail took a deep breath.

"I understand," James said. "What else?"

"That is more than enough for right now."

James realized at that moment his dream of sharing his life with Abagail was exactly that—a dream.

"It is not fair of me to make any commitments when I do not know what the future holds for me."

"None of us know what our future holds," James said.

"I do not have any idea about the most basic things of my past. I have to figure out who I am before anything else, do you understand?"

"Yes," James said sadly.

"I know I care for you," Abagail said. She walked over to James and sat down next to him.

They sat apart, staring into the fire. Abagail started to shiver. "Would you hold me, James?"

Without saying a word, James scooted very close to Abagail and put his arm around her shoulders.

Abagail leaned in and felt safe. They stayed in that position for a long time. Abagail pulled back for a second when memories of being forced flooded in. "This isn't easy for me."

"I know," James replied.

"I am confused and afraid."

"Do not be afraid. Nothing will happen that you do not want to happen."

They held each other until the fire burned down. "Should I build the fire up again?" James asked.

"Let us go inside," Abagail said, and without looking at him walked into the house and went straight into James' bedroom.

James joined her. They laid side by side with space between them. Their legs continued moving very slowly until the space between them disappeared.

Abagail started to tremble and tried to rid her mind of the monster who assaulted her. "What's wrong?" James asked. Then, in a whisper, "I'm nervous too." He put his arm around Abagail's shoulder and with his other hand caressed her face gently.

Abagail slowly melted in his embrace and as she relaxed the enormity of the events of the past months flooded her mind. Her past life with Margot in the palace seemed like it belonged to someone else. She cried for herself—not only for all that had happened to her but for the uncertainty of what may come. James held her and accepted her tears without asking for an explanation.

"We can lay like this for as long as you want," James said.

Abagail took his hand, squeezed it, and fell asleep.

James stared at the ceiling, not knowing if Abagail was awake. Her body lay completely still. Her breathing shifted into a slow, regular pattern. James thought how little he knew about Abagail and her life. Here he was with this young woman with her beautiful, thick hair and dark brown eyes. A fugitive brought up by the royal family, delivered to his doorstep. It seemed like a dream.

One hour later, they were both sleeping the sleep of two people who shed a lifetime of care. For one night all was perfect in the world. Abagail woke up in the middle of the night and bumped into a leg. She was startled, but only for a second, and then remembering, smiled and went back to sleep, her body lightly pressed against James'.

CHAPTER 37

It was the middle of the night and Margot lay in bed, eyes wide open. Although her body was exhausted, her mind demanded attention. Disturbing thoughts wouldn't leave her. Margot realized her life was built on a series of lies and nothing was what it seemed. Her mother's heartlessness had no limits. *If her mother could lock up her own sister and send her daughter to a foreign land to live the rest of her days in a loveless marriage, what else was she capable of doing?* Margot thought. Where is Abagail now—in jail, dead? Margot couldn't stop pondering the horror of what her mother did.

Margot pledged to herself that, when she became queen, people would be treated with decency and was struck again that she had no control of her life, but that was going to change. *When I am queen, I swear I will own my life, live a good life, and be kind to those around me,* she said to herself and fell into a deep, restful sleep.

Queen Henrietta also lay wide awake in her bed, knowing how the choices she made sounded to her daughter. But even now she didn't see any alternatives. People believe that as you gain power you have more say about the course of your life. In fact, the opposite is true. In Henrietta's experience, her life became more constricted as her power grew. Acting as the de facto ruler, her political power increased, but her life was more and more not her own. Rivals, rebels, and conspirators were on all sides and now, with the king too ill to rule, the decisions and great responsibilities of the realm fell to her. It was a tragic irony that her life of great privilege led to no real power. Royal obligations enslaved the queen. Margot would have to learn this bitter but important lesson in order to rule effectively.

Queen Henrietta tried to do her best to take care of her sister and her child but that ended in death and tragedy. And now she was in danger of alienating her daughter. What would Margot think when the whole story was revealed—the details of Abagail's imprisonment, her bloody escape, and the death of the queen's sister, Beatrice? The queen was reviled by those she cared for the most. Her sister forced her hand many years ago, starting the cascade of events leading to the present with her daughter viewing her as cruel. Beatrice's revenge...but the game was not over yet. It had fallen to her to preserve the monarchy and assure her family's continued rule. Her husband, the king, was unable to rule and the responsibility fell to her. What choice did she have?

CHAPTER 38

James and Abagail lived in a world that seemed to be of their own creation and it was the most perfect of all worlds. Like Adam and Eve, they felt newly born and totally complete. Days were long, and time stretched and folded into itself.

They spent their days working in James' garden, cooking, eating together, and talking politics, values, and how to live a moral life. James may not have been a priest, but he retained the morality of a certain kind of Christianity. Abagail felt her mind expanding by the hour. What joy to have the blinders removed and inhabit the world and see it for how it really was and to dream of what it could be. Simple things like feeding the chickens, letting the cow out to graze, cooking, washing dishes were all a revelation to Abagail. They made her feel part of life—*real* life.

Her life at court was cut off from everyday activities. Everything was done for the ladies of the court and offered to them on silver platters. Knowing where things came from and the work involved was a revelation. Abagail discovered that when all of your desires are immediately and completely satisfied just by making a request of others, an unreality permeates your entire life. *I feel rooted*, Abagail thought. *My life is real, and I am real.* She didn't say this to James because she didn't know how to put it into words, but she felt it in the deepest part of herself.

"Do you know how wonderful it is to have someone I can talk openly with about these issues?" James said over lunch one day. "It really helps me to figure out what I believe."

Abagail was surprised. "I thought you knew your beliefs."

"Yes and no," James replied.

"All right, tell me."

"There was a speaker at the last Leveler meeting. He called his group the true Levelers. I heard others call him a Digger.

He said to change society into a true democracy there must be economic equality along with political change."

"What does that mean?" Abagail asked.

"He argued that wealthy land-owners should have their land taken away and be given to the poorest peasants and that the right to vote should be extended to all adults with no restrictions based on property."

"When he says all adults does that include women?" Abagail asked excitedly.

"I think so. He never got a chance to fully explain, because there was such an uproar over the peasants getting the land there was no chance to talk about any other issues."

"So, where do you stand?"

"I don't know," James said. "The Digger ideas sound very radical to me but there is an underlying logic in their proposals."

"Which is what?"

"Remember when I asked if you believed that the king and queen's rule is divinely mandated?"

"Yes," Abagail said, "and we both agreed they are just people like us."

"Right, and therefore, they had no God-given right to rule. Well, if you apply the same logic to the rest of the aristocracy why should they have these huge estates while poor peasants are being forced off the land? Aristocrats are people like you and me who happened to be born in the right families."

"Who decides who gets the most or the best land according to the Diggers?" Abagail asked.

"I don't know."

"It sounds good but not very practical," Abagail said.

"Why not?" James asked.

"Why wouldn't it lead to a few aggressive and scheming individuals ending up with the largest parcels of land? Then we're back where we started with the few making the rules for the rest."

He understood Abagail's point and didn't have an answer. James rubbed his face and let out a deep sigh.

"It is complicated," Abagail said, "but I do have a solution."

"Tell me."

"It's only temporary."

"What is it?"

"Why don't we take the day off? Even the bible allows for a Sabbath." Abagail was beaming, drunk on her sense of freedom.

"Why?" James asked.

"We can spend the day any way we want. Imagine a day with no tasks, no responsibilities."

James thought for a moment and smiled. "Have I ever had a day, a whole day when my time was mine, where what I did, I did for myself? Have you ever had a day like that, Abagail?"

"I do not think so. I always had duties to complete. When I think about it now, it all seems so trivial and empty."

"More than empty, it is tragic. We've been slaves so long we don't even need a master to tell us what to do, we have the master inside us."

"But now, the world is only the two of us, if we let that slave master control us, we have only ourselves to blame," Abagail said with great feeling.

"Now, I have a very important question to ask you." James smiled and after a pause asked, "If you could do anything today, what would it be?"

Abagail let out a deep belly laugh. "Swim."

"Swim? Of all the things I would have guessed you might say that would be the last thing."

Like two kids playing, they splashed and dunked each other in the water. Being in the water was freeing. Like being in another world. They laughed so much their stomachs hurt. They held on to each other in a way they never did on land, looking for any reason to touch. There was magic being in the water.

Two hours later they were laying on a blanket in their wet undergarments, feeling the water evaporate from their bodies by the sun's warm rays. "I feel like the world is ours," Abagail said, "at least this little part of the world, which is enough for me."

"Like a king and a queen," James said.

Later in the afternoon they were once again laying down, fully dressed on James' bed. James was still smiling, thinking about the swimming and how close he felt to Abagail. He knew that he wanted to be with her and protect her.

Abagail trusted James as she hadn't trusted anyone since she escaped from the cave. She scooted closer to James, so their thighs were touching. "I'm ready, James," she said, and before he could ask for what she let him know. Abagail crawled under the blanket and slipped out of her clothes.

Afterwards, they both stared at the ceiling in that half-dream-like state from being physically and emotionally spent. Abagail sighed and stretched like a cat sunning itself.

"Why can't life be like this? All the misery and hardship there is in the world, does it have to be that way?" James asked.

"It would be lovely. Is it possible? Does it exist anywhere?"

James leaned over and kissed her. "I love you and want to spend the rest of my life with you to make our heaven here on earth."

Abagail laughed nervously and could tell James was expecting her to echo his sentiment and wanted to with all her heart but couldn't help but believe that this, too, would come to a bad end like everything else.

The couple molded their bodies as one, not knowing where one began and the other ended, their thoughts traveling through time and over distances.

"But there has to be more," James said.

"More what?" Abagail asked.

"More to life than work and obligation. Not more material

things. So maybe more is the wrong word but more happiness more what?"

"More control over our own lives," Abagail said enthuse-astically.

"Yes."

"You're a dreamer, James." She could feel his body tense. "I mean that as a compliment. To dream of a life with a higher purpose, otherwise how are we different than the animals in the field, if we just work, eat, and have offspring? That is all fine and part of life, but I agree there should be more."

CHAPTER 39

Abagail was at the back of the house near the barn, feeding the chickens, and she heard the noise first. She ran into the house. "Someone is coming. Should I hide?" Then, shuddering, she said, "I'm not going back to the cave."

"No, of course not," James said. "I wonder who it could be? It sounds like one horse. Go to the barn and cover yourself with hay."

Abagail ran out of the back door of the house, past the chicken coop, and into the barn.

James put away any sign of another person living with him and was ready when the knock came. He opened the door and was too shocked to speak when he saw who was standing in front of him.

"Hello, James, I know you must be very surprised to see me."

He didn't know what was more astonishing; the captain at his door or that he was out of uniform. Finally, he replied, "Why, Captain Nugent, what a surprise. Is there anything wrong?"

The captain blew on his hands. "It's getting a little chilly out here. Do you mind if I come inside?"

"Yes, welcome. Do you want something to eat or drink?"

"No, just a few minutes are all I need."

The captain seemed smaller out of uniform. He sat down at the table and looked embarrassed.

James sat down across from him and waited.

The captain took a deep breath. "When I was here last time on official business, I saw the books you had. I was wondering if it was all right with you if..." He stopped.

James saw the man squirming and would have liked to help him out, but he had no idea what he wanted. So, he just waited.

"Well, you see, I saw those books and I got to thinking that I would like to learn to read better." The captain had his eyes on the floor as he spoke. Now he looked up and met James' gaze. "I was wondering if you could teach me to read. I would pay you, of course. I heard that you studied to be a priest and left because you disagreed with the teachings of the church."

James got nervous. "Well, it's more complicated than that."

"That is what got me thinking about you teaching me," the captain said.

The captain leaned toward James, who unconsciously mirrored the captain's posture and shifted forward in his chair. "You have heard of the Levelers?" the captain asked.

"Yes, of course," James replied, getting very nervous. Did the captain recognize his Leveler pamphlets from the last visit? Was he going to be accused of wanting to overthrow the monarch?

"There are many of us in the army that are supporters of their cause. We are sick and tired of dying and killing our fellow citizens for the enrichment of a king or his wealthy opponents. I had a feeling about you when I first met you, a kindred spirit. Then I recognized the pamphlet by John Lullbiner and knew that you are one of us. What do you say?"

James didn't know what to say. Was this some part of an elaborate trap or was this man genuine? He seemed real enough in his beliefs, but could James really trust him? How could he say no?

"You cannot breathe a word of what I said to anyone—*anyone*. But I need to read so I can follow the pamphlets of our movement," Captain Nugent continued in a quiet voice.

Without thinking it all the way through, James heard himself ask, "When would you like to come?"

The captain reached in his pocket and handed James a coin. Stretching out his hand, he said, "We have a deal."

James shook his hand. "Yes, I guess we do."

The captain smiled and with a twinkle in his eye said, "And by the way, I know the woman everybody is looking for is here with you."

"Captain, sir..." James began, alarmed.

"No, don't deny it. Your secret is safe with me. I hope you can trust me. If I wanted to, I could have arrested you both. And now I must go, until our first class, next Tuesday at five o'clock, does that work for you?" He shook James' hand, walked out, and rode off without waiting for an answer.

James sat down at the table, too stunned to think. First Abagail dropped into his life and then this. *The world is indeed a mysterious and wondrous place.* His thoughts were interrupted when he heard someone opening the front door.

"Did you forget about me?" Abagail asked, shaking hay out of her hair. "What were you thinking, leaving me to wait for you out there? It's a good thing I heard the horse leaving."

"Abagail, you wouldn't believe who was just here and what he wanted."

Abagail was as shocked as James when she heard.

CHAPTER 40

Queen Henrietta and Princess Margot ate breakfast together. They entered into an unspoken agreement to act as if their discussion yesterday never happened.

"Your father is looking forward to seeing you." The queen hesitated. "Prepare yourself, he is not the man you remember." She cleared her throat and dabbed one eye.

It was agreed that Margot would visit her father alone. The king's bed chamber was dark and held a cloyingly sweet smell to mask the awful odors of a body close to death and already starting to decay.

Margot tried to prepare herself but was still shocked by the sight of her father. His body was almost invisible under his blanket, his face gaunt and pale, and his skin a sickly grey. Margot had to convince herself that this weak and fading man was really her father, the king. Memories of the king as a strong young man, always having time to play with Margot, and how she looked up to him came back to her. Unlike her mother, he was quick to laugh, and everyone remarked on how he spoiled his only child. But she was not his only child. He had to know about Abagail, and what about the queen's sister, Abagail's mother, rotting in prison? How well did she really know her father? How well did she know anyone?

Her father slowly held out his hand, his skin flimsy like easily torn paper. He tried to sit up but couldn't. Margot placed her hand on his back to support him and felt the bones of his spine protruding. With a great effort he was able to rise a little.

"It's yours," he whispered. Then he fell back to the bed and was absolutely still.

"Dad, dad," she implored him to explain what he meant. His unseeing eyes stared into the distance, then closed, and his breathing became labored.

She sat with him for what felt like hours, thinking about

the meaning; "It's yours." In all that time, he didn't move. Margot kissed her father on the top of his head and tip-toed out of the room.

"Oh, Mother," she said, falling into her mother's arms. The queen held her. It seemed like the earth held its breath and stood absolutely still while mother and daughter grieved.

Margot knew that this was the last time she would see her father alive and it was too much to bear, another loss to add to all the losses in her short life.

CHAPTER 41

Spencer spent the first few days at the Morton farm trying to figure these people out. There were just the two of them, no children. Ezra was a man of few words. Spencer was sure his silence was based on distrust. What man would invite a complete stranger into his home and let him sleep there while he was in the next room with his wife? Although Ezra said little, he was always polite and respectful when he did speak to Spencer.

Ruth was the opposite of her husband. She treated Spencer with an openness and warmth that initially made him uncomfortable. She explained to Spencer, "We are Puritans and we're against the Church of England, which is in love with gold, rituals, and the powerful priests who rule their follower's lives. But most of all we don't believe you need the church to communicate with God. Individuals can communicate directly with God, just as Jesus did. We are all equal in the eyes of the Lord."

Spencer didn't care about the conflicts between all these different religious groups. Religion to him was just another gimmick to separate people from their valuables. The one thing he agreed with, though, was their view of the state church as a gigantic scheme to bleed the poor of the little they had. When the Mortons bowed their heads before every meal to thank God for the food, Spencer made sure his head bowed as well but that was all. He was not thanking his new employers or God or anyone else for anything.

During his first two weeks at the farm, he busied himself with figuring out the valuables in the house and what he could carry when he snuck out. Everything in his life confirmed that this situation could not last. A couple taking in a stranger and letting him sleep in their home, knowing nothing about him, seemed as likely as his waking up one morning and learning to fly. He would lay in his bed at night and instead of praying or thinking about his life as other people might and would say to himself, *I will stay here for a while and when it's safe and I am ready I'll just go. I'll take what I need. I don't owe these people anything.*

Spencer convinced himself that he was only staying with the Mortons because it was the best place for him to hide out. Physical labor was not really for him. His back was stiff, his legs sore, and his arms ached. He was so tired after a long day working in the fields that he didn't have the energy to think long about robbing his hosts. Besides, he had three meals a day, a place to sleep, and, most importantly, a place to hide until the manhunt for him ended.

When he saw his reflection in their mirror, he saw that his beard had grown and covered up the scar almost com-pletely. *I'll just wait here,* he thought to himself. *The Mortons are not going anywhere, and I should probably stay out of sight.*

CHAPTER 42

For Abagail and James, time was elastic, expanding to allow the expression of their love and yet the days whizzed by. One night while lying in bed, James told Abagail how the death of his mother while giving birth to him had molded his life. "I was always under pressure to justify my life which directly led to my mother's death. I had no choice but to be the best-behaved child in the village, the perfect boy. Then of course excelling in school was expected along with going to the seminary to become a priest. I would still be a priest if my father hadn't died."

"What do you mean?" Abagail asked.

"I never could disappoint him. After all, my very existence meant the death of his wife." James gasped, feeling a sense of shock saying this out loud. Abagail held him tightly.

That same night, Abagail told James the story of killing the young guard. She recounted in detail the discovery of her mother and the horror of the cave, how the killing seemed almost justifiable.

"What choice did you have?" James asked. "It was you or him."

"I feel like I've lived three lives," Abagail said.

"What do you mean?" James asked.

"My first seventeen years living in the palace with the royal family. My second life was in the cave where I met my mother and began to learn about my past. And now..." Abagail stopped, not sure how to say it.

James waited. How would Abagail describe her present situation? Would he be included?

"My third life is living in the world with other people." Abagail stopped.

James held his breath.

"Especially one person." She leaned over and kissed James

softly on his cheek.

The next morning, James woke with a lightness. If the person he loved could love him after hearing the worst about him, he would never be lonely again. Abagail also felt a lightness, but for her it didn't feel as complete. She hadn't told James about the rape, not yet. There was the shame, and not being sure how he would react, but the largest barrier was the pain that always accompanied her talking about the rape. Every time she thought about it, it was like reliving it all over again.

Like so many before them, Abagail and James came to learn that pure happiness is not a permanent state and paradise is fleeting. Their Eden was not shattered by a serpent. The outside world came bursting through their door disguised as two innocent children.

The wagon pulled up and, before it stopped all the way, Theresa and Jeffrey jumped off and ran toward the house, yelling, "Uncle James, Aunt Abagail!" The new couple was wrenched back to the real world. They jumped out of bed and hurriedly dressed.

"Oh, we have so much to tell you," Theresa said.

"We went to the city, sold all of our soap, and I could buy any toy I wanted," Jeffrey chimed in, jumping up and down.

"And we ate in a tavern," Theresa giggled.

"We saw a puppet show," Jeffrey added excitedly.

"Slow down, children," Maria said, walking in the door and staring at her brother and Abagail. "You will have a chance to tell them all about your adventures later."

"Seeing the two of you is all they have been talking about since we started back," Frank said, walking in right behind his wife. "They could not wait to see Uncle James and Aunt Abagail."

Maria watched Abagail walk past James and touch his hand, squeezing his fingers. James squeezed back with a smile playing across his lips. That simple gesture confirmed what

Maria initially thought. They were a couple.

James couldn't help but resent the arrival of his sister's family. As much as he loved her and loved all of them, he knew that something precious was lost.

Abagail was getting some food out from the cupboard when Maria walked over to her. "So, it looks like things worked out with you and James. I guess you are not going back to our place after all."

Abagail turned away from Maria, feeling herself blush.

"How did the soap-selling go?" James asked Frank.

"We made all our deliveries." The two men laughed, and James clapped his brother-in-law on the back.

"You seem to be in a good mood," Frank said. "I wonder why?" he asked, raising his eyebrows.

James ignored the remark. In truth, he was trying hard not to show his disappointment that his time with Abagail had ended. He went over to his sister and gave her a big hug.

Maria released herself from the hug, stepped back, and took a long look at James.

"Frank, keep an eye on the children. James and I are going for a walk."

When they got outside, Maria blurted, "What were you thinking?"

James replied, "What do you mean?"

"You know exactly what I mean—you and Abagail."

"Why not me and Abagail?" he asked. "You're always going on about how I need to settle down with somebody, raise a family. I thought you would be happy."

"Use your common sense. Abagail was brought up in the palace. Do you think she would be happy living on a farm?"

"Yes, I do. Look where her life in the palace has gotten her. What is this about, Maria? I don't understand."

Maria whispered, "How well do you really know her? It has only been two weeks."

"One of the special things about us is that we've been

honest with each other. It is a relief to have someone you can talk to about important things."

"So, she told you about the guard who was killed during the escape. And that the palace has men looking for her?"

James stopped walking and took hold of his sister's arm. "I thought you would be happy for me."

"Abagail's life is so troubled and add your radical ideas to the mix, it sounds like a life destined for more troubles."

James let go of Maria's arm and walked away.

"Where are you going?" Maria yelled after him, but James kept on walking. "Are you coming back? We have to leave soon."

Maria returned to the house and saw Frank, the two children, and Abagail sitting in front of the fire, laughing and talking. The love and warmth of the scene was heartbreaking. She realized that she was wrong about her brother and Abagail. Had she ruined his and Abagail's chance to be together?

Abagail looked up from watching the children. "Where's James?"

Maria didn't answer. Without saying a word, she turned around and walked quickly out of the house. *What have I done? I am not his mother. He doesn't need my protection.* The more she thought about it the worse she felt, and her pace quickened, desperate to find him. Where could he be? Then it came to her in a flash. When James was a boy and was upset, he would go to the cave. And there he was, sitting on a log near the mouth of the cave.

"James," Maria said softly.

James almost jumped to a standing position. "Maria, you scared me half to death."

Maria walked over and sat beside her brother. "I am sorry."

He didn't reply and sat with his back to her.

"I should not have interfered."

"I do not know. Maybe you are right. I mean, what do we

have in common?"

"The two of you have not spent that much time together," Maria said. "How do you feel about her?"

"I love her," James said.

"And I can see that she loves you."

"Can you? Can you really?"

"Yes."

"Then why did you say what you did?"

"Maybe I was being over-protective, maybe I was jealous of your special relationship. I don't know."

"Jealous—but you and Frank..."

"Yes, I know. I love Frank but after being together for so many years it is just not the same as when you first fall in love."

"Oh, Maria," James said, putting his arm around her shoulder.

"Look, if you find real love in your life you should give it every chance. Let's go back to the house and be with the others," Maria said. They walked slowly back to the house, James thinking of his future, Maria reflecting on her past.

"You're leaving so soon. I thought you would stay at least one night," Abagail said. She looked at James, who was surprisingly quiet. As a matter of fact, he'd been quiet the whole evening. Abagail wondered why. *He is probably disappointed that his sister's family interrupted our time alone.* He looked at her and she smiled as if saying to him, *Don't worry my love, we have our whole life together.*

"Oh Mother, can we stay just one night?" Jeffrey pleaded.

Maria shook her head with a determined look on her face.

Frank knew that look and knew it meant there was no possibility of a compromise. So, he was ready with the answer when Theresa asked, "Please dad, just one night."

"You heard your mother. We have to get back to the farm. It will not take care of itself. Do we have everything? Oh right, I almost forgot. James, we have two packages for you to store until next time we see you. Can you help me bring them to the cave?" Both men left the house.

"All right, you kids play with your new toys while I talk to Abagail." Maria gave Abagail a big hug and whispered in her ear, "I hope all the best for the both of you. I am so happy, and I welcome you to our family."

When Abagail let go of Maria, there were tears in both of their eyes. "Thank you, Maria, that means a lot to me."

CHAPTER 43

The most undesirable aspect of the job as advisor to the royal family was to be the bearer of bad news. Rulers, more than most, are accustomed to controlling people and events and have great difficulty in acknowledging when they cannot. Blaming the messenger was always a possibility. The old man took a deep breath and knocked on the door to the queen's chamber.

"Enter," the queen said. She was in an intense conversation with Lucia.

"I have some sad news, your Majesty." The advisor hesitated, giving a chance for Lucia to leave. But she didn't make a move and the queen didn't ask her to.

"You can tell me. Tell me now," the queen said impatiently.

"The king has died quietly in his sleep last night, your highness. The physicians say he felt no pain."

Queen Henrietta sat absolutely still. After a moment she said, "You may go," with no emotion in her voice.

As soon as he left the room, the queen let out a terrible moan and collapsed into Lucia's embrace. Lucia's knees buckled as much from surprise as the physical weight of her grieving queen. In all the years she had served the queen, this was the closest physical contact they ever had. Lucia could feel the queen's body regain its strength as she pulled herself together.

The queen didn't have the luxury of properly mourning her husband, at least not now. This was a particularly vulnerable time for the monarchy and not the time to grieve. Her daughter needed to be informed, funeral arrangements made, and, most importantly, the coronation organized.

"Forget about..." the queen started to say, but her voice quivered and once it started, she could not control it. The quivering spread to her head, then her neck, and within seconds her whole body was shaking. "I need a few minutes," the queen said. "Wait outside, Lucia. I will call you in soon."

"Yes, your Majesty. Is there anything I can do for you?" Lucia asked, handing her a handkerchief.

"No."

The queen laid down on her bed. She felt so tired but also relieved to hand the burden of ruling the country to her daughter, but her responsibilities were not over yet. The handover of the crown to Margot would take planning. The queen hoped she had the energy for one more battle.

Queen Henrietta rang the bell and Lucia returned. "Now, where was I? Oh yes, we can forget about finding Abagail. She does not want to be found and it seems like we do not have the capability to find her. The incompetence of those searching for her actually has worked for us." The queen laughed bitterly.

Lucia felt the sting of the rebuke but held her tongue.

"As soon as Margot is on the throne, Abagail is no longer a threat."

"Yes, your Majesty," Lucia said.

"We will have the funeral procession in two days and Margot's coronation two weeks later," instructed the queen. "There will be no deviation from protocol that would cause anyone to question the legitimacy of Margot's succession. I want you to coordinate both." A tear slipped down the queen's cheek as she looked upon her loyal aide.

"Yes, my queen." Lucia bowed.

The queen touched Lucia's shoulder. "Thank you."

CHAPTER 44

The day of Captain Nugent's first reading lesson arrived. The two of them decided it would be better if Abagail was not in sight even though the captain knew she was staying with James. Abagail retired to the barn, where they had set up a comfortable place for her to spend the time reading Leveler pamphlets. Abagail had come to appreciate the barn. Staying comfortably in there made Abagail feel that the fears of her confinement in the cave were finally going away. It was a peaceful, restful place.

Captain Nugent approached James at the door of the house but didn't enter. "I rode out here to tell you that I am unable to take part in the tutoring. I am needed at my regi-ment. I am sure you understand, given what has happened."

"What has happened?"

"You really do not know? the captain asked, astonished.

James shook his head. "I am isolated here, tell me."

"The king is dead, and his daughter Margot is back in England and will succeed him. Or rather, she will unless something stops her." The captain hesitated. "I know you support the revolution and the Levelers. Am I right?"

"Yes," James said excitedly.

Captain Nugent looked around although they were completely alone. He spoke in a soft voice. "The time for theories and what-ifs is over. It is time for all patriotic men to act. Princess Margot is not known by the people and this puts the monarchy in a very weak position. We are having a planning meeting tonight at seven at the Red Oxen Tavern. Now is the time to act. I have to go and tell others. Will you be there?"

"Yes, of course."

"Good man. I knew I could count on you. See you tonight." He put on his hat, mounted his horse, and shouted, "To a free

England," and rode away.

"Abagail, Abagail," James called, running to the barn.

"What happened? Did something go wrong?"

James laughed, picked her up, and twirled her around.

"What is it?"

"The king is dead."

"What?"

"I said the king is dead."

Abagail's knees buckled. "Are you sure?" she asked with a quiver in her voice.

"Yes. Captain Nugent rode out here to tell me." James held her by the waist. "Are you all right?"

Abagail didn't answer.

"Abagail," James said. "What is wrong?"

"Nothing," she finally responded. "The king..." She hesitated. "My father."

"Oh, I am sorry." James immediately felt stupid.

Abagail took a deep breath. "I am fine," she said, but her mind flooded with memories of being picked up by the king and his joy in both her and Margot's squeals of laughter. He seemed so strong and powerful and now he was no more. The realization that he really was her father made her anger disappear into sadness.

"Are you sure?" James asked, noticing her eyes moisten.

"Yes," Abagail replied softly.

"The Levelers are going to act before the new queen's coronation to overthrow the monarchy. They're meeting to-night to decide on a plan of action and Captain Nugent wants me to participate." James tried to speak calmly and slowly but was unable to contain his excitement.

Abagail's thoughts went to Margot. She must be deva-9stated. Abagail questioned her own feelings. *Do I love the king, my father? I really don't know,* she thought.

"Abagail, are you sure you are all right?" James asked, putting his hand on her shoulder.

"I want to go to his funeral procession."

"Even after all they have done to you?" James asked.

"They are my family." Abagail took a step back from James. "I cannot just dismiss the people who raised me."

"What the queen did to you and your mother was terrible."

"Sometimes families hurt you as we both know. I have questions only the queen and Margot can answer before I can say goodbye to that part of my life."

"If you are recognized, you could be charged with the murder of that young guard and you could end up back in that cave, or worse."

"I will hide my face and blend in with the thousands of mourners." Abagail looked at James. "It would be best if I go alone."

"No, it is too risky."

"James, this is something I must do alone. I need to say goodbye to my father and find out why my life turned out the way it has."

"Even with the possibility of being thrown back into that hell hole?"

Abagail shivered as she hugged James' arm. "Yes, even with that possibility."

"I have to go with you."

"No, James, I must go alone."

"Abagail, it does not feel right," James said as he caressed her chin and looked into her determined eyes. He put his arms around her trembling body and softly said, "But I understand why it is important for you to go. I really do."

"I love you for being so..."

"I worry the world is separating us."

"What do you mean?" Abagail asked.

"You look to your past and the royal family for meaning in your life."

"Yes."

"I look to the future for meaning in my life and see ridding ourselves of all royal families as the solution."

"But cannot we each do what we have to do and still be together?"

"I do not know, Abagail. I do not see how."

"Oh, James." Abagail rested her head on James's shoulder.

James spoke quietly into Abagail's ear. "It is what you and I have been talking about and what I have been dreaming about all these years. Now is the time to act to make it real. As strongly as you feel you have to find answers, I feel about taking control of our country, our lives, our future."

"Why would that divide us? I believe in the same things as you."

"Abagail, if the Levelers move against the new monarch, will you stand beside me?"

"By the new monarch, you mean Princess Margot?"

James nodded. "Yes."

"You're asking me to turn my back on my oldest friend, my half-sister." Abagail took a deep breath. "If by some stroke of luck, I do get a chance to speak with Margot, it depends on how she answers my questions, but the chances are that she and I will never meet."

"Abagail, you haven't answered the question. Will you stand with me?"

"I believe in the ideas we've been discussing. But I will not stand by you if you plan to harm Margot."

"So, you will stand with me up to a point," James said. He took Abagail's silence as her answer.

They both felt the distance between them grow until it seemed like they were looking at each other from across an abyss.

CHAPTER 45

The royal funeral procession started in the palace and ended at the royal cemetery. One carriage transported the body of the king, followed by another carriage with Princess Margot. The route it took was a circuitous one through the city to allow the populace to say goodbye to their deceased king and to celebrate the continuation of the monarchy. The funeral was to be followed soon after by the coronation of the new sovereign. The queen was too ill to accompany the king's coffin, so it was only Margot who rode in the royal coach. The journey brought into sharp focus how alone Margot really was. Her father gone, her mother a shell of her former self, her husband in another country, she thought about Abagail and wondered where life had taken her.

At that very moment, Abagail stood at the side of the road, wearing a cloak that protected her from the drizzle and a red hat that hid most of her face. People craned forward to get a better look, pushing her into the king's soldiers. The soldiers pushed back.

"Stop pushing," someone yelled.

"I cannot help it," a man shouted back. "They are pushing me."

A soldier raised his rifle and yelled out, "Quiet, show some respect."

A very large woman next to Abagail said to no one in particular, "Respect, hah. Good riddance, no more kings."

A man standing next to her added, "Aye, it's time for a change."

"You better show some respect, you bloody peasants. That is your king who is passing by!" another man shouted.

"Aye, tell him. What are you, Papists?" another woman yelled. "What are you doing here if he was not your king?"

"I am here to say good riddance to the king. The last one

this country will ever have," the large woman said.

"You people are Papists, taking your orders from Rome." People around Abagail were repeating, "Papists, damn Papists."

A woman yelled, "Hey, watch your swearing, there are children here."

People started pushing into each other. A man's hat got knocked off, and when he bent down to retrieve it he was pushed to the ground. "What do you think you're doing?" He threw a punch at the man he thought was responsible, who leaned backwards to avoid the punch and shoved someone else, who took a swing at another man. The people were packed in so tight that anyone was liable to be hit.

During the fighting, the carriage carrying Margot passed. A large group of soldiers protected it. "Take six men with you and see about that fuss over there," the Captain of the Guard said, pointing to where Abagail stood. The soldiers used their horses to break up the crowd. Most of the citizens just wanted to avoid getting trampled by the horses, but a few tried to pull the soldiers off their horses and one soldier was dragged to the ground. The other soldiers rode quickly to his side, swinging their batons. The crowd began to break up. Abagail did not run. She was glued to the spot as it seemed Margot was looking directly at her.

Margot looked out the window of the carriage and was thrown back in her seat as if shot. She could just barely see the face of the woman with the red hat in the middle of the swirling mass, but there was something familiar in the way she moved. Could it be? No, Abagail was almost certainly long gone and far away, but Margot knocked twice on the side of the coach. The driver stopped at once.

The Captain of the Guard came galloping quickly. "Yes, your Majesty?" he asked in a worried tone.

"There is a woman in the crowd I must speak to." Margot pointed. "That is her, wearing a brown shawl and a red cap."

Margot leaned out of the carriage and saw the woman with the red cap running away. "She is the one running." Margot pointed again. "Bring her to the palace."

Abagail ran as fast as possible but was no match for a horse. Everyone scattered so as not to get crushed by the horse. She felt herself being swooped up onto the soldier's saddle as he galloped out of the crowd.

"Let me go. Where are you taking me?" Abagail shouted. She was seated in front of the soldier, and he held her with one arm around her waist as they rode at a fast gallop. She felt his grip tighten as they turned a corner, bringing back memories of that man who raped her. They were going in the direction of the city. Was he headed for the palace? At that moment, Abagail made a resolution to die rather than return to the cave.

James' warning came to her mind. It is too much of a risk, he said. But she insisted and the more he tried to reason with her, the more determined she became. *He was right. It was stupid to come to the funeral procession. Why did I insist? It's almost like I wanted to be caught,* Abagail thought.

They rode past the gate and under the archway into the entrance of the grounds leading to the palace. The soldier jumped off his horse and held out his hand like he was helping a lady dismount. The soldier didn't know Abagail's position in society and that made it impossible to know how to treat her.

Abagail shared the confusion of the escort. Legally, she was a fugitive wanted for escaping imprisonment and the murder of a guard. Was it going to be a reunion of long-lost friends, a meeting of half-sisters, or would she be locked up again, maybe even executed?

Abagail walked quickly through the corridors of her childhood feeling unexpectedly calm; it was her destiny and fate had brought her here. It wasn't until the escort left her at the queen's anteroom, where she saw a large man sitting on a small couch with his face in his hands, that she panicked. The couch was tiny, and the man was so large he dwarfed the piece of furniture. Abagail couldn't see his face, but his broad back and big shoulders looked very familiar. Then it came to her—he was the prison guard that brought them food until that fateful day when the younger guard took his place.

"The queen will see you now," an attendant said, waving his hand and bowing with a flourish. Abagail saw the large guard from the corner of her eye stand up. She turned away from him quickly, but not before catching him staring at her. She began to walk as quickly as possible but stopped suddenly, realizing she was going to meet the queen. *I'm not ready to see the queen*, she thought. It wasn't Margot who had her brought here—it was the queen. Abagail began to shake. The thought of being thrown back into the cave made her ill.

She sat on the closet chair.

The queen's attendant prompted Abagail with a whisper. "The queen is waiting."

"Just a moment, please."

"It is the queen," the attendant said more forcefully.

Abagail started to get up but stumbled and almost fell.

The door to the queen's chamber opened. "Where is she?" Margot demanded.

Abagail stood up. Everyone bowed deeply. Abagail snuck a quick glance over the bowed bodies and caught the big man staring at her with eyes ablaze. She turned toward Margot, putting the man and his hateful stare at her back, and took a deep breath. Believing she had been brought to Queen Henrietta, then seeing the incensed guard, and now facing Margot, the nightmares of the past were real and breathing right in front of her.

"Come in," Margot said, taking Abagail by the hand. They entered the throne room. "Please leave us alone," Margot said, and several people quickly and silently scurried out.

"When they said the queen will see you, I thought..." Abagail was so relieved she almost started crying.

At that moment Margot reached over and embraced Abagail. "I am so happy to see you. I never thought I would see you again." They held on to each other for a long time. Abagail kept her arms at her side and stood stiffly. As the embrace went on, Abagail relaxed and allowed herself to feel how much she missed her oldest, dearest friend. "I have so much to tell you and I want to hear about your life," Margot said, resting her hand on Abagail's arm. "Come, let's go someplace where we can be alone and talk."

CHAPTER 46

"That is all of it?" Spencer asked, staring at the few coins in his hand.

Ezra nodded.

Ruth nervously watched Spencer. "Sam, this is your share of the harvest as we talked about."

"My name isn't Sam," he spat out. "My real name is Spencer, and this money is..." He stopped and shook the few coins in his hand. "This money is a joke. This is not a man's wages. This is child's pay." He threw the coins against the wall and slammed the door as he left the cabin.

Spencer felt like a fool. All their prayers and concern for him was just a way to get him to work for almost no pay. They used me, he thought.

Spencer started walking and kept on walking with thoughts of murder filling his head. It was an hour before he stopped and looked up to see a tavern, the Red Oxen. He pushed the door open so hard it slammed into the wall. He stared at the men sitting around the wooden tables, daring someone to say something to him so he could bash their head in.

He sat in a corner and ordered the first drink of what he knew would be many. After three hours of drinking, Spencer's head was getting too heavy to hold up. He cradled his head in the bend of his arm when the door to the tavern opened and a large group of men walked in. Several of the newcomers had the look of military men, while others had an unmistak-able aristocratic bearing, and still others, young men, could have been apprentices. Spencer couldn't imagine what would bring such a group together in this out-of-the-way tavern. As more people arrived, Spencer grew more and more curious. He went up to the bar, asked for a large goblet of water, and took a big drink to clear his head. He changed tables to get a clear view of the back room. There must have been forty men crowding into that room. A husky man was positioned at the door, allowing some people in without any hesitation and stopping others.

Spencer ordered another glass of ale and laid his head in the crook of his arm. He seemed to be just another customer, passed out after drinking too much, but that was not the case. Spencer's senses were as sharp as they had ever been. The few phrases he heard were enough to let him know the general topic of the meeting.

Suddenly, the door swung open and the group poured out of the back room into the main bar area. Two men stood right next to Spencer's table. The older man had an elaborate moustache and a military bearing. He was speaking with great urgency to the younger man. "I know who she is, James," the older man said, and looked around to make sure nobody was near enough to hear—but Spencer heard every word. The older man continued, "If I know, how long do you think it will be before others find out? Do you think our comrades in there—" he pointed to the back room, "would look kindly on you living with a lady of the royal court who is being pursued by the queen?"

The young man rubbed his face. "What can I do? I love her and she feels the same way. I cannot and will not kick her out. I will not."

"All right, James, I will keep your secret, but you are taking a big risk. We all know our movement is riddled with spies and the queen would pay handsomely to anyone bringing that criminal to justice."

Spencer couldn't believe it. They must be talking about the same woman who ruined his life. All he had to do was follow this James to find the woman to get his revenge. *Maybe my luck*

is changing, Spencer thought. *The Mortons can wait.*

CHAPTER 47

Margot didn't seem to notice how stiffly Abagail stood as she hugged her. "I am so happy to see you, Abagail. It is a dream come true. Come in, sit down. I will get us tea." Margot started to raise her hand to have an attendant get some tea.

"No, I do not want tea," Abagail said, still standing.

"At least take a seat. I have so much to tell you." Margot gestured to a chair and started to sit but stopped when she saw Abagail still standing.

"I came to pay my respects to your father," Abagail said in a formal tone.

"Why were you in the crowd? Why not let me know where you were?"

"Because I had no idea what you might do to me."

"Do to you—oh Abagail, how could you say that?" Margot took a step towards Abagail.

"Because of what happened," Abagail said as she took a step back.

"I am so sorry for the whole horrible incident."

"Incident? It was my life and my mother's."

"I just learned about it when I returned to England."

"You mean you had no idea I was locked up and thrown into a cave with no explanation? My mother in rags, eating mush and living like an animal for fifteen years alone in the dark?"

Margot shook her head. "Please believe me, I had no idea."

"That is hard for me to believe. What did you think? Did you ask your mother where I disappeared to?"

"Of course, I asked her repeatedly. If the queen doesn't want you to know something, you are not going to know. I asked and asked. I was going through my version of hell, marrying Prince Leon..."

"Hell, you have no idea what hell is like," Abagail said.

169

"And now my father," Margot choked but was determined not to fall apart. Abagail was the last person from her past she could count on. "I am asking you to help me."

"Help you with what?" Abagail asked, examining closely the woman she had served and loved for the first seventeen years of her life. To the world, Margot carried herself as if born to lead but Abagail saw a frightened, desperate girl in over her head.

Margot laughed bitterly. "Help me with everything. Help me figure out where to live, how to survive, figure out my duty, and how to carry it out. I need someone I trust, someone I loved, who once loved me, someone I still love more than ever."

Abagail couldn't help but be touched by Margot's declaration of love. Not long ago it was what she would have wanted to hear more than anything. But too much had happened to Abagail, and Margot was not the only person whose life had changed.

"I am very sorry about what happened to you and your mother. It's horrible but I cannot dwell on the past. I am soon to be the sovereign of this country and I need all my wits about me to make this transfer from my father to me as smooth as possible. I have no one I trust that I can talk to."

"What about your mother?" Abagail asked.

"I'm afraid my mother will soon be joining my father. The doctors say she is run down. So, as you can see, I am alone." Margot looked directly into Abagail's eyes. "Can you join me and be my trusted advisor? Can you bury the past? I am offering you an official position in my court, a senior advisor with your own staff and a generous salary, a chance to control your destiny."

Abagail was amazed that Margot was pleading for her help. But the voice in her head advised caution. She thought about her mother and imagined her saying, *Don't repeat the mistakes of the past. That voice inside may help you figure out what not to do but it doesn't tell you what to do.*

"What do you say?" Margot asked.

Abagail replied, "I do not know."

"You do not know," Margot repeated and sighed. "I understand. Think it over and we will talk in two days. Is that enough time?" she asked.

"Yes."

"If you say yes to my offer you can live here in the palace with your own attendants. We can rule together."

CHAPTER 48

Albert pushed the attendant's hand away. "I can dress myself," he said. Looking at the large mirror, he had the odd feeling that it wasn't his reflection staring back at him. It wasn't just the strange clothes or even the fact that he lost considerable weight. There was something missing, something inside. He was face to face with the woman who had killed his son, destroyed his marriage, and ruined his life and he didn't attack her. He let her walk away. Of course, he was shocked when he caught sight of her. Imagine her walking in the palace like she owned it. What did it all mean? Was she in the palace the whole time? Was the whole escape a ruse? His son did not have to die. The questions kept coming. He could not make sense of it. His head hurt.

What was most upsetting was that he was no longer enraged with Abagail. To see her in the flesh was a shock—she was just a teenage girl. The longer Abagail eluded him, the larger her stature had grown until she became more of an idea than a person. And now that the pursuit of Abagail had ended, what was the purpose of his life?

Albert did not know it, but Lucia had a plan for his lost soul.

"Albert." He barely moved. Then, more loudly, "Albert." His head snapped straight up. "Look at me, Albert." He made eye contact. "I have a job for you." Lucia had his full attention. "You are to be the personal bodyguard to Princess Margot, who will very soon be Queen Margot, the ruler of this country. Do you understand?"

"Yes, I understand," Albert said, and as if by magic he seemed to grow an inch.

"Your job is to protect your sovereign Margot with your life. You are to see that no harm comes to her."

"Yes, ma'am," Albert said, clicking his heels.

"Good, now follow me," Lucia said, and off they went to meet with the soon-to-be-crowned Queen of England. Lucia had composed a list of things that had to be done and categorized them in order of importance.

"Wait out here," Lucia said to Albert, pointing to a chair.

"Shall I begin, your Majesty?" Lucia asked as she entered the royal chamber.

"Yes," Margot said.

"According to reports I've received, the rebels are planning to overthrow the monarchy."

Margot listened very closely without showing any alarm. Lucia admired her for that and thought, *There's the toughness of her mother. Lord knows she's going to need it.*

Margot was focused and present, thankful that her mother informed her about the dire political situation, so Lucia's news wasn't shocking.

"What can we do?" Margot asked.

"Exactly, my lady. That is the question."

"Let me think about this and get back to you," Margot said, thinking it might be too late for an early coronation. She must speak with her mother immediately.

CHAPTER 49

Many things were discussed at the Red Oxen meeting that James never thought he would hear out loud. Ideas like a country without a king or queen, no state church, the right to vote for all men, and the Diggers position to redistribute land to peasants were all topics of conversation. He couldn't wait to relate all he heard to Abagail.

James, drunk with all these heady ideas about the possibilities of a new future, didn't think of looking around him as he walked home. If he did, he would have seen Spencer Sykes trailing him forty yards away.

Spencer almost gave up following James. The younger man walked too fast and as the night turned cold Spencer's legs were barely able to move. *What am I doing anyway? I should go back to the Morton farmhouse and burn it down,* he thought. A smile came to his face imagining the scene, Ruth and Ezra Morton running out of their miserable little shack, screaming with their hair on fire. *A sucker, they made me a sucker.* He turned around, ready to walk in the direction of the Mortons, but knew after a couple of steps he'd never make it, not without a full night's sleep. He hiked to the crest of a nearby hill to rest until tomorrow. From the elevated vantage point, he saw James in the valley below, entering a small farmhouse. He forgot about the Mortons. They weren't going anywhere. He would take care of them after he took care of his business here. Keeping low, he crept down the hill to a grouping of trees overlooking the house, a perfect spot to observe without being seen. Spencer tried to stay awake, but the walking and the drink overcame him. He was fast asleep within a few minutes.

It was very early in the morning when James arrived back at the farm. He opened the door quietly, thinking Aba-gail would still be sleeping, and was surprised to find her awake at the kitchen table.

"You are awake," he said.

Abagail was in her own world, too exhausted to think but unable to let her thoughts go. "Oh," she said. "You are back. You must be hungry, let me make some breakfast."

James began pacing around the kitchen. He stopped abruptly and said, "You would not believe the things I heard."

"Tell me," Abagail said distractedly.

James was so excited about his news that he didn't notice her lack of interest or even remember her plan to go to the king's funeral. "It is really going to happen," he said.

"What is going to happen?"

"The revolution. We plan to march on the palace and demand the royal family give up the throne. England will be a republic, governed by the people. John Lilburn himself spoke. He said that a man should not give his loyalty to a country that would not give him a say in the ruling of that country."

"Every person living in England would have the vote?" Abagail asked as James' excitement about this extraordinary meeting captured her interest despite Margot's offer to join her in ruling the country.

"Oh yes, and a lot more," James went on. "There were proposals that the church would have to give up the land it was granted from the crown and for it to be distributed to the prior owners and, if prior ownership could not be estab-lished, the land would be given without cost to landless peas-ants. There would be no official state church of England and every citizen would have the right to worship openly, with-out fear of reprisal as they see fit. It was unbelievable—it was like, like, well I don't know what it was like."

"It sounds like the world turned upside down," Abagail said.

"Exactly," James said and repeated it, "the world turned upside down."

Abagail brought two plates with fried potatoes with

onions, a bit of leftover chicken, and a pitcher of water to the table. When he finished eating, James pushed his empty plate away and asked, "Tell me how it went for you at the king's funeral procession?"

Abagail told him about being brought to the castle to meet with Margot, who had apologized for what happened to her and her mother. She left out Margot's offer.

"Say that again. You were taken to the palace and met with Princess Margot. How did that happen?"

"The princess recognized me in the crowd and had a soldier bring me to her." Abagail paused. Could she tell James about Margot's offer? Where was her loyalty?

"Abagail, come, let's go sit outside and talk more about our extraordinary day." The sun was trying but its faint rays didn't warm the autumn air.

James gathered twigs to start a fire and handed them to Abagail, who placed them in the fire pit the way James taught her. It was one of thousands of small everyday acts that gave Abagail great pleasure. Living at the palace meant there was always someone whose job it was to do these small tasks. If she returned to that life, her days of feeding the chickens and planting in the garden would be over.

Meanwhile, Spencer groaned, awakened by voices drifting up the walls of the valley. His head pounded and his throat felt like it was lined with broken glass. He remembered the few coins he was paid by the Mortons and the anger focused his mind. Then he saw the reason why he was here. Once he saw it was her, the one who slashed his face, he became fully awake and alert. The lion refocused on his prey, and this time nothing was going to get in the way of the kill.

CHAPTER 50

Margot quietly opened the door and the heat hit her immediately. The fireplace was loaded with wood and roaring even though it was not cold outside. She stood in the doorway and saw her mother lying in bed, covered in thick blankets. "Mother," Margot said softly.

"Come in my dear." Queen Henrietta's eyes burned with fever and she shivered violently. "It is imperative that you are coronated immediately."

Margot had to bend down very close to her mother's mouth to hear. "Yes, Mother, I understand," she said, rubbing smoke and tears from her eyes.

"To delay is to give these traitors the chance to act in the name of saving the country from anarchy. They would never dare to confront a sitting queen who has been crowned as sovereign."

"Yes, Mother, I am only too aware of the situation. Lucia gave me a full report."

"What was the conclusion?"

"The opposition is strong, stronger than we are at the present time, and truthfully, the prospects are not good."

Queen Henrietta seemed to sink into herself. "What is to be done?"

"We are considering several ideas. One is for me to meet with the moderate individuals in the parliament."

"Not a prudent move. That would give the rebels instant credibility. Once you meet with them, you give up your natural position of superiority. You lose and they have won before any negotiation begins."

"You are probably right," Margot said, "but we also have to be realistic. Our support among the populace is spotty. The wars and the resulting taxes have eroded the loyalty of many of our subjects."

Queen Henrietta heard the criticism embedded in her daughter's words but didn't have the energy to debate past choices. "The question is, what can be done now?"

"I do not know, Mother."

The queen was quiet. She felt like everything in her life led to this moment—the birth of her daughter, her sister's imprisonment and death, and now the fate of the monarchy. And she had no answers, no plan. Queen Henrietta felt her attachment to the living world fray. Was this really what would happen? The end of the monarchy despite all her efforts?

At the moment princess Margot most needed wise counsel, there was no one to guide her. Her life and the life of the country depended on her making the right choices. Margot sat down at her desk and wrote a letter.

Dearest Husband,

I miss you very much.

From the day I arrived there has been one crisis after another. My father's death has emboldened the rebellious forces in the kingdom to such a degree that there is talk of abolishing the monarchy. My mother is close to death and I fear for my life. According to my mother's most trusted advisor, the opposition forces are capable of defeating the loyalists.

I need your help. Whatever you can do short of an invasion. An invasion by Spanish forces would unite the country and validate the charges brought against my mother and implicitly me, of supporting the Catholic Church.

If I can suggest, a small band to ferry me out of the country until the loyal forces can organize an army to defeat these traitors and make it safe for me to return.

Yours with love,

M

Margot wondered how she could get the letter to Spain without it being intercepted. She needed to find out who in the court were loyalists and who supported the rebels. Margot rang for Lucia, the one person she could trust.

"I want you to deliver this letter to my husband personally as soon as possible. It is of the utmost importance," Margot said, handing the letter to Lucia.

"Yes, my lady." Lucia reached for the envelope. "I'll leave immediately," she said, but made no move to leave.

"Is there anything else?" Margot asked.

"I would like one person, Albert, the former prison guard, to accompany me. Is that acceptable?"

"Yes," Margot assented.

Again, Lucia hesitated. "Should I wait for a response?"

"Yes, absolutely."

"Would it be advisable for me to read and memorize the contents of the letter?"

"Why?" Margot asked impatiently.

"Just in case I am detained," Lucia replied, "and the letter is discovered on my person or it falls into the wrong hands due to some other mishap."

"I see. Yes, that does make sense."

"Yes, my lady. I will read it, memorize it, and then destroy it."

"Leave as soon as possible and God speed."

It wasn't until Lucia left that Margot realized the magnitude of what she proposed to her husband. The implications of her so-called plan were reckless and desperate. Could she really sneak out of the palace and go to Spain without being detected? If caught, then what? What would happen to the monarchy? Who would support a queen who was caught slinking away to a foreign land; who, until a few months ago, was the enemy?

If her escape was successful it may even have more dire consequences. What made her think she would even return? The news of her escape would inflame her subjects and lend credence to the radicals' claim that the monarchy did not represent them and was only interested in their own survi-val. The populace would demand revenge and the only re-maining person who could satisfy the mob would be the queen, Margot's mother. *How could I even contemplate it?* Margot reached for the cord to summon Lucia but hesitated. *What choice do I have? Can I really sit by passively and hope for a miracle?* Margot stood up and walked to her mother's bed chamber. This was too big of a decision for her to make on her own.

CHAPTER 51

"You understand the likely consequences if my plan succeeds?" Margot looked intently at her mother.

"Yes," Queen Henrietta said. "I fully appreciate that after your escape I become the sole symbol of the monarchy and the target of all this treasonous hate toward our family. My body is breaking down but thank the Lord my mental facilities are still functioning."

"I do not know what to say, Mother." Margot's eyes began to water.

"I am not going to pretty things up to make any of us feel better." The queen closed her eyes and laid back down.

Margot sat looking at her mother for what was likely the last time.

Her mother sat up. Her eyes snapped open. "Do you remember the talk we had months ago in this very room, the day you found out you were going to marry Prince Leon?"

"Yes," Margot said in a small voice. "It was about not owning your life."

"Yes, and we are talking about it right now?"

"Yes, for the both of us, I see that." Margot stood. "Mother, I have to pack and prepare to leave."

"There's just one more thing," her mother said. "I heard Abagail has come to see you."

Margot immediately felt accused and wondered briefly how her mother found out. Then it came to her—it had to be Lucia.

"So, where does it stand between the two of you?" Queen Henrietta asked.

"What do you mean, Mother?"

"Margot, don't be coy with me. Is she coming back to your household?"

"I honestly do not know. I left it up to her." Margot had a

strong sense there was something more behind the question.

"And does she know about your plan to escape?"

"No. Why the interest, Mother?"

Queen Henrietta smiled. "Perhaps Princess Abagail has a part to play in this final drama. Now I have to sleep, my daughter. Promise me that we will have the opportunity to bid each other farewell."

"I promise." Margot leaned over and kissed her mother on her cheek.

"One more thing, dear."

"Yes, Mother?" Margot said.

"Has Lucia left for Spain yet?"

"I do not think so, why?" Margot replied.

"Ask her to come see me."

"Yes, Mother." The tears Margot had been holding back slipped down her cheeks. She knew that this image of her fading mother trying to figure her way out of a seemingly impossible situation would be seared in her mind forever.

CHAPTER 52

"Spain?" Albert asked. "We are to travel to Spain?"

"Yes, we have a message to give to Princess Margot's husband, the King of Spain."

Albert was shocked into silence.

"The future of the monarchy depends on our successful delivery of this message," Lucia continued.

"When do we leave, how do we get there, and who is to accompany us?" Albert asked, recovering.

"This is a secret mission. There will only be the two of us so as not to arouse suspicions." Lucia stopped, waiting to make sure Albert was present and able to take in what she had to say next. "We will travel as husband and wife. Albert, I want you to understand this trip is very dangerous. We have to be on constant alert. Do you understand?"

Albert didn't hear what Lucia said after the statement about traveling as husband and wife. *What does that mean*, he wondered? Would they be sharing the same room, the same bed? He wasn't sure if he was flattered or insulted by the off-hand way she informed him. It was as if it was just another detail to be arranged, like what clothes they should bring. Was that how Lucia saw him, as just another item to take on the journey? His wounded pride was offset by his excitement. What would this woman be like in bed?

"If we are caught and the message is discovered, it will mean the end of our lives and possibly the monarchy. If you choose to go with me on this trip you must promise not to drink. Not one drop while we are in England."

"I promise," Albert said solemnly.

The sun was just beginning to rise as the large man and the petite, dark-haired woman left the palace on horseback. The empty city streets echoed the clomp, clomp, clomp of the two steeds. It had rained earlier in the day, which made everything sparkle in the waning moonlight. Albert was not fooled by the glistening streets and the little stalls and shops. *Goodbye and good riddance*, he said to himself. This city was the place where the remnants of his life's missteps resided—the deaths of his innocent children, a failed marriage, and a failed life.

Albert let out a loud sigh when he entered the forest as if expelling his old self and leaving it in the city he once called home. He made a promise to himself that from this day forward he would be true to the man he could be and not the one he once was. Albert considered how much his life had changed in the last few months. He grappled with the disturbing reality that his life had become much better since his son's death. *How can that be?* It seemed wrong to be rewarded for the awful crime made possible by his own lust and selfishness.

Lucia was lost in her thoughts. *Do I want to devote my life to Margot, another queen?* Lucia knew in her heart that she was done with living for someone else. She looked over at Albert and wondered why she wanted him of all people to accompany her on this mission. Was this trip a test to see if he could stay sober and be a part of her new life? She smiled. At least she would find out how big and strong this big, strong man really was.

They rode all day, only stopping to give their horses and themselves a quick break. They drank some water, ate an apple, and then were back on their mounts, galloping across the country. They didn't see another soul all day. It was so peaceful you would never know that the world was threatening to come tumbling down.

"Where are we going to sleep for the night?" Albert asked.

"Soon..." Lucia said, then stopped.

Soldiers appeared out of nowhere. Every tree seemed to have a soldier behind it.

"Who are you and where are you going?" one soldier

demanded.

Albert and Lucia looked all around but they couldn't tell which soldier was speaking.

"Dismount," the voice ordered, "and keep your hands in front of you where I can see them. Search them," the voice commanded. Two soldiers ran their hands over Albert and Lucia's clothes and checked all their pockets.

"They are unarmed sir," one of the soldiers said.

"We are just on a journey..." Lucia started to say.

"Silence," the leader shouted. "You will speak when you are asked a question. Do you understand?" Lucia shook her head. "What about you, big man, do you understand?" Albert stared and didn't reply. "Oh, a tough man. I'm going to ask you one more time—do you understand?" Albert hesitated for a few seconds then nodded.

"Take their horses and the two of you follow us." He pointed to four soldiers. Lucia and Albert walked behind their horses, led by two soldiers in front of them and four behind.

"Hey, big man," one of the soldiers said softly so only Albert could hear. "You don't like taking orders, do you? Well, you better watch yourself if you want you and your lady to get out of here alive."

Albert turned and looked at the soldier. He didn't say a word. He just stared at his face as if trying to memorize it.

"You think I am afraid of your stare?"

"Let it go." his comrade said.

They walked in silence.

Uncertain what was waiting for them, the only thing Albert knew for sure was that he was going to knock out the soldier with the big mouth if he got the chance.

Lucia's thoughts were centered on one question: were these soldiers loyal to the throne or were they rebels? She was glad that she took the extra precaution of hiding the queen's seal in an inner dress pocket against her thigh. Now the question was, should she show the seal? It could be their way to pass through or it could be a death sentence.

They entered a large encampment embedded deep in the forest. Soldiers were everywhere, some eating, others sharpening their swords, while still others washed their clothes. Everybody stopped what they were doing and froze when they saw Albert and Lucia. They stared at Lucia in a way that infuriated Albert. He wasn't sure how much more he could take before he would explode. The procession stopped. Lucia and Albert were too far back to see what was going on in the front.

"Bring the prisoners forward," the captain yelled.

The soldier who taunted Albert grabbed him roughly by the arm. "Anytime you want, we can dance," the soldier whispered in Albert's ear.

Albert turned his head toward the soldier and growled back, "I would like that, yes, I would like that very much."

They were bought into a tent. "Untie them," an older man with grey hair and a beard said. "Have a seat. Tell me what brings the two of you out riding in this desolate place."

Lucia looked at the bearing of the man, the clothes he wore, and how those around him took on the attitude of servility and knew he was an aristocrat. "God save the Queen," she said and, when he repeated, "God save the Queen," Lucia let out a long breath. They were safe.

All Lucia had to do was present the queen's seal, and the soldiers began to treat them as comrades. The Duke insisted the couple dine with him and spend the night in his encampment. After dinner, Lucia explained to the Duke the situation in the city, the queen under house arrest, and parliament in control. The Duke became increasingly agitated.

"My men will scatter these rebels like the vermin they are," he stated with great confidence.

Lucia tried to describe the layout of the city, but the Duke wasn't interested. He was too taken with his army and assured of his victory to listen to a female prattle about the strength of his foe.

This was not where Lucia imagined the first time sleep-ing with Albert would be. Looking at the sky awash with stars, she had to admit that making love outdoors had its advantages. Albert was strong and, when he realized Lucia wasn't a delicate porcelain doll, their passion lasted long and went deep, leading to a restful sleep.

Albert did not fall asleep after he and Lucia finished. The memory of the smirk on that soldier's face wouldn't let him sleep. He quietly got up so as not to wake Lucia, found the soldier who taunted him, woke him up, and gave him the beating of his life. Now, he could sleep.

They left the next morning, well-rested and with a saddlebag full of fresh food.

Lucia noted Albert's smile and chuckled. "You're in fine spirits this morning. Nothing like a good night's sleep."

CHAPTER 53

"You know what they say about seasickness," the old man said to Albert, not waiting for a response. "At first you are afraid you are going to die. Then after a while you are afraid you are not going to die." The old man laughed loudly. "People who do not know think the Bay of Biscay is a smooth, easy ride. This water can get pretty nasty. Would you agree, son?"

Albert, who had never been on a boat, was bent over, every part of his body screaming out in pain. His stomach was empty after vomiting, sleep impossible, too dizzy to stand, and sitting only made the rocking worse. It was the longest two days of Albert's life.

By the time they docked at the Santander port in Northern Spain, Albert would have given anything to walk on solid ground.

"We have no time to waste," Lucia said, quickly scanning the shops on the main street. Albert, still weak, shakily followed behind her. "Aha," she said, walking up to a stable.

"Can I help you?" a boy of about ten asked.

"Yes, where is your master?" Lucia asked.

The boy ran off.

Albert, still rocking from the movement of the water, couldn't stand any longer and plopped down on a bale of hay.

The boy returned with an attractive young woman, dressed in workmen's clothes, who asked, "Can I help you?"

Lucia turned her back to everyone and pulled up her dress, taking out Princess Margot's seal.

The young woman's eyes got big. "What do you need?"

"Two horses," Lucia said, and twenty minutes later they were in the saddle again, heading towards Madrid.

After a day of hard riding, they found an inn, registered as husband and wife, and went straight to their room. They cleaned themselves, ate a large evening meal, and did not leave their room until the next morning, when they got up at dawn and rode again all day. They were both sore every night but that didn't stop them from getting to know each other. After three days of hard riding, they arrived at the Palace. The royal seal opened all doors like a magic wand. The prince summoned them. Lucia presented Princess Mar-got's message in Spanish.

Albert didn't understand a word, but he didn't have to speak the language to know the prince was visibly upset. "And how is my wife? Is she in danger?"

"Not at the moment but the situation is volatile, your Majesty, anything can happen," Lucia replied.

Prince Leon looked at the large man and petite woman in front of him. They made an odd pair. It was clear the small woman was in charge. "You must be exhausted. Sleep, and tomorrow you will return to your country with my reply."

They were both shown to their respective rooms. Albert was relieved they would not be husband and wife tonight. He just wanted to sleep, and truth be told Lucia's passion coupled with the long days of riding was wearing him out. In his room was a small table with a tray filled with food. A whole roasted chicken, a loaf of bread, cheese, apples, grapes, and even a bottle of red wine. He promised Lucia that he would not drink while they were in England. But he never said anything about Spain. He ate, enjoying every morsel, and drank the bottle of wine, barely making it to bed, where he immediately fell asleep.

Lucia let Albert sleep. She left her room and went to see the prince, who gave her his reply. She didn't have to be told to memorize it.

My dearest wife,

We have to remove you from your current situation. I think you are correct that if it was discovered by your countrymen that a sizeable Spanish force had landed in your country, we would be at war again. The best way to proceed is for you to leave under the cover of night with two or three of your most trustworthy aides.

This action has risks but there are also things that work in our favor. The very audacity of this action is its greatest asset. Your mother, the queen, is seen as the head of state and all eyes are on her. She can be a diversion. You have a few weeks before the whole world knows that you are the reigning queen, and it would be much more difficult for you to leave.

Your aide can lead you to a location on the coast where in three nights a ship will be moored, waiting to pick you up and bring you to safety, back to me.

I am certain the situation will change soon, and you will be welcomed back to your country and assume your rightful place on the throne. For the present, the goal is to keep you safe.

All my love,

Leon

CHAPTER 54

"Yes, tonight," James said. "We plan to overtake the palace guards and arrest the royal family. The time is now while the queen is too ill to move against us while her daughter…" James stopped and looked at Abagail closely, "has not yet been crowned. We have to take advantage of this opportunity. It will not last much longer."

"Then what?" Abagail asked.

"What do you mean?"

"What happens to Margot and the queen?"

"There will be a trial," James replied.

"And you want to know if I will support you and this trial?" Abagail asked. In a soft voice, she continued, "If I say no, what then?"

James didn't reply. He felt his future—his whole life—was being decided at this very moment.

"Is this trial just a way to execute Margot and her mother?"

"I don't know of any such plan. The idea is to see what comes out at the trial. I cannot tell you the verdict before-hand."

"You cannot guarantee Margot's safety?"

Once again James didn't reply.

The more Abagail thought about it, the more hopeless the situation looked. No matter her course of action, someone she loved was threatened. Warn Margot and James could be arrested and probably executed, the revolution defeated. Could she live with the possibility of Margot being hurt or imprisoned?

"I need to go for a walk," Abagail said, grabbing her shawl. The sky was beginning to turn from deep black to gray. She shivered and wrapped the shawl tightly around her body.

Spencer ducked behind a bush just as the front door of the

house opened. His target walked out, alone. He waited for the man to join her. He didn't. This was his chance. He followed her, crouching low.

Like the first time, Abagail was once again unaware she was being stalked. Spencer watched her with all the concentration of a hunter tracking his prey. He had no doubt it was the bitch who stabbed him in the face and now here she was, walking by herself. Unconsciously rubbing his scar, he crept closer to her.

Abagail came to a decision, turned, and started to walk back to the house. A twig snapped. She turned and there he was, her recurring nightmare come alive, running towards her like a wild animal.

Abagail felt for her wooden spoon, but it was in the house. She picked up two big rocks, spread her legs to brace herself, and threw one rock towards him. He laughed, looking up at the rock coming down, and easily dodged out the way—and that's when Abagail threw the second rock. This one was aimed directly at his chest. It hit him with a thud and stopped him, but only for a second. He was coming to kill her.

Abagail looked for another rock, but it was too late. He was less than ten feet from her. She grabbed a stick and swung it at him, but Spencer leaned out of the way and threw it on the ground. She yelled at the top of her lungs, "James!" and then he was on her. He tackled her to the ground and began to beat her with his fists. He tore at her clothes. Abagail fought back, scratching his face with her nails, trying to get to his eyes. Then he grabbed her by the throat and squeezed. Abagail, gasping for air, hit him with her fists and reached for his face, clawing at his wound. He screamed in pain and his hands left her throat, going to the bleeding wound. Their eyes met for a second and Abagail saw raw hate reflected in his glare. The pain energized him to choke her harder. She saw lights and then darkness. Then the pressure on her neck miraculously gone. Abagail rolled over. James stood above

Spencer, holding a large rock. The rock dripped blood in James' shaking hand.

James bent down, still shaking, and without a word held Abagail in his arms.

Spencer moaned and tried to get up. His eyes were closed and, no matter how hard he tried, they wouldn't open. He lay back on the ground. He could feel his hair stuck to his scalp. There was someone standing above him. Abagail was speaking, but he couldn't make out a word. Spencer's last memory of the world was screaming "no" as a rock came down on his face and he sank into the dark.

Abagail fell to her knees and sat on the wet grass.

"Are you hurt?" James asked, his voice trembling.

"I don't know," Abagail replied. She checked her limbs. There was blood on her hands but couldn't tell if it was or the attacker's.

"Who was that man?"

"I don't want to talk about it, not now."

"All right," James said, staring at the still body. "I think I've seen him before. Yes, now I remember. He was at the tavern where last night's meeting was held. He must have followed me—why would he do that?"

"I have to lay down, James." Abagail started to stand but staggered, almost falling.

"I have you," James said as he held her up. "Just lean on me." Together they walked slowly to the house. James guided her to the bedroom, where she collapsed on the bed. "You rest and I'll clean up out there." Abagail didn't respond.

James went to the back of the house and got the wheelbarrow. He was surprised at how heavy the body was. He wheeled the body slowly to the cave. Once inside the cave, the ground sloped downward so the wheelbarrow did all of the work. On reaching the bottom, he found a corner and dug a hole. James turned the wheelbarrow to one side and the body rolled into the shallow grave. In less than an hour, a man had disappeared from the face of the earth. Not a trace left.

James walked to the pump and washed the dirt and blood from his hands. He felt calm, no second thoughts. Then, in the short walk back to the house, the enormity of what had happened crashed down on James. He killed a man and had no regret. Now he knew what he was capable of and James wasn't sure he was happy about it. He thought this may not be the last time he would be involved with violence. The talk at the Red Oxen would soon lead to action. James did not believe that the overthrow of the monarchy would be bloodless. He murdered someone who was trying to kill his love. Would he commit murder for a cause? Were there other, as-of-yet unknown reasons to kill? James was very uncomfortable about his drift into this moral morass.

He looked in on Abagail, who was sleeping soundly. He crawled next to her, careful not to wake her and, not even removing his shoes, tried to sleep.

The sunlight streaming through the window woke the both of them. They both laid very still until Abagail broke the silence. "Where is he?"

"He's gone," James said.

"What do you mean gone?"

"Buried in the cave, out of sight, like he never existed."

Abagail shuddered and James put his arm around her. "It's all right," he said, wiping away her tears. "You don't have to worry about him ever again."

"That man, he did terrible things."

"You don't have to tell me, Abagail," James said.

"I must tell you everything," Abagail insisted. It wasn't until the story ended that James realized he had been holding his breath.

Abagail took a deep breath. "What do you think of me now?"

"I don't know what to say."

"I don't blame you," Abagail said. "I understand. Who

would want to be with a person who did those terrible things?"

"No, that's not what I am thinking, not at all."

Abagail waited.

"I do not think you are terrible. I think terrible things happened to you."

"But still..." Abagail started to say.

"I admire you for facing your life and trying to change it."

"Oh, James, if I could believe that."

"It is true," he said. "You are incredibly strong. Most people who have gone through what you did would have given up."

"James, you have saved my life twice in one day."

"And you have saved me from a bitter, lonely life."

As they held each other, Abagail felt closer to James than she had to anyone in her life. Her decision already made; was solidified. Love trumps luxury. Beatrice would be proud of her.

"I have to leave soon to prepare for tonight," James whispered, slowly pulling away from Abagail. He waited for her to say something. "We're meeting again at the Red Oxen and then there will be a general assembly in the central square."

Abagail was not yet ready to face the world. Her eyes remained closed.

"Then we march to the palace," James continued.

"I love you, James," Abagail said and rolled over to be close to him.

"I love you too," James said, sliding his arm around her. A few minutes went by and then he sat up. "Will you warn the royal family?"

"I don't know what I am going to do, but I won't betray the revolution."

"Are you going to the palace?" he asked.

"Yes. I think so. I cannot just stand by and not do anything. I have to talk to Margot face to face and close this chapter in my life."

"It may be dangerous."

"Yes, for both of us." Abagail kissed him long and deep. "I love you, James," she said again.

"And I love you, Abagail," James replied. He stood up, put on his jacket, and without another word walked out. Abagail left the bed, washed her face, changed her clothes, and with a new resolve headed for the palace, hoping the two-hour walk would give her time to work out what she would do.

CHAPTER 55

Margot was remarkably calm after Lucia recited the contents of her husband's letter. She had only one concern—leaving her mother behind. "Lucia, is there any possibility my mother can join us?"

"I know it is very difficult, your Majesty, but realistically we would need an entire regiment to transport the queen, and to be frank, even with that much support she may not be strong enough to survive the trip."

"Yes, but to leave her here, so vulnerable and defenseless. It is immoral, criminal."

"Your mother understands that the larger the party accompanying you the more likely you will be caught and then you, your mother, and the monarchy are in danger. Secrecy is our only hope."

The most difficult part of the plan for Lucia to carry out was to prepare Margot's escape without alerting anyone in the palace. Clothes had to be packed, incriminating documents and letters destroyed. Money, jewels, and other items of value needed to be safely tucked away. Theoretically, only three people knew of the plan; herself, Princess Margot, and Albert. But Lucia knew of at least two supporters of the rebels in the palace. And there were countless more who would eagerly divulge the details of the escape for a few coins. The more the escape was delayed the more likely it would be revealed.

All Abagail had to do to enter the palace was show the guards Margot's seal. Certain of what had to be done, she walked with confidence, as if she belonged. This self-confidence radiated from her and no one challenged her or even stopped her to ask where she was going or what she was doing. Abagail walked right up to the two soldiers who always stood guard over any room occupied by a member of the royal family. "Tell her highness Abagail needs to speak with her. It is of the utmost importance." One of the guards started to say something but the other opened the door and without saying anything entered the room. Abagail didn't move. She and the remaining guard stared at each other for a few seconds.

"Princess Margot will see you now," the guard announced as soon as he opened the door.

Abagail walked into the royal chamber, which was a smaller version of the throne room, more informal and suitable for a smaller number of people. Margot was talking intently with a woman Abagail recognized, Lucia. Their heads bent so close together their foreheads almost touched.

Margot hadn't noticed Abagail enter the room. Abagail decided to take this opportunity to look at Margot closely. Did they look like sisters? Margot had long, straight golden hair, while Abagail's hair was darker and curly. Abagail grew up thinking Margot was much more attractive than her. Now she wasn't so sure. They did look like they could be sisters, remarkably so. Abagail thought nothing was how it used to be. This was her first time seeing Margot as a half-sister and, in a way, she couldn't explain it—it was like seeing herself for the first time.

Margot straightened and waved for Abagail to approach.

"Hello," Lucia said in an unfriendly manner. "You had a lot of people wondering where you were. Some of us were hurt trying to find you."

"There was a lot of pain for a lot of people and a brutal death as well," Abagail replied in an equally cold tone.

"I think there was more than one death. At least three deaths related to your escape that I am aware of." Lucia did not take her eyes from Abagail. She felt a river of hate course through her body.

"I am sorry for your pain, but I experienced pain as well. I lost my mother," Abagail said, meeting Lucia's gaze. The world disappeared as the two women locked into their rage.

"All right," Margot said, breaking the deadlock. "Lucia, you have a lot to do and Abagail and I have a lot to talk about."

"Yes, your Majesty," Lucia said as she bowed, staring at Abagail one last time before she walked briskly out of the room.

"I was afraid you would not return. I cannot say I would have blamed you," Margot said. "My request is still the same but there is one change. It is a major change. I do not think I can tell you about the change unless you agree with my request."

"Your Majesty..." Abagail hesitated.

"Yes, tell me. Will you accept my offer and return to the royal court with me where you belong?"

"Well, your Majesty—Margot," Abagail said and faltered again, unable to get the words out.

"Abagail, yes or no, which is it?"

"No," Abagail said and let out a big breath. "But I came today to bring you some very grave news."

Margot went slack as her last remaining support was pulled out from under her. "Yes, what news?" she asked disinterestedly.

"The rebels will be storming the palace tonight and will put your mother on trial. Your life is in danger." There, she said it, but Margot's lack of reaction puzzled her. "Do you understand your life is in danger?"

"Abagail, are you sure about this? They are coming tonight?"

"Yes, I am sure."

"This is not some rumor you heard?"

"No, this comes straight from the rebels."

"I am not going to ask how you know this, but if what you say is true, you are right, we have to leave tonight. Think again, Abagail, do you want to..."

"No, Margot. I am certain. My life is here."

"Why do you tell me this and yet refuse my offer to return to court?"

"Well, I no longer support the monarchy, but I still love you." Abagail stopped.

"I see," Margot said. She pulled a cord and a page appeared. "Tell lady Lucia I need to see her right away."

The page bowed. "Yes, your Majesty," he said, and left hurriedly.

Margot walked toward Abagail with her arms outstretched and said, "Well, I suppose this is goodbye."

Abagail didn't move.

"You look surprised," Margot said. "What did you expect to happen? You tell me I must flee. My life is in danger and you refuse to come with me. What is left for us but to say goodbye?"

"You are right, of course you are, but I never thought this through. Not to have you in my life, well, it seems strange. There will be an empty space."

"I know. Even though we have not seen each other for these past months, you have been a constant companion in my mind."

"Exactly," Abagail replied. "I think about you and your mother every day."

Margot sighed. "Yes, my mother will not be coming with me on this journey."

"Why not? You know they plan on putting her on trial."

"My mother would not survive the trip." Margot hesitated. "I wonder if you could visit her. I think it would do her good and she has expressed regret for the actions taken against you and your mother."

"I do not know," Abagail replied. Confronting the queen and avenging her mother's death was one of the dreams that kept Abagail alive during this whole ordeal. Her thoughts of revenge never formalized into a plan. Abagail could not imagine she would ever see the queen again. Now, given a chance to avenge her mother's imprisonment, she hesitated. Any act of violence seemed repugnant. Abagail took a deep breath, remembering her oath not to forget her mother. "Yes, I will meet with the queen."

CHAPTER 56

Abagail slowly opened the door and quietly walked in. The room was dark and dank, reminding her of the cave. She waited for her eyes to adjust and saw a bed on the opposite wall. Walking towards it, a shadowy figure came into focus.

"Is that you, Margot?" the queen said in a hoarse whisper.

"No, it is Abagail."

"I'm glad you came. I have been waiting for you. Now, I know you do not have much time so let us get down to business."

Abagail, confused, asked, "What kind of business?" This was not the kind of greeting she expected. She moved closer to the bed and bent down to enter the queen's line of vision. The queen looked directly at Abagail, but her eyes didn't register. They were lifeless as they stared out, unblinking.

"I have a list of people—friendly people to our cause—for you to contact when you arrive in Spain."

Now she understood; the queen was confused. "I am not Margot. I am Abagail." Abagail had to remind herself: this was the woman who kept her mother from her and was responsible for her death. Any feelings of pity for the queen and her decline had to be squashed.

"It is also important that you set up a way to communicate with the loyalists in this country."

"This is Abagail, not Margot," Abagail repeated.

The queen went on as if Abagail hadn't spoken. "It is crucial that the message you convey is that you expect to return shortly and assume your rightful place on the throne."

Abagail stared at the old woman who had ruined her life. The most shocking thing about the queen was how ordinary, fragile, and impotent she appeared. The list of accusations Abagail practiced delivering to the queen evaporated. She remembered James' question about the divine nature of the queen. Here was the answer. The queen who ruined her and her mother's lives was a frail, dying old lady who could not distinguish her own daughter from someone she had known her whole life.

"Come, my dear, kiss your mother goodbye," the queen said plaintively.

Abagail bent down to give the dying woman a kiss, then stopped suddenly. The queen looked up expectantly at who she thought was her loving daughter. Abagail realized this was the moment she had dreamt about. Abagail picked up a pillow and held it above the queen. It would be so easy. *Just put it on her face. Make sure to cover her mouth and nose.* Abagail's heart raced and sweat poured down her face.

Then something extraordinary happened. In the dark, the queen's face transformed into Abagail's mother. Abagail's heart stopped for a moment and she grabbed onto a chair so as not to fall. After a few moments, her breathing slowed, and her heart began to beat normally again Abagail took a deep breath and came to a decision. She was not going to kill this defenseless old lady in her bed. She bent down and placed the pillow ever so carefully on the floor as if it was a bomb ready to explode.

"Margot, Margot," the queen whispered. "Kiss me and tell me you forgive me."

I am not going to kill you, Abagail thought. *But you are not getting away without feeling some pain.*

"Kiss me farewell, my daughter," the queen implored.

"No, mother, never," Abagail said, turned away, and walked out of the room, ignoring the cries of, "Margot, Margot!" from the heartbroken queen.

CHAPTER 57

Abagail left the palace determined to tell James that Margot knew about the timing of the insurrection. She did not know how he would react or whether it would end their relationship, but there was no alternative.

The Red Oxen Inn looked like a thousand other inns. It had one feature that made it the perfect meeting place for a large group. There was a very large room set discreetly in the back of the tavern that could accommodate up to thirty men. This night there were two times that number crammed in.

Abagail, ignoring the stares of the men sitting at tables in the tavern, walked directly to a man standing at the door of the meeting room and put her hand on the doorknob. The man stepped sideways to block her entrance.

"Excuse me, I have an important message for somebody at the meeting." Abagail tried to walk around him, but he did not budge. "You do not understand—I have crucial informa-tion."

"Sorry miss, no one is allowed in without an invitation," the man said firmly.

"Do you know James Collier?"

"No, I do not, miss. I am sorry. You cannot stand here."

Abagail walked away. She had to come up with another way to contact James. It was clear they wouldn't let her in. Then it came to her. Abagail walked back to the door.

The man sighed. "Miss, I told you..."

Abagail interrupted him, "I'm sure you know Captain Nugent."

He stared at her but didn't deny it.

Abagail walked up to the bar and asked the bartender for a paper and a quill.

"Aye," he said, "but it will cost you a half-crown." He smiled so wide that Abagail got a view of his few black teeth.

Abagail gave him a dirty look, but there was no other

choice. She reached into her pocket and felt two quarter crowns. "All I have is one quarter crown," she said, pulling one of the coins out.

The bartender shook his head.

Abagail placed the coin in her open hand so he could see it.

Staring at the coin, the bartender said, "All right, for a pretty lady like you, you can have it for a quarter crown."

Abagail sat at the bar and wrote.

Captain Nugent,

I am staying with James Collier. I am the fugitive you were looking for when you came to his house. It is imperative that I speak to James and you. I have vital information about the palace you can use tonight. Come out to the tavern. I will be waiting for you.

Abagail

Turning the paper over, she drew a map on the back then folded it in half, making sure the map was not visible, and gave it to the man at the door. "I'm sure Captain Nugent will want to see this letter immediately."

The man sighed and opened the door a crack. "Give this letter to Captain Nugent," he said, handing the letter off to someone in the room. Abagail could hear someone speaking but couldn't make out the words. She angled her head to catch a view of the room, but the man at the door blocked her vision.

Abagail turned around and saw an empty table, only then realizing she was the only woman in the tavern. Every man had his eyes glued on her. Sitting at the empty table, she purposefully did not make eye contact with anyone. She was very hungry but couldn't buy anything without revealing her other quarter crown. She sat and waited. The scene in the queen's chamber came to mind. There was no sense of satisfaction or of a promise kept to her mother, only sadness about the whole situation—her mother, the young guard, the king, and now the queen more dead than alive. Closing her eyes and laying her head on the table, Abagail felt the weight of all these ghosts from her past.

It seemed like only a few seconds passed since she closed her burning eyes when someone shook her shoulder.

"Miss, wake up."

Abagail emerged from the deep, dark sleep to feel someone touching her breasts. For a second, only half-awake, the awful thought of that evil man attacking her played in her mind. She opened her eyes, and the bartender came into focus. "Get your hands off me. What do you think you're doing?" Abagail's body shook. She pulled out the wooden spoon.

The man took a step back, holding his hands up to defend himself. "We're closing, miss. Whoever you are waiting for has already left." The bartender held a tankard of ale. "Here, drink this. It is late and dark outside. An attractive lady like you should not be walking around by herself this time of night."

"I can take care of myself, sir. Now you take a step back, so I can leave." The barkeep took one small step back, forcing Abagail to brush past him as she stood up from the table. She gave him a push and strode quickly out of the tavern. Once outside, she took a deep breath. *What is it with men?* Abagail walked briskly towards home, feeling stronger with every step.

After an hour of walking, Abagail could see the house, but there was something wrong. The house was dark. She ran the last few hundred yards and burst in. "James, James," she called out, but no answer. Running to the back yard and looking in the barn, she still found no one. *Maybe they're already marching to the palace.* Why didn't James come and get her from the tavern when Captain Nugent got her note? Did James not believe what was in the letter—or worse, did he think she would betray him? There was only one way to find out. Abagail put on a warmer shawl and began walking back to the palace.

CHAPTER 58

It was the heart of the night, but the streets of the city were as crowded as if it was the middle of the day. Thousands were marching, many carrying lighted torches that illuminat-ed the city. The marchers were festive, singing, laughing, and carrying handmade signs painted on wooden boards. The mood of the thousands who filled the street was more cele-bratory than revolutionary, making the evening feel like a night-time fair.

Abagail tried to push through the crowd, looking for James, thinking he would be close to the front of the march.

James was, in fact, at the head of the demonstration, marching with the Levelers from the Red Oxen. He could tell what other groups were participating by the banners they waved. Different groups of apprentices, men wearing their military uniforms, members of parliament, Levelers, Diggers, and even clergy were all represented. He walked alongside Captain Nugent, who seemed to know half of the marchers by name.

"There's only one thing that's bothering me," James said.

"What? I can't hear you with all this noise."

James put his mouth close to the captain's ear and said loudly, "I am worried about Abagail. I don't know where she could be." He feared she was in the palace.

"Oh, how can I be so foolish?" Nugent said, looking in his pockets. "I have a letter for you."

"A letter?"

"Back at the Red Oxen someone gave me a letter. He said it was from a young woman and she asked for a James Collier. He told her he did not know anyone by that name, so she said to give it to me." Captain Nugent retrieved the letter, handing it to James, and said, "I never opened it."

I need to talk to you tonight before you and your friends

take any action. *It is of the utmost importance.* He read it again and then it became clear Abagail did not want to include any details in the letter in case it was intercepted. He started to put it in his back pocket when he noticed writing on the back of the page. It was a map of the palace, crudely drawn, but it seemed accurate. And on the map was a door, with a caption underneath that said, "The way in." James' hand started to shake. It meant they could get inside the palace without any fighting. It also meant that Abagail chose him and the revolution over life in the palace.

"Well, what does it say?" Captain Nugent asked.

"The letter is very general but there is this," James turned the letter over, showing him the map.

Captain Nugent stared at the map intently. "If this is accurate, we have a way into the palace." He handed the map back to James, who didn't take it.

"You keep it. I will catch up to you. I'm pretty sure Abagail is here somewhere, and I have to find her."

"I understand," said the captain. At that moment they turned a corner, and a platoon of cavalry came into view. The crowd turned quickly from festive and boisterous to panicked.

James had his back turned to the horsemen peering over the heads of people, but the crowd continued to push him forward as it lurched toward the palace.

Abagail, boxed in by a solid wall of people, hadn't moved in what felt like an hour. Then suddenly the crowd thinned out. The march fragmented. Abagail couldn't figure out why until the soldiers on horseback came into view. This was her chance to get to the front of the crowd where she was certain James would be. Walking against the tide of frightened marchers hurrying away from the palace toward safety slowed her progress.

The soldiers on horseback forced James to divert his attention. Weapons appeared out of nowhere. People around him pulled out axes, hoes, knives, and the occasional gun from under their coats. James' eye caught sight of a familiar face in the churning crowd.

"Abagail" he shouted, but to no avail. It was too noisy, and she was too far away.

Captain Nugent, in uniform with his regal bearing, stood as still as a statue as the crowd ebbed and flowed around him. He turned to his aide standing next to him. "We must get into the palace now. This will turn ugly soon. If this map is accurate, twelve men should be enough. Sergeant, gather our men and bring them here."

"All right, men," Nugent said as the men formed a circle around him. "We have reliable intelligence identifying a way into the palace and directions to where the queen is. We can take the queen as our prisoner and save countless lives. This is a dangerous enterprise and if anyone decides not to participate, you will not be ostracized." He looked around at the group of men. Nobody moved and or said a word.

James pushed against the crush of marchers. He was forced to turn and change direction. Soon he was drenched in sweat, exhausted, and no closer to Abagail. Frantically searching the crowd, he saw Captain Nugent leading a group of soldiers. Even though they were only one street away, James couldn't buck the press of the crowd, which was pushing him away from Nugent. They began their approach to the palace without him.

Nugent's men ran down several streets until they came to a rise. Crouching behind some hedges, Nugent took out the map and unfolded it. He whispered to the others, "According to the map there are usually soldiers guarding the entrance. It doesn't specify how many."

Captain Nugent pointed to the sergeant. "Go up there and see how many soldiers there are."

The rest of the group sat down without making a sound.

The sergeant returned after a few minutes. "Just two guards, Sir."

"Very good. Take three men with you, tie the two guards up, and signal us when it's done."

"Yes, Sir."

Less than five minutes later they heard a whistle. The group ran up the hill. The two guards were tied up, frightened but unhurt.

The men walked quickly and silently until they came to a door hidden behind a thick growth of vines just as the map illustrated. The door opened easily and they found themselves inside the palace. Nugent looked at the map. "Follow me," he said quietly, running up several flights of stairs. They came to a room where every inch of wall was covered with shelves loaded with books. Captain Nugent stood very still, then walked over to the far wall and pushed. The wall gave way and a small, almost invisible door opened. They walked through into the main corridor of the palace. It was bedlam. Groups of soldiers, aides, and servants rushed every which way.

The rebels walked in unseen, just another group of soldiers walking quickly in the crowded chaos of the palace.

When they got to the door of the queen's chamber, two soldiers stood guard. "Halt," one ordered, holding up his arm. The other guard reached for his sword, but before he could draw it from the scabbard, the rebels surrounded them with drawn swords.

"Take their weapons," Captain Nugent said. "Tie them up. The two of you—" he pointed at two men, "wait out here and act as guards. Don't allow anyone in the room. If there is a problem, knock on the door three times loudly."

The room was completely dark. The group stood quietly, waiting for their eyes to adjust.

"Who's there?" an old woman asked in a wavering voice from the corner of the room. "What do you want? Answer me. Who is it?"

"Your Majesty, my name is Captain Nugent and in the

name of parliament and the people I have come to arrest you."

In an eerily calm tone, the queen replied, "I have been expecting you."

"I want all of you to leave this room and guard the door. I will stay with the queen," Captain Nugent said.

The soldiers milled around, confused by the captain's order. "But, Captain, should not all of us remain here to guard the queen?" the sergeant asked.

"Did you not hear me? Outside all of you, now," the captain said sternly.

The soldiers looked to the sergeant and when he walked through the door, they followed.

The queen steeled herself, ready for anything. *Whatever this man is planning to do to me, I will not grovel or beg for mercy.* "Do what you wish," the queen said, "but make it quick."

The captain approached the queen's bed and did the most extraordinary thing. He crouched down on one knee and bowed deeply. "Your Majesty, I am and will always be your loyal servant."

The queen was shocked. "Rise, young man, tell me your name and how you came into my service."

"My name is Peter Nugent, and I am a captain in the royal army. I have been an agent of the crown working with Lucia these last two years."

Queen Henrietta struggled to sit up and put her hand on his forearm. "You are a brave and noble man. When this business is over you will be properly rewarded," she said with great effort, then sank back into bed. Her prayers were answered. Margot was safely out of the country and the future of the crown was intact at least for now.

Captain Nugent's arm tingled where the queen touched it. He vowed that, as long as he lived, no harm would come to his queen.

CHAPTER 59

The members of the House of Commons were in an uproar. The Speaker brought his gavel down so hard it sounded like a gunshot. "Gentlemen, gentlemen," the Speaker yelled over the members' shouting, which slowly subsided as they took their seats. The Speaker cleared his throat. "Queen Henrietta has a statement she would like entered into the official record of this trial."

"No, she may not," a member from the back benches called out loudly. The parliament once again erupted a torrent of noise.

"Order, order," the Speaker repeated, banging his gavel. "Where is the honorable gentleman who first shouted no?" His eyes roamed the hall until they landed on a member standing with his arm raised.

"Explain yourself," the Speaker said.

Everyone turned in their seats to get a clear view of the handsome young man who behaved so boldly.

"My name is John Saunders. I represent East London. My constituents have suffered under this monarch. Even so, they are divided over the fate of the queen. Some want a restricted monarchy and others want her to pay the highest cost for the pain she has caused. The one thing I promised them was that the queen's fate will be decided by laws that are fair. The same laws that would apply to ordinary people will apply to the royal family. Is a regular citizen able to submit a statement before they go to trial? The answer is no. The same rules and protections apply to the queen—no monarch is above the law, therefore the answer is no. No statement," he finished with a flourish and sat down.

Before Saunders' bottom touched the seat, an outpouring of shouts—"treason, regicide, criminal!"—cascaded against an opposing chorus of support—"hear, hear, go to trial, the will of the people!"

"I demand to be heard." A booming voice filled the large chamber. A distinguished-looking man with a mane of white hair started speaking, "I dare say all of you know me. I am the Earl of Essex. What we are contemplating doing today is unthinkable and will come back to haunt this country for years to come. Regicide is a sin against God and the natural order. You speak of putting her Majesty on trial. It is treason."

A wall of sound bellowed from the opposition. The Earl took a deep breath and said in his loudest voice, "I refuse to be a party to this outrage. I am walking out of this assembly and will not return until the rightful monarch is occupying the throne. I urge all loyal Englishmen to follow me." And with that, the Earl left the hall with a third of parliament following. The remaining members looked around at the empty seats. A heavy silence fell throughout the hall.

John Saunders stood and said, "Let them go. They represent the aristocracy, not the people." The spell was broken and once again the building itself seemed to rock with the crashing waves of accusations and counteraccusations. Those members who supported the monarchy left the assembly, so the remaining members largely supported John Saunders' position of no pre-trial statement from the queen. But the noise of the excited legislators continued.

"Order, order," the Speaker shouted again. Even with his banging the gavel he could not be heard above the ocean of sound. Knowing that he could not compete with the deafening roar, the Speaker put down his gavel and began to make his way slowly out of the chamber. The shouting finally diminished as members watched the Speaker turn around and return to his appointed chair.

"We have a historic task before us," the Speaker began. The raucous bedlam quieted to a murmur, then silence. The Speaker continued, "The future of our country is as much on trial as is the monarchy. Whatever the verdict, we must act in a thoughtful and deliberate manner and not bring shame on our country and this house.

"I am now asking for a vote," the Speaker said. "The question before this body is, can Queen Henrietta have a statement read aloud and entered into the official record of this trial? Yea or nay."

"May we have some time to discuss this matter before we take this momentous step?" John Saunders asked.

"Are there any objections?" the Speaker asked, looking around the assembly. "So, to you sir, what objections do you have?"

John Saunders exhaled. "I have concerns more than objections. We are faced with a dilemma. By extending to the queen the right to make a statement to this body, are we giving up our power before the trial begins? On the other hand, her request to make her statement seems fair and also it legitimizes our endeavor. So, there you have it, a paradox."

"How does it legitimize our endeavor?" the Speaker asked.

Saunders rose again. "By stating publicly whatever she will about our assembly, she implicitly recognizes our authority."

"So, your recommendation is?"

"My recommendation is for us to be very polite to the woman, not deferential but respectful, and we do our duty to the citizens of our country without fear or favor."

"Whatever the outcome," the Speaker intoned solemnly.

"Whatever the outcome," Sauders echoed. He took a deep breath and continued, "There is no one who is above the law. The queen must stand trial."

Nobody moved, nobody breathed. Every person in that hall knew they were embarking on a journey into the un-known. The unprecedented act of putting a sitting monarch on trial took their breath away. Beheadings of royalty had numerous historical precedents. But it was always the aristocracy killing one of their own in their campaign to wear the crown. Parliament was heading down a road without precedent. The heroic certainty bred by the passion of the movement gave way to the reality of what they were contemplating—the imprisonment and possible killing of a queen. Accompanying the fear of their present course was a sense of wonder, a new world being born.

Saunders stood. "This trial is revolutionary regardless of the outcome. The principle of no one being above the law and accountable to the people is established. If a ruling monarch is subject to the law as is every citizen of this country, then we have won. The world is watching us. The aristocracy of every country is holding their breath, hoping we fail. That is why we must be scrupulous in our proceed-ings." Shouts of "hear, hear" rang out. The matter was settled before the vote was taken.

CHAPTER 60

The court doctors were flabbergasted at the queen's recovery. They all tried to take credit for her turnaround. Ironically, it was the rebel's confinement that gave her the opportunity to regain her strength. Unburdened by the unrelenting demands of ruling the country, the queen conserved her energy for a more important task—saving the monarchy. The queen may have been confined to the royal bedroom and the adjoining sitting room, but she still had a hand to play in this game. First, she sent for Lucia, recently returned from Spain.

There was also a statement to write for those fools in parliament to terminate this so-called trial. Every word on the page used up a little bit of her declining energy, but it was an opportunity to state her case.

To the Traitorous Rebels,

The throne does not recognize the legitimacy of the proceedings of this "trial." Who are you to sit in judgement of your monarch? For a thousand years past and a thousand more to come this country has been and will continue to be governed by the Lord Almighty represented on earth by your monarch. The divine right granted by God cannot be undone by man. To do so is not only treasonous it is an act against the All Mighty.

Therefore, I refuse to attend these illegal, blasphemous meetings. I urge all believing Christians to likewise absent themselves.

Beware the wrath of God!

Queen Henrietta

My husband would be proud of me, the queen thought, feeling more in control now than she had in the past several years. *This was why I survived*, she mused, *to be here now to protect the country and restore the monarchy to its rightful place. It is my destiny.* Her plan was bold and audacious, but with the help of God, it would succeed.

CHAPTER 61

Lucia was back in the palace, but it was not the palace she knew. The rebels were now in control. It took her almost three hours to be admitted. Soldiers walked in the corridors without regard to anyone else. Now that the rebellion suc-ceeded and the palace belonged to the people, commoners were free to roam the corridors, gawk at the portraits on the walls, hold their children's hands, and even sit on the fancy furniture as if they were visiting a zoo.

"My queen," Lucia said, bowing deeply. "You look well." It was true. The queen was transformed. Her eyes were bright, her speech clear and strong, and even her hair was more lustrous.

"Yes, it is surprising how well I feel. There is no better medicine than regaining control of one's life. I have a plan and I need your help."

"I am at your service," Lucia said.

"It is complicated and there are many things that have to be put in place. But it is the only way to save the monarchy."

"I am ready to do what has to be done."

"We must make Abagail the heir to the throne."

Lucia caught her breath and wondered whether her queen's mind was affected by her illness. Her face must have shown her confusion because the queen smiled.

"You see, if Abagail is seen as the next in line for the throne, she diverts attention from Margot, who becomes just a spare to the heir. Only we use the spare first to save the heir."

"How do we do that, your Majesty?" Lucia asked, reeling from the news.

"We change her past." The queen's eyes brightened with the fever of inspiration.

"Change her past?" Lucia asked. "Is that possible?"

"It is," the queen replied.

Lucia wondered if there were things even a monarch couldn't do. *Is the queen trespassing on God's domain bending reality, turning the clock back?* Lucia felt a chill rise through her body, but a lifetime of loyalty overruled her doubts.

"Now listen carefully," the queen continued, her bright eyes shining as she twisted a piece of fabric in her hands. "Abagail has the same father, the king, and her mother is my sister, Beatrice. Abagail was born two months after Margot. All we have to do is change her birth date and she is next in line. It is possible—far-fetched, but possible. Abagail will assume the role of the queen-to-be, while we make sure she is captured by the rebels with Margot safe in Spain. For this to succeed, no one can know her true past."

Lucia now understood why it was so important for Albert to remain in Spain. Anybody who knew about Abagail's imprisonment and escape had to be silenced so as not to contradict the account of her being the heir to the throne.

"I know it is a desperate plan and there are many ways for it to fail but if all goes well, we can save the monarchy."

Lucia walked out of the queen's room, animated by her mistress' excitement but still unsure if her queen's plan was brilliant or mad. Regardless of which it was, Lucia knew her duty; to carry out the queen's wishes.

CHAPTER 62

John Saunders had to admit he looked good this morning, checking the hall mirror again, wearing his best suit. He was able to tame his unruly light brown hair and the suit high-lighted his broad shoulders and narrow waist. Meeting with the queen was a circumstance he had never envisioned. But here he was, waiting outside the queen's chamber. Everything he learned about the queen confirmed that she was a determined, experienced adversary and he had to admit—if only to himself—he was nervous. Saunders, the only child of a lowly clerk, in the position of not only meeting the queen but deciding her fate. His charge was to convey the wishes of parliament and persuade the queen that it was in her interest to participate in a trial that would most likely end a thou-sand-year rule. There were rumors she was near death, but nevertheless he assumed she would be a powerful adversary and do everything to prevail, including asserting her power to make him wait.

He had to counter her power with his own, which was not granted to him by birthright but conferred on him by his constituents, the people. Determined not to start at a disad-vantage, he was not going to begin this business by letting the queen call the shots. He had been waiting forty minutes. Enough waiting, Saunders knocked on her door loudly and said, "Your Majesty, I cannot wait any longer."

The door opened and a petite woman with curly, raven-black hair said, "Her Majesty will see you now."

Head held high, back as straight as possible, the queen looked anything but frail and sickly. John Saunders felt a combination of disinterest and forbearance in her gaze. Stop-ping himself from bowing, Saunders stood tall to meet her gaze. "Your Majesty," he started to say, but stopped; he was meeting the queen as a member of the House of Commons of the duly elected parliament, and thus began, "I come as a representative of the people of this land. I have a document ordering you to appear at a tribunal before parliament."

The queen sat absolutely still. Saunders went on, "The tribunal begins in a week's time. You can be represented by the counsel of your choice. Do you have any questions?" he asked.

"My decision," the queen said, handing an envelope to the dark-haired woman, who attempted to deliver it to Saunders.

Saunders didn't offer his hand to take the envelope. Never taking his eyes off the queen, he said, "I understand you want a statement read. That matter is under discussion and a decision has not yet been reached whether or not to allow it." He noticed a flicker of emotion cross the queen's face. The dark-haired woman held the document in front of him, waiting for him to take it. Finally, he took the envelope, looked around the room, and placed it on a small table. Without saying another word, he turned and left the room. It wasn't until he was outside that he realized his shirt was stuck to his back with sweat.

The queen, pale, all her energy spent, slumped in her chair. Lucia, worrying that she may slip off, ran to her mistress. The queen raised her hand. "I'm fine, just help me to the sofa and fetch me some water."

CHAPTER 63

Lucia decided that the best place for a meeting with Nugent was in the queen's private room, the same room she had used with Albert. Lucia never fully trusted Nugent. She always viewed him as self-serving, but Lucia thought using this secret room would convey that she had the full backing of her Majesty.

"I don't understand," Captain Nugent said. "You want me to arrest Abagail?"

"Not you personally," Lucia said abruptly, immediately regretting her tone.

Nugent didn't say anything, but Lucia could tell he felt hurt. She had to make up for her mistake. There weren't many agents willing to work for the throne now that the rebels had the upper hand. She thought bitterly of all the coins she handed out to those who professed loyalty to the crown. Where were they now? Captain Nugent was well placed to help their cause. As the leader of the men who actually captured the queen, he was held in high regard by the rebels and hailed as a hero by the people.

"Her Majesty the queen is very grateful for your timely intervention on her behalf and your loyalty. That is why she is entrusting you to carry out this plan to save the mon-archy."

Captain Nugent smiled and his chest expanded. He leaned forward in his eagerness. "I said to her Majesty that fateful day that I am her loyal servant for life and will do whatever she needs."

"We will save the monarchy by placing Abagail in the sights of the rebels. She will be a distraction."

"Ah," he said, "a sacrificial lamb."

"Exactly," Lucia said. "And to do that we have to modify her history by eliminating all witnesses who could contradict the idea that Abagail was a queen in waiting. You are perfectly placed to drop a few words to the rebels regarding Abagail as the true heir to the throne and our agents will do the rest."

"Brilliant," Nugent said.

"Yes." Lucia smiled. He was back on board.

CHAPTER 64

James was exhausted from pushing through the crowd as he looked for Abagail. He was ready to give up. It seemed like every person living in the city was out in the streets celebrating. It was only yesterday when news of the capture of the queen became public knowledge. The queen was no longer in charge and many people thought that no queen meant no law, so they acted like children. Schools were closed and youngsters ran through the streets. Merchants abandoned their stores, apprentices their workshops, and civil servants poured out of the government buildings.

It was a people's holiday. James felt out of place in this frenzied celebration. All the work, all his dreams of a new world seemed hollow. He knew he should feel the joy that others felt but now that the victory he yearned for was real, James felt empty.

Two questions consumed him. Where was Abagail, and what was her decision—a life with him or with Margot? There were rumors that Princess Margot escaped to Spain during the confusion of the rebel's attack on the palace. Is that where Abagail was, on the road to Spain?

It was time to go home and see what Abagail had decided. James' slow gait home turned into a fast trot when he saw smoke coming out of the chimney. He pictured Abagail sitting in the kitchen. James burst through the front door, almost tripping over his own feet when he saw who sat at the kitchen table.

"Welcome home," Captain Nugent said with a big smile. "I hope you don't mind, I let myself in and made a cup of tea. Do you want a cup?"

"Uh," James said. "What are you doing here? I thought you were in the palace guarding the queen."

"I'm on a special assignment." Nugent sipped his tea,

looking as comfortable as if he was sitting in his own kitchen.

"A special assignment," James repeated, feeling a pit expand in his stomach.

"I am charged by a parliament committee to apprehend Abagail," Nugent continued.

James grabbed hold of a nearby chair back to steady himself. "Why? Why does parliament want Abagail?" he said in a shaky voice.

"Abagail is the true heir to the throne."

"No, that can't be. The queen threw her in prison."

Nugent jumped up, knocking over his chair. He bounded toward James until his face was so close James could almost taste his breath. "Where is Abagail, James?"

James took a step back. "You know it is a lie. It was Abagail's map that got you and your men into the palace." He saw doubt in Nugent's eyes. "I do not know where she is. You know that. I was with you when I went looking for her. What is really going on, Captain Nugent?"

"Abagail is wanted for questioning. It seems you haven't been told the whole story. She is next in line for the throne. I could tell by the way you walked in here that you expected her to be sitting here."

"Yes, when I saw the smoke from the chimney, I assumed it was Abagail. And the fact that she's not here should confirm that I do not know where she is. Now if you could please leave my house, Captain Nugent." James opened the door.

Nugent shook his head and strode toward the door. "I believe you, James, but I want your word; if Abagail contacts you, you will come to the proper authorities." The captain ran his fingers through his hair. "Think about it, James. The revolution is a sham if all we accomplish is substituting one monarch for another. Is that what we fought for?"

James didn't respond.

"James, did you hear what I said?"

"I heard, Captain," James responded as he shut the door.

He sat down heavily and let his head fall into his hands. Where was Abagail, and could it be true? Was she really the next in line to be queen?

CHAPTER 65

"Your Majesty, the plan is in the beginning phase, but the pieces are starting to fall in place." Lucia lowered her voice and looked behind her, although she knew they were alone in the queen's private room. "The first major news is that Captain Nugent has convinced the rebels that Abagail is the true heir to the crown."

"Have they found her?" the queen asked.

"Not yet," Lucia replied.

"That girl has a knack for not being found."

"Captain Nugent is pretty sure she will go to the ex-priest's house sooner or later."

"What ex-priest?"

"It seems Abagail was discovered by the ex-priest's sister and her husband when she was nearly dead from hunger. They nursed her back to health, and she has since moved into the ex-priest's home."

"What about the sister, what does she do?"

"The sister, her husband, and two children sell soap."

"Sell soap," the queen said loudly. "We have her. She is disobeying the king's edict limiting soap selling to the trade alliance only." The queen paused. "I am certain they could not pay the licensing fee to sell soap. There are still some loyal soldiers in the capitol?"

"Yes, Your Highness," Lucia replied.

"Have the soap-selling woman and her husband arrested and put the children in the royal orphanage. Do it quietly."

"If I could ask why, your Majesty?"

The queen raised her eyebrows, unaccustomed to explaining to her trusted aide the thinking that underlied her strategy. "Two reasons, Lucia—first, we must recreate Abagail's past as a queen in waiting. The priest's sister and her family knew her and could contradict our account. It's unlikely they would be believed but why take the chance. There is also leverage. We may need this ex-priest and his family to lure the elusive Abagail to London."

CHAPTER 66

It took all of Albert's courage to approach Princess Margot. He wanted to know why he was forbidden to return to England. Couldn't he better serve the crown and protect the queen there? Princess Margot didn't need him for protection. In Spain she was guarded by a platoon of soldiers befitting a princess and a queen-to-be. He practiced what he planned to say so many times he could recite it in his sleep. And now here he was, standing outside Princess Margot's chamber, waiting to be summoned. *Breathe and speak slowly*, he told himself.

"The princess will see you now," an attendant said. And just like that, he was in front of Princess Margot. He bowed long and low and when he looked up at Princess Margot, her husband, Prince Leon was sitting next to her.

The practiced words flew out of his head. Albert was sure that the prince was glaring at him. Of course, he didn't know Princess Margot and never remembered uttering a word to her, but by spending time with her on the journey to Spain he saw evidence of her kindness. The prince, on the other hand, he knew nothing about. He heard the rumors of his flashes of anger and general ill-temper. And there he was glowering at Albert as if he was guilty of some unimaginable crime.

The princess smiled.

The prince glared then cleared his throat. "*Si*," he said.

Albert looked at Princess Margot, his voice trapped deep in his throat. His mouth dry and tongue swollen, drops of sweat ran down his face. Talking at that moment was as foreign as flying.

"Yes, Albert, you wanted to see me," Princess Margot said, breaking the spell.

The princess knew his name; that fact brought his courage back. "Yes, your Majesty—majesties," he added quickly, not looking at the prince. "I ask for your permission to return to my country of birth." He cursed himself for speaking too quickly.

Princess Margot rested her chin on her hand and seemed to think about it.

During the time that passed, Albert rehearsed the rest of his speech.

The prince made a sound like, "humph."

"Yes, you can return to England and Godspeed to you," Princess Margot said.

Albert, surprised by the quick approval, didn't move until an attendant took his elbow and guided him out of the chamber.

While packing his few belongings, Albert heard a knock on his door. "The princess requests your presence."

Oh no, he thought, *the princess has changed her mind.*

To his great relief, the princess was alone. "There is something you can do that would be of great value to me."

"Yes, your Majesty," Albert replied.

Princess Margot handed him an envelope. "This is a crucial message for the queen. It is to be delivered to the queen or Lucia only. Nobody else. Do you understand?"

"Yes, your Majesty."

"If this letter falls into the wrong hands..." Princess Margot hesitated. "If this letter falls into the wrong hands it would be the end of my mother and the monarchy. By taking this letter you are agreeing to pledge your life on the receipt of it only by those two."

"I understand," Albert said. He immediately left the palace, riding his horse hard. He was going to see Lucia and couldn't wait.

When he arrived in England, it was not the country he had left. Peasants had taken over their lord's lands. Soldiers sauntered down the streets and their comrades stumbled out of taverns, looking for someone to fight. He galloped without stopping and reached the palace in two days. The land he once called home seemed foreign. At first, he couldn't gain entry to the palace. Then he thought to go by the back door leading to the cells. The man standing on guard remembered Albert from his days working with the prisoners. Once inside the prison, it was an easy path to the main staircase.

"What? You must be mistaken," Lucia said, looking up from a pile of papers on her desk when the attendant informed her of who had arrived.

"No, my lady, he is right outside your door, insisting he see you. He says he just returned from Spain."

Lucia looked at the attendant with astonishment not only at the message he conveyed but even more so at his disrespectful tone.

"Tell me your name," Lucia said in her most haughty manner.

"Joseph," he squeaked out.

"Joseph what? What is your family name?"

"Smith, my lady. Joseph Smith."

"Well, Joseph Smith, when you address one of your betters you do so in a respectful way. Do you understand?"

"Yes, my lady," the attendant said and started to walk out when he turned. "Do I show the gentleman in, my lady?"

"Show him in." Was that a smile on his face as he turned back towards the door? *When things get back to normal,* Lucia thought, *we are going to have a complete review of the palace staff.*

When the door opened, Lucia heard a familiar voice. "I know you wanted me to stay in Spain, but I have come to help you any way I can." Albert was confused by Lucia's silence. He took a step toward her, then stopped abruptly. "I have something for you," he said, but before he could finish Lucia jumped in.

"I did not believe it when I heard—but here you are," Lucia said.

"Yes, I..."

"Has everyone gone crazy?"

Albert was almost thrown off his feet by her voice. Her tone was so full of scorn. "What do you mean?"

"What do I mean, you thunderhead? You had orders not to return and to safeguard the princess in Spain and you disregarded those orders and come walking in here as if you are the hero of the moment."

"But your lady, Lucia, Princess Margot is perfectly safe in Spain. I just thought I could be of service here and..."

"You are not to think you are to obey, now leave. I have important work to do."

"Here," Albert said in a wavering voice, handing Lucia the letter from Princess Margot. *Great*, Lucia thought, *I have to keep him from being seen by Queen Henrietta*. Who knew what she would do if his presence in the palace became known. Her instructions were clear—no one should be able to challenge her story about Abagail being the heir to the crown. Lucia shuddered, imagining Albert locked away in some dungeon or worse.

CHAPTER 67

James never felt worse in his life. Everything he valued that gave his life meaning was now a source of confusion and pain. The success of the revolution he yearned for had left him hollow in a way he couldn't explain and his relationship with Abagail was in doubt. Nugent's story was improbable but was it any more fantastic than Abagail's? Now that he thought about it, being thrown into a cave, meeting her long-lost mother, escaping, and killing a guard all sounded too outlandish to be true. Was Abagail only with him so she could live safely tucked away from all this turmoil? But why the map that got them into the palace if she was really who Nugent said she was? And Nugent—who was he really? What had turned his friend into an enemy? Was he ever a friend? Everything was in doubt and the certainties of James' life melted away.

The more he thought, the more confused he became. James couldn't figure out what was real and what wasn't. The walls of the kitchen closed in on him. He went outside to clear his head. In the back of the house near the barn, he heard rustling in the bushes.

"Who's there?" He found a long stick and picked it up.

"It's me," a familiar voice replied.

James dropped the stick. Out walked Abagail.

"I was hoping with all my heart to see you again," James said. She looked as beautiful as ever. He was overcome with emotion. "I thought, I thought...." He faltered. "I thought I would never see you again. Oh, Abagail..." He started to walk towards her but stopped in his tracks. "What is the matter?" he asked.

Abagail stood absolutely still, her arms at her side. "I saw you at the march last night, but I couldn't reach you. I kept calling out your name but the crowds..."

"I know. I saw you too and called out to you. Why were

you hiding in the bushes?"

Abagail didn't meet James' eyes. "I came back to the house to be with you. I looked through the window and saw Captain Nugent sitting at the kitchen table. There were two soldiers on horses hiding out of sight by the barn. I made sure they did not see me. Something wasn't right about the whole scenario so rather than walk into a trap I hid in the bushes. Is my fear real or have I been running from people for so long that I am suspicious of everyone? What is going on, James?"

"I wish I knew," James said. "Nugent told me the most fantastic story." He glanced at Abagail. "He said that you are the heir to the throne, not Margot, and the rebels are searching for you."

"What?" Abagail felt the ground move under her. "That's crazy. I mean..." She stared at James. "You don't believe that, do you?"

James hesitated for a moment.

"Oh," Abagail said softly and sat down after feeling her legs start to buckle.

James sat next to her, putting his arm around her shoulder. "No, I don't believe it. But why would Nugent say that?" He felt Abagail stiffen.

"I don't know." Abagail felt a weariness that went right down to the marrow of her bones. Maybe it was time to give up. If James didn't believe her, where else could she turn?

Her mother sprang to life in her mind, speaking directly to Abagail. The message was clear and unambiguous. "*Never give up.*"

"Abagail, Abagail," James said, worried that she seemed so far away. He grasped her shoulder.

Abagail's eyes returned to focus. She turned to James and asserted, "You have a choice—either you believe me, or you believe Nugent. You decide, but I have to know now."

James' head was about to explode with two unthinkable thoughts, either the woman he loved was not who she said she was, or the revolution he believed in was riddled with falsehoods.

There was nothing else for her to say. Using her mother as her guide, Abagail put one foot in front of the other. Abagail was so sure of James' answer that she didn't hear him when he did make his feelings known.

CHAPTER 68

John Saunders was back in the queen's room. "Ma'am," he said, trying to be respectful without acknowledging her royalty.

Queen Henrietta sat up in her bed, propped up by pillows, managing to look regal and powerful even while reclining. "Yes, Mr. Saunders," the queen said with a faint smile.

Saunders had the strong impression that the queen knew what he was going to say before he said it. "The executive committee has decided to allow your statement to be read and recorded into the minutes of the trial." He watched her closely, curious to see her reaction.

Queen Henrietta flinched at the word *trial*, but quickly regained her composure. "Good," she said, pointing to the table where Saunders had left the statement the last time they spoke.

Saunders didn't move.

"Is there anything more?"

"Yes, ma'am; we are in pursuit of Princess Abagail."

Queen Henrietta immediately straightened up. "Have you found her?"

"Not yet, but we will."

The queen didn't say anything.

"She was reportedly hiding in a remote farmhouse."

"Yes?"

"So far she's managed to elude our efforts." Saunders hesitated.

The queen, noticing his hesitation, asked, "What?"

"Abagail was living in this farmhouse with a man, James Collier, an ex-priest."

"And?"

"They appear to be living together as husband and wife." Saunders cleared his throat. "Did you know of this arrangement?"

"Mr. Saunders, what are you implying? Princess Abagail was fleeing for her life—from you rebels, I might add. I am sure there is a reasonable explanation for this unusual living condition. This may shock you but given the extreme circumstances, Princess Abagail has my full support to do whatever she had to in order to survive."

"Ma'am," John Saunders said, stopping himself from bowing as he turned to leave.

"Don't forget my statement," the queen said, pointing to the envelope on the table. Saunders picked it up on his way out. *This queen is full of surprises,* he thought and, despite his politics, he admired her intelligence and courage.

CHAPTER 69

Maria and her family had been home nearly two weeks since they finished their last soap delivery. It was good to be home. Even the children welcomed their daily routines once they calmed down from the trip. Maria was in front of the house with a basket full of wet clothes when she saw them. "Frank, get the children," she shouted.

"What is it?" Frank said as he ran out of the house. Then he saw them. A squadron of soldiers, maybe twenty, maybe more, riding toward them at a fast clip. "Theresa, Jeffrey, come quickly."

Both children ran to their father. "Now you go hide in the woods. You know where."

"Why, poppa, why?" Jeffrey asked.

"Just do it," Frank said sharply. "Go with your sister and hide inside the big tree." Jeffrey started to cry. "Theresa, take your brother's hand. Go, now, and do not come out until we tell you, run, go." Frank watched as the two of them ran into the forest.

He walked over to his wife. "What do you think they want?" he asked.

"I don't know. But it's not good, Frank." Maria reached out to hold his hand. She could feel his hand tremble and was about to reassure him when she realized it was her hand shaking.

The horses stirred up a cloud of dust as they rode into the front yard. One of the soldiers, sporting an elaborate moustache—obviously the leader—brought his mount close to the couple. "Frank and Maria Eagleton, you are under arrest," he declared, his voice booming.

"Under arrest what for?" Maria demanded.

"You will be apprised of the charges soon enough. Where are your children?"

Maria and Frank froze.

The head soldier dismounted and walked right up to Maria. He was inches from her face. "Where are your children?" he shouted.

"You cannot talk to my wife like that," Frank said, grabbing the soldier by the arm. The entire squad jumped down from their horses. Two men grabbed Frank and roughly pinned his arms back.

"We are arresting you both and taking your children."

Jeffrey came running out of the woods. "Leave my daddy alone," he shouted, hitting the soldiers who held his father's arms.

"Grab him," the leader said, pointing at Jeffrey.

Theresa joined her brother, swinging at the soldiers.

"You better tell your brats to stop, or I will tie them up."

Maria felt her body seize up. She couldn't move. Talking was beyond her capability.

"All right, children, stop fighting," Frank said.

The soldiers tied the children's arms behind their backs.

"Ow, that hurts," Jeffrey said, trying to hold back tears.

"Don't worry, dear," Maria said. "This will all get worked out. Everything will be fine." Her family was being torn apart in front of her eyes. Maria remembered Abagail's stories of the cave. A shiver passed through her as if she was already there. *I should have known that the soap business would blow up at some point. As long as they don't find the religious literature. I pray they do not find it. That could be the gallows.* The children, Frank, her family, her life, and the earth started to spin.

"Mount," the head soldier said. Maria willed herself not to faint. Two soldiers hoisted Maria and Frank on two of the horses. The children were pulled up by a soldier and each placed in front of the rider.

It took all of Maria's control not to scream. It was scary enough for the children without their mother becoming hysterical. A thought came to her. Maybe it was not the soap. The soldiers hadn't searched the farm or mentioned a thing about illegal trade. What else could it be? As soon as Maria asked the question, the answer emerged clear as day—Abagail.

CHAPTER 70

"We cannot stay here," James said. "It is just a matter of time until Nugent and his men return."

Abagail was thinking the same thing. "Where can we go?"

"I know," James said. "Maria's; we will go to my sister's and figure out our next move. We have to be very careful. There are soldiers everywhere."

"Pack only what you need," James said, but then did something strange. He had a feeling he was leaving his house forever. So, in his bag he packed two books and, for a reason he couldn't explain, his priestly clothes.

"It will take two hours to walk there and we should travel at night."

As they walked, even in the dead of night the sky was a bright orange from the flames of burning houses. The landscape was empty, devoid of buildings, people and animals gone. Neither one spoke of it, but they seem to be walking towards the war. What would they find at Maria's house?

"Oh my God," James said when he saw the laundry scattered over the front yard. He ran into the house, calling his family's names. The odor of burnt food seeped into every corner. A pot of burnt stew with a skin of congealed fat sat over a dead fire.

Abagail followed close behind, suddenly realizing what happened. They both stood in the deserted little kitchen that should have been full of life and laughter.

"What now?" James asked, sinking heavily onto a wicker chair.

"Maybe if I go to the palace, they will let Maria and Frank go. They haven't done anything. It's me they want."

"No, that's impossible," James replied. "It is suicide."

"Do you have a better idea?" Abagail asked.

He didn't answer as his mind frantically searched for

alternatives and just as quickly dismissed them as impractical.

Abagail's mind returned to the cave. *Would I really go back there?* Her breath caught in her chest. She felt the room spin around her as her heartbeat swelled like crashing ocean waves, and had the sensation of looking down at herself from above. Her head seemed to be disconnected from her neck. Without warning, she found herself laying on the floor, the back of her head throbbing.

"What happened? How did I get here?" Abagail asked a blurry James standing over her.

"You fainted," he said.

"I'm all right," Abagail said, propping herself on her elbows and into a sitting position.

James grabbed her around the shoulders to help her up off the floor. They sat together at the kitchen table.

"I don't think we are in any shape to travel tonight," James said. "They may come back to look for us but not until tomorrow. We can stay here tonight and leave early in the morning."

"I am exhausted," Abagail said. She started to walk to the bedroom, then turned, walked back to James, and, leaning down, gave him a kiss on the cheek.

"I am going to stay up a little more," he said. As soon as he was alone, James touched his cheek. He tried to remember the days when it was just the two of them. The swimming, their talks, just spending their days doing everyday activities of life. It seemed like another lifetime. Now he might lose her forever.

Abagail was tired but sleep eluded her. She closed her eyes, but her mind had too much work to do to let her take a break. The longer she lay in bed, her certainty strengthened that turning herself in was the only workable solution. When James came to bed, Abagail didn't move. She couldn't let the family who saved her life, who showed her nothing but kindness, suffer because of her. James would not allow her to turn herself in. She had to do it alone. Why couldn't the world leave her alone? She remembered her mother saying, "The past defines who we are in the present." The past felt like a heavy metal chain weighing her life down.

James didn't move a muscle as Abagail got out of bed and tiptoed out of the bedroom. Slipping her sweater on, she gathered a jug of water, a piece of bread, and a slab of cheese before carefully opening the front door. Abagail patted her pocket, checking for her wooden spoon. She took a deep breath and began to walk to what she knew would be a return to hell.

CHAPTER 71

James woke up feeling her absence before he opened his eyes. There was no evidence of Abagail's existence. He ran out the front door in his bedclothes. "Abagail, Abagail, where are you?" Even as he called out her name, he knew it was fruitless. When he went inside and saw the water jug missing, that clinched it. Abagail was turning herself in. He was alone. First his sister's family was locked up, now Abagail. He felt like the last person alive in the world.

Maybe he should turn himself in and get locked up so he could join all the people he cared about. *That's crazy*, he told himself. *The only way I can help those I love is by remaining free. I have to do what I can.*

James remembered where his sister hid her money. He walked to the back of the house, found the big tree, and dug until his fingers touched a tin box. He lifted the box out of the dirt, took out all the coins, and put them in an inside jacket pocket.

It was a beautiful day as James started toward the capitol, but the warm sun and refreshing breeze did not register. He had no plan, no next move, and no hope. James walked the entire way without stopping. He nibbled on bread and cheese while on the move. The sun started to set when he reached the outskirts of the city. The streets were uncommonly empty. Even the major thoroughfares were deserted.

James found a tavern full of life, but before entering he extracted two coins from his pocket. A blast of loud voices, laughter, and music hit him as he walked through the door. He found an empty table.

"Ale please," he said to the waitress. When she brought him a jug, he gulped it down with one long swallow. He didn't realize until that moment how thirsty and hungry he was. He ordered another ale and a shepherd's pie. The tavern patrons were working folk—he guessed laborers and appren-tices. At the other side of the room, two men shouted at each other. A menacing looking character bellowed in a booming baritone, "They all should be hanged, the whole lot of them. What did any of them do for the working man, eh?"

"Don't they deserve a trial like anyone else?" the other, shorter, wiry man replied.

"Aye, they could have a trial just as long as it ends in hanging." The big man laughed and many of the onlookers joined in.

The shorter man waited for the laughter to end. "You always talk about equality and fairness. Now that we have the power, where is your precious fairness?"

"Thomas, I know you are one of us. We fought together the glorious night we took the queen. If I did not know better, I would think you were a royalist." The big man took a step towards the smaller one.

The little man didn't back down. "I am a rebel," he said, "and I am damn proud of it. What I'm saying is I did not risk my life to change one set of tyrants for another."

"Hear, hear," some patrons shouted in support, while others applauded.

"We are all equal before the law. All means all," the shorter man continued.

"What should we do if the queen and her daughter, Abagail, refuse to go on trial?" the big man asked.

James didn't wait for the other man's answer. He left the two coins on the table and walked out. Once outside, he went down a deserted alley. Once alone, he donned his priestly garb.

CHAPTER 72

James found the side door to the palace Abagail had indicated on her map. To his surprise, he walked right past a guard dressed like a working man who barely looked at him. James figured he went unchallenged due to his priestly disguise. Once inside, James followed the corridor to the stairs leading down to the cave. Abagail had described it so vividly it was like she was walking beside him. Two rebel guards sat on the floor playing a game of cards.

"I am here to see the prisoner," James said to the guards with more confidence than he felt.

"I was not told about any visitors, were you?" one guard asked the other.

"No, but what harm would it be?" the younger guard answered.

"Search him good," the first guard said.

"Sorry, Father," the guard apologized as he felt through James' clothes. "He's unarmed."

"All right, let him in. You have fifteen minutes, no more. Do you understand?"

"Yes," James said, entering a different world—Abagail's world. The stories Abagail told of the odor, the sound of water dripping, the feeling of being utterly alone in this alien world came back to him. Abagail told him that her mother was imprisoned down here for fifteen years. The thought of it made James shiver. He tried to picture the two of them wrestling with the guard and killing him. For a moment he forgot why he was there.

The cave seemed empty. He was ready to call out to the guard to let him out when a shadowy figure walked ever so slowly towards him. "Abagail?" he asked. No answer. He looked again "Maria?" James almost choked on her name.

Maria stared blankly at him as if she didn't know who he

was.

"James," he said softly. "It's James, your brother."

Maria fell into his arms. "Oh James, it really is you."

They hugged, holding each other up.

"The children," Maria said. "Where are they?"

James looked for a place to sit and together they sank to the cold, damp floor. His sister looked twenty years older. The light in her eyes was gone. He had to stop himself from staring and screaming.

"I don't know yet," he said.

Maria's hand went to her mouth and she let out a sob.

"I will find them. I promise," he said. "Tell me what happened. Did they say why you were arrested?"

"No one said a thing. I have no idea why." Maria looked around then whispered, "They didn't ask about the soap or..." her voice dropped, "the leaflets."

James didn't know whether he should tell Maria about Captain Nugent's claim that Abagail was the heir to the throne or her decision to turn herself in.

As if reading his mind, Maria said, "I think all this may have something to do with Abagail. Find the children and have them released to you."

The door creaked. "All right Father, it is time."

James whispered to his sister, "I promise I will find them."

CHAPTER 73

"Every crisis presents an opportunity if you know how to use it," Queen Henrietta said to her three confederates. "This is a perfect example." None of them knew what she was talking about, but Lucia was confident in the end it would all make sense.

The queen held up a sheet of paper. "This letter from my daughter is a plan to rescue me. I believe the plan was devised by her husband, Prince Leon." Albert smiled and glanced at Lucia, feeling proud he had carried the plan from Spain. "The plan is doomed to fail." Albert lowered his head.

The queen read the letter to them. "'A squad of Spanish soldiers dressed as English civilians will infiltrate the palace and whisk you away.'" She laughed. "We'd be lucky to make it outside my chambers alive and if by some miracle we did, imagine the reaction of my subjects when it was discovered Spaniards helped their queen escape. It would guarantee the end of the monarchy." She crumpled the letter into a tiny ball and tossed it to the floor.

"Now we don't have time to send messengers back and forth to devise a workable escape plan. The absurd trial is progressing, the verdict is already decided, so time is of the utmost importance. We will use Prince Leon's proposed plan with a slight modification. It won't be me the Spaniards rescue but a decoy, Princess Abagail. Whether she's caught or not is immaterial. If she dies in the escape attempt, or if by some miracle avoids capture, all eyes will be on her. We will plan my escape to coincide with hers."

Lucia looked at Albert and Nugent, who, if anything, seemed even more confused than she felt. "How will it happen?" Lucia asked for herself as well as the other two.

"Captain Nugent, being a military man, will act as liaison with the Spanish rescuers. We will coordinate the two escapes and he will verify that it is in fact Abagail going with the Spaniards. You and Albert will coordinate my escape. This will all take place at precisely the moment those loyal to the crown will counterattack and storm the palace." Queen Henrietta's color had returned to her face and her fevered eyes sparkled. "We will use the chaos to slip out of the palace and meet a small contingent of soldiers once we are outside. Then we ride to the coast to meet the ship to Spain."

"Brilliant, your Majesty," Nugent said. "You have the mind of a battle-tested military man."

"Thank you," Queen Henrietta said sarcastically, her lips curling. "I have received word that the attack by loyalists will take place tomorrow night."

Lucia gasped.

Queen Henrietta sharply eyed Lucia. "Another positive factor is the perception I am too weak to escape. Saunders, the parliament's messenger boy, seems convinced I am on death's doorstep. I will be the last person he'd imagine escap-ing. But even with all these factors in play, this is a risky strategy. I am open to hearing alternate plans."

Queen Henrietta looked at her three confederates. No one said a word.

CHAPTER 74

James promised Maria that he would find Theresa and Jeffrey, but in truth he didn't have a clue how to begin. Every idea seemed likely to reveal his deception. His mind raced. *Why not try the most straightforward way?* he thought.

"Thank you very much for allowing me to visit the prisoner," he said to the young guard.

The guard bowed slightly and crossed himself. "It was my duty to assist you in your good work."

James saw his chance. "I was wondering if you could tell me where the woman's children are being held?"

The guard looked around and whispered, "They are staying in the Royal Orphanage. We rebels aren't the heartless heretics we are accused of being."

"I can see you are a good Christian, my son," James said in his most clerical tone. He decided to go for it. "And pray," he continued, "do you happen to know where Princess Aba-gail is residing?"

"What are you going to do, Father—minister to all of them, or try to help them escape?"

I've done it now, James thought. *I went too far.*

"I am kidding, Father," the guard chuckled.

James joined in the merriment. "Very funny, my son, helping them escape."

The guard stopped laughing and looked at James intently.

James tried to look pious and calm. "Thank you again for your kind assistance. May God bless you." He turned away.

"Father," the guard said.

James pretended not to hear and kept walking. He felt a tug on his cassock. He turned, not sure what to expect.

"Father," the guard said. "Do you want to know where Princess Abagail is?"

"Yes," James said, his heart pounding with excitement.

"She's on the top floor of the palace in the rear chamber." The guard beamed as he waited.

James put his hand on the man's head and, looking closely, saw the face of a boy, sixteen or seventeen at most. James felt bad for a moment for tricking this lad who so obviously wanted approval from an authority figure. "God bless you, my child," he said and walked away.

CHAPTER 75

The following evening, the Duke sat high on his horse, surveying his army. Banners flapping in the breeze and hundreds of foot soldiers in military formation was quite a sight, but even more impressive were the horsemen who represented the best of the best. The Duke had known a good percentage of them since they were young boys. They were the landed gentry of his county, the best of England.

He ruled his part of the country as he imagined the monarch ruled the entire land, firm but fair. He was born to rule. That was the natural order of the universe. The gentry followed his lead and, of course, his peasants did as well, willingly. They didn't want the turmoil and uncertainty of a revolution of apprentices and shopkeepers.

When he raised his sword, he felt the weight of his position, the admiration of his soldiers, his family pride, and God's blessing. Fortified by the absolute belief in the righteousness of his cause, he could not imagine anything but total victory for his army and glory for himself. He recalled his speech to his officers, all fellow aristocrats, before the night sky gave way to the rising morning sun.

"We go today to defeat those rebels who hold our sovereign hostage. Who, if given the chance, would take our land, appropriate our worldly possessions, and ravage our wives and daughters. They would destroy our holy church and bring our fair and beautiful country to ruin. We fight today to restore the natural order of things, between men and men, and between men and the almighty. We fight for God, England, and the crown. You are the last remaining bulwark of civilization. Let us inflict severe punishment on these cowardly dogs. Let them feel the deadly steel of our swords. Onward for the king, for England, for God."

The Duke, heart full of dreams of glory and fueled by his

own inspiring words, unsheathed his sword, held it up high, and yelled, "Forward to victory!"

Three hundred horsemen followed by one thousand infantrymen thundered toward the city. The Duke felt invincible. They galloped right up to the outer wall surrounding London. Not one arrow was shot, nor one rebel encountered. The royalist army rode unopposed to the heart of the city where the wide boulevards gave way to narrow streets that seemed to run haphazardly. Some streets led to dead ends while others switched back onto themselves in circles. The soldiers split up into smaller groups, following the narrow streets, looking for the invisible enemy. The further into the city they rode without meeting their adversary, the more confident the Duke felt. He imagined the sight of his army so intimidated the rebels that they all ran back to their taverns and shops.

Was this talk of a rebellion a hoax? The Duke turned in his saddle and asked his aide-de-camp, "Where are they?" The answer came as a hail of arrows fell upon the mounted horsemen. The aide-de-camp, along with dozens of others, was struck by arrows and fell to the ground. The soldiers desperately looked around but could not see any archers.

"Where are those arrows coming from?" the Duke yelled at one of his generals. The men didn't know what to do. How can you fight an enemy you can't see? As their comrades fell to their death all around them, the Duke's men panicked. Horses without riders ran into each other, adding to the general chaos. The same horses that hours earlier symbolized the army's superiority became a hindrance, too big for the narrow streets. The still-mounted horsemen were trapped by their fallen comrade's steeds and became stationary targets for the rebel archers. It seemed like the very houses of the city leaned in to tighten the noose on the Royalist army.

The arrows sailing through the air like flocks of birds kept up their deadly volley.

"Sir," a general yelled. "We must leave this area and regroup."

The Duke glared at the general. "We will never retreat."

"Not a retreat. We have to regroup and fight as a single army. We are getting picked off and..."

"You are talking treason, General. I will have none of it. Do you hear?"

"Look around you, sir, in a short time you will not have an army."

The Duke saw the bodies of his men, lying dead and dying on the ground, pierced with arrows. The horses, his pride, running aimlessly in circles. "All right general, sound the retreat."

As the troops rode, ran, and limped out of the city, they were attacked by the city's defenders. Every street had a series of obstacles blocking the way out. The rebels had built barricades behind the troops as they entered the city. Their way out was blocked. Soldiers had to dismount their horses and dismantle the hastily made barricades while under constant attack by deadly arrows.

The army that finally amassed on the outskirts of the city was not the same force of a few hours before. The Duke, unhurt but badly shaken, sent his officers to assess the losses. Their report was devastating. The casualty rate was horrendous, especially among the horsemen. One-quarter of all the officers were killed or severely wounded and no one knew how many of his foot soldiers were still alive, trapped in the narrow city streets.

The Duke did not know what to do. His desire to avenge the cowardly tactics of the enemy was curtailed by the knowledge that another defeat may be the end of his army. He met with his senior officers and in his most commanding voice said, "We will coordinate our attack on the rebels with other forces loyal to the crown. Gentlemen, do not be disheartened. We will return. Justice will prevail."

The officers applauded their leader's words, grateful to be alive and going home.

CHAPTER 76

Abagail heard men shouting and people running in the corridor outside her room. She smelled smoke and tried to open the door, but it didn't budge. It was locked from the outside. She banged on the door with both fists until her wrists became weak. She brought her arms down just when the lock turned. Abagail felt for her wooden spoon, running her thumb across the sharpest part. *I will not be taken to the cave without a fight, she thought. I am a woman now and if I die, I die fighting.*

The door flew open and a dozen men not in uniform stormed into the room.

Her mind went back to the last time men stormed her bedroom and dragged her down to the cave. This time Abagail was not bound and gagged. She would fight.

One of the men bowed deeply and said, "Your Majesty, we are here to rescue you."

"Who are you?" Abagail asked, "And where are you planning on taking me? I am not going with you until you tell me where you are taking me."

"Your Majesty, we are taking you to safety," the head man explained.

"Where is that?"

"We are to accompany you to a ship for your safety. Please come with us." The man held out his hand.

"I will not."

"You are in great danger here. Can you hear the sounds of battle and smell the smoke of the fires?"

Abagail crossed her arms and shook her head.

"You leave me no choice. My orders are to take you away any way I have to. We do not have time to argue. Are you coming peacefully, or do we have to carry you out?"

Abagail didn't know what to say.

"The two of you, put her on a horse. Tie her hands if she fights you."

"All right, I will go with you. Get those men away from me."

In a daze, Abagail followed the men down the smoke-filled hallway to the staircase leading to the hidden door. Outside, the courtyard was empty, but the sounds of battle raged nearby. It was chaos—smoke hung in the air, men screamed, and horses cried out in pain.

A soldier held out his hand to help Abagail mount an awaiting horse. There was something familiar about his mustache; it was Captain Nugent. Before she had a chance to ask him what was going on, the horseback rescue party escorted her away.

CHAPTER 77

"Are you ready, your Majesty? It is time." Lucia put a plain black cloak over the queen's head and, walking slowly, entered the hallway. The queen was bent over, her breathing labored.

The hallways were full of people running in all directions. Albert met them at a door leading to a staircase that led to a palace exit. Once outside, Albert brought a horse to the queen. Queen Henrietta summoned all her strength and will but could not mount the horse herself. Albert looked at Lucia, who nodded, and picked the queen up and placed her in the saddle. He was amazed by how little she weighed. For a brief moment he saw her eyes open wide, but the look was quickly replaced by her usual aloof gaze.

Queen Henrietta sighed, almost whispering, "We better be going." When the horse moved, she shifted to the side of her saddle.

"I think a carriage may be more suitable, your Majesty," Lucia called as she caught up to the horse and took the reins.

"You are right, I am too visible out in the open. A carriage will be better," the queen said.

"I will be right back," Albert said, finally feeling useful. He ran to the palace stables and found the perfect coach—one with no royal crest or any other sign of the crown.

"I will stay inside and ride with her majesty," Lucia said.

Albert took hold of the reins and, ten minutes later, the carriage with its royal passenger was speeding to the coast and the waiting Spanish ship.

"Stop the carriage," Lucia yelled to Albert from inside the carriage.

"Whoa, whoa," he called to the horses pulling back on the reins. Lucia held her mistress, who was pale and shivering.

"Water, please I need some water," the queen said softly as if it took all her strength to speak.

"Yes, your Majesty," Lucia said. Albert looked in on them. "The queen is very weak, Albert. She needs water."

"We left the provisions in the saddlebags when we took the carriage," Albert said.

"We must do something," Lucia said, trembling as she cradled the queen. "It's like she is..." She couldn't finish the sentence.

"I'll find some water somewhere. I'll be back," Albert said, sprinting away from the carriage.

The queen let out a deep sigh. "I want to write a letter to Margot before I pass from this world."

"But your Majesty, your time is not up."

The queen waved her hand. "Do you have paper and ink?"

"Yes, your Majesty."

"Write this word for word."

My dearest daughter,

I am puzzled by your hostility toward me the last time we spoke. I assume it is because of your unhappiness about the course your life has taken. I understand and wish I could change it for you, but it is out of my hands. All I can say is do the best you can with what life gives you. Know that you were loved by both your parents. I cannot wish you any more than to be happy in the fulfillment of your duties as wife, mother, and sovereign of your country of birth. I will never know my grandchildren but remember me and tell them stories about the happy times at court. I will see you in God's kingdom.

Your loving mother,
Queen Henrietta

"Where is the water?" were the last words Queen Henrietta uttered.

Albert burst into the carriage. "I have the water..." He stopped. The queen lay very still, her head on Lucia's lap. Lucia gazed down at her pale face as if under a spell. Her eyes seemed to focus on a point beyond this world. She jumped, startled by Albert's sudden return. She stared at him as if not recognizing who he was. Lucia laid the queen's head gently on a pillow, then sprang through the carriage door and pounced on Albert. She threw wild punches with both hands, screaming, "Where were you? What took you so long? You killed her. You never brought the water."

Albert let the first few punches land but soon grabbed her arms and pinned them back.

Lucia flailed, trying to free herself from his grip, but eventually stopped. Her arms went slack. Albert let her go. Lucia crumpled to the dusty ground and let out a terrible wail that chilled Albert's blood. It reminded him of the sound his wife made when he told her about their son's death. He did with Lucia what he couldn't do with his wife. He took her in his arms and hugged her as she leaned heavily into him.

CHAPTER 78

James headed toward where he guessed the rear chamber of the palace was. The Duke's army and the rebels were fighting just outside. Soldiers, servants, and court attendants ran in all directions. He grabbed a servant by the collar and shouted, "Where are the queen and princess?" The man gave James a dumbfounded stare, his eyes darting from side to side, looking close to passing out. James released him. The man slumped against the hallway wall and slid to the floor.

A group of rebel soldiers ran down the corridor. "The queen has escaped," one of them called out. Another soldier said, "The princess, too." James followed them outside to the courtyard. Swords and arrows covered the ground. Men screamed in pain and others quietly moaned. Corpses lay in grotesque poses, sprawled out in impossible positions, while others seemed to be sleeping peacefully.

"Where is the princess?" James asked the first soldier he met.

"They're gone," the soldier said.

"How do you know?" James asked.

The soldier stared at him, unable to speak.

"Where?" James raised his voice.

"I don't know, Father."

James fell to his knees. He was finished, empty—what was there to live for? Abagail, his love, was out of his life, gone. She came into his life as if from another world and now she had vanished like she never existed.

James felt a tap on his shoulder.

"Father, Father."

James picked his head up to see a soldier with a blood-soaked rag on his head. "Father," the man repeated. "We need you." He hesitated. "We need you to minister to the dead and wounded."

"I cannot," James said haltingly.

"You must," the soldier insisted. "We need you."

"You do not understand—I cannot."

As they were talking, wounded soldiers from all around saw James—a priest, to them—and slowly crawled towards him. The crowd of soldiers around him grew as dozens turned into hundreds, some of them limping, others dragging their broken bodies. Those who couldn't walk were carried by their comrades.

James, stricken by the sight of the carnage, looked down. The courtyard was full of soldiers following his lead. They stood perfectly still with bowed heads.

"Father, please," the soldier said again.

James looked into the soldier's pleading eyes, seeing a reflection of the desperation he felt. He opened his mouth to speak, to say something, anything to ease their pain. *What could I possibly say? I'm not even a priest.* Then something extraordinary happened. He started to speak, and his words formed sentences.

"I look out among you all and see the living and the dead. I see the soldiers of the rebellion and those who support the monarchy. I see the mighty lords of the land, the shop keepers, the apprentices, and peasants, and I know in my heart of hearts that all those differences are meaningless. I don't know if there is a god, but whether he exists or not I do know that we are all brothers. A lord and a peasant, we are all born the same in blood and pain, loved by our mother, and as we can see, all men regardless of their station in life die the same way, with blood and pain. Who gives these men love? Some may say God. I really don't know." He shrugged his shoulders.

James' speech was met with absolute silence. His gaze took in the throngs of soldiers looking up at him. Then he realized they were waiting for a miracle, an answer, and they wanted him to provide it. He felt their need for comfort and solace. Embarrassed by his poor attempt at a speech, James wanted nothing more than to leave and find Abagail.

Two soldiers standing next to him dropped to their knees. He didn't know what to do. He placed his hands on their heads. The soldiers who listened to his speech formed a long line and one by one knelt in front of James, who placed his hand on their heads. The soldiers bowed their heads and said a prayer. The line of wounded soldiers snaked around the corner. More soldiers joined the slowly moving line.

James touched each soldier. He felt transformed by the experience. The belief that these desperate men had in him did not inflate his sense of self. Just the opposite; he was humbled. It wasn't God working through him but something greater that touched him as he comforted the wounded.

CHAPTER 79

"Margot, please sit. You will wear yourself out," Prince Leon said, smiling. He put his arm protectively around his wife. "I hear from my sources that your mother's escape was successful and even your childhood friend, Abagail, is safe and en route to you. You should be pleased." He put his hand under his wife's chin, raising her head. He kissed her on her forehead and she dutifully kissed him on the cheek.

"I am pleased, my husband," Margot said. "I am very pleased, and deeply appreciate your efforts on my behalf."

The prince was puzzled by his wife's formality. Her tone had changed since returning from England, increasing the distance between the two of them. It felt like his wife was exerting some new kind of power, but he couldn't quite put his finger on it.

Margot had changed. After trying so hard to be the perfect mate, she decided to be more aloof; to not try so hard to make the marriage work. This change led to her feeling less angry and more in control. One of the unexpected reactions to Margot's retreat was more attentiveness and affection from her husband. The previous night, for the first time, she outright rejected his sexual advances, claiming an upset stomach. He pouted but eventually left her room unsatisfied.

Margot laid in bed, enjoying her newly discovered power over her husband. And there was a major secret that gave her a sense of power in the marriage. Margot was waiting for her mother to join her at court before she announced her pregnancy. The court doctor assured her it was a boy, a male heir. Margot had the court doctor swear to secrecy, but it didn't take long for her secret to reach the prince.

Prince Leon played along as if he didn't know. He respected his wife's decision to keep the pregnancy to herself. In the past he would have been furious at her for keeping this secret, but the prince had also changed. The prospect of being a father changed him. He vowed to give up his selfish behavior. No more drunken nights of pleasure. It was time to take on the responsibility of parenthood and the duties of his office.

CHAPTER 80

What James witnessed in the palace courtyard was repeated throughout the city. Soldiers with horrible wounds, crushed limbs, writhing in pain, crying out for help, pleading for water, moaning, and dying like slaughtered animals in the street.

James wandered the city, trying to ignore the mayhem. His clerical clothes attracted attention and he was repeatedly asked to comfort those in pain. Everywhere he went people were desperate to talk, asking for forgiveness or for James to say a prayer for their dead or wounded relatives. He tried to refuse at first, but the people he met were so desperate that he gave up resisting their entreaties. It took a small amount of effort on his part to bring the wounded and their loved ones some comfort.

He heard all the rumors swirling around about the queen. Some said she was seen leading a royal army heading to storm the city. Another report insisted she was living in Spain and planning an invasion with Spanish troops; others were certain she was already dead, killed by the rebels.

The speculation of the queen's fate was matched by the silence about Abagail. James wandered the streets searching for her, but it was as if Abagail had disappeared. He couldn't bear the endless presence of death. Two days of caring for the wounded and the cruel effects of the battle wore him down. He was losing himself in the role of the comforting priest. He had to escape the pain and misery in the city. He told himself he was still looking for Abagail, but in truth he was fleeing from the carnage and destruction of the city. But however deep into the forest he went, he could not escape the images of men dying, limbs hanging unnaturally, and blood, everywhere blood.

James walked for days. When he couldn't find an

abandoned hut or barn for the night, he slept in caves or right on the ground. The images of the dead and dying continued but not as vividly. For the first time since the slaughter of the Duke's army, James wasn't startled awake by a nightmare.

James walked into a town that looked like every other town he'd seen in his travels. Cows and chickens ambled down the main street. A child ran up to him. "You are the wandering priest, Father James," the boy said loudly. People started to gather around him. They all wanted to see this thin man of God. With his sunken eyes and hollowed cheeks, James seemed to embody the pain of the people. Villagers touched him, kissed his hand, and murmured, "Bless you, Father, God bless you."

A big-bellied man with an enormous moustache walked through the crowd to stand right in front of James and stuck out his hand. "We have been waiting for you," he said in a booming voice. He looked around as the crowd of people grew and held out his arms as if he had conjured up this priest.

"Waiting for me?" James quietly asked.

"Welcome to our humble village, Father. We're honored."

"I think you are confused. I am not..."

"Your modesty and humility are well known," the big man said as he scanned the crowd. "I should say we know by your Christian..."

"Stop talking, will you?" someone shouted from the crowd and half of the people laughed hardily while the rest covered their mouths.

"Let the priest say something."

"If it would not be asking for too much," James hesitated.

The crowd was absolutely quiet.

"Yes," the big-bellied man said.

"Well, you see, I haven't eaten in two days, and if it's not too much..."

The man loudly said, "Why of course, how rude of us."

And that is how it began. Details changed from town to

town, but the general pattern was the same. James would enter a town, word would spread of his arrival, and the population would gather to meet the wandering priest. The people fed him and provided a modest place to sleep. James would minister. The days rolled into weeks and James, wandering from town to town, became Father James, or just Father as he was most often called.

Word spread of the wandering priest who provided comfort to a confused, fearful, and mourning peasantry. The fact that he wasn't connected to any church actually bestowed more credibility on James. Puritans viewed him as one of theirs, as did the followers of the Church of England, and even Catholics welcomed him to their homes.

Then one morning without warning, the village people would wake up to find their wandering priest gone. They were puzzled but felt lucky to have him as long as they did. They understood his disappearance; he had the whole country—nay, the whole world—to serve.

CHAPTER 81

Lucia's breathing finally slowed and became rhythmic. Albert ever so carefully laid her head on the floor of the carriage. Her eyes didn't open, and he knew she was asleep. He leaned his head against the side of the carriage, certain he wouldn't sleep, but he must have, for when he opened his eyes the sky was light. He stretched and tried to stand up, hitting his head on the carriage roof. Lucia looked peaceful, but Albert, remembering last night, knew her peace was going to be short-lived.

"I thought it was a terrible dream, but it wasn't, was it?" Lucia said with her eyes still closed.

"No, it wasn't," Albert answered.

"The queen, where is she?"

Albert nodded his head toward the back of the coach.

"Oh my god," Lucia said quietly, putting her hand to her mouth. "What do we do now?"

"Do we take her to Spain or bury her here?" Albert asked.

Lucia quietly considered the two options. "I am afraid what the rebels would do to her if they had her body. We must bury her. Yes, bury her here. That way no one can ever find her." Lucia reached into her skirt and pulled out a bag full of coins. "Can you find a coffin maker and a shovel? I'll wait here with her Majesty."

Albert took the coins and left without saying a word.

Lucia sobbed when Albert left. "My queen, my queen," she moaned. As she sat near her mistress, Lucia's mind roamed over the years she served the queen. *The queen, feared by most, was well known to me*, Lucia thought. *No, she was not perfect, and could be cold and calculating, but was never mean for the sake of being mean. The queen was someone who believed in duty and obligation and lived her life that way right to the very end.*

Queen Henrietta had one more message from beyond the grave for Lucia to deliver. It was her duty to carry out her final obligation and she would deliver her last letter to Princess Margot, whatever the cost. Lucia heard Albert riding up and knew what had to be done.

Albert was breathing hard. "I bought a shovel and found a coffin maker. The man's son is bringing it in his carriage. Here he comes. What do we tell him?"

Lucia looked at this big, sweet man and couldn't imagine her life without him.

Albert waited for her response, taking the faraway look on her face as her reaction to the queen's death. "Lucia," he said. "What do we tell him?"

"Just that my mother died unexpectedly." She choked on the words and had to brace herself so as not to fall.

Albert grabbed her by the elbow and embraced her. "Lucia I..." He was about to declare his love for her when the carriage carrying the coffin appeared. The coffin maker's son had the look of a professional mourner even at his young age. "I am sorry for your loss," the boy said as a matter of professional courtesy as he dismounted from the driver's seat. In a respectful tone full of concern he asked, "Where should I put the coffin?"

"Right here next to the carriage," Lucia said.

When the boy left, Lucia pointed to a rise with a large oak tree and said, "I think that would be a good spot for her, don't you?" And the Queen of England was buried in a simple, unadorned plot in the middle of the forest.

Albert and Lucia were wrung dry by the physical effort of digging the grave and the enormity of what they had witnessed—the death of a queen. Albert, though exhausted, couldn't rest until he asked the question plaguing him; "What happens now, Lucia?"

"What do you mean?"

"With us?" Albert asked quietly.

"I will return to Spain and serve Margot." Lucia stopped. "And you, what will you do?"

"What do you want me to do?" Albert asked.

"That is for you to decide," Lucia answered.

He shuddered as he thought, *I cannot take that boat ride again, but what about Lucia?*

CHAPTER 82

Abagail vowed that no one would ever control her life again. Yet here she was, once again snatched by force, torn from her life. Abagail was a different person now than when she was dragged down into the cave the first time. She reminded herself that if she could escape the cave, she would find a way out of this. She needed to wait, watch, and when it was time to act, be decisive.

The men rode hard the first day and Abagail remained totally silent. They didn't know what to make of her. They had the court's guarantee of protection. Was she a prisoner they captured or a victim they rescued? They interpreted her silence as passivity, which was fine with her.

She remembered what her mother had said when planning their escape. "They could not imagine an old woman and a young girl would even try to escape." Surprise was her secret weapon. While Abagail slept the first night, she dreamed of killing her captors rather than being upset. She wanted to hold on to her rage as fuel. *Watch and wait—you'll know when it's time to act,* she told herself.

The second night, Abagail listened as the two soldiers guarding her tent talked softly. She rested her ear on the flap of the tent.

"Tomorrow we're free of this, whatever this is," one soldier said.

The other soldier laughed. "I will be damned if I know what we are doing, kidnapping some girl."

"This is not soldiering—I feel like a bandit. But tomorrow we ride to Portsmouth and load her on the ship to Spain and our part will be done."

Spain, the country ruled by Margot. Abagail felt sick to her stomach. She was not going to be a part of another royal court to serve at the pleasure of the princess after all she had been through. No.

Tonight was the time to escape. Once on the ship, there would be no way out. It had to be tonight. Abagail willed herself to stay awake and listened as the voices of the two soldiers became softer, then waited until it was quiet. Rising carefully from her bed, Abagail simply left the tent and walked away. She kept walking until the sun appeared. She slept in the hollow of a very large tree and woke herself after a few hours to put more distance between her and her captors.

Abagail hiked to a small hill, surveying what direction to take, when she saw hundreds of peasants walking in a large field.

It was as if an entire town had grown legs and began to walk. A seemingly endless line of people stretched to the horizon, carrying all their possessions in overloaded wagons. The wagons moved slowly, sagging from the weight of a lifetime. There were piles of bedding, rocking chairs, tables, and farm tools. Pots and pans hung off the sides, clanging and banging as the wagons rode over bumps and ruts in the road. Children tried to find a place to sit on the impossibly loaded wagons, squeezed in between the family's pitiable keepsakes and grandmas too old to walk. Chickens and even pigs— potential meals—were given prized spots. Several cows walked alongside the wagons, often led by a child.

It was a town on the move. The country was at war. Not with another country, but a more deadly war—at war with itself, a civil war. Like their ancestors, the peasants were mostly ignorant of the grand causes of the war, whether the issue was king versus parliament, the people versus the aristocracy, or which god you believed in. It made no difference to these people who had the misfortune to live on land that became the waystation to roving armies. Their only goal was to survive and that meant they had to move. They marched with no destination. They marched to stay alive.

Abagail joined the long line of stragglers as they made

their sad way across fields and through forests. She did not look directly at any of the others, especially avoiding the eyes of the few men. Most people were too involved in their own personal tragedies to notice one more

dirty, bedraggled woman joining the pitiable procession. They all walked with their heads down.

Several times, groups of soldiers on horseback passed the ragged caravan but, sensing there was nothing worth stealing, they rode on and took no notice. The long line of refugees became part of the background like the hills and the trees.

Abagail didn't know where she was going or what her plan was. The first and most important thing was to avoid capture. Her immediate plan was to hide among people, become just another refugee woman whose husband had gone off to war.

The caravan stopped as if it had a mind of its own. Abagail stopped with everyone else. It was only then, when the exhaustion hit her, that she wondered where her next meal would be coming from. Then something strange happened. There weren't different campfires, only one huge fire, everyone busy doing something to prepare the meal. Even the youngest children ran back and forth to the fire with armfuls of wood. One group of women prepared vegetables—peeled carrots, washed potatoes, sliced onions—and others washed plates and forks and put them on a large wooden table. No one seemed to be in charge. There must have been a dozen people involved in the preparation of the meal. Abagail couldn't believe these were the same people who walked so dejectedly. Now they resembled an efficient army, everyone dutifully doing their tasks.

The contents in the two huge pots started to boil and the aroma of the food drew Abagail to the fire. She stood transfixed, not just by the presence of food but also by the calm and efficiency of how the whole meal proceeded. With-out any announcement, two orderly lines formed. People walked past a table where they picked a large piece of bread and an empty bowl. Three women stood at each large pot. One took the bowls and held them out for another to serve the soup while another handed the full bowl to the waiting person. Two women made sure there was bread for everyone. It all happened without any conflict or even discussion. Aba-gail had never seen anything like it.

A woman walked over to Abagail. "Would you like to join us?"

Abagail stared, dumbstruck. The woman's blue eyes sparkled and her warm smile reassured Abagail.

The woman asked again. "Would you like to have supper?"

"Yes, very much," Abagail said.

The woman took Abagail's hand and led her to the stack of bowls. Abagail joined the line and handed her bowl to a woman dishing out the stew. "Welcome," the woman said to Abagail. Abagail was touched by the very simple, human gesture.

"Thank you very much. This is very kind of you."

Another woman gave her a piece of bread. She looked for a place to sit when the woman who first approached her waved her over. "Come, sit down," she said, scooting over to make room. "My name is Naomi."

With the warm bowl in her hand, Abagail remembered the bowls of gruel she ate with her mother, and then the image of her mother lying dead on the cave floor came flooding back. Her body trembled and tears came to her eyes. At first ashamed, Abagail tried to hide her tears—but if anyone noticed, they didn't say anything. The food and the warmth of the fire relaxed her. But it was the kindness of the people that touched something deep inside her. Taking a deep breath, Abagail felt herself let go. She realized she had been running and hiding for what seemed like her whole life. Maybe, just maybe, she could learn from these people how to live a happier life.

Abagail looked around the fire at the people eating and

talking quietly. The light of the flames softened their faces, making them look angelic. The children, their bellies full, started to laugh and play. They reminded Abagail of Theresa and Jeffrey. Someone took her empty bowl and spoon and a group of women walked to a nearby creek to wash them. Abagail stood up to follow, determined to do her part, but Naomi placed her hand on Abagail's shoulder. "This is your first meal with us. You do not have to contribute tonight. Tomorrow we can talk about you getting involved with the community. What is your name?" she asked as she gathered some empty bowls.

Abagail started to say her name and then stopped. *Should I give my real name?* She didn't know if those soldiers would be looking for her. "My name is Anna."

"Rest well, Anna."

After eating, Abagail's lack of sleep caught up with her. She found a spot without too many rocks and curled up, not sure if sleep would come to her. The word *community* was her comforting companion. Tomorrow she would find out more about this community and, accompanied by that reas-suring word, she fell into a deep, restful sleep.

CHAPTER 83

"Gentlemen, this is how history turns into myth and myth is transformed into truth." John Saunders wanted his opening remarks to parliament to get his audience's attention, and it seemed he had. For once, they were not shouting at each other but were quietly listening. *All right, John,* he said to himself, *speak slowly and make it short and to the point.*

"Queen Henrietta is more powerful since she has disappeared than when she was on the throne. She is the most powerful adversary of our movement. Her sway over the people of this country is significant and every day that the queen eludes us, her reputation and power increase." He felt himself speeding up as the torrent of his thoughts propelled his speech. "The triumph of the people's will over monarchial tyranny is in doubt as long as the queen's fate is unknown. The hunt for her is on. No one knows her location or even if she is still alive."

The assembled members of parliament shouted their reactions, "Hear, hear. Yes, it's true. Something must be done."

Saunders took a deep breath, then continued. "Rumors abound. It is said she is in hiding, conspiring with noblemen to storm the capital, reclaim the throne, and kill all of us. Others say she is in Spain amassing an army to invade England. Still others swear the queen has reunited with her long-lost king and the death of the two monarchs was all an elaborate hoax. Even more fantastic, it is rumored they have both come back from the dead."

"Nobody here is arguing with you, sir," Oliver Cromwell said, standing. "What can we do to counter these ridiculous rumors? It is gossip. Why should we spend our time contesting it?"

"We must put an end to this royalist campaign to keep her

image alive," Saunders replied. He knew that Cromwell was not just questioning him about this specific issue but was using the opportunity to challenge his authority in parliament.

"Yes, yes, we all know that," Cromwell stated, "but sir, we are past the point of diagnosing the problem. We are at the point of formulating a plan of action to eradicate the problem."

"We must make our case in a public arena that will get the public's attention and how we do that..." Here John Saunders hesitated.

"How we do that, sir," Cromwell said with a sneer, "is to fulfill our promises to the people, defeat the royalist army, and set about making a new society."

"That is well and good but first we have to assure the public that the queen or any other aristocrat will not return from exile or the dead to reinstate the monarchy."

"And how do you propose to do that, sir?" Cromwell inquired.

"We try her in absentia," Saunders replied angrily.

The members of parliament were initially stunned into silence, but soon the murmuring began. "How can that be? Is it possible?" Cromwell asked. "Do we call witnesses from the great beyond?" Laughter echoed throughout the hall. "What you are suggesting is blasphemy."

"Yes, it is possible, to try the queen without her presence," a voice from the back benches rang out. Everyone looked to see a thin man with large Adam's apple stand up and, in a strong voice, say, "It is not only possible, it is brilliant." He continued when he saw he had parliament's attention. "We put the queen on trial as a way to make the case this is the end of the monarch's destructive rule and publicly expose the folly of all monarchs." Some members started to applaud.

Cromwell interrupted the applause. "Now wait a minute, young man," he said. "That going too far. What is your name, sir?"

"Tom Perry, representing Manchester."

"Why do I not recognize you?" Cromwell asked.

"I just was elected to parliament during the last election."

"I see," Cromwell said. "I am not certain how things work in Manchester, but in this body you must be granted the right to speak by the Speaker." *This was further proof there had been too many elections since the queen was detained,* Cromwell thought to himself.

"Mr. Speaker, I believe I still have the floor?" John Saunders asked.

"Yes, you do," the Speaker said.

"Then I yield it to Mr. Perry from Manchester."

"Mr. Perry, you have the floor," the Speaker said.

"Thank you, Mr. Speaker." Perry cleared his throat. "It is fairly simple. If it's the image of the queen we have to contend with, then that image is what must be put on trial."

The politicians began shouting again.

"Gentlemen, gentlemen, order please," the Speaker implored.

Saunders stood up. "I propose that we vote on the matter now. A yes or no."

"I second it," Tom Perry said.

"Vote on what, exactly?" Cromwell asked as he shot up out of his seat.

"I propose that the new government carry on with the original plan to put the monarchy on trial with or without the physical presence of a monarch," Saunders proposed.

"Do we continue with the search for the queen?" Cromwell asked.

"Of course, and Princess Abagail as well," Tom Perry replied.

"And the entire court," Saunders added. "The queen's agents, members of the royal household—in other words, we indict the entire court."

"Yes, the entire old system must be cleansed if we are to make a truly new society composed of free men," Tom Perry continued.

The chamber erupted into a wall of noise as members cheered and there were shouts of "hear, hear." What most didn't notice were the ones who clapped politely and those who sat on their hands, but Tom Perry took a picture with his mind's eye to remember who they were for the future fights.

"Then we better pray that we don't find any of them," Cromwell said softly enough that only those sitting around him heard.

The session ended and John Saunders quickly walked out of parliament, also committing to memory the members who were restrained in their reaction and especially those who shook their heads and looked towards Cromwell. He was in his own world when he felt someone touch his shoulder.

"I have been calling your name, sir." It was Tom Perry, the new member of parliament.

"Oh, Mr. Perry, Thank you for your support today."

"It was my pleasure, sir," Perry said. "I wonder if we could have a chat?"

"Yes, I would like that. When?"

"Let's meet for lunch in an hour at the Wild Ginger café," Tom Perry said.

"Write down the address and I'll meet you there in an hour," Saunders said.

CHAPTER 84

Albert was lost. When the search for his son's killer ended, his life lost its purpose. He hoped that by catching the murderer, Abagail, he could right his unforgivable wrong that had led to his son's murder. Albert was not a believer, but deep within him the fears of having to pay for his sins were coming to life.

Then he met Lucia, and everything changed. When Lucia joined him at the queen's behest to find the murderer, he had a chance for redemption and more, much more. Lucia, exciting Lucia, became his lover. Through her he glanced the world of the aristocracy. He was never going to live in that world, but he did visit it, and it changed him. Albert could never comfortably inhabit the brutish world of poverty and want again. He was a man between two worlds. The life he led before Lucia now seemed coarse and alien to him. The concerns that ruled his life were animal-like. The satisfactions of the body; food, drink, casual sexual activity were all part of being human, but what of the beauty of objects and the finer points of philosophy and poetry? He spent his career working in the castle but came to realize he was basically working in the servant quarters, the prison. He would catch a glimpse of the royals and their staff, but they were like gods, superhumans seldom seen. Living among them, even for the short while that he did, showed him a completely different way of life. He now realized that he always knew it couldn't last. How could this wonderful turn of events result from the murder of his son?

Albert's world had been destroyed. His life was without direction or purpose. No family—his wife made it very clear about never wanting to see him again. The queen was dead and with her death the pursuit of his son's murderer ended. Lucia was in Spain serving the queen's daughter, Margot. He was left behind in a country riven by civil war and he was on the losing side. He was aware of the death, pain, and destruction that surrounded him, but it didn't concern him. He was already dead, dead inside.

He saw hundreds driven from their homes, bent over and dragging their pitiable possessions, trying to escape the carnage. And like these bedraggled armies of peasants, he was on the move without a definite destination. The difference was the peasants were fleeing from an external threat. Albert was fleeing from a threat that was internal—a threat he could never outrun. One day folded into the next as Albert let his feet guide him. He roamed the countryside and one day he looked up and he was standing in front of his family home. He didn't remember deciding to go there, but here he was. He stood and looked at the house where he had once lived with Claire and their children. The memories returned; the death of Frederick, the accusations of his wife, and how he walked out and left his family to fend for themselves. He was still eager to be with Lucia, but could he desert his wife and children? *Can I face my wife and my children? Will she take me back? Can I win back her trust?* Albert felt an overwhelm-ing desire for a drink. *Just one, maybe two,* he thought. He turned his back to his house and walked to the nearest tavern. He was disgusted with himself, sickened by his cow-ardice and failure to act.

The taste of the ale only made Albert feel his sense of loss more acutely. The drink that used to be a treat almost made him gag, coarse compared to the wines he and Lucia shared. But this tavern of the working man sold ale only. *Where do I belong? Have I lost myself?* Albert wondered.

By the time the waitress brought the second tankard of ale, Albert made up his mind. He vowed to change his life and become the man he aspired towards; a man who was righteous and moral. His house was still standing. His family needed him. He started to get up and then stopped suddenly and swallowed the last of the ale, wiped his mouth, and almost ran out of the tavern. On his way out, he bumped into a customer walking in.

"Hey, watch where you're..." The aggrieved man stopped mid-sentence when he noted Albert's size.

Albert, his courage fortified by the alcohol, didn't hesitate. He was ready to face his wife, accept her anger, be contrite and ask for forgiveness even if it was unlikely forth-coming. He walked up to his cottage, took a deep breath, and pushed the door open. Where his family should have been, he saw a man and woman, both strangers, sitting in his kitchen. The man was stoking a fire.

"What are you doing in my house?" Albert yelled furiously.

The woman screamed.

The man jumped up and brandished the stick he was using to tend the fire. "Do not come any closer," he said with a quiver in his voice. His hand shook.

Albert looked at the woman and saw she was nursing an infant.

"We do not mean any harm," the man said. "We just needed to get out of the cold. The baby was coughing something terrible. We saw there was no one in this house so we came in. We plan to stay only one night."

Albert looked around the house and saw that all the dishes, cups, and silverware were gone. He walked into the bedroom and saw the beds were stripped clean. He opened up the closet and found it empty except for his dress shirt and a pair of his pants. He walked back into the kitchen. His rage petered out.

The two people hadn't moved as he walked through the house. "You can put that stick down," Albert said.

The man lowered the stick but still held onto it. "I am very sorry we used your house but..."

"I understand. You have to take care of your family, right? After all, that is what a man does." Albert swallowed. "By any chance do you know where the people who lived here went?"

"No," the man said.

"There was a battle nearby and some of the soldiers rode into town and did some terrible things," the woman said.

"When?" Albert asked.

"Two days ago," the man answered.

"Most of the town left after that," the woman continued. "We could not leave because this one—" she nodded toward her infant, "decided to enter the world at that very moment. That's why we could not leave with the others and needed to find a warm place to stay."

Albert felt frozen to the spot. The next thing he knew, he was outside. His ears were ringing. He didn't remember leaving the house.

Where was his family—were they still alive? It was unthinkable to face the possibility that they had been killed. If that is what happened, it was Albert's fault. He was not there to protect his family. He would make sure he got the punishment he deserved. The sentence would be carried out because he would be his own executioner. His worst fears were coming true. He was ready to make amends and there was no one to make them to. He didn't know what to do. The desertion of Lucia to Spain has taken his soul. He passed another tavern and wandered in. Then he stopped suddenly, turned, and rushed out as if being chased by a ghost, which in fact was exactly what happened. The ghost was his past; the past where he senselessly inflicted pain upon his wife and all but killed his son. He had not kept his vow to kill or at least capture his son's murderer. What vow had he ever kept? None. He was full of hot air and full of himself. He was all bluff and no substance. The only conclusion he could come to was "I don't deserve to live. I should be dead already." As he heard his words spoken out loud, he knew how false they sounded. Suicide wasn't the act of a brave man. It was the cowardly way out for someone who couldn't face life. The way for him to redeem himself was to live with the pain and try to make amends. The first person he must do that with was Claire, his wife. And he must do it in the face of her rage, knowing that no matter what he said that she would reject him. How could she not reject him when all he brought her was pain and suffering? He had to think. Where would she go? He needed a plan. He walked back into the tavern and sat at a table. He took out the leather purse the queen gave him. The purse was half full, judging by the weight of it. He knew that was more than enough for what he was going to do.

He called out to the waitress. "An ale, make it a large one." *I will sit here until I come up with a plan rather than running off without any rhyme or reason.* He drank the large ale quickly. "Bring me another ale, make sure it's a large one," he said, feeling himself calm down.

What Albert failed to see were three men sitting a few tables away who were staring at the big man with his purse heavy with money. They didn't have to speak. They knew the way all predators know—when to strike. They would wait for the right moment. Albert drank and the three of them watched closely for signs; for when he was weak enough to be taken down.

CHAPTER 85

Maria heard someone shouting her name. Thinking it was a dream, she rolled to her other side. The straw mattress was too uncomfortable to lay in one position for an extended time.

"Maria Eagleton, are you there?"

Maria, groggy from lack of sleep and spending too much time lying in bed, got up slowly.

"Maria Eagleton, are you there?"

Now she was awake. "Yes," Maria shouted back. "What do you want?" Silence. She rose from her bed and tried to stretch out the aches and pains. "Yes, what is it?" Again, no response.

Maria walked to the entrance of the cave to find the door wide open. It made her anxious, but she walked out of the cave. A stranger approached her and announced loudly in an official tone, "Maria Eagleton, the people have declared a general amnesty. All prisoners incarcerated during the illegitimate reign are free."

Maria didn't move.

"That means you are free to go."

"My children, do you know where they are?"

"Waiting for you in the courtyard."

"Mother!" the two children cried when they saw their mother, running into Maria's arms.

Maria held them tight, feeling their faces wet with tears. "Are you all right?" she asked.

"Yes, but I never want to go back there again," Jeffrey said. "Children cried all night, and the beds were so hard. We all slept in one big room. The biggest room I ever saw. The food..."

"Where is Father?" Theresa asked.

The children held on tighter when their mother didn't answer.

Theresa pulled away first, wiping her eyes. "Where is

Father?" she asked again.

Jeffrey stopped sobbing when he heard his sister's question. The two children stared at their mother, waiting for her answer.

Unable to speak, Maria's arms fell to her side.

"Mother," Theresa said with a tremor in her voice. There had never been a time when her mother was unable to answer a question. "Mother, please answer me. Where is daddy?"

"I do not know," Maria responded, and tried but failed to hold back a sob. "The soldiers separated us. I have not heard a word about him." She could not hold it in anymore. The children embraced their sobbing mother, trying to comfort her.

"Mother, it will be all right," Jeffrey said softly. "Father will come back soon, you will see, right, Theresa?"

When Jeffrey looked over at his older sister for support, Theresa was silent and turned her head away from her brother's hungry gaze.

Jeffrey was not able to put a name to it, but something inside him moved. He knew his life would never be the same. His stomach did a flip and heat radiated into his chest and then into his head. He felt dizzy and collapsed to the ground when his legs could no longer support him.

Maria picked her son up from the ground and embraced him.

"What do we do now, Mother?" Theresa whispered.

Maria sighed. She couldn't think of an answer. Wiping her eyes, she took a deep breath and said the exact two words the children wanted to hear: "Go home."

"Yes, Father will meet us there," Theresa said, and Maria tried to believe her daughter's hopeful words—but in her heart, she sensed the awful truth.

CHAPTER 86

James was a searcher who lost what he was searching for. But the search continued.

Every time James closed his eyes, images of dying men flooded his brain. He couldn't sleep without having nightmares. He couldn't explain it, but he had to keep moving, as if he could outrun the ghosts of the past.

He wandered the countryside in his priestly garb, listening to people's woeful stories. The need to be heard was overwhelming. He was just one man and couldn't begin to give the peasants he met what they wanted and deserved. The need of people to talk and be understood was enormous and he was afraid it would swallow him up. He was just one man. Then he came up with the idea of establishing what came to be called campfire meetings. As night arrived, the people would build a large bonfire in the town square. Any adult who wanted to could sit by the fire at night and talk about whatever they needed to.

The campfire meetings were held at night, partly for the practical feature of the children being asleep, so their parents could talk freely. And there was another unexpected advantage about sitting in the darkness surrounded by your neighbors—people could talk about the most intimate topics and then, just by leaning back, they could retreat into the blackness of night and not be embarrassed by revealing their most secret fears and dreams. The fire invited deep sharing and profound connections were forged. These voiceless peasants were listened to. Their lives had value and meant something.

The first meeting sputtered at the start. The peasants were looking for James to preach. But he refused and kept repeating, "This time is yours, use it any way you want." And tentatively, in halting speech, people told their stories. These stories were invariably of loss; loss of family members killed in the civil war, loss of land and home. James never expressed the usual church bromides about God having a plan or how all this suffering was for a greater cause. He listened. That's all he did—listened and encouraged the villagers to talk to each other, and that seemed good enough. The next meeting, he talked less, and even less the following night until he was silent for the entire time. Then he moved on, usually in the middle of the night while people slept.

James became Father James as his reputation grew. The peasants adored him and treated him as God's representative. His poverty coupled with his sad countenance seemed to be the living embodiment of the country's ills. For the nation to find any peace, thousands had to be heard, and the way to begin was to encourage them to speak. The campfire meetings turned out to be a powerful way for simple people to find their voice.

Once the campfire meeting was established in a village, James disappeared without warning. He walked for days until he came to another village, where he repeated the whole process.

CHAPTER 87

"I cannot believe it," Margot said in a barely audible voice. "Are you certain?"

"Yes, your Majesty," Lucia said as gently as she could. "Albert and I were there at the end. We buried her."

"Tell me, did she suffer? What were her last words?"

"My dear, are you sure you want to know that kind of detail?" Prince Leon asked. "It will only upset you..."

"Yes, I want to know all the details." Margot glared at her husband icily.

Lucia took a deep breath. "The queen was in a weakened state before the escape. The demands of traveling without a rest proved too taxing." She hesitated.

"Tell me all. Omit nothing," Margot insisted.

Lucia told Princess Margot the whole story of Queen Henrietta's death with one exception—the question that plagued the queen to the very end of why her daughter was so cold to her during their last conversation. The reason, Lucia learned, was that Margot wasn't in the queen's room that last day; it had been Abagail. And it was Abagail who deceived the queen into thinking her daughter was spurning her. Lucia couldn't bear to relate how the queen was so cruelly tricked by Abagail as she was dying. Lucia had the queen's letter to Margot with her and hadn't yet decided what to do with it. Now witnessing how upset Margot was, she chose not to disclose it. Lucia knew if Margot found out she was withholding the letter she would face serious conse-quences.

Margot sat absolutely still for what seemed like hours. Lucia waited, observing her new mistress. Any signs of her girlhood had disappeared. The princess looked like a younger version of her mother with the intense gaze that made others feel judged and not up to par. She was also like her father in the way she came to a decision. Lucia could almost hear her mind working. Queen Henrietta's greatest strength as a ruler was her ability to assess a situation and act quickly—sometimes too quickly. King Charles was more deliberative. He would not have thrown his sister in a prison then imprisoned her daughter in the same cell.

Lucia's thoughts were interrupted.

"I want her body brought back to Spain, so she has a proper funeral and a final resting place befitting her position." Margot looked directly at Lucia as she spoke.

"Yes, your Majesty," Lucia said.

"Whatever you need to accomplish this, tell me and you shall have it," Margot said. "You will leave tomorrow." She looked at her agent closely. "How many men will you need to accomplish this mission?"

"We don't want an international conflict. We are not prepared to fight another war at the present time," Prince Leon interjected. "If we even send a small force and they are captured it would..."

"This is my mother," Margot retorted.

"Your Majesty," Lucia said softly, "if I may."

"Go on, speak freely," Prince Leon said.

"Thank you," Lucia said, responding to the prince but never taking her eyes from Margot. "I do not need anyone to accompany me."

"That is ridiculous," the prince said. "Of course you will need assistance, moving the body and transporting it without being discovered."

"What do you have in mind, Lucia?" Margot asked.

"I still have contacts in the country, agents and friends of the crown who have remained."

"Ah yes, that large prison guard, I remember him," Margot said.

"And others, your Majesty—I mean majesties," she quickly corrected herself.

"You really think you have enough support to carry this

out?" the prince asked.

"I do, your Majesty," Lucia replied.

"Lucia," Margot said. "If you succeed in this enterprise you will be freed of your service to this crown and will be sufficiently compensated so that you can live your life without concern about money."

"Your Majesty, I am deeply grateful and touched by your generosity. I am overwhelmed." Lucia bowed deeply and left the throne room.

CHAPTER 88

Albert stumbled out of the tavern mumbling to himself. If he could be understood in his advanced state of drunkenness you would hear words like *duty, husband, failure, I swear*. He walked a small distance and fell flat on his face, landing in a pile of mud.

The three men who had been watching him drink himself to the point of total oblivion followed him and, when he fell, they pounced. Without speaking, they knew they had to get him out of sight so they could do their work in private. "This guy is heavy," one of the three said. "Maybe we can drag him."

"Too much to drink," one of them said, smiling at a well-dressed couple who, upon seeing the three men dragging one of their own, quickened their pace. They steered Albert into an alley and went to work. His jacket and vest were removed. The pockets emptied. The leather purse with the coins was passed between the three thieves.

"Let's go," said one of them. "He has nothing else worth taking."

"Oh yeah?" one of the thieves said and pulled the queen's seal out of an inside vest pocket. The three of them bent over to stare at the seal.

"How did he end up with the queen's seal?"

"I don't know but this is not a good time to be the queen's man," the first thief said.

"You are right," the other thief replied and threw the seal in the mud puddle.

The three thieves walked out, feeling like it was a good night's haul, and to celebrate they returned to the same tavern where they first saw Albert and proceeded to drink their stolen loot.

Except later that night, one of them returned to the mud puddle and felt around in the dark until he found what he was looking for. He smiled and thought how easy it was to talk those two dummies out of keeping the seal.

CHAPTER 89

Abagail opened her eyes. Her clothes were wet from sleeping on the grass and her back was sore. Not yet ready to get up, she rested on the grass for a few more minutes. It was delicious, the height of luxury. The camp was waking up around her. People stirred, greeting each other with "good morning" as children got up to run and play. Abagail stood up slowly and stretched. People everywhere stretched and moved their bodies gingerly. Most had slept on the ground like her. Others crawled out from under their wagons and a few climbed down from within them. People shook out their arms, others slowly twisted, trying to loosen their backs. Only the children were up and running the way children do, going from dead asleep to full steam ahead in a matter of seconds. Abagail realized that she had become more observant of children since becoming pregnant.

She remembered the previous night when the women made dinner and how everyone worked together. It was all so organized. Abagail looked around for the woman, Naomi, who promised to show her around the community.

Abagail could see a line starting to form as groups of women handed out pieces of bread, bowls of hot mush, and cups of milk. Abagail joined the line. The line moved quickly and soon Abagail was sitting on a log with her meal, eating with great relish. When she finished and returned her bowl and cup, she was determined to join the wash-up crew. Abagail spotted Naomi walking in her direction.

"Sleep well, Anna?"

In the daylight, the woman looked younger than Abagail remembered, but there was something in her eyes that gave her the look of an older woman, someone deeply embedded in life.

"Are you alone?" Naomi asked.

"Yes," Abagail said.

"We have a lot of women traveling by themselves." Naomi sighed. "What we don't have is men. Well, what I mean is young men."

"Where are they?" Abagail asked.

Naomi looked surprised by the question. "They are off fighting of course."

"Of course," Abagail replied quickly with an awkward laugh.

Naomi gave her a curious look. "We're going to be packing up and leaving soon. You are welcome to join us. I will tell you more about us as we walk."

"Yes, thank you," Abagail said nervously.

"I have some things to take care of. I will catch up with you," Naomi said.

This time Abagail didn't ask. Walking up to where breakfast was served, she gathered some cups, took them to the stream, and washed them. With her few belongings in tow, Abagail joined the procession. The ragtag line of survi-vors Abagail had seen walking yesterday transformed in her eyes into a community of powerful women.

Soon Naomi appeared at Abagail's side, matching her stride for stride.

CHAPTER 90

James had the dream again. He was walking in a meadow and the green grass was wet. It felt like morning dew but soon the water was rising. It was up to his ankles. He looked down and the water was bright red; it wasn't water, it was blood. He felt the current pulling at him. It was carrying him away. He was jolted awake, sweating and breathing hard.

James got up from the bed he shared with the young boy who lived with his two sisters and their recently widowed mother in a one-room cottage. Everyone else slept deeply, the only sound their breathing. It seemed to James the cottage breathed in time with the occupants.

He gulped in the fresh air and walked to the widow's well. The sky had changed from inky black to light blue. He pulled up a bucket of water to pour over his head and first checked to make sure it was not red. He shook his head to banish the dream. His hair dripped with water and he took a long, delicious drink. It was time to move on.

"Good morning, Father," a child said.

James jumped. Two boys stood next to him. He hadn't seen them approach.

"Good morning," the taller boy said again, his eyes downcast. "You are leaving us?"

"Yes," James answered with a sigh, expecting to be asked to minister someone. "How can I help you?"

"We want to go with you," the boy answered.

"What do you mean go with me? Go with me where?"

"Wherever you go. We want to learn from you, help you."

"Thank you for your offer but it is not possible."

"Why not?" the taller boy asked. "We want to help people like you do."

"Do your parents know about this?"

"Our parents are dead," the boy said matter-of-factly.

"Someone must take care of you."

"We have no family. We take care of each other."

"I cannot take care of anybody. I am not sure where I am going to be next, where or when I am going to eat next. It's not a life for two young boys."

"The life we have is not a life for us either."

"I am sorry, but it is just not possible," James said. He gathered his few belongings and began to walk. Two hours later, he stopped by a stream to rest and drink some water. He saw the two boys following him.

James hoped the two boys would tire and turn back, but after fifteen minutes he looked over his shoulder and saw they were still there. He walked on at a brisk pace and when he checked again there was no one. He was surprised that he felt disappointed when he did not see them. *It is for the best. I can't care for other people's children*, he thought.

The sun quickly dropped behind the horizon and the air became cold. It was time for James to find a place to spend another night alone. *It would be nice to have company. It's better this way,* he told himself as he found a comfortable spot under a tree with a large canopy and soft moss covering the ground. He started a fire for warmth. He took out an apple, a piece of bread, and a slab of cheese. He lay on his back looking at the stars when he heard rustling in the bushes. He picked up his staff and waited as quietly as possi-ble, poised to strike.

"Father," the taller of the two boys said.

James let out a lungful of air. "Come, sit, you must be tired and hungry."

"I've never been more tired and hungry in my whole life," the taller boy said.

James laughed. "I have some food and you can sleep here next to the fire."

"Thank you, Father," the boy said.

"What are your names?" James asked the taller boy.

"Will," he said, then pointed to the smaller boy, "and this

is my younger brother Lee."

James smiled. "How old are you, Will?"

"Fourteen," Will said, standing up straight.

"And you, Lee?"

"He is eleven, but he cannot talk. Nobody knows why but since our farm was burned down, he stopped talking."

"What happened to your family?" James asked.

Will hesitated.

"You do not have to talk about it now. When you want to tell me you can, all right?"

"Yes, thank you, sir," Will said with great relief.

"You can call me James."

Will ran his fingers through his hair and his eyes clouded over.

"What's the matter?" James asked.

"Uh, uh…"

"What is it, Will?"

"How about Father James—is that good?"

"Fine, that is fine. Now it is time for us to sleep. But tomorrow we are going to talk about you following me."

"All right, Father James," Will said.

"Good night, Will, and goodnight to you, Lee."

CHAPTER 91

John Saunders hesitated before he walked into the restaurant. By the dress of a group of men leaving the restaurant, it was clear they were from the working classes. *This cannot be the restaurant Tom Perry had in mind,* John thought. Walking from the bright sunlight into the dark, John Saunders was momentarily blinded. As his eyes adjusted, he saw someone waving to him from a corner table. John navigated the small spaces between tightly crammed tables, carefully making his way over.

"Some place you picked," John said, looking around at the restaurant's plain décor—no paintings on the walls, the tables shoved close together, as many as could fit. The restaurant conveyed the sense of a no-nonsense place whose main attraction was good, honest food at reasonable prices.

"Yes, no one would ever imagine we would meet in this place. We're safe here from prying eyes." Tom laughed, handing John the menu. "What will you have? I was so hungry that I ordered already."

"I'll have whatever you're having."

"Great," Tom said and gestured to a passing waiter. "Make that two orders of today's special."

"I want to thank you for supporting me in parliament today," John said. "I really do not know why Cromwell was so dead set against trying the queen in absentia."

"You really do not know why?"

"No," John replied.

Tom leaned forward and kept his voice low. "He is not really anti-aristocracy. Cromwell would support a monarch if that king was more capable."

John pulled back in his chair like he was hit in the face. He frowned and shook his head.

"You are surprised?" Tom said.

"I am. I thought if you support the revolution you are by definition a supporter of democracy."

"Democracy, what is your concept of democracy?" Tom stopped talking as the waiter appeared at the table with their food.

"Gentlemen," he said. "Shepherd's pie and the house ale."

"Thank you," Tom said, "It smells delicious." He broke through the crust with his fork and a cloud of steam billowed.

John followed the example of his lunch mate and the smoke carried the aroma from John's pie, making his stomach groan. He hadn't realized how hungry he was.

"Let us continue talking after we eat," Tom said.

"I could not agree more," John said.

Both men ate with gusto. They finished at the same time and pushed their plates away.

"Now, where were we?" Tom asked. "Right, I remember, democracy. What is your definition of democracy?"

John knew he was entering a trap. He took a long drink of his ale and decided to play along, eager to hear how Tom defined democracy. "Well, it is one man one vote, is it not? That is the central tenet?"

"You mean men of property, don't you?"

John shook his head. "No, I meant what I said. One man one vote as long as he is of age."

"I am surprised," Tom said. "Good for you, but are we really all equal in this country?"

"If there is a policy that every adult male has the vote, then I would say that yes we are all equal."

"When it comes to voting, maybe, but when you include economic equality, this country is dominated by the few very wealthy landowners. Although they are a very small minority, they wield much more power than the rest of us."

"What are you proposing?"

"We are not proposing—we have already started. The Diggers have organized poor and landless peasants to work the idle fields of the lords."

"Why would they want to work their master's land?" John asked, feeling like he was entering dangerous territory.

"Precisely. The land would no longer be their masters. The ownership would transfer to those who work it."

"That is theft. Certainly, you do not endorse those illegal seizures and who are these Diggers?" John asked.

"They are..." Tom stopped. "What I mean to say is we are a group that wants to apply the principles of the revolution consistently."

John frowned, "I do not know what you mean."

"Do you endorse hungry children dying of diseases that can be prevented? Their parents working a farm their whole life to find themselves forced off the land and out of their home. Why? Because the lord wants more acres to hunt foxes or decides to grow a more profitable crop. A vote is meaningless without a basic change in this economic circumstance."

"Of course I do not support those policies," John said, "but taking someone's property by force is a criminal offense. We are members of parliament and cannot condone it."

Tom gripped the table, leaned forward, and in a strained voice said, "So, you value the law over people's lives."

"We don't have a perfect form of government but with-out the law we cannot exist. I will not be a party to this campaign of lawlessness directed by these Diggers." John counted out some coins and stood, ready to leave.

Tom grabbed his arm and said, "What would you think if your precious democracy leads to the return of a monarch?"

John smiled. "You really believe after all that has been sacrificed, we can go back to being ruled by a king?"

"That is exactly what I think. We can have a monarchy without a king."

John sat back down. "Come on, Tom. How is that possible?"

"Look at Oliver Cromwell."

"He has done as much or more for the revolution than anyone. What do you have against him?"

"I do not trust him," Tom said.

"Why not?"

"There are many who are opposed to the monarchy that I do not trust."

"But why, are we not all on the same side?" John asked.

"Yes," Tom replied, "as long as we have a common enemy."

"But..."

"Just a minute, let me explain. We were all on the same side because circumstances compel us to bury our differences and now that we have won, those differences reemerge."

"What differences do you hear? All I hear are disagreements about strategy," John said.

"Yes, the debates in parliament center around strategy but strategy on a larger scale is ultimately about what you believe in."

"I am not sure what you are talking about."

"Let me give you an example," Tom said. "Cromwell is always going on about how important it is to have a strong military to defend the revolution."

"He is only stating the obvious. If our armies are defeated, the revolution is defeated."

"Yes," Tom said. "But what is underneath what he is saying?"

"I don't understand," John replied.

"Cromwell is lobbying to be the head of this expanded army."

"Yes," John said. "I have heard that."

"And if he is, he becomes the most powerful person in the country."

"I do not think..." John began to say.

"It is clear that he does not have the support of parlia-ment or the people, but who can stand up to the army and its leader? You, John Saunders, with your oratorical skills and your fervent defense of democracy, you can be a true leader in parliament in a way that Cromwell could only dream about. The army fits Cromwell to a tee. Its hierarchical struc-ture mimics a monarchy. Soldiers are taught to obey their commanders without questioning. There is not the rough and tumble of debate that we value as MPs. The civil war is not only between royalists and rebels it is also being played out between former allies." Tom Perry looked over at his lunch mate, ready to counter any argument John Saunders may make. What he saw was John Saunders sitting completely still. It was the one response he had not counted on. So, he matched John's posture and became still.

When confronted with new ideas, John Sanders would quiet himself. He would instruct his body to be still and quiet his mind. He learned it from his father, a free thinker who valued being open to new ideas over everything else.

Tom Perry couldn't sit in silence anymore. "Let me ask you a question." He kept his eyes on John. "Are you against this king or all kings?"

John did not answer.

Tom asked again, speaking louder and slower. "John, are you against this king or are you against all kings?"

John shook his head and in a raspy voice said, "All kings, of course."

"What if I told you that Cromwell is not against all kings? If this is true would you say you and Cromwell are on the same side?"

CHAPTER 92

People began walking. The horses pulling wagons neighed and snorted and then the caravan community was on the move. No one shouted any orders but, like a flock of birds responding to some unseen signal, they knew it was time to leave. *Will I discover I cannot raise a child on my own like my mother?* Abagail asked herself for the thousandth time as she joined the long line of refugees.

Abagail was so lost in her thoughts that it took a few minutes for her to realize Naomi was walking alongside her. Abagail looked at the woman and smiled. "I am sorry," she said. "I did not see you."

"Yes, I could see that. You had the look of someone with a lot on your mind." Naomi sighed. "We all are traveling with our ghosts."

"I am," Abagail agreed, not ready to relate her story, not yet.

"Let me tell you how I got here," Naomi said. "I went to my son's regiment to see if I could persuade him to come home. He just turned eighteen and volunteered to fight in the rebel army without asking me. I appealed to his commanding officer and was surprised how understanding he was. He invited me to take my case all the way to the very top. I met with General Cromwell, who said that he only wanted soldiers who believed in the cause and stated that if Joseph, my son, wanted to, he could leave the army and come home. Of course, I was thrilled, but Joseph would not consider leaving."

"Why not?" Abagail asked.

"Being in the army he is part of a family he said, and he would not desert his family." Naomi took a deep breath and seemed to decide to relate more of the story. "Joseph's father deserted us when Joseph was a little boy. Our home life has been rocky. So, I understand his adoption of a new family."

"It must have been hard on you."

"Yes, it still is." Naomi's voice caught, and she wiped her eyes. "And now I am on my way home," she continued.

Home, Abagail thought. *I am alone in the world, without a family or a home. Alone with a past based on a bed of lies, a present over which I have no control, and an uncertain, frightening future.*

Abagail shook her head and said to Naomi, "Tell me about this community."

"It's really very simple. We are mostly women and children uprooted by the war and thought that the best chance for us to survive is to band together."

"What does that mean?" Abagail asked.

"We are just starting out, so it is all new but for right now we've decided to work together as if we were one family. As you saw last night and this morning, we share our food, and share watching the children."

Abagail kept walking, looking straight ahead.

Naomi was the first to break the silence. "What do you think of our community?"

"I am not sure what to say. The way you described it makes the community out to be a simple convenience. But I feel it is more than that—much more." Abagail replied.

"You are right. It is more than convenience. Every adult in this community is a parent to every child. We are a family of families. Tragedy may have brought us together, but we are trying to create something loving and supportive."

"I think it's the most wonderful idea I have ever heard. Who came up with it, you?"

Naomi laughed. "No, not me. Have you heard of Father James?"

Abagail almost fell from the shock. "Father James," she said, her voice trembling.

"Yes, he is this wandering priest. I think he's a priest, although he insists he is not. He is not like any priest I have ever met. He doesn't talk about God or quote from the bible. He travels the countryside offering comfort to those who have lost somebody. And who hasn't lost a husband, father, or a son to this war? Who hasn't been uprooted, torn from our land?"

"But how did this Father James help you come up with the idea of community?" Abagail felt her face turn red with excitement. Could this wandering holy man be her James?

"Very simply; he preached that instead of looking for the church to give us the answers, we should look to ourselves."

Now Abagail knew for certain that this was her James. She could almost hear his voice expressing these very ideas.

Father James—it was like he came back from the dead. *A man dressed like a priest, who swears he's not a priest but minsters to everyone. It could only be James.* Abagail had a purpose other than survival, to find James.

"Anna, where did you go?" Naomi asked.

"Uh..." was all Abagail could say.

"You had this far-away look in your eyes. Are you ill?" Naomi asked.

"No, I feel fine," Abagail said, but she was thinking of James. *What will he think about having a baby?*

"How far along are you?" Naomi asked as if reading her mind.

Abagail's hands went right to her stomach. "How did you know? I didn't think I was showing."

"Well, young lady, it's my business to know, I am a midwife." Naomi laughed. Her blue eyes sparkled.

"I think four or five months," Abagail said.

"And the father?" the older woman asked.

Abagail tried not to cry but could feel her chin quiver.

"That's all right, dear. I know these are terrible times."

The two women continued their walk without talking, Abagail in her own world and Naomi quietly respecting her need to be alone.

CHAPTER 93

Lucia's stomach matched the rhythm of the rocking boat as it rose and fell with the surf. The movement of the boat didn't bother her at first but as the sea got rougher, she started to feel nauseous and her small cabin seemed to close in on her. It was difficult to breathe, like she was drowning in the tiny room. Needing space, she pushed the cabin door open, bolted up the stairs to the deck, and took a deep breath of the sea air. Feeling alive for the first time all day, Lucia remembered the last time she had the feeling of drowning. It was when that man they were looking for knocked her out and Albert carried her back to the palace and saved her life.

The sea breeze was delicious, sweet and salty. Her head cleared. The sky looked like it exploded with a million stars shining through the layer of blackness. Was it the light of heaven poking through the covering in the sky like her father told her or were they planets? Other worlds with people living on them. Did they have kings and queens, and did the kings and queens on these distant planets have someone like Lucia who lived to serve them? She wondered if Queen Henrietta was looking down on her from somewhere in the sky. For the life of her she couldn't picture what heaven looked like no matter what the priests said. But she could see the queen, her old mistress, sitting on a throne up in heaven from where the stars shone. Lucia smiled, picturing her queen trying to outthink God. *Watch out, God, you have some competition.*

Lucia's mind wandered and landed in the most unexpected place. She hadn't thought about her mother or father in a long time. She missed them but didn't miss the life they lived. Every day there was the question of whether there would be enough to eat and more often than not the answer was no. Lucia would lie in the bed she shared with her brother and sister and try to comfort them after going to bed without supper again.

Lucia remembered lying in bed listening to her parents talk about a stranger asking to call on the family to meet Lucia and discuss her future. The next morning, a man rode right up to their house on the most beautiful horse Lucia had ever seen. He wasn't asking for her hand in marriage after all. He worked for the queen and asked Lucia's parents whether they would allow their daughter to live and work in the palace as an aide to the queen. Lucia left home the next day and never saw her parents again—and, to be truthful, never even thought about them. The queen became her mother and Lucia loved her mistress. Over the years, she did whatever the queen asked her to.

It is only now, after losing her second royal family, that her first family came to mind. Lucia remembered when her mother died, she didn't cry. The queen was as much a mother to her as her real mother, maybe more so. To her horror, she couldn't remember what her real mother looked like. Lucia closed her eyes and, though she tried as hard as possible, her mother's face was gone to her. Her eyes started to water but even now she couldn't say which mother she was crying for.

Now returning on her own to carry out this latest task for her new mistress, Margot, the Spanish queen-to-be, Lucia thought about what might be waiting for her in England. *Has the country changed now that there is no king or queen? Is Albert still drinking or is he sober? Is he back with his wife?* Maybe he was arrested for helping the queen escape. The first mate said they should be able to dock sometime late tomorrow. Lucia looked up at the sky one last time, said goodbye to her queen, to God, and the people who lived on the stars. She climbed the stairs to the deck below and as she curled up in her bed, an unbidden thought came to her—*this is my last assignment. After this I will break free from Margot and be my own person and live my life. Could it be with Albert?* she thought.

CHAPTER 94

"Money for a new military campaign? Have we forgotten already that our revolution was a revolt against endless war? The toll the Spanish war took on our country was unbearable. The treasury emptied, people taxed beyond their limit, fees paid to the crown for every activity, and of course, the loss of human life. I cannot believe that we fought the revolution to turn around and finance more wars." Saunders sat down, feeling triumphant. Westminster was buzzing. Every member of parliament felt the gravity of the moment.

Cromwell, his hand raised, stood up quickly.

The Speaker said, "I recognize Mr. Cromwell."

"The rebels in Ireland are using the turbulence in our country to mobilize against us. We must quash this rebellion. If we do nothing, they will succeed, and Scotland will be next demanding their independence."

"Never!" members yelled.

Cromwell cleared his throat. "And who knows what will follow. I fear for the continued existence of our great country. I know that I did not fight to overthrow the monarchy to relinquish our duty to protect the integrity of our country." He sat down as parliament erupted around him.

"What is to be done?" someone called out from the back row.

"Are you addressing me, sir?" Cromwell asked.

"Yes, I am, sir. What is to be done?" the member replied.

"We have no choice," Cromwell intoned. "We must defend the motherland and that means war."

Saunders jumped up. "What was the revolution about? Why did we risk everything? Not to end up in the same place where we were."

"What do you suggest, Mr. Saunders?" Cromwell replied.

"War should be the last response, not the first one, Mr.

Cromwell. What about negotiations?"

"The Irish rebellion is based on the demand that they be granted complete independence. They have rejected any negotiations. I for one will not sit idly by as our country is picked apart by every group that wants independence. I will not let our great land die." Cromwell stood with his arms crossed. His body seemed to expand as parliament erupted into shouts of "hear, hear" and applause rained down.

"Call the question," someone shouted.

"Is there a second?" the Speaker asked.

Several members shouted, "I second."

"The motion is seconded," the Speaker brought the gavel down. "All those in favor..."

"Wait, just wait. What exactly are we voting on?" Tom Perry called out from the back benches.

"The proposal is that an army will be fully funded by this parliament," Cromwell said, "to engage in military action against the Royalist army in this country and their supporters, the rebel army in Ireland. Mr. Speaker, can we have the vote?"

"All those in favor of raising an army to defend the revolution and defeat the Irish rebels from breaking away from England say 'aye.'" *Ayes* rang out. "All those opposed to this proposal say nay." A few scattered *nays* were heard. "The ayes are in the majority. The proposal passes," the Speaker said. "Clerk, make a note of this."

"One more thing," Cromwell interjected. "I propose that I lead this army to guarantee that the ideals of the revolution will guide us during this campaign."

"I second that," a member shouted.

Another member shouted, "It should be by proclamation."

Several members shouted, "I second."

Perry saw Saunders stand up and leave as the Speaker began to ask for the proclamation installing Cromwell as General of the revolutionary army. He ran after him but by the time he clambered down the stairs Saunders was gone.

CHAPTER 95

"Yes, come in," Cromwell said. He stood with a group of officers, all of them bent over a map covering a large table. "What is it?" he asked his aide de camp in irritation.

"Sir, Captain Nugent has arrived."

"Show him in," Cromwell said without looking up from the map.

"He is already here, General," the aide said sheepishly.

Cromwell looked up. His aide took a step to the side, allowing a figure to emerge from the shadows. "Well, well, I have been looking forward to meeting you, good sir." Cromwell walked up to Captain Nugent, who saluted smartly. Cromwell returned the salute in perfunctory manner. "You led the group who captured the queen?"

"Yes, sir," Captain Nugent replied.

"I understand you suffered no casualties—remarkable. What was your secret?"

"I was fortunate to happen upon a map of the castle. We were able to circumvent the defenders, sir."

"You are too modest."

Nugent smiled.

"You are one of the heroes of the rebellion."

Nugent, not sure if Cromwell was being sarcastic, just nodded.

Cromwell continued, "I also heard that as the captain of a platoon in the service of the monarchy, you were an agent of the rebellion."

"True enough," Nugent replied, knowing that Cromwell's casual tone did not make this first meeting anything other than what it was, a vetting.

Cromwell walked up to the captain, never diverting his eyes, and whispered in his ear, "We will have to utilize your skills in deception." Cromwell was a big man. Nugent heard about Cromwell's intimidation tactics and tried to adopt a respectful yet not obsequious stance.

"We would like you to continue your career in subterfuge," Cromwell went on, "but this time openly in the service of the revolution. Are you fully committed to the ideals of the revolution?"

Captain Nugent nodded, uncertain how to respond.

"The ideals being the elimination of the papist influence and the promulgation of puritan religious practices throughout the country?"

Nugent swallowed, nodded, and said with as much enthusiasm as he could muster, "Yes, sir."

Cromwell seemed to relax and, with a big smile, said, "Now the good news: I understand that you are receiving a promotion." Never taking his eyes from Nugent, Cromwell opened a leather pouch and unfolded a letter, which he read out loud. "'The members of parliament in recognition of the noteworthy courage and the important contribution made by Captain Nugent to the victorious campaign against the tyranny of the crown are pleased to promote him to the rank of major.'"

"Congratulations, Major," Cromwell said as he pinned a star on Nugent's lapel.

"Thank you, sir. It is a great honor," Nugent said with emotion.

"As part of your new rank you will be assigned to special operations." Cromwell firmly shook Nugent's hand. "Welcome to the inner circle of the citizens' new army."

Several officers came up to Nugent and shook his hand, offering their congratulations.

"There are two assignments I want you to take on," Cromwell said. "The first is to verify the death of Queen Henrietta, which is crucial in dispelling the myth once and for all that she will somehow restore the monarchy." Cromwell took a deep breath. "Secondly, I want you to locate and arrest

Princess Abagail. We cannot have her alive and wandering through the country. The royalists can use her as a symbol for their supporters to rally around. Do you have any questions, Major Nugent?"

"No, I understand, sir," Nugent said.

As Nugent walked out of Cromwell's tent, his mind was going full speed. For a moment he had to remind himself what side he was on. He wondered if he was getting in over his head and then he smiled. Nugent was working for Nugent and whatever side was winning would have his allegiance and now he was working for Cromwell. Albert and Lucia were the only ones who knew whether the queen was dead or alive and where she was hiding or buried. He hadn't heard anything about Lucia since that night she escaped with the queen. Albert, on the other hand, was not difficult to find. As a matter of fact, he was hard to miss. He would assign an agent to track the big man. Sooner or later that little lady would show up to meet with Albert and lead him to the queen whether she still breathed or not. The way to accomplish the second part of his assignment seemed equally straightforward—find Abagail, find James.

Major Nugent, he liked the sound of that. And if he captured the queen and apprehended two royal agents, Colonel Nugent may be in the offing. And if he delivered Abagail to the rebels, who knew what the rewards would be. So far this revolution business was a good one if he played his cards right. But he had to be very careful. The meeting with Cromwell affirmed what he had heard about him. He was not someone Nugent wanted as an enemy. There was a fanaticism in his eyes that shook Nugent.

Nugent knew Lucia's and Albert's destination and the route they would have taken when they helped the queen escape. Once Lucia and Albert led him to the queen they would be arrested. He was vulnerable to being exposed by them as a royal agent. The only guarantee that he would not be exposed was their execution. He was certain the rebels would sentence them to death, doing his work for him.

Then, once he captured Abagail and James and they were executed, there would be nobody left who could expose him as a double agent. *Brilliant,* he told himself. He smiled, marveling once again at how this revolution provided a perfect opportunity for an intelligent man to make some-thing of himself.

CHAPTER 96

Albert tried to move but his body would not cooperate. It felt like someone was hitting his head with a hammer from the inside. He opened his left eye first, then his right. The sun was bright, and the light hurt his eyes. He noticed people walking by walked a little faster when they passed him. Most of them looked away but a few stared and shook their heads. Everything in his body ached. He had a terrible thirst. The last thing he remembered was leaving the tavern, then he started to recall being set upon by three men. He panicked and went through his pockets. It was gone, his leather purse with his coins. He checked again and realized the queen's seal was also gone. He put his elbows on the ground and tried to lift himself, but fell back to the ground. His thirst drove him to try again. He took a deep breath and got to his feet. He tottered but before he fell down again, he leaned against a wall to prop himself up. He began to slide down the wall and wished he could just disappear.

"Albert, Albert," someone was calling him from what sounded like a long distance.

He opened his eyes and like a wish come true he saw her. The person he most wanted to see in the world.

Lucia put her hand under his arm to support him.

"Is it you?" He blinked, unbelieving. "You have come back. I am sorry," he said, "so sorry." Tears welled up in his eyes. "I have made a mess of my life..." He began to sob. "A mess."

"We have work to do, if you are up to it," Lucia said, her tone serious but a teasing smile on her face. "What happened to you?"

"I do not know. I do not know," Albert repeated with his head hanging.

"What, what is it you do not know?"

"I know nothing. I do not remember where I was last night

or who robbed me. I do not know where my family is. I do not know if they are all right or even if they are alive. I do not know what I should be doing, what is next, or why I am alive."

"Well, I have the answer to all your questions."

"You do?" Albert asked, lifting his head.

"Yes, we have a job to do—or rather, we have a job to finish," Lucia told him. "We have to bring the body of Queen Henrietta to Spain so there can be a proper funeral befitting a queen." Lucia looked at Albert tenderly. "Are you ready to work with me to do that?"

"Yes," he answered immediately.

"We start tomorrow but first we have to get you cleaned up."

None of this escaped the notice of Nugent's spy, who immediately reported back to Major Nugent.

It wasn't until later that night, with Lucia's arm draped across his chest and after a good meal without alcohol when Albert thought, *Once again I am being rescued from my miserable life by someone's death, first my son and now the queen.* A shiver went through his body. He closed his eyes and thankfully, by morning, the thought disappeared in the light of the rising sun.

CHAPTER 97

It was the middle of the day when the caravan stopped. Abagail, with no one to distract her, spent the morning trying to digest the news about James, asking herself how she could find him.

Naomi returned and said, "You are too far gone to walk all day. We do not want anything to happen to your baby. I found a place for you in a wagon. It is not fancy, but it will spare you from walking."

Squeezing into a tight corner with a basket of dirty, smelly clothes on one side and a tottering pile of loose potatoes, onions, and cabbages on the other side, Abagail felt very fortunate to occupy that small space.

A very old, wrinkled, toothless woman sat in a rocking chair a few feet from Abagail.

"Hello," Abagail said, and the old woman smiled at her. Abagail was still not used to her body. The constant aches, swollen feet, her expanding belly, and the sway of the wagon made for a rough ride, but still Abagail was extremely grateful to Naomi and the family who allowed her to stay in their wagon. She vowed to somehow return the kindness shown to her. With these pleasant thoughts and the slow rhythmic movements of the wagon, Abagail fell asleep.

The days ran together for Abagail as in a dream. Riding in the back of the wagon, each day was like the one before. It reminded her of when she and James were together on his farm. Was it really only four months ago? It seemed like a lifetime. The time when they went swimming, their long talks about politics and the future—*their* future—and how nervous they both were the first time they slept together seemed like yesterday's memories.

Naomi stuck her head in the wagon. "So, how are you, Mom?"

"Fine," Abagail said, startled. Caught up in her own thoughts, she had not realized the wagon stopped.

"I have something for you—well, actually for the both of you," Naomi said. She placed a piece of fabric on the floor of the wagon.

"It is beautiful," Abagail said, holding it up.

Naomi laughed. "You do not know what it is, do you?"

"I do not," Abagail said, "but it is very pretty. Thank you."

"I will show you how to use it." Naomi took the material and wrapped it around Abagail's shoulder, tucking the other end under the opposite arm. "It is a baby pouch. You can carry your baby and have your hands free."

Abagail smiled. "How clever. It is wonderful. Did you make it?"

"Yes."

Abagail leaned over and took Naomi's hand. "You are the kindest person." Tears came to her eyes. Naomi started to pull her hand away, but Abagail held on. "I mean it; you really are a special and loving person. You have done so much for me."

"It gives me much joy to help you." Naomi seemed nervous.

"I hope I do not make you feel uncomfortable," Abagail said.

"No, there is something else on my mind. You see, I am leaving the community soon and I wonder...well, you do not have to decide today. It will probably be in the next two days that I will be going...you see, my sister lives close by and my plan is to live with her. She has a house and a small farm."

"I understand. Of course, you have to go," Abagail tried to say calmly as her stomach did a somersault.

"No, you do not understand. I would like you to come with me."

"Really? That would be—what can I say?" Abagail leaned over and touched Naomi's shoulder. "I would love that more than anything."

"It is a small farm and a tiny house but there is a nice sized kitchen and two bedrooms. There are two cows, a few chickens, a horse, and a good-sized garden."

"It sounds like heaven. Thank you, thank you."

"Then you are interested?"

"Oh yes, very much so."

"Oh, good. I have to go now and help get dinner organized. After dinner we can talk, and I'll tell you more about the house and my sister."

CHAPTER 98

John Saunders walked as quickly as he could, believing it undignified for a member of parliament to run in the halls of Westminster. This was one committee meeting he did not want to miss. The Military Affairs committee chair banged his gavel to open the session just as Saunders made his entrance.

"All right, all right, gentlemen, we have much to cover today. Please take your seats." The chairman cleared his throat. "We have a report from General Cromwell on the military situation. Unfortunately, the General is unable to attend due to his responsibilities. However, his adjunct is here to represent him. Colonel Standish, please come up to the table."

A soldier with bushy sideburns in full military uniform marched up to a table facing the committee. He saluted then sat in a ramrod fashion. The chairman cleared his throat. "It is an honor to have you before our committee, sir," the chairman said.

"The honor is mine, sir," Standish said.

"First I want to praise the fine work of the new army. You should know—and I hope you convey this to General Cromwell—that we are all in his debt. The continued existence of our revolution is due in no small measure to your success on the battlefield. Now I will open up to questions from committee members."

Tom Perry raised his hand.

"Yes, Mr. Perry," the chairman said.

"Thank you, Mr. Chairman." Tom Perry cleared his throat and looked down at a pile of papers. "Colonel Stand-ish, thank you for coming to clarify some questions and to hear our concerns." Perry looked up and met Standish's gaze. "The first concern is regarding prisoners taken during battle. Colonel Standish, what is the policy of the new army regard-ing the treatment of prisoners captured during a battle?"

Standish looked toward the chairman, who did not meet his eyes. "The policy is to treat prisoners captured during combat in a humane manner," he replied.

"Which means what exactly? Please be specific."

"Well," Standish cleared his throat, "specifically they should be fed and cared for medically."

"And that is the policy of General Cromwell's army, correct?"

"Yes, I already told you that's the policy," Standish said with irritation.

"Then what do you make of the eye-witness accounts of prisoners being shot execution-style by soldiers in the new army under Cromwell's command?"

"That is a lie, sir," Standish shouted as he bolted out of his chair.

Cries of "traitor" and "how dare he" rang out in the chamber.

"Order," the chairman said, banging his gavel loudly. "Order, we will have order."

Perry stood up. "May I continue?" He lifted a stack of papers. "I have statements from eye-witnesses." He waved the papers as if they were alive. "Statements that they personally witnessed Royal soldiers being lined up and shot by a firing squad."

"Who are these liars?" Standish bellowed.

"So, you deny the veracity of these accounts?" Perry asked.

"Absolutely," Standish said.

"You deny that on June second of this year, under General Cromwell's command, captured Royal soldiers were executed?"

"Where would our revolution be if it wasn't for the military genius of General Cromwell and the bravery of our soldiers? It is easy to sit here and judge but until you have been in battle you have no idea what it is like," Standish said.

"You have not answered my question Colonel Standish," Perry said in a measured tone. "The events of June second, sir."

Standish's voice shook as he answered, "I am not participating in the besmirching of a hero's reputation. A man who makes it possible for all of you to sit here," he waved his hand, taking in the whole chamber, "and under-mine the efforts of those who risk their lives." He quickly rose from his seat and stalked out.

"Answer the question, Colonel," Perry shouted after him.

Standish kept walking.

A stunned silence descended as members of parliament sat frozen in their seats.

"I think we have our answer," Tom Perry said calmly. He gathered up his papers and slowly left the chamber.

John Saunders returned to his small office and collapsed in his chair. Were Tom Perry's accusations true? If they were, what did that say about the revolution? He had to find Tom and discover the truth. He was just leaving when a page handed him a note marked urgent. *Meet me at the restaurant, one o'clock, signed T.*

CHAPTER 99

"Come closer," James said to the boys. "Warm yourself by the fire."

Will and Lee scooted toward the fire and leaned into the warmth. The three of them sat in companionable silence. Like people since the beginning of time, they stared into the flames, mesmerized by the miracle of fire.

"So, tell me your story," James said in a soft voice. "What happened to your family?"

He looked at Will, expecting him to speak for the two brothers.

"The soldiers came and killed our mother and father." It wasn't Will but his younger brother, Lee, who spoke up. "Then they burned our house down."

James was taken aback.

Lee's simple statement hung in the air, naked and stark. His lack of emotion highlighted the horror of what he said. James looked at these two boys, alone in the world without a family, victims of terrible events, and realized the three of them shared much. They all reeled from horror and loss; had witnessed unspeakable events and were trying to find some peace. He was disappointed with himself for treating the boys like they were a threat to him and his seclusion.

Will yawned and Lee's head dropped so that his chin rested on his chest.

"Time to go to sleep," James said, getting up slowly. His knees hurt and his back was stiff. He laid down on his blanket. The boys curled up near the fire. He could hear by their heavy breathing they were already asleep.

James gazed up at the sky. *How can I help Lee and Will with the loss of their parents?*

I have no magic words to take their sadness away. James himself was living with inexplicable sadness and loss. He was reminded how much he had in common with the people who so desperately looked to him for answers. He had no an-swers, and this made him feel like a fraud. It was not because he wasn't an ordained priest. His secret was he felt himself beginning to heal from the horrors he'd seen in the war by helping others express their fears and sadness.

CHAPTER 100

While riding through the forest with Lucia, Albert realized he was a different person when he was with her—a better person, the kind of person he always dreamed of being; a man of honor and dignity.

"Albert, stop," Lucia cried out. "This is the place. I am sure of it."

Albert rubbed his chin. "I do not know," he said.

"You remember the hill over here, and look, there is the tree."

"If you are certain."

"I am," Lucia said.

Albert slid off the wagon seat and grabbed the shovel from the flatbed. "Where do I start?"

Lucia pointed to the spot without hesitation.

Albert began digging. "I do not know, Lucia. I do not feel anything. Did we dig this deep?" At that moment his shovel hit something solid.

They both froze and looked at each other. There was something sacrilegious about digging up the corpse of a dead queen.

Lucia broke the silence. "Let me have that." She grabbed the shovel from Albert and continued digging. The top of the coffin started to appear.

Albert leaped into the grave. He angled the coffin just enough so he could get his shoulder under it. It was ex-tremely heavy. He bent down and with tremendous effort lifted the coffin. It was half out of the grave. He crouched down again and with one last push shoved the coffin out. The night air was cool, but Albert dripped with sweat. He sat down a distance from the coffin. Lucia wiped his brow with her handkerchief and handed him some water, which he gulped greedily.

"I am ready," he said, standing to carry the coffin to the

wagon when he stopped suddenly. "Do you hear that?" Albert asked in a hushed tone, scanning the surrounding area.

Just then, soldiers crashed out of the forest. Two of them grabbed Albert's arms, pinning them to his sides. Two other soldiers grabbed hold of Lucia's wrists.

From atop a horse, their leader announced, "I arrest you in the name of the people for subversion and treason."

Albert and Lucia gasped. The man on the horse was their old comrade, Captain Nugent.

CHAPTER 101

"The situation with the army is worse than you can imagine." Tom leaned forward and whispered in John's ear. "There are stories of rapes and looting."

"I cannot believe it," John said.

"And just yesterday I got a visit from two soldiers who came to my door and threatened me. They warned me that certain elements of the army were upset about my questions and they could not vouch for my safety if I continue the hearings of the military affairs committee."

"No, that cannot be, threatening a sitting member of parliament. It is unthinkable. You must do something." John's voice got louder, and his face turned a deep red. "Have they threatened anyone else on the committee?"

"Not as far as I know," Tom replied.

"Why are you being targeted? You are just one member of the committee."

"I am asking uncomfortable questions. Cromwell knows I am not only opposed to his leadership with the army, but I also have grave concerns about his threat to our democracy. He knows who I represent and how we envision our new society without any aristocracy at all." Tom leaned back in his chair and took a long drink of ale.

"Tom, your beliefs are known to Cromwell and everyone else. You do not keep your opinions to yourself," John said with a smile.

Tom laughed. "I wanted us to have lunch because I need to talk to you," he went on. "What we talk about has to stay between us."

"Of course." John nodded.

Tom looked around the restaurant. Once satisfied no one could hear him, he leaned in and said, "The queen's body has been found."

"No, really, when, who? Why was this information not made public?"

"Those are some of the many questions about this whole affair," Tom said.

"What do you mean? What other questions?"

"It was one of Cromwell's top aides who apprehended the conspirators."

John shook his head. "What are you implying? You are accusing Cromwell of what exactly?"

"You doubt me," Tom said.

"I have to say that your obsession with Cromwell and his political ambitions make your accusations less credible."

"What do you mean?" Tom hissed, his face turning red.

"You cannot accuse Cromwell of treason because he is carrying out the wishes of parliament, our wishes. You and I were very vocal about the importance of recovering the body of the queen."

"Yes, of course, but..."

"And that is what Cromwell did and now you are accusing him of some crime for succeeding in the mission given to him by parliament. No matter what he does he is guilty in your eyes." John rose from his chair, placed some coins on the table, and walked out.

Tom was at a loss for words. He was struck dumb by John's reaction. He wondered if John was in Cromwell's pay but quickly dismissed the idea. *I am truly in this by myself,* he realized.

CHAPTER 102

"We are almost there. The town is not too far," James said to the boys trailing behind him.

"Do you know this town, Father?" Will asked.

"Yes, I have been here before and the people were very welcoming. I am sure we will find food here. You may be able to find a family to take you in."

"No, Father, we want to stay with you. Don't we, Lee?"

Lee nodded his head vigorously. He hadn't said a word since he spoke about the murder of their parents the previous night.

"We are very close—it is just beyond the rise." James pointed to a small hill a few hundred meters away. It was nearing evening and they had been walking all day. They were tired, thirsty, and very hungry. Their pace quickened without them realizing it. Finally, they reached the top of the hill, where they could see the green valley, but there was no town, only rubble. James asked himself if he was mistaken about the location. As they got closer, James saw it was no mistake. Where houses had once stood and people once walked, there were burnt-out structures and empty streets. They walked into the empty town but the only life they saw was a pack of wild dogs. Every building destroyed, every store empty, every window broken. There was not a soul in sight. All the energy drained from James' body.

"Now what?" James said out loud. "What are we going to do?"

"Do not worry, Father, we will find food."

"But how, where?" James asked.

"If there is any food in this town we will eat tonight. Come on, Lee," Will said. He ran down the deserted street with his younger brother trailing behind.

James sat on a rock in the middle of the town. Had he come

to a dead end? As long as he was only responsible for himself, he could indulge in this journey. It was immoral to let these young boys live in these conditions. Another day without food. He couldn't let two boys starve with him. It was time to go home.

CHAPTER 103

"You," Lucia said. She was so shocked all she could do was to stare at Nugent.

Nugent didn't flinch. "You, you, and you," he barked at three soldiers, "put that coffin in the wagon." Everyone watched as the three men tried to lift the coffin, but it was too heavy; it twisted and almost fell to the ground. "Help them," Nugent shouted, and two more soldiers jumped from their mounts and the five of them slowly carried the heavy coffin to the wagon Lucia and Albert had driven.

Nugent ordered his men to tie the two of them up.

Nugent imagined what it would be like when he presented his catch to Cromwell. He knew Cromwell was hesitant about trusting him, but his value would have to be appreciated now. He could not believe his good fortune. He had the queen's corpse and had captured the two royalist spies in the act of digging her up. General Nugent, now that had a real ring to it. He had to remind himself he wasn't home free yet. There was still the problem of being identified as a royal agent by Lucia and Albert. They were prisoners and his word would carry more weight than theirs, but why take the chance? It was a loose end. Why let there be any doubt about his loyalty to the revolution?

How to silence them occupied his mind during the ride back to the palace. By the time they reached the palace, he had the broad outlines of a plan. *Yes*, he thought. *I will not have to eliminate Lucia or her big dumb boyfriend, they will put themselves in harm's way. All I have to do is set the stage. Others will do my work for me. On the other hand, if I am lucky it all won't even be necessary. They just might hang them both on the spot without a trial.*

The stairs down to the cell were steep and wet. Lucia slipped and almost fell. One of the soldiers holding her arms caught her before she fell, and he touched her breast. "Oh, my lady," he said with a smile, "be careful. You do not want to get hurt. You have to be in good shape when they hang you."

Lucia glared at him.

"Oh, you do not like it when I touch you?" He pressed his hand against her breast again.

Lucia kicked him in the shin.

"Ow, you bitch," he yelped and slapped her across the face.

The other soldier laughed. "Serves you right."

The soldier went to raise his hand again, but the second soldier grabbed his comrade's arm and stopped him. "Enough, let us drop her off at the cell and then we can go to the tavern." The soldier's hand, still raised, shook. His eyes locked on Lucia.

Lucia did not flinch. She glared at him with hatred.

"Here we are," the second soldier said.

A guard walked up to the soldiers. "Is this the one caught with the queen's body?"

"Yes, and she is all yours. My partner and I are going to celebrate."

The two soldiers turned and walked away when the first soldier turned back and pointed at Lucia. "This is not over," he said.

CHAPTER 104

Parliament buzzed with rumors about Queen Henrietta. Even the most senior and distinguished members spread the most outlandish rumors. Conjecture and conspiracy theories flourished in the void created by the absence of information. Wild speculation ruled the day.

"I heard that they were going to remove her body from the coffin and bring it to Spain," one member whispered to a colleague.

"Is it true?" the other distinguished member asked.

The two parliament members' heads were so close their foreheads almost touched. There were small groups of members scattered throughout the great hall, whispering about the capture of the two royal agents who had been found digging up the queen's corpse.

The most outlandish rumors became more reasonable the more they were repeated.

"Well, someone from Cromwell's inner circle told a good friend of mine they were going to prop her up on a horse and have her lead the Royalists in battle."

"No, really?"

"I'm just reporting what I heard."

"Gentlemen, please take your seats. Gentlemen, please," the Speaker implored. "The trial is about to begin. As soon as the members are seated, we will let the public in." The speaker took a deep breath. He looked over the chamber. "All right, Sergeant at Arms, open the doors."

People poured into the great room, hurrying to claim a good spot. It only took a few minutes for all the seats to be occupied. There was electricity in the air, a steady buzz. The fact that the accused was no longer of the living made the proceedings more compelling. The penny broadsides and sheets were filled with tales of the demise of the queen. How did she die? Who killed her? How did she escape in the first place? Who was this couple caught digging up her body? Some papers speculated the queen was a witch being brought back to life. Other papers asserted the queen's corpse had magical properties which made as much sense as any other explanation to many people. The broadsides also speculated about this handsome new member of parliament, John Saunders, who was appointed to be the prosecutor for parliament.

"Ladies and Gentlemen," the Speaker intoned. "This is the house of the people and we are here to do the people's work. I ask you not to react verbally to what you see here. This is not a theater performance, no applause and keep talking to a minimum."

"Now the charges are treason for the two defendants. Mr. Saunders, would you begin?"

"Thank you, your honor. The prosecution will demonstrate that the two defendants, Albert Westbrook and Lucia Fanelli, worked for the enemy in their attempt to undermine the lawful government of this land. In short, they are accused of treason." Saunders pointed to Lucia and Albert. People craned their necks to get a good look at the accused and some people stood. There were gasps from the crowd.

"Quiet," the Speaker said. He waited a few seconds and looked to John Saunders, saying, "You may continue."

Saunders nodded. "The two defendants attempted to remove Queen Henrietta from her grave with the aim to take her body to Spain on the orders of the queen's daughter, Princess Margot of Spain."

A low buzz emanated from the public seats.

"Furthermore, we will reveal the assistance they received in this country to first help Queen Henrietta escape from her confinement in the palace during the uprising as well as those who aided in this latest attempted grave robbery."

Major Nugent, as the arresting officer, was ordered to

attend the trial to be a witness for the prosecution. He stood off to the side. Did Saunders look at him when he mentioned the assistance Lucia and Albert received? he wondered. No, it was his imagination. But the thought would not go away. Nugent reviewed all that happened, but he could think of only two other people in the whole world that could tie him to the queen—James and Abagail. And according to the latest reports of his agents, James was wandering the countryside, still masquerading as a priest, and Abagail seemed to have fallen off the end of the world. He was uneasy. Maybe just to be on the safe side, it was time to implement the plan. He would find out whether Saunders spoke to Albert and Lucia and discover whether his name came up.

The first day of the trial was devoted to opening state-ments by the prosecution, laying out the charges and the defense's rebuttal. The defense argued that the prosecution's case was all circumstantial. The only charge that could be proved was that the two defendants were apprehended digging up a body. All the rest of the charges were hearsay and speculation. The defense may have had a strong case legally, but the emotional charge of treason overwhelmed the judicial rules of evidence. There was a need for the public to put a face on the overthrown regime. Since the king and queen were dead, these two agents of the crown would have to suffice.

Later that evening, Saunders sat down in his new, larger office, one befitting a prosecutor of royalty, and took a deep breath. The first day was over and no big mistakes. This was only the beginning. He was still undecided on what to do with what he learned yesterday interviewing Lucia Fanelli. Could he believe her? What would be her motivation for naming Major Nugent as an agent for the monarchy?

Saunders recalled the horrible conditions of the cell below Westminster where he had interviewed mistress Fanelli. As he descended, he could not shake the sense of being buried alive. He felt sweaty and chilled and it only got worse.

John decided to interview her in her cell to try to establish some rapport with the prisoner and encourage her cooperation. He was shocked to see the conditions of the cell. She was clearly wearing the same clothes since her arrest. There was no light and no place to sit but a mattress on the floor made of thin cloth sheets with pieces of straw sticking out. He saw a bucket in the corner. He could not bring himself to ask what it was for and at the same time could not ignore it. It could only be there for one purpose. He gagged.

Lucia was on her feet when he entered the cell. Her hands balled in a fist, her legs spread apart, poised to counter an attack. On her left cheek was a large black and blue mark.

Saunders stopped. "I am a lawyer," he said and held out his hands to show her he was not armed. "What happened to your face?"

Lucia didn't move and kept her eyes on him.

"I'm not here to hurt you. I want to hear your story."

Lucia didn't move a muscle.

"It is pretty rough in here. Can I do something to make it a little better? Do you mind?" he asked and sat down on the bed. "How did you get that bruise?" he asked again.

Lucia shrugged her shoulders and took a cautious step towards him. "You want to make things a little better for me—that is why you are here?" She laughed bitterly.

"You know you are being charged with treason and you know the penalty?"

"Yes," Lucia replied.

"Perhaps if you could identify who assisted you with the queen's escape there could be some leniency."

"I would be happy to identify that person."

Saunders waited but the prisoner didn't respond. He asked, "What do you want in exchange?"

"There is only one thing I want. Promise you will undergo a complete and honest investigation of the person I name regardless of who it is."

"I will. I promise."

Lucia took a deep breath. "Major Nugent is a royal agent."

"No, I don't believe it."

"Yes, the hero of the revolution has been an agent for the crown for years."

"Are you certain? How do you know this?" Saunders asked.

"I know because I was the person he reported to."

CHAPTER 105

Can it really be true? A home for me and my baby? But it was not guaranteed, not yet. Naomi, who had been nothing but generous and honest, deserved to know Abagail's whole story, with no parts left out, starting with her real name. *I do not want a home based on a lie.* Later that night, Naomi knocked on the side of the wagon and climbed in. "Are you ready for tomorrow? We will have to take a carriage to my sister's house."

"How are we going to find one? I do not have the means to pay," Abagail said.

"It is all taken care of. One of the members of the community will bring us."

"How wonderful," Abagail said. "I have something to tell you. Actually, I have a lot to tell you." The words stuck in her throat.

Naomi waited.

"I want to be open and honest with you..." Abagail began. "I have lived most of my life surrounded in lies. My whole life was a lie, and I swore to myself that from now on I would live an open and honest life."

"We all have to lie sometime in our life," Naomi said. "Believe me, I know."

"That is not what I mean." Abagail took another deep breath. "Let me start with my name. My name is not Anna— my given name is Abagail."

Naomi's face didn't change expression, but Abagail could see her body tense.

"I understand this is a shock but when you hear my story you will understand why I had to lie. Of course, you can choose not to let me live with you and your sister once you hear me, but I need to tell you my story."

"All right," Naomi said.

Abagail related the story of her life from the beginning up until she joined the wagon community, not leaving out one part. "Well, what do you think?" she asked when she had finished, exhausted and elated.

"I do not know what to think. I need time to take all this in," Naomi said, sitting very still.

Abagail sat quietly but her mind was racing. *What happens if she takes back her invitation? Where do I go?*

What did Naomi really think about what she'd been through? The choices she made. The shame she felt about her mother's imprisonment and her part in the conspiracy of silence. The rage towards that monster and not feeling any remorse about killing him. The baker and Maria's family, and of course there was James. What did Naomi think about having a child outside of marriage?

"I would understand if you change your mind. I really would." Abagail had a powerful sense that once more the direction of her life would be determined by someone else, but surprisingly felt all right with this because it was her decision to tell Naomi the truth. She was taking responsibility for what happens in her life. *This is what it means to own your life,* Abagail thought.

"You have had a remarkable life," Naomi said.

Abagail nodded.

"The things you have experienced are remarkable."

"I am exhausted. After seventeen years being treated like a pampered, spoiled court pet, I was not ready for the world. I did not think I was entitled to a life."

"And now?" Naomi asked, smiling.

"And now, I think I can survive."

Naomi shook her head. "Oh, I think you have done that and more."

"Do you really think so?" Abagail asked, feeling stronger and more in control of her life. "Thank you for that, Naomi, I really appreciate it." And without thinking, Abagail went over, kissed Naomi on the cheek, and gave her a big hug. Naomi returned the hug.

Abagail laid down that night feeling lighter and stronger.

CHAPTER 106

Nugent's worst fear stared him in the face. John Saunders' page handed him a note asking for a meeting the following morning to discuss the pending case against Lucia Fanelli and Albert Westbrook. *Now is the time to take action,* he thought. He could not allow Lucia to testify in court. He knew he must visit one of the agents and set his plan into motion.

Nugent didn't remember it being so damn cold and wet on the stairway to the cells. He shivered on his descent. He would kill himself rather than live in this place.

A guard who looked like he was sleeping almost knocked his chair over when Nugent appeared. "Yes, sir," he said. "How can I help you?"

"I am here to interview prisoner Westbrook."

"I am sorry sir, but do you have a letter verifying..."

"Do you know who I am?" Nugent asked.

"Yes," the guard replied softly, "but..."

"And you know of the trial."

The guard nodded.

"Then you know why it is important for me to interview the prisoner."

The guard hesitated. "I will accompany you. It is not allowed for anyone to go to the cells without being accompanied by a guard."

"Fine," Nugent said—as long as he got to be with Albert alone. He followed the guard even further underground and shivered. They finally made it to the door of the cell. Nugent held out his hand for the key. "I can find my way from here."

The guard hesitated, holding on to the key tightly.

Neither one moved until, impatient, Nugent shook his hand with palm up.

The guard dropped the key in Nugent's hand.

"What are you doing here?" the big man roared as he tried to grab Nugent, but chains attached to the wall held him back. "I ought to kill you. You betrayed us," Albert spat at Nugent.

Nugent turned to the guard. "You can leave us alone now."

"Are you certain? This man is dangerous. It took four men to get him inside the cell. That is why he is chained."

"I will be careful," Nugent said and turned his back to the guard as if he ceased to exist.

"Make sure you wait for me to escort you out," the guard said.

"I will."

"Where is Lucia?" Albert yelled. "If she is hurt you will pay."

"Lucia is the reason I am here."

"You are a liar, a bastard." Every one of Albert's muscles strained to break free.

"If you stop for a minute, I will tell you why I came." Nugent leaned closer to Albert and whispered, "We are still on the same side."

"What do you mean? I..."

Nugent looked around to ensure the guard was gone. He reached into his pocket and pulled out a key.

Albert stared at the key.

"This key will unlock your chains." Nugent held the key in his palm. He crouched down next to Albert to put the key in the shackle locks, freeing Albert.

Albert rubbed his wrists. He couldn't take his eyes from the key.

"This key is just for the chains. The jailor has the key to yours and Lucia's cell. I assume he brings you food and has to walk in your cell."

Albert was dumbstruck.

"Well, he does, right?"

"Yes," Albert confirmed.

"I suggest you act like you are chained to the wall. Wait

until he comes into the cell. You know what to do."

Albert nodded.

"There will two horses waiting for you in the side courtyard," Nugent whispered, "God speed." He walked away. When the guard yelled after him that he was supposed to wait for an escort, Nugent just kept walking.

CHAPTER 107

Lucia lay in her dark cell with her eyes closed, half-dead, half-alive, ready to leave this world but not yet in the other world. She floated above it all. Her body shivered as people from her past, long dead, came to life as they paid their respect to her. Queen Henrietta unexpectedly hugged Lucia. The queen was about to say something when Lucia heard the bang of metal hitting metal. *No, I want to sleep. I want to sleep forever,* her mind cried out. *Someone is calling me—stop, stop,* but they did not. Forced to open her eyes, Lucia saw Albert.

"Hurry, we must go before the guards find out," he said.

Lucia finally found her voice. "How did you get here?"

"Nugent," he whispered. "I'll tell you about it later, now we have to get out of here."

"How?"

"There are two horses outside the side castle door." Albert took her hand and led her to the staircase. They went past a guard lying motionless on the floor. They moved quickly, hugging the wall until they reached the stairs. Once at the stairs they ran up to the landing.

"I know how to go from here," Lucia said, taking the lead. She grabbed his hand and they bounded up the stairs.

Albert stopped suddenly. "Do you hear that?" he asked.

"No, I..."

"Listen," he said.

The sound of men shouting came from the cells down below. They had been discovered. They listened for footsteps.

"I do not hear anyone coming up the steps, do you?" Albert asked.

Lucia listened carefully. "No, they probably think we went the other way thinking we are going down. We might have some time, but we have to hurry. Come on." They ran up more stairs, then Lucia stopped. She ran her hands against the wall, finding a loose stone, and pulled it out. The wall opened into a small room with a simple wooden desk and two chairs.

Albert recognized the room. This was where he met privately with Queen Henrietta and the very room where he first met Lucia. He was sure they would get out of this predicament, like all the other situations in the past, and they would laugh about the coincidence.

"We have to get down to the end of the hallway. There is a window we can climb out of," Lucia said.

"All right," Albert said and kissed Lucia fully on the lips. He brimmed with confidence and was thankful he was with Lucia.

Lucia pulled away and smiled. "Later. Follow close behind me."

The two of them walked quickly down the hallway. Albert saw the window.

"Halt," someone shouted behind them.

They both turned around. A group of soldiers at the other end of a long hallway ran towards them. They broke into a run, but the soldiers were catching up to them. Lucia got to the window first and lifted her leg onto the window-sill, ready to jump. She looked back and saw the soldiers gaining on Albert.

"Come on," she yelled.

"Go, go," Albert yelled and turned to face the on-rushing soldiers.

Lucia hesitated, one leg hanging out of the window, the other still on the floor.

"Go," Albert said again. The soldiers were on him and then he fell to his knees, still fighting, holding them back.

Albert fought ferociously but seven men would subdue one man, no matter how strong. He looked at the window and didn't see Lucia. Ge smiled. His last thought was, *My debt is paid.*

Lucia saw the soldiers stand up over Albert's inert body.

She jumped, hit the ground hard, and quickly mounted the smaller of the two horses, thinking that a big man like Albert needed a horse that could take his weight. She galloped out of the courtyard, past the houses and shops in the town, and into the forest. After two hours she stopped so her horse could rest. Only then did she realize why her face was wet. She'd been crying for the last two hours.

CHAPTER 108

Abagail and Naomi left right after breakfast. Everyone in the caravan, adults and children alike, lined up to say goodbye to Naomi. She hugged each person, wishing them luck and good fortune.

An old carriage pulled up to them, driven by a man who may have been the same age as the carriage. "Are you ready ladies?" he asked, jumping down gracefully from his high seat. He removed his hat and bowed, making a sweeping movement with the hat. "Anna," the old man said, looking at Abagail, who seemed confused.

"Are you going to answer the man, Anna?" Naomi laughed while drawing out her name.

"Oh, right yes, Anna," Abagail replied.

The driver held out his hand and helped Abagail up to the carriage. "You are carrying precious cargo there," he said, pointing to her stomach.

Naomi got in after her. "If all goes well, we should get there before dinner," she said, settling in.

They rode through deep green forests and long, open meadows for four hours. Abagail got more excited as the carriage forged ahead. Naomi seemed to relax as the carriage ate up the miles.

"We are almost there," Naomi said. "Just over the next rise."

On the way down from the rise, a house appeared. It seemed small and plain, just as Naomi said. As they got nearer and walked into the gated yard, a woman burst out of the house and hugged Naomi. The two women embraced for a long time. When they unlocked their arms, they both had tears in their eyes. They held each other's faces in their hands, their gazes locked, and hugged again.

Abagail stood off to the side quietly watching, her eyes

welling up.

"Oh, Rachel this, is Abagail," Naomi said, beckoning Abagail over.

Rachel cleared her throat and wiped her eyes. "Welcome," she said.

"Thank you, it is very generous of you..." Abagail started to say.

Rachel cut in, "Any friend of Naomi's is welcome." She hugged Abagail. "Did I feel a kick?" she said, holding Abagail back so she could look at her stomach. "Your baby is getting ready to enter the world. How wonderful, a baby born in our house. Come inside. You both must be exhausted and hungry."

As plain as the house was on the outside, the inside was beautiful. Abagail walked through the front door into a kitchen big enough for a dining room table with four chairs and a good-sized fireplace. Off the kitchen were two small bedrooms. Each bedroom had a bed and a dresser. It was furnished simply but the walls were covered with beautiful drawings of nature and windows lined every room. The house was drenched in sunlight and simple vases held wild-flowers in each bedroom.

"Come with me, I want to show you something." Naomi took Abagail's hand and exchanged looks with Rachel. "This will be your bedroom," Rachel said.

"Thank you so much. The two of you have been most generous."

"This is not the surprise," Rachel said. And with a flourish she opened the door all the way. Hiding in a corner was a rocking chair.

"Oh my," was all Abagail could say.

"It will come in handy when the baby wakes in the middle of the night or when you are feeding him or her."

"Thank you again," Abagail said. Sitting down in the chair, she realized how tired she was. "I will just rest my eyes for a few minutes." She fell asleep. When Abagail opened her eyes, she was initially disoriented but everything slowly came back to her. She left her new bedroom and walked into the kitchen. "Oh, I am sorry. Falling asleep like that. I..."

"Do not worry. Treat this house as if it was your own," Rachel said.

Abagail did not know what to say. She sat quietly and wondered about these two women. They did not look alike except for the same twinkle in their eyes. "Where is Naomi?" Abagail asked.

"Resting also. You must be very hungry," Rachel said.

"Yes, I am," Abagail replied.

Rachel walked to the fireplace and served Abagail a steaming bowl of chicken stew from a big pot.

"It is delicious," Abagail said, waving her hand to cool the top of her mouth.

Rachel poured water in a glass from a large bucket and handed it to Abagail.

"Was this your parent's house?" Abagail asked.

"No, we bought it together, Naomi and me," Rachel said.

"Oh." Abagail did not understand. She looked down at her bowl and ate some more. The silence was awkward. Abagail searched for something to say. "I just thought since you are sisters..."

"Sisters, where did you get that idea? Oh, I know. That is the story Naomi tells people."

"I do not understand," Abagail said.

"We live together like husband and wife," Rachel said, keeping her eyes on Abagail.

Abagail was silent, trying to understand. "Why would Naomi tell me a story?"

Rachel let out a soft laugh. "Some people—no, I would say most people—see us as sinful, two women living together as husband and wife."

Abagail finally understood and blushed. She needed to think it over. "I think I need to get some more sleep."

Lying in her bed, Abagail thought about what Rachel said about two women living together as wife and husband. What did that even mean? But fatigue overtook her confused thoughts and sleep came.

CHAPTER 109

Parliament was in an uproar. The capture of the two royal agents was huge news and now their daring escape leading to the killing of one and the disappearance of the other made the story even bigger. The papers asked how it happened, which quickly turned into the question of who made it happen. Predictably there had to be someone to blame. They must have had supporters in the palace or may-be the guards were paid off. Were there co-conspirators? Adding to the conspiracy theory was the fact that they escaped the night before they were to testify, all very suspicious.

The broadsheets trumpeted the news throughout the city. "Spies Escape—Who Aided Them?" and "Is There a Traitor in The Palace?" The story of the big escape, as the broadsheets called it, was selling a lot of newspapers. There were too many juicy tidbits for the story to be ignored. And the penny sheets were feeding the public a steady diet of rumors and speculation. A consensus began to form around the idea it had to be an inside job.

Tom Perry sat alone at his corner table at the back of the restaurant, his nose so far into a book he hadn't noticed John Saunders until he stood right next to him.

John cleared his throat and Tom almost flew out of his chair. "For God's sakes, man, you could scare a man half to death."

"Sorry," John said. "I just need to talk with you."

"Sit down," Tom said, feeling very pleased. John was seeking him out.

John looked around and, satisfied they were out of earshot, leaned in. "You might have been correct about Cromwell."

"What has happened?"

"Those two agents who escaped last night—" John hesitated, "I know who helped them." He looked around again and in an even lower voice said, "Major Nugent."

Tom's eyes were wide open now. "How do you know this?"

"There were only two visitors to the cells on the night in question—Nugent and me."

"Are you sure?"

"Yes, I examined the sign-in log for visitors."

"Major Charles Nugent, the rebel hero who captured the queen during the great uprising, is a spy for the monarchy," Tom said.

"And," John hesitated again, "he is on Cromwell staff. But we do not have hard evidence it was him."

"The question is, did Nugent do this at the order of Cromwell or was he acting at the direction of another royal agent?" Tom pondered.

"Or on his own. One way to determine Cromwell's guilt or innocence is how protective he is of Nugent," John said.

"Even if he was acting under Cromwell's orders you will not be able to incriminate Cromwell."

"No man is above the law. It is one of the principles of the revolution."

"We will see," Tom said. "We will see."

CHAPTER 110

Abagail opened her eyes. Her sheet was wet and sticky like blood. She suddenly saw her mother lying on the cold floor with blood coming out of her mouth, the blood spurting out of the young guard's mouth, the blood on her thighs when the monster attacked her, and his bloody, smashed face. All these pictures flashed by and lingered at the same time. Pain jerked her into consciousness. The pain was so bad she saw lights like the sun exploded. She screamed.

Rachel burst into the bedroom first. "Oh dear," she said, seeing the blood, and turned to fetch Naomi, who was right behind her.

"Heat some water and bring some clean sheets," Naomi said. Then she looked at the sheet, red with blood, and said, "Forget the sheets."

Taking Abagail's hand, Naomi said in a gentle tone, "This is what you were waiting for. Now I want you to take slow breaths. Take regular breaths, good. Now relax until I tell you to push, then push as hard as you can."

Sweat poured down Abagail's face. Rachel stood by Abagail's head and wiped the sweat from her face. What a mistake to get pregnant without a husband or a place to live. Abagail couldn't stop those thoughts from circling around her brain. *I am being punished.* "Ahh," Abagail screamed. Something was ripping her in half. *Stop, stop, please tell them to stop.*

"Try to relax, Abagail." Rachel said, wiping her forehead. "Breathe, that's right. Here comes another push. Push, Abagail, push."

Abagail let out another terrible scream. "Am I going to die? Dying would be better than this."

"Relax," Rachel said. "Breathe."

Abagail thought, *You try to relax with all this.* Another

sharp stab of pain.

"Push, Abagail, push," Naomi said.

Abagail was being torn in half. "Oh God," she said, pushing through the pain, sure she was dying.

"Here it—no wait, not it—here *he* comes," Naomi said with glee.

A loud, angry cry rose, like the baby was fighting against being dragged into the cold world.

"Look, mom, you have a baby boy," Rachel said.

"But he is ugly and all bloody," Abagail said, feeling nauseous.

Naomi laughed. "We all come out that way. It may not be a long journey, but it is a hard one. Wait, I will clean him up and then you can see your beautiful baby boy."

"Oh, he is adorable," Rachel said.

Naomi walked over holding the newborn and very carefully laid him on Abagail's chest. Abagail had never experienced anything like it. Her new baby stopped squirming and buried his face into her shoulder and fell asleep. "I have never seen anything more beautiful in my life," she said, starting to cry. The infant molded into her, his body matching perfectly with Abagail's. Through the tears, she repeated, "Thank you, the both of you, so much. You will forever be part of my family."

Rachel started crying. Naomi walked over and hugged her. The two women approached the bedside and, each hold-ing one of Abagail's hands, leaned over to look at this new being.

CHAPTER 111

At the moment Abagail gave birth to their son, the boy's father went through his own rebirth. James woke very early. All night he tossed and turned. There was a fight going on inside him which didn't allow sleep. He started to dress but he couldn't put on his priestly garb. The clothes didn't fit. He hadn't lost or gained any weight since yesterday. His clothes no longer fit his body because they no longer fit his life. Father James was no more, there was only James.

Could he just leave the boys? He owed them an explanation. He couldn't explain what he didn't understand. He only knew he couldn't continue assuming this false identity and running away from what he was afraid of by giving answers to others he didn't have for himself. No more disguises, no more false identities. Everyone he ever cared about may be in danger, hungry, frightened, or worse. It is time to take care of those he loves. He walked quietly to where the boys were sleeping to say a silent goodbye. Watching them sleep, he knew that the time to change was now.

"Will, Lee, get up boys."

"Father James," Will said, rubbing his eyes. "Where are we going?"

"Home, boys, we are going home."

First, I must find Maria's family then locate Abagail, he thought. The sky was still dark when he quietly walked away from his life as a minister. He felt incredibly lighter shedding his priestly disguise but also more vulnerable. He no longer had the special protection that the clerical attire afforded him. He felt naked and unsure and it terrified him. The only thing he was sure of was his decision to rejoin the world.

James looked back and saw two beaming faces. Will and Lee, ready to follow Father James anywhere, eager to hike to a place called home.

CHAPTER 112

"Mother, when is Father coming home?" Jeffrey asked as he did every morning since the three of them had reunited.

Maria pretended not to hear him and didn't answer. It hurt her every time he asked.

"Mother, when is..."

"Mother does not know, Jeffrey. Do you understand? She does not know," Theresa said impatiently.

"You mean he is never coming back," the little boy said. "Why? Did he stop loving us?"

"I am sure there is a reason why your father is gone," Maria said. "He loves us very much. You will see, he will come home soon."

"Maybe he is at our house," Jeffrey said hopefully. "Maybe he is waiting for us, right, Mother?"

"He might have gone there looking for us, but you remember the house burned down. We no longer have a house." Maria had to bite her lip to hold back the tears. The children should not see their mother cry. Every night when the children were asleep the tears poured out. "That is why we are staying at Uncle James' house." Maria gave Jeffrey a hug and motioned for her daughter to join them, but Theresa pretended not to see them and stood apart with her arms crossed.

Maria sighed and wondered what would become of her family. Jeffrey was acting younger and younger since Frank's absence. Her daughter refused to talk to her and was angry all the time, blaming her mother. Maria was exhausted. She had to struggle every day just to do the normal things of life. She was aware that without the children it would be easy for her to give up, but because of them it was not an option.

CHAPTER 113

James found he couldn't separate his thoughts about his house without thinking of Abagail. *What has happened to her? Is she still in England or in Spain with Margot? Is she alive?* The more he thought of her the faster he walked.

His two young companions matched his stride. "Are we almost there?" Will asked.

"Almost," James replied.

It was late in the afternoon when James stopped abruptly. The three of them caught their breath as they stood hidden in the trees. They watched a woman hugging a boy about the same age as Lee in front of a small cottage and an older girl standing by herself.

"Is that your house?" Will asked hopefully.

"Yes, it is," James answered in a whisper.

"Why did you have to sleep outdoors?"

"It is a long story, Will. Maybe I will tell you about it sometime," James said.

James froze and realized he dreaded this moment as much as he dreamed of it. To see his sister and her children set off a cascade of upsetting emotions; disappointment at not finding Abagail, failing to keep his promise to Maria about rescuing Frank and the children, and most of all deserting his sister's family, a betrayal. James, concealed by the trees, was unable to move.

"Father, are we going?" Will asked.

"Yes, yes we are. You go ahead. I will follow."

Maria, Jeffrey, and Theresa turned to see two unfamiliar young boys running towards them.

Maria saw her brother first and softly said, "James." Then she shouted his name and started to run towards him.

"Uncle James," the two children yelled, following their mother to the grove of trees, the three of them holding on tightly. They were laughing and crying.

"It is so good to see all of you," James said. "I am so relieved." He pulled back. "Jeffrey, you have grown so much, you are a big boy, and Theresa, you are a young woman. What happened to the two children I knew?"

"Do you know where my father is?" Jeffrey asked.

"No, I do not," James said, looking at Maria.

"Our house burned down," Jeffrey said.

"Well, it is a good thing you can live with me."

"I see you brought company with you," Maria said.

"Yes, this is Will and Lee. This is my sister Maria and her children, Theresa and Jeffrey."

They all said hello. Even Lee managed a whispered greeting. The six of them stood in the yard awkwardly. Maria and James walked a few feet away.

"I think we should rebuild our house," Maria said.

"Why?" James asked. "You know this house is as much yours as it is mine."

"Yes, but we want to go home so we can be there when Frank returns."

"I understand," James said. "But it would be easier to add on to this house rather than starting from scratch."

Maria bit her lip. "But..." she started to say and then stopped. "Are you sure? What about Frank?"

"He will come once he sees your place." What James thought but would not say was, *Frank is almost certainly dead. What other reason would there be for his disappear-ance?* "It would be safer for all of us to be together. Even if we decide to rebuild your house, you will need a place to live as we work on it," James said hopefully.

"I suppose you are right. What about the two boys?" Maria asked quietly, tilting her head in Will and Lee's direction.

"We will figure it out," James said as he put his arm around his sister.

Maria rested her head on her brother's shoulder and

almost smiled.

CHAPTER 114

"This is a colossal waste of valuable resources," Cromwell thundered to the members of parliament. "We are wasting time and funds to continue with a trial that has long ago ceased to have a purpose. There is no queen to try, no spies to interrogate for information, no witnesses to accuse anyone of anything. This so-called investigation and trial should end right now. We have real work to do. We have our revolution to defend from enemies. We know who the enemies from the outside are." Cromwell lowered his voice. "We also have enemies on the inside. I am not referring to those incompetent royalist agents, dead and gone. We have them right here in parliament. What else would we call those who insist on spending our energies on a futile inquiry with no possible resolution?" Parliament was so quiet the members could hear Cromwell's heavy breathing.

"Now I understand that there are accusations whispered in the hallways of this assembly regarding an aide of mine, Major Nugent. These vicious, slanderous rumors are just that. Ask yourselves who benefitted from us fighting among ourselves? To accuse this man of murder is itself a crime. This is the man who, with a small band, of soldiers penetrated the castle and captured the queen, ending the fighting, saving lives, and guaranteeing our victory. That is not all. This same Major Nugent has also captured the two royalist spies in the act of digging up the body of the queen with the aim of using her corpse to arouse sympathy for their cause. And this is the same man that is being accused of murder. This will not stand. I demand a vote to an immediate halt to the investiga-tion of Major Nugent."

Cromwell sat down as members of parliament stomped the floor, shouting "hear, hear," and "yes, the investigation must end." He sat with his arms crossed, looking grave.

"A vote was called; are there any seconds?" the Speaker intoned.

"I second," two dozen men called out.

John Saunders rose from his seat as quietly and quickly as possible. He left the chamber. Out of the corner of his eye he saw Tom Perry leaving. Their eyes met and they gave each other a slight nod. They both knew where they were headed.

Tom got to the restaurant first and took his regular seat at the back table. John walked in a few minutes later.

"We just witnessed a declaration of war, the end of the revolution, and the beginning of the dynasty of Cromwell," Tom said.

John didn't reply. What he heard was so demagogic and distorted he was incapable of speaking.

"You had better be careful, my friend. This country is going to be a dangerous place for anyone who is seen as an enemy of Cromwell," Tom continued.

"And what about you?" John asked.

"Me," Tom laughed. "I will be out of danger by tomorrow."

John was confused. "How?"

"Because, my friend, I am leaving these fair shores. I am going to the new world."

"But what about working here for the issues you believe in—*we* believe in?" John asked.

"I suggest you come with me," Tom said. "This country is not ready for real change. The new world, from what I hear, may be more receptive to my ideas."

"My fight is here. I loathe to see you go but I must stay," John said.

"I do not believe in martyrdom. Think seriously about what I am saying, John Saunders. Having Cromwell as an enemy can be deadly. There are some exciting developments in the colonies. I reserved a place for you on the ship I am taking."

"Tom, I am touched by your offer. I really am."

"Think about it. Just think about it."

"There are still things to do in this country."

"If you show up tomorrow morning at nine o'clock, the captain will let you board. If you do not arrive, well, I wish you the best, John."

"God speed," John said, getting up from the table. He walked back to Westminster.

As the two members of parliament said their farewells, Oliver Cromwell was meeting with a trusted aide.

"I do not understand, sir. I just heard you defend Major Nugent from those slanderous charges."

"That was for public consumption. There are too many unanswered questions about our good Major Nugent. Has anyone ever found out how he came upon a way to enter Windsor castle the night of the revolution? And I heard from soldiers that were with him that night he insisted on being with the queen by himself. What did they talk about? There are other concerns. How did he know where to find those two royalist agents? And to capture them just as they were digging up the corpse of Queen Henrietta? He has too much inside information—where does he get it from? In the meantime, I want you to have him followed. I have a feeling he will lead us to this pretender to the throne, Abagail."

CHAPTER 115

"Has it really been one year?" Abagail asked, slicing the cake Rachel made for James' birthday.

"It seems like it was just a month ago when the two of you entered our life," Naomi said.

"And yet it feels like the four of us have been together a lifetime," Rachel added.

Naomi leaned across the dining room table and gave James a package wrapped in brown paper. James excitedly took the package. He tore the paper into strips, throwing pieces on the kitchen floor. "If you like the paper that much, wait until you see what is inside." James cried when Naomi took the paper away to unwrap the gift.

"There, there, big man, it is fine," Naomi said and gave James the paper back. He sniffled and took the paper, happily playing with it until he saw what Naomi was doing. Wrapped inside the paper was a cup attached to a wooden rod and a long string with a ball at the end. James stared.

"Do you know how it works?" Rachel asked Naomi.

"I have no idea," Naomi replied.

"How about you, Abagail? Ever see one of these?"

"No, how does it work?"

"Let me show you," Rachel said, taking the toy by the rod and flipping the ball up. The ball made a loud noise as it hit the side of the cup. "The idea is to get the ball in the cup," Rachel said and tried again. "It is not easy." With a laugh, she tried it a third time. The wooden ball landed in the cup.

"Me, me," James yelled excitedly.

Later that night after James finally went to sleep, Abagail went outdoors. The air was cool. Abagail was restless and needed to walk. She felt warm inside thinking about the good things in her life—her love for her son and gratitude for these two women who comprised her family. But a restless feeling would not go away, growing inside of her. A sense of things, important things, not finished, questions unanswered, something missing. She thought these disturbing thoughts would have gone away by now. *Maybe if I still feel this way tomorrow, I will go for a horseback ride. Going for a ride will clear my head.*

"Sure, take the day off," Rachel said when Abagail brought up the idea the following morning.

"Go for a ride," Naomi chimed in. "We will watch James and have a good old time, right, James?"

James was concentrating on playing with his birthday gift. The ball went in every direction but the cup. He held his birthday gift out toward Rachel. When she took it and got the ball in the cup, James laughed and clapped, as excited as if he had done it himself.

"You see," Rachel said, "we are going to have a great time, right James?" Abagail was already out of the house, walking to the stable, when she heard James laughing.

The horse seemed as happy as Abagail to be galloping through the forest. No destination, no obligations, free. *This is magical,* she thought. Go left, go right, turn here, no go straight. Her body was working with the horse and her mind was at peace. The road looked familiar, but Abagail could not remember ever being on it. And then she saw it, a sign for the Red Oxen Inn. "Whoa," she said, "whoa." She dismounted, walked up to the door, and turned the handle. It was locked. But without question it was the same Red Oxen Inn. "James," she said out loud and realized he was at the root of her restlessness. Abagail turned around and galloped home.

Naomi and Rachel were sitting, talking quietly on the front porch of the house. "Did you have a good ride?" Rachel asked.

"James is in bed. He tried to wait for you but fell asleep right after supper." Naomi laughed.

"There is something I need to talk to you about," Abagail said.

Both women nodded and by the tilt of their bodies invited Abagail to speak.

"Today I came upon an inn that is just a couple of miles from where James lives. I had no idea we were so close. I want to go and see if he is there. I do not know what I will do if he is, but I must find out." Abagail took a deep breath.

Neither Rachel nor Naomi said anything for a minute.

Am I looking for their permission, their blessing? Abagail asked herself.

Then Naomi said, "I think you have to go and speak to him, then decide what you must do."

The next morning after breakfast, Abagail set off. She took the most direct route to the Red Oxen Inn, turned left, and, pushing her horse to a fast gallop, headed to James. Saying his name brought back memories, mostly happy but some sad ones too. Feeding the chickens, sitting and talking by the fire, and swimming. More than anything she remembered the feeling of being understood and loved by James. *He has probably changed. I know I have,* she thought. Her mind raced with questions. *Does James still love me? Does he still want us to live together? Would I leave Rachel and Naomi? I will not tell him about his son. That way whatever decision he makes will be about us and not some paternal obligation.*

All these questions did not weigh her down. The unknown did not scare her. Just the opposite, she felt exhilarated. For the first time in her life, Abagail was heading towards a future that would be created by her facing life head-on. No ancient quarrel between sisters, no living in a web of lies, no being snatched and imprisoned, but a life of her own choosing.

Abagail arrived at James' before she was ready and was suddenly afraid. There he was, alone, working in the garden. Reluctant to reveal her presence, Abagail dismounted quietly, tethered the horse, and found a spot where she could watch James without being seen. Watching James without his knowledge was thrilling and yet it seemed unfair. James looked different. He seemed older, more grounded. *Come on,* she told herself. *What are you afraid of? Is he the same man I loved? I am not the same person I was.*

Abagail took a deep breath walked out of the forest towards James, who dropped his hoe and stared.

"Abagail," James said and took a step toward her.

Abagail couldn't speak but took a step toward him. "James," she finally whispered.

They came face to face, only inches apart, frozen with fear, then fell into each other's arms.

ABOUT ATMOSPHERE PRESS

Atmosphere Press is an independent, full-service publisher for excellent books in all genres and for all audiences. Learn more about what we do at atmospherepress.com.

We encourage you to check out some of Atmosphere's latest releases, which are available at Amazon.com and via order from your local bookstore:

The Embers of Tradition, a novel by Chukwudum Okeke

Saints and Martyrs: A Novel, by Aaron Roe

When I Am Ashes, a novel by Amber Rose

The Recoleta Stories, by Bryon Esmond Butler

Voodoo Hideaway, a novel by Vance Cariaga

Hart Street and Main, a novel by Tabitha Sprunger

The Weed Lady, a novel by Shea R. Embry

A Book of Life, a novel by David Ellis

It Was Called a Home, a novel by Brian Nisun

Grace, a novel by Nancy Allen

Shifted, a novel by KristaLyn A. Vetovich

ABOUT THE AUTHOR

Steven Mendel is a psychologist with a practice in NYC and has published over three dozen works, including a dozen short stories, poems, essays ranging from politics to cultural criticism, group psychotherapy, and travel pieces. He has also published a self-help book titled *Love is not Enough: Making your Marriage Work* (Lulu Press 2008) and a novel titled *Welcome to the Revolution* (Muse It Up Press 2019).

CPSIA information can be obtained
at www.ICGtesting.com
Printed in the USA
LVHW020041121021
700156LV00002B/140